THE FALL OF DARKNESS

Concealed and ignored at the time, the Freeholders' rebellion was a signal that the Empire's long afternoon was drawing to a close. However, other vigorous folk, both human and non-human, had learned the same lessons from history and were individually preparing to survive their effete overlords.

Yet sunset could not be postponed forever. Terra and Merseia wore each other into oblivion. Their exhausted dominions were devastated by rebellions from within and attacks from without. By the middle of the fourth millennium, the fearful Long Night fell . .

Also by Poul Anderson in Sphere Books:

The Long Night

POUL ANDERSON

SPHERE BOOKS LIMITED
London and Sydney

First published in Great Britain by
Sphere Books Ltd 1985
30–32 Gray's Inn Road, London WC1X 8JL
Copyright © 1983 by Poul Anderson
First published in the United States of America by Tor Books
1983

Acknowledgements: The stories contained herein were first
published and are copyrighted as follows:
'The Star Plunderer,' *Planet Stories*, © 1952 by Love
Romances Publishing Co., Inc.
'Outpost of Empire,' *Galaxy*, © 1967 by Galaxy Publishing
Corp.
'A Tragedy of Errors,' *Galaxy*, © 1967 by Galaxy Publishing
Corp.
'The Sharing of Flesh,' *Galaxy*, © 1968 by Galaxy Publishing
Corp.
'Starfog,' *Analog*, © 1967 by Conde Nast Publications Inc.
Prologue and interstitial material © 1979 by Sandra Miesel.

Set in Sabon

Printed and bound in Great Britain by
Collins, Glasgow

CONTENTS

PROLOGUE

In the bright noontide of the Polesotechnic League, bold merchant-adventurers swarmed across the starlanes exploring, trading, civilizing, zestfully – and profitably – living by their motto, 'All the Traffic Will Bear.'

The hugely successful 'League of Selling Skills' emerged in the twenty-third century in response to the challenges of the Breakup, mankind's faster-than-light explosion into space. Like its prototype, the European Hansa of a thousand years earlier, this mercantile union aided its members' quest for wealth. Backed by its own sound currency and powerful fleet, the League was the expansionist, ecumenical, optimistic vanguard of Technic civilization. During its heyday, its impact was generally beneficial because it exchanged cultural as well as material goods among the stars. Prosperity followed the League's caravel flag across a whole spiral arm of Earth's galaxy and beyond.

But the higher any sun rises, 'the sooner will his race be run/ the nearer he's to setting.' The long lifespan of the era's greatest merchant prince, Nicholas van Rijn, also saw the shadows of institutional mortality lengthen. Despite van Rijn's efforts, the League faded from a vigorous self-help organization to a sclerotic gang of cartels during the twenty-fifth century. Protectionism stifled opportunity. As the traders became more and more entangled with Earth's corrupt government, intervention, exploitation, and expedience dictated policies toward extraterrestrial humans and aliens alike. With mutual advantage blotted out, profit withered. The slow waning of trade disrupted communications and invited anarchy. By 2600, the League had collapsed and the dismal Time of Troubles had begun.

The nadir of this sorrowful and poorly chronicled period was the sack of Earth by the Baldic League, a horde of spacefaring

1

barbarians originally armed by some greedy human gunrunner. Afterwards, the alien Gorzuni raided the Solar System at will, seeking slaves and treasure to expand their burgeoning realm.

So deep had darkness fallen, few dared to dream of dawn.

THE STAR PLUNDERER

The following is a part, modernized but otherwise authentic, of that curious book found by excavators of the ruins of Sol City, Terra – the Memoirs of Rear Admiral John Henry Reeves, Imperial Solar Navy. Whether or not the script, obviously never published or intended for publication, is a genuine record left by a man with a taste for dramatized reporting, or whether it is pure fiction, remains an open question; but it was undoubtedly written in the early period of the First Empire and as such gives a remarkable picture of the times and especially of the Founder. Actual events may or may not have been exactly as Reeves described, but we cannot doubt that in any case they were closely similar. Read this fifth chapter of the Memoirs as historical fiction if you will, but remember that the author must himself have lived through that great and tragic and triumphant age and that he must have been trying throughout the book to give a true picture of the man who even in his own time had become a legend.

Donvar Ayeghen, President of
the Galactic Archeological
Society

They were closing in now. The leader was a gray bulk filling my sight scope, and every time I glanced over the wall a spanging sleet of bullets brought my head jerking down again. I had some shelter from behind which to shoot in a fragment of wall looming higher than the rest, like a single tooth left in a dead man's jaw, but I had to squeeze the trigger and then duck fast. Once in awhile one of their slugs would burst on my helmet and the gas would be sickly-sweet in my nostrils. I felt ill and dizzy with it.

3

Kathryn was reloading her own rifle, I heard her swearing as the cartridge clip jammed in the rusty old weapon. I'd have given her my own, except that it wasn't much better. It's no fun fighting with arms that are likely to blow up in your face but it was all we had — all that poor devastated Terra had after the Baldics had sacked her twice in fifteen years.

I fired a burst and saw the big gray barbarian spin on his heels, stagger and scream with all four hands clutching his belly, and sink slowly to his knees. The creatures behind him howled, but he only let out a deep-throated curse. He'd be a long time dying. I'd blown a hole clear through him, but those Gorzuni were tough.

The slugs wailed around us as I got myself down under the wall, hugging the long grass which had grown up around the shattered fragments of the house. There was a fresh wind blowing, rustling the grass and the big war-scarred trees, sailing clouds across a sunny summer sky, so the gas concentration was never enough to put us out. But Jonsson and Hokusai were sprawled like corpses there against the broken wall. They'd taken direct hits and they'd sleep for hours.

Kathryn knelt beside me, the ragged, dirty coverall like a queen's robe on her tall young form, a few dark curls falling from under her helmet for the wind to play with. 'If we get them mad enough,' she said, 'they'll call for the artillery or send a boat overhead to blow us to the Black Planet.'

'Maybe,' I grunted. 'Though they're usually pretty eager for slaves.'

'John — ' She crouched there a moment, the tiny frown I knew so well darkening her blue eyes. I watched the way leaf-shadows played across her thin brown face. There was a grease smudge on the snub nose, hiding the little freckles. But she still looked good, really good, she and green Terra and life and freedom and all that I'd never have again.

'John,' she said at last, 'maybe we should save them the trouble. Maybe we should make our own exit.'

'It's a thought,' I muttered, risking a glance above the wall.

The Gorzuni were more cautious now, creeping through the

trampled gardens toward the shattered outbuilding we defended. Behind them, the main estate, last knot of our unit's resistance, lay smashed and burning. Gorzuni were swarming around us, dragging out such humans as survived and looting whatever treasure was left. I was tempted to shoot at those big furry bodies but I had to save ammunition for the detail closing in on us.

'I don't fancy life as the slave of a barbarian out-worlder,' I said. 'Though humans with technical training are much in demand and usually fairly well treated. But for a woman – ' The words trailed off. I couldn't say them.

'I might trade on my own mechanical knowledge,' she said. 'And then again, I might not. Is it worth the risk, John, my dearest?'

We were both conditioned against suicide, of course. Everyone in the broken Commonwealth navy was, except bearers of secret information. The idea was to sell our lives or liberty as exorbitantly as possible, fighting to the last moment. It was a stupid policy, typical of the blundering leadership that had helped lose us our wars. A human slave with knowledge of science and machinery was worth more to the barbarians than the few extra soldiers he could kill out of their hordes by staying alive till captured.

But the implanted inhibition could be broken by a person of strong will. I looked at Kathryn for a moment, there in the tumbled ruins of the house, and her eyes sought mine and rested, deep-blue and grave with a tremble of tears behind the long silky lashes.

'Well – ' I said helplessly, and then I kissed her.

That was our big mistake. The Gorzuni had moved closer than I realized and in Terra's gravity – about half of their home planet's – they could move like a sunbound comet.

One of them came soaring over the wall behind me, landing on his clawed splay feet with a crash that shivered in the ground.

A wild 'Whoo-oo-oo-oo!' was hardly out of his mouth before I'd blown the horned head off his shoulders. But there was a gray mass swarming behind him, and Kathryn yelled and fired into the thick of another attack from our rear.

Something stung me, a bright sharp pain and then a bomb exploding in my head and a whirling sick spiral down into blackness. The next thing I saw was Kathryn, caught in the hairy arms of a soldier. He was half again as tall as she, he'd twisted the barrel off her weapon as he wrenched it from her hands, but she was giving him a good fight. A hell of a good fight. Then I didn't see anything else for some time.

They herded us aboard a tender after dark. It was like a scene from some ancient hell – night overhead and around, lit by many score of burning houses like uneasy torches out there in the dark, and the long, weary line of humans stumbling toward the tender with kicks and blows from the guards to hurry them along.

One house was aflame not far off, soaring blue and yellow fire glancing off the metal of the ship, picking a haggard face from below, glimmering in human tears and in unhuman eyes. The shadows wove in and out, hiding us from each other save when a gust of wind blew up the fire. Then we felt a puff of heat and looked away from each other's misery.

Kathryn was not to be seen in that weaving line. I groped along with my wrists tied behind me, now and then jarred by a gunbutt as one of the looming figures grew impatient. I could hear the sobbing of women and the groaning of men in the dark, before me, behind me, around me as they forced us into the boat.

'Jimmy. Where are you, Jimmy?'

'They killed him. He's lying there dead in the ruins.'

'O God, what have we done?'

'My baby. Has anyone seen my baby? I had a baby and they took him away from me.'

'Help, help, help, help, help – '

A mumbled and bitter curse, a scream, a whine, a rattling gasp of breath, and always the slow shuffle of feet and the sobbing of the women and the children.

We were the conquered. They had scattered our armies. They had ravaged our cities. They had hunted us, through the streets and the hills and the great deeps of space, and we could only snarl and snap at them and hope that the remnants of our navy might pull a miracle. But miracles are hard to come by.

So far the Baldic League had actually occupied only the outer planets. The inner worlds were nominally under Commonwealth rule but the government was hiding or nonexistent. Only fragments of the navy fought on without authority or plan or hope, and Terra was the happy hunting ground of looters and slave raiders. Before long, I supposed bitterly, the outworlders would come in force, break the last resistance, and incorporate all the Solar System into their savage empire. Then the only free humans would be the extrasolar colonists, and a lot of them were barbaric themselves and had joined the Baldic League against the mother world.

The captives were herded into cells aboard the tender, crammed together till there was barely room to stand. Kathryn wasn't in my cell either. I lapsed into dull apathy.

When everyone was aboard, the deckplates quivered under our feet and acceleration jammed us cruelly against each other. Several humans died in that press. I had all I could do to keep the surging mass from crushing in my chest but of course the Gorzuni didn't care. There were plenty more where we came from.

The boat was an antiquated and rust-eaten wreck, with half its archaic gadgetry broken and useless. They weren't technicians, those Baldics. They were barbarians who had learned too soon how to build and handle spaceships and firearms, and a score of their planets united by a military genius had gone forth to overrun the civilized Commonwealth.

But their knowledge was usually by rote; I have known many a Baldic 'engineer' who made sacrifices to his converter, many a general who depended on astrologers or haruspices for major decisions. So trained humans were in considerable demand as slaves. Having a degree in nuclear engineering myself, I could look for a halfway decent berth, though of course there was always the possibility of my being sold to someone who would flay me or blind me or let me break my heart in his mines.

Untrained humans hadn't much chance. They were just flesh-and-blood machines doing work that the barbarians didn't

7

have automatics for, rarely surviving ten years of slavery. Women were the luxury trade, sold at high prices to the human renegades and rebels. I groaned at that thought and tried desperately to assure myself that Kathryn's technical knowledge would keep her in the possession of a nonhuman.

We were taken up to a ship orbiting just above the atmosphere. Airlocks were joined, so I didn't get a look at her from outside, but as soon as we entered I saw that she was a big interstellar transport of the Thurnogan class, used primarily for carrying troops to Sol and slaves back, but armed for bear. A formidable fighting ship when properly handled.

Guards were leaning on their rifles, all of Gorzuni race, their harness worn any way they pleased and no formality between officers and men. The barbarian armies' sloppy discipline had blinded our spit-and-polish command to their reckless courage and their savage gunnery. Now the fine-feathered Commonwealth navy was a ragged handful of hunted, desperate men and the despised outworlders were harrying them through the Galaxy.

This ship was worse than usual, though. I saw rust and mold on the unpainted plates. The fluoros were dim and in places burned out. There was a faint pulse in the gravity generators. They had long ago been stripped and refurnished with skins, stolen hold goods, cooking pots, and weapons. The Gorzuni were all as dirty and unkempt as their ship. They lounged about gnawing chunks of meat, drinking, dicing, and looking up now and then to grin at us.

A barbarian who spoke some Anglic bellowed at us to strip. Those who hesitated were cuffed so the teeth rattled in their heads. We threw the clothes in a heap and moved forward slowly past a table where a drunken Gorzuni and a very sober human sat. Medical inspection.

The barbarian 'doctor' gave each of us the most cursory glance. Most were passed on. Now and then he would look blearily at someone and say, 'Sickly. Never make trip alive. Kill.'

The man or woman or child would scream as he picked up a sword and chopped off the head with one expert sweep.

The human sat halfway on the table swinging one leg and whistling softly. Now and again the Gorzuni medic would look at him in doubt over some slave. The human would look closer. Usually he shoved them on. One or two he tapped for killing.

I got a close look at him as I walked by. He was below medium height, stockily built, dark and heavy-faced and beak-nosed, but his eyes were large and blue-gray, the coldest eyes I have ever seen on a human. He wore a loose colorful shirt and trousers of rich material probably stolen from some Terran villa.

'You filthy bastard,' I muttered.

He shrugged, indicating the iron collar welded about his neck. 'I only work here, Lieutenant,' he said mildly. He must have noticed my uniform before I shed it.

Beyond the desk, a Gorzuni played a hose on us, washing off blood and grime. And then we were herded down the lone corridors and by way of wooden ladders (the drop-shafts and elevators weren't working, it seemed) to the cells. Here they separated men and women. We went into adjoining compartments, huge echoing caverns of metal with bunks tiered along the wall, food troughs, and sanitary facilities the only furnishings.

Dust was thick on the corroded floor, and the air was cold and had a metallic reek. There must have been about five hundred men swarming hopelessly around after the barred door clanged shut on us.

Windows existed between the two great cells. We made a rush for them, crying out, pushing and crowding and snarling at each other for first chance to see if our women still lived.

I was large and strong. I shouldered my way through the mob up to the nearest window. A man was there already, flattened against the wall by the sweating bodies behind, reaching through the bars to the three hundred women who swarmed on the other side.

'Agnes!' he shrieked. 'Agnes, are you there? Are you alive?'

I grabbed his shoulder and pulled him away. He turned with a curse, and I fed him a mouthful of knuckles and sent him lurching back into the uneasy press of men. 'Kathryn!' I howled.

The echoes rolled and boomed in the hollow metal caves, crying voices, prayers and curses and sobs of despair thrown back by the sardonic echoes till our heads shivered with it. 'Kathryn! Kathryn!'

Somehow she found me. She came to me and the kiss through those bars dissolved ship and slavery and all the world for that moment. 'Oh, John, John, John, you're alive, you're here. Oh, my darling – '

And then she looked around the metal-gleaming dimness and said quickly, urgently: 'We'll have a riot on our hands, John, if these people don't calm down. See what you can do with the men. I'll tackle the women.'

It was like her. She was the most gallant soul that ever walked under Terran skies, and she had a mind which flashed in an instant to that which must be done. I wondered myself what point there was in stopping a murderous panic. Those who were killed would be better off, wouldn't they? But Kathryn never surrendered, so I couldn't either.

We turned back into our crowds, and shouted and pummeled and bullied, and slowly others came to our aid until there was a sobbing quiet in the belly of the slave ship. Then we organized turns at the windows. Kathryn and I both looked away from those reunions, or from the people who found no one. It isn't decent to look at a naked soul.

The engines began to thrum. Under way, outward bound to the ice mountains of Gorzun, no more to see blue skies and green grass, no clean salt smell of ocean and roar of wind in tall trees. Now we were slaves and had nothing to do but wait.

* * *

There was no time aboard the ship. The few dim fluoros kept our hold forever in its uneasy twilight. The Gorzuni swilled us at such irregular intervals as they thought of it, and we heard only the throb of the engines and the asthmatic sigh of the ventilators. The twice-normal gravity kept most of us too weary even to talk much. But I think it was about forty-eight hours after leaving Terra, when the ship had gone into secondary drive and was leaving the Solar System altogether, that the man with the iron collar came down to us.

He entered with an escort of armed and wary Gorzuni who kept their rifles lifted. We looked up dull-eyed at the short stocky figure. His voice was almost lost in the booming vastness of the hold.

'I'm here to classify you. Come one at a time and tell me your name and training, if any. I warn you that the penalty for claiming training you haven't got is torture, and you'll be tested if you do make such claims.'

We shuffled past. A Gorzuni, the drunken doctor, had a tattoo needle set up and scribbled a number on the palm of each man. This went into the human's notebook, together with name, age and profession. Those without technical skills, by far the majority, were shoved roughly back. The fifty or so who claimed valuable education went over into a corner.

The needle burned my palm and I sucked the breath between my teeth. The impersonal voice was dim in my ears: 'Name?'

'John Henry Reeves, age twenty-five, lieutenant in the Commonwealth navy and nuclear engineer before the wars.' I snapped the answers out, my throat harsh and a bitter taste in my mouth. The taste of defeat.

'Hmmm.' I grew aware that the pale chill eyes were resting on me with an odd regard. Suddenly the man's thick lips twisted in a smile. It was a strangely charming smile, it lit his whole dark face with a brief radiance of merriment. 'Oh, yes, I remember you, Lieutenant Reeves. You called me, I believe, a filthy bastard.'

'I did,' I almost snarled. My hand throbbed and stung. I was unwashed and naked and sick with my own helplessness.

'You may be right at that,' he nodded. 'But I'm in bad need of a couple of assistants. This ship is a wreck. She may never make Gorzun without someone to nurse the engines. Care to help me?'

'No,' I said.

'Be reasonable. By refusing you only get yourself locked in the special cell we're keeping for trained slaves. It'll be a long voyage, the monotony will do more to break your spirit than

11

any number of lashings. As my assistant you'll have proper quarters and a chance to move around and use your hands.'

I stood thinking. 'Did you say you needed two assistants?' I asked.

'Yes. Two who can do something with this ruin of a ship.'

'I'll be one,' I said, 'if I can name the other.'

He scowled. 'Getting pretty big for the britches you don't have, aren't you?'

'Take it or leave it,' I shrugged. 'But this person is a hell of a good technician.'

'Well, nominate him then, and I'll see.'

'It's a her. My fiancée, Kathryn O'Donnell.'

'No.' He shook his dark curly head. 'No woman.'

'No man, then.' I grinned at him without mirth.

Anger flamed coldly in his eyes. 'I can't have a woman around my neck like another millstone.'

'She'll carry her own weight and more. She was a j.g. in my own ship, and she fought right there beside me till the end.'

The temper was gone without leaving a ripple. Not a stir of expression in the strong, ugly, olive-skinned face that looked up at me. His voice was as flat. 'Why didn't you say so before? All right, then, Lieutenant. But the gods help you if you aren't both as advertised!'

It was hard to believe it about clothes – the difference they made after being just another penned and naked animal. And a meal of stew and coffee, however ill prepared, scrounged at the galley after the warriors had messed, surged in veins and bellies which had grown used to swilling from a pig trough.

I realized bleakly that the man in the iron collar was right. Not many humans could have remained free of soul on the long, heart-cracking voyage to Gorzun. Add the eternal weariness of double weight, the chill dark grimness of our destination planet, utter remoteness from home, blank hopelessness, perhaps a touch of the whip and branding iron, and men became tame animals trudging meekly at the heels of their masters.

'How long have you been a slave?' I asked our new boss.

He strode beside me as arrogantly as if the ship were his. He

12

was not a tall man, for even Kathryn topped him by perhaps five centimeters, and his round-skulled head barely reached my shoulder. But he had thick muscular arms, a gorilla breadth of chest, and the gravity didn't seem to bother him at all.

'Going on four years,' he replied shortly. 'My name, by the way, is Manuel Argos, and we might as well be on first name terms from the start.'

A couple of Gorzuni came stalking down the corridor, clanking with metal. We stood aside for the giants of course, but there was no cringing in Manuel's attitude. His strange eyes followed them speculatively.

We had a cabin near the stern, a tiny cubbyhole with four bunks, bleak and bare but its scrubbed cleanliness was like a breath of home after the filth of the cell. Wordlessly, Manuel took one of the sleazy blankets and hung it across a bed as a sort of curtain. 'It's the best privacy I can offer you, Kathryn,' he said.

'Thank you,' she whispered.

He sat down on his own bunk and looked up at us. I loomed over him, a blond giant against his squatness. My family had been old and cultured and wealthy before the wars, and he was the nameless sweeping of a hundred slums and spaceports, but from the first there was never any doubt of who was the leader.

'Here's the story,' he said in his curt way. 'I knew enough practical engineering in spite of having no formal education to get myself a fairly decent master in whose factories I learned more. Two years ago he sold me to the captain of this ship. I got rid of the so-called chief engineer they had then. It wasn't hard to stir up a murderous quarrel between him and a jealous subordinate. But his successor is a drunken bum one generation removed from the forests.

'In effect, I'm the engineer of this ship. I've also managed to introduce my master, Captain Venjain, to marijuana. It hits a Gorzuni harder than it does a human, and he's a hopeless addict by now. It's partly responsible for the condition of this ship and the laxness among the crew. Poor leadership, poor organization. That's a truism.'

I stared at him with a sudden chill along my spine. But it was Kathryn who whispered the question: 'Why?'

13

'Waiting my chance,' he snapped. 'I'm the one who made junk out of the engines and equipment. I tell them it's old and poorly designed. They think that only my constant work holds the ship together at all; but I could have her humming in a week if I cared to. I can't wait too much longer. Sooner or later someone else is going to look at that machinery and tell them it's been deliberately haywired. So I've been waiting for a couple of assistants with technical training and a will to fight. I hope you two fit the bill. If not – ' He shrugged. 'Go ahead and tell on me. It won't free you. But if you want to risk lives that won't be very long or pleasant on Gorzun, you can help me take over the ship?'

I stood for some time looking at him. It was uncanny, the way he had sized us up from a glance and a word. Certainly the prospect was frightening. I could feel sweat on my face. My hands were cold. But I'd follow him. Before God, I'd follow him!

Still – 'Three of us?' I jeered. 'Three of us against a couple of hundred warriors?'

'There'll be more on our side,' he said impassively. After a moments' silence he went on: 'Naturally, we'll have to watch ourselves. Only two or three of them know Anglic. I'll point them out to you. And of course our work is under surveillance. But the watchers are ignorant. I think you have the brains to fool them.'

'I – ' Kathryn stood, reaching for words. 'I can't believe it,' she said at last. 'A naval vessel in this condition – '

'Things were better under the old Baldic conquerors,' admitted Manuel. 'The kings who forged the League out of a hundred planets still in barbaric night, savages who'd learned to build spaceships and man atomblasts and little else. But even they succeeded only because there was no real opposition. The Commonwealth society was rotten, corrupt, torn apart by civil wars, its leadership a petrified bureaucracy, its military forces scattered over a thousand restless planets, its people ready to buy peace rather than fight. No wonder the League drove everything before it!

'But after the first sack of Terra fifteen years ago, the

14

barbarians split up. The forceful early rulers were dead, and their sons were warring over an inheritance they didn't know how to rule. The League is divided into two hostile regions now, and I don't know how many splinter groups. Their old organization is shot to hell.

'Sol didn't rally in time. It was still under the decadent Commonwealth government. So one branch of the Baldics has now managed to conquer our big planets. But the fact that they've been content to raid and loot the inner worlds instead of occupying them and administering them decently shows the decay of their own society. Given the leadership, we could still throw them out of the Solar System and go on to overrun their home territories. Only the leadership hasn't been forthcoming.'

It was a harsh, angry lecture, and I winced and felt resentment within myself. 'Damn it, we've fought,' I said.

'And been driven back and scattered.' His heavy mouth lifted in a sneer. 'Because there hasn't been a chief who understood strategy and organization, and who could put heart into his men.'

'I suppose,' I said sarcastically, 'that you're that chief.'

His answer was flat and calm and utterly assured. 'Yes.'

In the days that followed I got to know more about Manuel Argos. He was never loath to talk about himself.

His race, I suppose, was primarily Mediterranean-Anatolian, with more than a hint of Negro and Oriental, but I think there must have been some forgotten Nordic ancestor who looked out of those ice-blue eyes. A blend of all humanity, such as was not uncommon these days.

His mother had been a day laborer on Venus. His father, though he was never sure, had been a space prospector who died young and never saw his child. When he was thirteen he shipped out for Sirius and had not been in the Solar Sytem since. Now, at forty, he had been spaceman, miner, dock walloper, soldier in the civil wars and against the Baldics, small-time politician on the colony planets, hunter, machinist, and a number of darker things.

Somewhere along the line, he had found time to do an astonishing amount of varied reading, but his reliance was always more on his own senses and reason and intuition than on books. He had been captured four years ago in a Gorzuni raid on Alpha Centauri, and had set himself to study his captors as cold-bloodedly as he had studied his own race.

Yes, I learned a good deal about him but nothing of him. I don't think any living creature ever did. He was not one to open his heart. He went wrapped in loneliness and dreams all his days. Whether the chill of his manner went into his soul, and the rare warmth was only a mask, or whether he was indeed a yearning tenderness sheathed in armor of indifference, no one will ever be sure. And he made a weapon out of that uncertainty. A man never knew what to await from him and was thus forever strained in his presence, open to his will.

'He's a strange sort,' said Kathryn once, when we were alone. 'I haven't decided whether he's crazy or a genius.'

'Maybe both, darling,' I suggested a little irritably. I didn't like to be dominated.

'Maybe. But what is sanity, then?' She shivered and crept close to me. 'I don't want to talk about it.'

The ship wallowed on her way, through a bleak glory of stars, alone in light-years of emptiness with her cargo of hate and fear and misery and dreams. We worked, and waited, and the slow days passed.

The laboring old engines had to be fixed. Some show had to be made for the gray-furred giants who watched us in the flickering gloom of the power chambers. We wired and welded and bolted, tested and tore down and rebuilt, sweltering in the heat of bursting atoms that rolled from the radiation shields, deafened by the whine of generators and thud of misadjusted turbines and the deep uneven drone of the great converters. We fixed Manuel's sabotage until the ship ran almost smoothly. Later we would on some pretext throw the whole thing out of kilter again. 'Penelope's tapestry,' said Manuel, and I wondered that a space tramp could make the classical allusion.

'What are we waiting for?' I asked him once. The din of the

generator we were overhauling smothered our words. 'When do we start our mutiny?'

He glanced up at me. The light of our trouble lamp gleamed off the sweat on his ugly pockmarked face. 'At the proper time,' he said coldly. 'For one thing, it'll be while the captain is on his next dope jag.'

Meanwhile two of the slaves had tried a revolt of their own. When an incautious guard came too near the door of the mens' cell one of them reached out and snatched his gun from the holster and shot him down. Then he tried to blast the lock off the bars. When the Gorzuni came down to gas him his fellow battled them with fists and teeth till the rebels were knocked out. Both were flayed living in the presence of the other captives.

Kathryn couldn't help crying after we were back in our cabin. She buried her face against my breast and wept till I thought she would never stop weeping. I held her close and mumbled whatever foolish words came to me.

'They had it coming,' said Manuel. There was contempt in his voice. 'The fools. The blind stupid fools! They could at least have held the guard as a hostage and tried to bargain. No, they had to be heroes. They had to shoot him down. Now the example has frightened all of the others. Those men deserved being skinned.'

After a moment, he added thoughtfully. 'Still, if the fear-emotion aroused in these slaves can be turned to hate it may prove useful. The shock has at least jarred them from their apathy.'

'You're a heartless bastard,' I said tonelessly.

'I have to be, seeing that everyone else chooses to be brainless. These aren't times for the tender-minded, you. This is an age of dissolution and chaos, such as has often happened in history, and only a person who first accepts the realities of the situation can hope to do much about them. We don't live in a cosmos where perfection is possible or even desirable. We have to make our compromises and settle for the goals we have some chance of attaining.' To Kathryn, sharply: 'Now stop that snuffling. I have to think.'

She gave him a wide-eyed tear-blurred look.

'It gives you a hell of an appearance.' He grinned nastily.

'Nose red, face swollen, a bad case of hiccoughs. Nothing pretty about crying, you.'

She drew a shuddering breath and there was anger flushing her cheeks. Gulping back the sobs, she drew away from me and turned her back on him.

'But I stopped her,' whispered Manuel to me with a brief impishness.

* * *

The endless, meaningless days had worn into a timelessness where I wondered if this ship were not the Flying Dutchman, outward bound forever with a crew of devils and the damned. It was no use trying to hurry Manuel, I gave that up and slipped into the round of work and waiting. Now I think that part of his delay was on purpose, that he wanted to grind the last hope out of the slaves and leave only a hollow yearning for vengeance. They'd fight better that way.

I hadn't much chance to be alone with Kathryn. A brief stolen kiss, a whispered word in the dimness of the engine room, eyes and hands touching lightly across a rusty, greasy machine. That was all. When we returned to our cabin we were too tired, generally, to do much except sleep.

I did once notice Manuel exchange a few words in the slave pen with Ensign Hokusai, who had been captured with Kathryn and myself. Someone had to lead the humans, and Hokusai was the best man for that job. But how had Manuel known? It was part of his genius for understanding.

The end came suddenly. Manuel shook me awake. I blinked wearily at the hated walls around me, feeling the irregular throb of the gravity field that was misbehaving again. More work for us. 'All right, all right,' I grumbled. 'I'm coming.'

When he flicked the curtain from Kathryn's bunk and aroused her, I protested. 'We can handle it. Let her rest.'

'Not now!' he answered. Teeth gleamed white in the darkness of his face. 'The captain's off in never-never land. I heard two of the Gorzuni talking about it.'

That brought me bold awake, sitting up with an eerie chill along my spine. 'Now – ?'

18

'Take it easy,' said Manuel. 'Lots of time.'

We threw on our clothes and went down the long corridors. The ship was still. Under the heavy shuddering drone of the engines, there was only the whisper of our shoes and the harsh rasp of the breath in my lungs. Kathryn was white-faced, her eyes enormous in the gloom. But she didn't huddle against me. She walked between the two of us and a remoteness was over her that I couldn't quite understand. Now and then we passed a Gorzuni warrior on some errand of his own, and shrank aside as became slaves. But I saw the bitter triumph in Manuel's gaze as he looked after the titans.

In the power chamber where the machines loomed in a flickering red twilight like heathen gods, we found three Gorzuni standing there, armed engineers who snarled at us. One of them tried to cuff Manuel. He dodged without seeming to notice and bent over the gravity generator and signaled me to help him lift the cover.

I could see that there was a short circuit in one of the field coils, inducing a harmonic that imposed a flutter on the spacewarping current. It wouldn't have taken long to fix. But Manuel scratched his head, and glanced back at the ignorant giants who loomed over our shoulders. He began tracing wires with elaborate puzzlement.

He said to me: 'We'll work up to the auxiliary atom-converter. I've fixed that to do what I want.'

I knew the Gorzuni couldn't understand us, and that human expressions were meaningless to them, but an uncontrollable shiver ran along my nerves.

Slowly we fumbled to the squat engine which was the power source for the ship's internal machinery. Manuel hooked in an oscilloscope and studied the trace as if it meant something. 'Ah-hah!' he said.

We unbolted the antiradiation shield, exposing the outlet valve. I knew that the angry, blood-red light streaming from it was harmless, that baffles cut off most of the radioactivity, but I couldn't help shrinking from it. When a converter is flushed through the valve, you wear armor.

Manuel went over to a workbench and took a gadget from it

which he'd made. I knew it was of no use for repair but he'd pretended to make a tool of it in previous jobs. It was a lead-plated flexible hose springing from a magnetronic pump, with a lot of meters and switches haywired on for pure effect. 'Give me a hand, John,' he said quietly.

We fixed the pump over the outlet valve and hooked up the two or three controls that really meant something. I heard Kathryn gasp behind me, and the dreadful realization burst into my own brain and numbed my hands. There wasn't even a gasket –

The Gorzuni engineer strode up to us, rumbling a question in his harsh language, his fellows behind him. Manuel answered readily, not taking his gaze off the wildly swinging fake meters.

He turned to me, and I saw the dark laughter in his eyes. 'I told them the converter is overdue for a flushing out of waste products,' he said in Anglic. 'As a matter of fact, the whole ship is.'

He took the hose in one hand and the other rested on a switch of the engine. 'Don't look Kathryn,' he said tonelessly. Then he threw the switch.

I heard the baffle plates clank down. Manuel had shorted out the automatic safety controls which kept them up when the atoms were burning. I threw a hand over my own eyes and crouched.

The flame that sprang forth was like a bit of the sun. It sheeted from the hose and across the room. I felt my skin shriveling from incandescence and heard the roar of cloven air. In less than a second, Manuel had thrown the baffles back into place but his improvised blaster had torn away the heads of the three Gorzuni and melted the farther wall. Metal glowed white as I looked again, and the angry thunders boomed and echoed and shivered deep in my bones till my skull rang with it.

Dropping the hose, Manuel stepped over to the dead giants and yanked the guns from their holsters. 'One for each of us,' he said.

20

Turning to Kathryn: 'Get on a suit of armor and wait down here. The radioactivity is bad, but I don't think it'll prove harmful in the time we need. Shoot anyone who comes in.'

'I – ' Her voice was faint and thin under the rolling echoes. 'I don't want to hide – '

'Damn it, you'll be our guard. We can't let those monsters recapture the engine room. Now, null gravity!' And Manuel switched off the generator.

Free fall yanked me with a hideous nausea. I fought down my outraged stomach and grabbed a post to get myself back down to the deck. Down – no. There was no up and down now. We were floating free. Manuel had nullified the gravity advantage of the Gorzuni.

'All right, John, let's go!' he snapped.

I had time only to clasp Kathryn's hand. Then we were pushing off and soaring out the door and into the corridor beyond. Praise all gods, the Commonwealth navy had at least given its personnel free-fall training. But I wondered how many of the slaves would know how to handle themselves.

The ship roared around us. Two Gorzuni burst from a side cabin, guns in hand. Manuel burned them as they appeared, snatched their weapons, and swung on toward the slave pen.

The lights went out. I swam in darkness alive with the rage of the enemy. 'What the hell – ' I gasped.

Manuel's answer came dryly out of blackness: 'Kathryn knows what to do. I told her a few days ago.'

At the moment I had no time to realize the emptiness within me from knowing that those two had been talking without me. There was too much else to do. The Gorzuni were firing blind. Blaster bolts crashed down the halls. Riot was breaking loose. Twice a lightning flash sizzled within centimeters of me. Manuel fired back at isolated giants, killing them and collecting their guns. Shielded by the dark, we groped our way to the slave pens.

No guards were there. When Manuel began to melt down the locks with low-power blasting I could dimly see the tangle of free-floating naked bodies churning and screaming in the vast gloom. A scene from an ancient hell. The fall of the rebel

21

angels. Man, child of God, had stormed the stars and been condemned to Hell for it.

And now he was going to burst out!

Hokusai's flat eager face pressed against the bars. 'Get us out,' he muttered fiercely.

'How many can you trust?' asked Manuel.

'About a hundred. They're keeping their heads, see them waiting over there? And maybe fifty of the women.'

'All right. Bring out your followers. Let the rest riot for a while. We can't do anything to help them.'

The men came out, grimly and silently, hung there while I opened the females' cage. Manuel passed out such few guns as we had. His voice lifted in the pulsing dark.

'All right. We hold the engine room. I want six with guns to go there now and help Kathryn O'Donnell hold it for us. Otherwise the Gorzuni will recapture it. The rest of us will make for the arsenal.'

'How about the bridge?' I asked.

'It'll keep. Right now the Gorzuni are panicked. It's part of their nature. They're worse than humans when it comes to mass stampedes. But it won't last and we have to take advantage of it. Come on!'

Hokusai led the engine room party – his naval training told him where the chamber would be – and I followed Manuel, leading the others out. There were only three or four guns between us but at least we knew where we were going. And by now few of the humans expected to live or cared about much of anything except killing Gorzuni. Manuel had timed it right.

We fumbled through a livid darkness, exchanging shots with warriors who prowled the ship firing at everything that moved. We lost men but we gained weapons. Now and again we found dead aliens, killed in the rioting, and stripped them too. We stopped briefly to release the technicians from their special cage and then shoved violently for the arsenal.

The Gorzuni all had private arms, but the ship's collection was not small. A group of sentries remained at the door, defending it against all comers. They had a portable shield

22

against blaster bolts. I saw our flames splatter off it and saw men die as their fire raked back at us.

'We need a direct charge to draw their attention, while a few of us use the zero gravity to soar "overhead" and come down on them from "above",' said Manuel's cold voice. It was clear, even in that wild lightning-cloven gloom. 'John, lead the main attack.'

'Like hell!' I gasped. It would be murder. We'd be hewed down as a woodsman hews saplings. And Kathryn was waiting – Then I swallowed rage and fear and lifted a shout to the men. I'm no braver than anyone else but there is an exaltation in battle, and Manuel used it as calculatingly as he used everything else.

We poured against them in a wall of flesh, a wall that they ripped apart and sent lurching back in tattered fragments. It was only an instant of flame and thunder, then Manuel's flying attack was on the defenders, burning them down, and it was over. I realized vaguely that I had a seared patch on my leg. It didn't hurt just then, and I wondered at the minor miracle which had kept me alive.

Manuel fused the door and the remnants of us swarmed in and fell on the racked weapons with a terrible fierceness. Before we had them all loaded a Gorzuni party charged us but we beat them off.

There were flashlights too. We had illumination in the seething dark. Manuel's face leaped out of that night as he gave his crisp, swift orders. A gargoyle face, heavy and powerful and ugly, but men jumped at his bidding. A party was assigned to go back to the slave pens and pass our weapons to the other humans and bring them back here.

Reinforcements were sent to the engine room. Mortars and small antigrav cannon were assembled and loaded. The Gorzuni were calming too. Someone had taken charge and was rallying them. We'd have a fight on our hands.

We did!

I don't remember much of those fire-shot hours. We lost heavily in spite of having superior armament. Some three hundred humans survived the battle. Many of them were badly wounded. But we took the ship. We hunted down the last Gorzuni and flamed those who tried to surrender. There was no mercy in us. The Gorzuni had beaten it out, and now they faced the monster they had created. When the lights went on again three hundred weary humans lived and held the ship.

* * *

We held a conference in the largest room we could find. Everyone was there, packed together in sweaty silence and staring at the man who had freed them. Theoretically it was a democratic assembly called to decide our next move. In practice Manuel Argos gave his orders.

'First, of course,' he said, his soft voice somehow carrying through the whole great chamber, 'we have to make repairs, both of battle damage and of the deliberately mishandled machinery. It'll take a week, I imagine, but then we'll have us a sweet ship. By that time, too, you'll have shaken down into a crew. Lieutenant Reeves and Ensign Hokusai will give combat instruction. We're not through fighting yet.'

'You mean – ' A man stood up in the crowd. 'You mean, sir, that we'll have opposition on our return to Sol? I should think we could just sneak in. A planet's too big for blockade, you know, even if the Baldics cared to try.'

'I mean,' said Manuel calmly, 'that we're going on to Gorzun.'

It would have a meant a riot if everyone hadn't been so tired. As it was, the murmur that ran through the assembly was ominous.

'Look, you,' said Manuel patiently, 'we'll have us a first-class fighting ship by the time we get there, which none of the enemy has. We'll be an expected vessel, one of their own, and in no case do they expect a raid on their home planet. It's a chance to give them a body blow. The Gorzuni don't name their ships, so I propose we christen ours now – the *Revenge*.'

It was sheer oratory. His voice was like an organ. His words were those of a wrathful angel. He argued and pleaded and bullied and threatened and then blew the trumpets for us. At the end they stood up and cheered for him. Even my own heart lifted and Kathryn's eyes were wide and shining. Oh, he was cold and harsh and overbearing, but he made us proud to be human.

In the end, it was agreed, and the Solar ship *Revenge*, Captain Manuel Argos, First Mate John Henry Reeves, resumed her way to Gorzun.

In the days and weeks that followed, Manuel talked much of his plans. A devastating raid on Gorzun would shake the barbarian confidence and bring many of their outworld ships swarming back to defend the mother world. Probably the rival half of the Baldic League would seize its chance and fall on a suddenly weakened enemy. The *Revenge* would return to Sol, by that time possessed of the best crew in the known universe, and rally mankind's scattered forces. The war would go on until the System was cleared –

' – and then, of course, continue till all the barbarians have been conquered,' said Manuel.

'Why?' I demanded, 'Interstellar imperialism can't be made to pay. It does for the barbarians because they haven't the technical facilities to produce at home what they can steal elsewhere. But Sol would only be taking on a burden.'

'For defense,' said Manuel. 'You don't think I'd let a defeated enemy go off to lick his wounds and prepare a new attack, do you? No, everyone but Sol must be disarmed, and the only way to enforce such a peace is for Sol to be the unquestioned ruler.' He added thoughtfully: 'Oh, the empire won't have to expand forever. Just till it's big enough to defend itself against all comers. And a bit of economic readjustment could make it a paying proposition, too. We could collect tribute, you know.'

'An empire – ?' asked Kathryn. 'But the Commonwealth is democratic – '

'Was democratic!' he snapped. 'Now it's rotted away. Too bad, but you can't revive the dead. This is an age in history such as has often occurred before when the enforced peace of Caesarism is the only solution. Maybe not a good solution but better than the devastation we're suffering now. When there's been a long enough period of peace and unity it may be time to think of reinstating the old republicanism. But that time is many

25

centuries in the future, if it ever comes. Just now the socio-economic conditions aren't right for it.'

He took a restless turn about the bridge. A million stars of space in the viewport blazed like a chill crown over his head. 'It'll be an empire in fact,' he said, 'and therefore it should be an empire in name. People will fight and sacrifice and die for a gaudy symbol when the demands of reality don't touch them. We need a hereditary aristocracy to put on a good show. It's always effective, and the archaism is especially valuable to Sol just now. It'll recall the good old glamorous days before space travel. It'll be even more of a symbol now than it was in its own age. Yes, an empire, Kathryn, the Empire of Sol. Peace, ye underlings!'

'Aristocracies decay,' I argued. 'Despotism is all right as long as you have an able despot but sooner or later a meathead will be born – '

'Not if the dynasty starts with strong men and women, and continues to choose good breeding stock, and raises the sons in the same hard school as the fathers. Then it can last for centuries. Especially in these days of gerontology and hundred-year active lifespans.'

I laughed at him. 'One ship, and you're planning an empire in the Galaxy!' I jeered. 'And you yourself, I suppose, will be the first emperor?'

His eyes were expressionless. 'Yes,' he said. 'Unless I find a better man, which I doubt.'

Kathryn bit her lip. 'I don't like it,' she said. 'It's – cruel.'

'This is a cruel age, my dear,' he said gently.

Gorzun rolled black and huge against a wilderness of stars. The redly illuminated hemisphere was like a sickle of blood as we swept out of secondary drive and rode our gravbeams down toward the night side.

Once only were we challenged. A harsh gabble of words came over the transonic communicator. Manuel answered smoothly in the native language, explaining that our vision set was out of order, and gave the recognition signals contained in the codebook. The warship let us pass.

26

Down and down and down, the darkened surface swelling beneath us, mountains reaching hungry peaks to rip the vessel's belly out, snow and glaciers and a churning sea lit by three hurtling moons. Blackness and cold and desolation.

Manuel's voice rolled over the intercom: 'Look below, men of Sol. Look out the viewports. This is where they were taking us!'

A snarl of pure hatred answered him. That crew would have died to the last human if they could drag Gorzun to oblivion with them. God help me, I felt that way myself.

It had been a long, hard voyage even after our liberation, and the weariness in me was only lifted by the prospect of battle. I'd been working around the clock, training men, organizing the hundred units a modern warcraft needs. Manuel, with Kathryn for secretary and general assistant, had been driving himself even more fiercely, but I hadn't seen much of either of them. We'd all been too busy.

Now the three of us sat on the bridge watching Gorzun shrieking up to meet us. Kathryn was white and still, the hand that rested on mine was cold. I felt a tension within myself that thrummed near the breaking point. My orders to my gun crews were strained. Manuel alone seemed as chill and unruffled as always. There was steel in him. I sometimes wondered if he really was human.

Atmosphere screamed and thundered behind us. We roared over the sea, racing the dawn, and under its cold colorless streaks of light we saw Gorzun's capital city rise from the edge of the world.

I had a dizzying glimpse of squat stone towers, narrow canyons of streets, and the gigantic loom of spaceships on the rim of the city. Then Manuel nodded and I gave my firing orders.

Flame and ruin exploded beneath us. Spaceships burst open and toppled to crush buildings under their huge mass. Stone and metal fused, ran in lava between crumbling walls. The ground opened and swallowed half the town. A blue-white hell of atomic fire winked through the sudden roil of smoke. And the city died.

We slewed skyward, every girder protesting, and raced for the next great spaceport. There was a ship riding above it. Perhaps they had been alarmed already. We never knew. We opened up, and she fired back, and while we maneuvered in the heavens the *Revenge* dropped her bombs. We took a pounding, but our forcescreens held and theirs didn't. The burning ship smashed half the city when it fell.

On to the next site shown by our captured maps. This time we met a cloud of space interceptors. Ground missiles were arcing up against us. The *Revenge* shuddered under the blows. I could almost see our gravity generator smoking as it tried to compensate for our crazy spins and twists and lurchings. We fought them, like a bear fighting a dog pack, and scattered them and laid the base waste.

'All right,' said Manuel. 'Let's get out of here.'

Space became a blazing night around us as we climbed above the atmosphere. Warships would be thundering on their way now to smash us. But how could they locate a single ship in the enormousness between the worlds? We went into secondary drive, a tricky thing to do so near a sun, but we'd tightened the engines and trained the crew well. In minutes we were at the next planet, also habitable. Only three colonies were there. We smashed them all!

The men were cheering. It was more like the yelp of a wolf pack. The snarl died from my own face and I felt a little sick with the ruin. Our enemies, yes. But there were many dead. Kathryn wept, slow silent tears running down her face, shoulders shaking.

Manuel reached over and took her hand. 'It's done, Kathryn,' he said quietly. 'We can go home now.'

He added after a moment, as if to himself: 'Hate is a useful means to an end but damned dangerous. We'll have to get the racist complex out of mankind. We can't conquer anyone, even the Gorzuni, and keep them as inferiors and hope to have a stable empire. All races must be equal.' He rubbed his strong square chin. 'I think I'll borrow a leaf from the old Romans. All worthy individuals, of any race, can become terrestrial citizens. It'll be a stabilizing factor.'

28

'You,' I said, with a harshness in my throat, 'are a megalo-maniac.' But I wasn't sure any longer.

It was winter in Earth's northern hemisphere when the *Revenge* came home. I walked out into snow that crunched under my feet and watched my breath smoking white against the clear pale blue of the sky. A few others had come out with me. They fell on their knees in the snow and kissed it. They were a wild-looking gang, clad in whatever tatters of garment they could find, the men bearded and long-haired, but they were the finest, deadliest fighting crew in the Galaxy now. They stood there looking at the gentle sweep of hills, at blue sky and ice-flashing trees and a single crow hovering far overhead, and tears froze in their beards.

Home.

We had signalled other units of the Navy. Some would come along to pick us up soon and guide us to the secret base on Mercury, and there the fight would go on. But now, just now in this eternal instant we were home.

I felt weariness like an ache in my bones. I wanted to crawl bear-like into some cave by a murmuring river, under the dear tall trees of Earth, and sleep till spring woke up the world again. But as I stood there with the thin winter wind like a cleansing bath around me, the tiredness dropped off. My body responded to the world which two billion years of evolution had shaped it for and I laughed aloud with the joy of it.

We couldn't fail. We were the freemen of Terra fighting for our own hearthfires and the deep ancient strength of the planet was in us. Victory and the stars lay in our hands, even now, even now.

I turned and saw Kathryn coming down the airlock gangway. My heart stumbled and then began to race. It had been so long, so terribly long. We'd had so little time but now we were home, and she was singing.

Her face was grave as she approached me. There was something remote about her and a strange blending of pain with the joy that must be in her too. The frost crackled in her dark unbound hair, and when she took my hands her own were cold.

29

'Kathryn, we're home,' I whispered. 'We're home, and free, and alive. O Kathryn, I love you!'

She said nothing, but stood looking at me forever and forever until Manuel Argos came to join us. The little stocky man seemed embarrassed – the first and only time I ever saw him quail, even faintly.

'John,' he said, 'I've got to tell you something.'

'It'll keep,' I answered. 'You're the captain of the ship. You have authority to perform marriages. I want you to marry Kathryn and me, here, now, on Earth.'

She looked at me unwaveringly, but her eyes were blind with tears. 'That's it, John,' she said, so low I could barely hear her. 'It won't be. I'm going to marry Manuel.'

I stood there, not saying anything, not even feeling it yet.

'It happened on the voyage,' she said, tonelessly. 'I tried to fight myself, I couldn't. I love him, John. I love him even more than I love you, and I didn't think that was possible.'

'She will be the mother of kings,' said Manuel, but his arrogant words were almost defensive. 'I couldn't have made a better choice.'

'Do you love her too?' I asked slowly, 'or do you consider her good breeding stock?' Then: 'Never mind. Your answer would only be the most expedient. We'll never know the truth.'

It was instinct, I thought with a great resurgence of weariness. A strong and vital woman would pick the most suitable mate. She couldn't help herself. It was the race within her and there was nothing I could do about it.

'Bless you, my children,' I said.

They walked away after awhile, hand in hand under the high trees that glittered with ice and sun. I stood watching them until they were out of sight. Even then, with a long and desperate struggle yet to come, I think I knew that those were the parents of the Empire and the glorious Argolid dynasty, that they carried the future within them.

And I didn't give a damn.

Thus Manuel Argos, a hero as unconventional as van Rijn, traded the iron collar of slavery for the vitryl ring of mastery. He found the imperial signet a perfect fit for his heavy hand.

The Terran Empire he proclaimed was eagerly welcomed as a force for interstellar peace. Both ravaged worlds and those that had escaped harm chose to join the new imperium. Terra's protection brought security without loss of local autonomy. At its zenith, the Empire ruled 100,000 inhabited systems within a sphere four hundred light-years in diameter.

But size and complexity could not avert the doom that ultimately faces any human enterprise. The original worthy goal of security became a crippling obsession, especially after Terra collided with furiously ambitious Merseia. Worries about foes without masked decadence within. Knaves and fools sought to preserve their threatened authority by unjust means. To many thirty-first century citizens, the vaunted Pax Terrena had become a Pax Tyrannica.

Yet despite the impossible odds against them, the stubbornly independent settlers of Freehold vowed that Terra would not make of their world a desert, and call it peace.

OUTPOST OF EMPIRE

'No dragons are flying – '

Karlsarm looked up. The fog around him was as yet thin enough that he could glimpse the messenger. Its wings sickled across nightblue and those few stars – like diamond Spica and amber Betelgeuse – which were too bright and near to be veiled. So deep was the stillness that he heard the messenger's feathers rustle.

'Good,' he murmured. 'As I hoped.' Louder: 'Inform Mistress Jenith that she can get safely across open ground now. She is to advance her company to Gallows Wood on the double. There let someone keep watch from a treetop, but do not release the fire bees without my signal. Whatever happens.'

The sweet, unhuman voice of the messenger trilled back his order.

'Correct,' Karlsarm said. The messenger wheeled and flew northward.

'What was that?' Wolf asked.

'Enemy hasn't got anyone aloft, far as Rowlan's scouts can tell,' Karlsarm replied. 'I instructed – '

'Yes, yes,' growled his lieutenant. 'I do know Anglic, if not bird language. But are you sure you want to keep Jenith's little friends in reserve? We might have no casualties at all if they went in our van.'

'But we'd have given away another secret. And we may very badly want a surprise to spring, one of these times. You go tell Mistress Randa the main body needs maximum cover. I'm after a last personal look. When I get back, we'll charge.'

Wolf nodded. He was a rangy man, harsh-faced, his yellow hair braided. His fringed leather suit did not mark him off for what he was, nor did his weapons; dirk and tomahawk were an ordinary choice. But the two great hellhounds that padded black at his heels could only have followed the Grand Packmaster of the Windhook.

He vanished into fog and shadow. Karlsarm loped forward. He saw none of his hundreds, but he sensed them in more primitive ways. The mist patch that hid them grew tenuous with distance, until it lay behind the captain. He stopped, shadow-roofed by a lone sail tree, and peered before and around him.

They had had the coastal marshes to conceal them over most of their route. The climb by night, however, straight up Onyx Heights, had required full moonlight if men were not to fall and shatter themselves. This meant virtually no moon on the second night, when they entered the cultivated part of the plateau. But with a sidereal period of two and a third days, Selene rose nearly full again, not long after the third sundown, and waxed as it crossed the sky. At present it was hardly past maximum, a dented disk flooding the land with iciness. Karlsarm felt naked to the eyes of his enemies.

None seemed aware of him, though. Fields undulated away to a flat eastern horizon, kilometer after kilometer. They were planted in rye, silvery and silent under the moon, sweet-smelling where feet had crushed it. Far off bulked a building, but it was dark; probably nothing slept within except machines. The fact that agriculture took place entirely on robotized latifundia made the countryside thinly populated. Hence the possibility existed for Karlsarm of leading his people unobserved across it after sunset – to a five-kilometer distance from Domkirk.

Even this near, the city looked small. It was the least of the Nine, housing only about fifty thousand, and it was the second oldest, buildings huddled close together and much construction underground in the manner of pioneer settlements. Aside from streets, its mass was largely unilluminated. They were sober folk here who went early to bed. In places windows gleamed yellow. A single modern skyscraper sheened metallic beneath Selene, and it too had wakeful rooms. Several upper facets of the cathedral were visible above surrounding roofs. The moon was so brilliant that Karlsarm would have sworn he could see color in their reflection of it.

33

A faint murmur of machinery breathed across the fields. Alien it was, but Karlsarm almost welcomed the sound. The farmlands had oppressed him with their emptiness – their essential *lifelessness*, no matter how rich the crops and sleek the pastured animals – when he remembered his forests. He shivered in the chill. As if to seek comfort, he looked back westward. The fogbank that camouflaged the center of his army shimmered startlingly white. Surely it had been seen; but the phenomenon occurred naturally, this near the Lawrencian Ocean. Beyond the horizon, barely visible, as if disembodied, floated the three highest snowpeaks of the Windhook. Home was a long march off: an eternal march for those who would die.

'Stop that, you,' Karlsarm whispered to himself. He unshipped his crossbow, drew a quarrel from his quiver, loaded and cocked the piece. Hard pull on the crank, snick of the pawl were somehow steadying. He was not a man tonight but a weapon.

He trotted back to his people. The fog was thickening, swirling in cold wet drifts, as Mistress Randa sent ever more of her pets from their cages. He heard her croon a spell –

Shining mist, flow and twist,
fill this cup of amethyst.
Buzzing dozens, brotherlings,
sing your lullaby of wings.
Ah! the moonlight flew and missed!'

He wondered if it was really needed. Why must women with Skills be that secretive about their work? He heard likewise the tiny hum of the insects, and glimpsed a few when Selene sparked irridescence off them. They kept dropping down to the ryestalks after they had exuded all the droplets they could, filling up with dew and rising again. Soon the cloud was so dense that men were almost blind. They kept track of each other by signals – imitated bird calls, chirrs, cheeps, mews – and by odor, most of them having put on their distinctive war perfumes.

Karlsarm found Wolf near the red gleam of one hell-hound's eyes. 'All set?' he asked.

'Aye. If we can keep formation in this soup.'

'We'll keep it close enough. Got a lot of practice in the tidelands, didn't we? Very well, here we go.' Karlsarm uttered a low, shuddering whistle.

The sound ran from man to man, squad to squad, and those who knew flutecat language heard it as: 'We have stalked the prey down, let us leap.'

The fog rolled swiftly toward Domkirk; and none in the city observed that there was no wind to drive it.

* * *

John Ridenour had arrived that day. But he had made planetfall a week earlier and before then had crammed himself with every piece of information about Freehold that was available to him — by any means necessary, from simple reading and conversation to the most arduous machine-forced mnemonics. His whole previous career taught him how little knowledge that was. It had amused as well as annoyed him that he ended his journey explaining things to a crewman of the ship that brought him thither.

The *Ottokar* was a merchantman, Germanian owned, as tautly run as most vessels from that world. Being short of bottom on the frontiers, the Imperial Terrestrial Navy must needs charter private craft when trouble broke loose. They carried only materiel; troops still went in regular transports, properly armed and escorted.

But Ridenour was a civilian: also on time charter, he thought wryly. His job was not considered urgent. They gave him a Crown ticket on Terra and said he could arrange his own passage. It turned out to involve several transfers from one ship to another, two of them with nonhuman crews. Traffic was sparse, here where the Empire faded away into a wilderness of suns unclaimed and largely unexplored. The Germanians were of his own species, of course. But since they were a bit standoffish by culture, and he by nature, he had rattled about rather alone on what was to be the final leg of his trip.

Now, when he would actually have preferred silence and solitude, the off-duty steward's mate joined him in the saloon and insisted on talking. That was the annoyance — with Freehold in the viewscope.

'I have never seen anything more ... *prachtig* ... more magnificent,' the steward's mate declared.

Then why not shut your mouth and watch it? grumbled Ridenour to himself.

'But this is my first long voyage,' the other went on shyly.

He was little more than a boy, little older than Ridenour's first son. No doubt the rest of the men kept him severely in his place. Certainly he had hitherto been mute as far as the passenger was concerned. Ridenour found he could not be ungracious to him. 'Are you enjoying it ... ah, I don't know your name.'

'Dietrich, sir. Dietrich Steinhauer. Yes, the time has been interesting. But I wish they would tell me more about the port planets we make on our circuit. They do not like me to question them.'

'Well, don't take that to heart,' Ridenour advised. He leaned back in his chair and got out his pipe – a tall, wiry, blond, hatchet-faced man, his gray tunic-and-trousers outfit more serviceable than fashionable. 'With so much loneliness between the stars, so much awe, men have to erect defenses. Terrans are apt to get boisterous on a long voyage. But from what I've heard of Germanians, I could damn near predict they'd withdraw into routine and themselves. Once your shipmates grow used to you, decide you're a good reliable fellow, they'll thaw.'

'Really? Are you an ethnologist, sir?'

'No, xenologist.'

'But there are no nonhumans on Freehold, except the Arulians. Are there?'

'N-no. Presumably not. Biologically speaking, at any rate. But it is a strange planet, and such have been known to do strange things to their colonists.'

Dietrich gulped and was quiet for a few blessed minutes.

The globe swelled, ever greater in its changing phases as the *Ottokar* swung down from parking orbit. Against starry blackness it shone blue, banded with blinding white cloudbanks, the

36

continents hardly visible through the deep air. The violet border that may be seen from space on the rim of any terrestroid world was broader and more richly hued than Terra's. Across the whole orb flickered aurora, invisible on dayside but a pale sheet of fire on nightside. It would not show from the ground, being too diffuse; Freehold lacked the magnetic field to concentrate solar particles at the poles. Yet here it played lambent before the eye, through the thin upper layers of atmosphere. For the sun of Freehold was twice as luminous as Sol, a late type F. At a distance of 1.25 a.u., its disk was slightly smaller than that which Terra sees. But the illumination was almost a third again as great, more white than yellow; and through a glare filter one could watch flares and prominences leap millions of kilometers into space and shower fierily back.

The single moon hove into view. It was undistinguished, even in its name (how many satellites of human-settled worlds are known as Selene?), having just a quarter the mass of Luna. But it was sufficiently close in to show a fourth greater angular diameter. Because of this, and the sunlight, and a higher albedo – fewer mottlings – it gave better than twice the light. Ridenour spied it full on and was almost dazzled.

'Freehold is larger than Germania, I believe,' Dietrich's attempt at pompousness struck Ridenour as pathetic.

'Or Terra,' the xenologist said. 'Equatorial diameter in excess of 16,000 kilometers. But the mean density is quite low, making surface gravity a bare ninety per cent of standard.'

'Then why does it have such thick air, sir? Especially with an energetic sun and a nearby moon of good size?'

Hm, Ridenour thought, you're a pretty bright boy after all. Brightness should be encouraged; there's precious little of it around. 'Gravitational potential,' he said. 'Because of the great diameter, field strength decreases quite slowly. Also, even if the ferrous core is small, making for weaker tectonism and less outgassing of atmosphere than normal – still, the sheer pressure of mass on mass, in an object this size, was bound to produce respectable quantities of air and heights of mountains. These different factors work out to the result that the sea-level atmosphere is denser than Terran, but safely breathable at all altitudes of terrain.' He stopped to catch his breath.

'If it has few heavy elements, the planet must be extremely old,' Dietrich ventured.

'No, the early investigators found otherwise,' Ridenour said. 'The system's actually younger than Sol's. It evidently formed in some metal-poor region of the galaxy and wandered into this spiral arm afterward.'

'But at least Freehold is old by historical standards. I have heard it was settled more than five centuries ago. And yet the population is small. I wonder why?'

'Small initial colony, and not many immigrants afterward, to this far edge of everything. High mortality rates, too – originally, I mean, before men learned the ins and outs of a world which they had never evolved on: a more violent and treacherous world than the one your ancestors found, Dietrich. That's why, for many generations, they tended to stay in their towns, where they could keep nature at bay. But they didn't have the economic base to enlarge the towns very fast. Therefore they practiced a lot of birth control. To this day, there are only nine cities on that whole enormous surface, and five of them are on the same continent. Their inhabitants total fourteen and a half megapeople.'

'But I have heard about savages, sir. How many are they?'

'Nobody knows,' Ridenour said. 'That's one of the things I've been asked to find out.'

He spoke too curtly, of a sudden, for Dietrich to dare question him further. It was unintentional. He had merely suffered an experience that came to him every once in a while, and shook him down to bedrock.

Momentarily, he confronted the sheer magnitude of the universe.

Good God, he thought, if You do not exist – terrible God, if You do – here we are, Homo sapiens, children of Earth, creators of bonfires and flint axes and proton converters and gravity generators and faster-than-light spaceships, explorers and conquerors, dominators of an Empire which we ourselves founded,

whose sphere is estimated to include four million blazing suns . . .
here we are, and what are we? What are four million stars, out on
the fringe of one arm of the galaxy, among its hundred billion;
and what is the one galaxy among so many?

Why, I shall tell you what we are and these are, John Ridenour.
We are one more-or-less intelligent species in a universe that
produces sophonts as casually as it produces snowflakes. We are
not a hair better than our great, greenskinned, gatortailed
Merseian rivals, not even considering that they have no hair; we
are simply different in looks and language, similar in imperial
appetites. The galaxy – what tiny part of it we can ever control –
cares not one quantum whether their youthful greed and
boldness overcome our wearied satiety and caution. (Which is a
thought born of an aging civilisation, by the way.)

Our existing domain is already too big for us. We don't
comprehend it. We can't.

Never mind the estimated four million suns inside our borders.
Think just of the approximately one hundred thousand whose
planets we do visit, occupy, order about, accept tribute from. Can
you visualize the number? A hundred thousand; no more; you
could count that high in about seven hours. But can you conjure
up before you, in your mind, a well with a hundred thousand
bricks in it: and see all the bricks simultaneously?

Of course not. No human brain can go as high as ten.

Then consider a planet, a world, as big and diverse and old and
mysterious as ever Terra was. Can you see the entire planet at
once? Can you hope to understand the entire planet?

Next consider a hundred thousand of them.

No wonder Dietrich Steinhauer here is altogether ignorant about
Freehold. I myself had never heard of the place before I was asked
to take this job. And I am a specialist in worlds and the beings that
inhabit them. I should be able to treat them lightly. Did I not, a
few years ago, watch the total destruction of one?

*Oh, no. Oh, no. The multiple millions of . . . of everything
alive . . . bury the name Starkad, bury it forever. And yet it was a
single living world that perished, a mere single world.*

No wonder Imperial Terra let the facts about Freehold lie

unheeded in the data banks. Freehold was nothing but an obscure frontier dominion, a unit in the statistics. As long as no complaint was registered worthy of the sector governor's attention, why inquire further? How could one inquire further? Something more urgent is always demanding attention elsewhere. The Navy, the intelligence services, the computers, the decision makers are stretched too ghastly thin across too many stars.

And today, when war ramps loose on Freehold and Imperial marines are dispatched to fight Merseia's Arulian cat's-paws – we still see nothing but a border action. It is most unlikely that anyone at His Majesty's court is more than vaguely aware of what is happening. Certainly our admiral's call for help took long to go through channels: 'We're having worse and worse trouble with the hinterland savages. The city people are no use. They don't seem to know either what's going on. Please advise.'

And the entire answer that can be given to this appeal thus far is me. One man. Not even a Naval officer – not even a specialist in human cultures – such cannot be gotten, except for tasks elsewhere that look more vital. One civilian xenologist, under contract to investigate, report, and recommend appropriate action. Which counsel may or may not be heeded.

If I die – and the battles grow hotter each month – Lissa will weep; so will our children, for a while. I like to think that a few friends will feel sorry, a few colleagues remark what a loss this is, a few libraries keep my books on micro for a few more generations. However, that is the most I can hope for.

And this big, beautiful planet Freehold can perhaps hope for much less. The news of my death will be slow to reach official eyes. The request for a replacement will move slower yet. It may quite easily get lost.

Then what, Freehold of the Nine Cities and the vast, mapless, wild-man-haunted outlands that encircle them? Then what?

* * *

Once the chief among the settlements was Sevenhouses; but battle had lately passed through it. Though the spaceport continued in use and the *Ottokar* set down there, Ridenour

40

learned that Terran military headquarters had been shifted to Nordyke. He hitched a ride in a supply barge. Because of the war, its robopilot was given a human boss, a young lieutenant named Muhammad Sadik, who invited the xenologist to sit in the control turret with him. Thus Ridenour got a good look at the country.

Sevenhouses was almost as melancholy a sight from the air as from the ground. The original town stood intact at one edge; but that was a relic, a few stone-and-concrete buildings which piety preserved. Today's reality had been a complex of industries, dwelling places — mainly apartments — schools, parks, shops, recreation centers. The city was not large by standards of the inner Empire. But it had been neat, bright, bustling, more up-to-date than might have been expected of a community in the marshes.

Now most of it was rubble. What remained lay fire-scarred, crowded with refugees, the machinery silenced, the people sadly picking up bits and pieces of their lives. Among them moved Imperial marines, and warcraft patrolled overhead like eagles.

'Just what happened?' Ridenour asked.

Sadik shrugged. 'Same as happened at Oldenstead. The Arulians made an air assault — airborne troops and armor, I mean. They knew we had a picayune garrison and hoped to seize the place before we could reinforce. Then they'd pretty well own it, you know, the way they've got Waterfleet and Startop. If the enemy occupies a townful of His Majesty's subjects, we can't scrub that town. At least, doctrine says we can't ... thus far. But here, like at Oldenstead, our boys managed to hang on till we got help to them. We clobbered the blues pretty good, too. Not many escaped. Of course, the ground fighting was heavy and kind of bashed the town around.'

He gestured. The barge was now well aloft, and a broad view could be gotten. 'Harder on the countryside, I suppose,' he added. 'We felt free to use nukes there. They sure chew up a landscape, don't they?'

Ridenour scowled. The valley beneath him had been lovely, green and ordered, a checkerboard of mechanized agroenter-

41

prises run from the city. But the craters pocked it, and high-altitude bursts had set square kilometers afire, and radiation had turned sere most fields that were not ashen.

He felt relieved when the barge lumbered across a mountain range. The wilderness beyond was not entirely untouched. A blaze had run widely, and fallout appeared to have been heavy. But the reach of land was enormous, and presently nothing lay beneath except life. The forest that made a well-nigh solid roof was not quite like something from ancient Terra: those leaves, those meadows, those rivers and lakes had a curious brilliance; or was that due to sunlight; fierce and white out of a pale-blue sky where cumulus clouds towered intricately shadowed? The air was often darkened and clamorous with bird flocks which must number in the millions. And, as woodland gave way to prairie, Ridenour saw herds of grazers equally rich in size and variety.

'Not many planets this fertile,' Sadik remarked. 'Wonder why the colonists haven't done more with it?'

'Their society began in towns rather than smaller units like family homesteads,' Ridenour answered. 'That was unavoidable. Freehold isn't as friendly to man as you might believe.'

'Oh, I've been through some of the storms, I know.'

'And native diseases. And the fact that while native food is generally edible, it doesn't contain everything needed for human nutrition. In short, difficulties such as are normally encountered in settling a new world. They could be overcome, and were; but the process was slow, and the habit of living in a few centers became ingrained. Also, the Freeholders are under a special handicap. The planet is not quite without iron, copper and other heavy elements. But their ores occur too sparsely to support a modern industrial establishment, let alone permit it to expand. Thus Freehold has always depended on extraplanetary trade. And the system lies on the very fringe of human-dominated space. Traffic is slight and freight rates high.'

'They could do better, though,' Sadik declared. 'Food as tasty as what they raise ought to go for fancy prices on places like Bonedry and Disaster Landing – planets not terribly far, lots of metals, but otherwise none too good a home for their colonists.'

Ridenour wasn't sure if the pilot was patronizing him in revenge. He hadn't meant to be pedantic; it was his professional habit. 'I understand that the Nine Cities were in fact developing such trade, with unlimited possibilities for the future,' he said mildly. 'They also hoped to attract immigrants. But then the war came.'

'Yeh,' Sadik grunted. 'One always does, I guess.'

Ridenour recollected that war was no stranger to Freehold. Conflict, at any rate, which occasionally erupted in violence. The Arulian insurgency was the worst incident to date – but perhaps nothing more than an incident, *sub specie aeternitatis*.

The threat from the savages was something else: less spectacular, but apt to be longer lasting, with more pervasive subtle effects on the long-range course of history here.

Nordyke made a pleasant change. The strife had not touched it, save to fill the airport with ships – and the seaport, as its factories drew hungrily on the produce of other continents – and the streets with young men from every corner of the Empire. The modern town, surrounding Catwick's bright turbulent waters, retained in its angular architecture some of the starkness of the old castle-like settlements on the heights above. But in the parks, roses and jasmine were abloom; and elsewhere the taverns brawled with merriment. The male citizens were happily acquiring the money that the Imperialists brought with them; the females were still more happily helping spend it.

Ridenour had no time for amusement, even had he been inclined. Plain to see, Admiral Fernando Cruz Manqual considered him one more nuisance wished on a long-suffering planetary command by a home government that did not know its mass from a Dirac hole. He had to swing more weight than he actually carried, to get billeted in a float-shelter on the bay and arrange his background-information interviews.

One of these was with an Arulian prisoner. He did not speak any language of that world, and the slender, blue-feathered, sharp-snouted biped knew no Anglic. But both were fluent in the principal Merseian tongue, though the Arulian had difficulty with certain Eriau phonemes.

'Relax,' said Ridenour, after the other had been conducted into the office he had borrowed, and the Terran marine had gone out. 'I won't hurt you. I wear this blaster because regulations say I must. But you aren't so stupid as to attempt a break.'

'No. Nor so disloyal as to give away what would hurt my people.' The tone was more arrogant than defiant, as nearly as one could make comparisons with human emotions. The Arulian had already learned that captives were treated according to the Covenant. The reason was less moral than practical – the same reason why his own army did not try to annihilate Nordyke, though Terra's effort was concentrated here. Revenge would be total. As matters stood, the prisoners and towns they held, the other towns they could destroy, were bargaining counters. When they gave up the struggle (which surely they must, in a year or two), they could exchange these hostages for the right to go home unmolested.

'Agreed. I simply want to hear your side of the story.' Ridenour offered a cigar. 'Your species likes tobacco, does it not?'

'I thank.' A seven-fingered hand took the gift with ill-concealed eagerness. 'But you know why we fight. This is our home.'

'Um-m-m . . . Freehold was man-occupied before your race began space flight.'

'True. Yet Arulian bones have strengthened this soil for more than two centuries. By longstanding agreement, the Arulians who lived and died here did so under the Law of the Sacred Horde. For what can your law mean to us, Terran – your law of property to us who do things mutually with our phero-monesharers; your law of marriage to us who have three sexes and a breeding cycle; your law of Imperial fealty to us who find truth's wellspring in Eternal Aruli? We might have compromised, after Freehold was incorporated into your domain. Indeed, we made every reasonable attempt to do so. But repeated and flagrant violation of our rights must in the end provoke secessive action.'

Ridenour started his pipe. 'Well, now, suppose you look at the matter as I do,' he suggested. 'Freehold is an old human colony, although it lies far from Terra. It was founded before the Empire and stayed sovereign after the Empire began. There was just no special reason why we should acquire it, take on responsibility for it, while the people remained friendly. But needing trade and not getting many human visitors, they looked elsewhere. The Merseians had lately brought modern technology to Aruli. Arulian mercantile associations were busy in this region. They had the reputation of being industrious and reliable, and they could use Freehold's produce. It was natural that trade should begin; it followed that numerous Arulians should come here to live; and, as you say, it was quite proper to grant them extraterritoriality.

'*But.*' He wagged his pipestem. 'Relationships between the Terran and Merseian Empires grew more and more strained. Armed conflict became frequent in the marshes. Freehold felt threatened. By now the planet had – if not a booming industry – at least enough to make it a military asset. A tempting target for anyone. Sovereign independence looked pretty lonely, not to say fictitious. So the Nine Cities applied for membership in the Empire and were accepted – as much to forestall Merseia as for any other reason. Of course the Arulian minority objected. But they were a small minority. And in any case, as you said, compromise should have been possible. Terra respects the rights of client species. We must; they are too many for suppression. In fact, no few nonhumans have Terran citizenship.'

'Nevertheless,' the prisoner said, 'you violated what we hold hallowed.'

'Let me finish,' Ridenour said. 'Your mother world Aruli, its sphere of influence, everything there has lately become a Merseian puppet. No, wait, I know you'll deny that indignantly; but think. Consider your race's recent history. Ask yourself what pronouncements have been made by the current Bearers of the Horns – as regards Merseia versus Terra – and remember that they succeeded by revolutionary overthrow of the legitimate heirs. Never mind what abuses they claim to be correcting; only recall that they are Merseian-sponsored revolutionaries.

'Reflect how your people here, on this planet, have always

45

considered themselves Arulians rather than Freeholders. Reflect how they have, in fact, as tensions increased, supported the interests of Aruli rather than Terra. Maybe this would not have occurred, had the humans here treated you more fairly in the past. But we were confronted with your present hostility. What would you expect us to do – what would you do in our place – but decree some security regulations? Which is the prerogative of His Majesty's government, you know. The original treaty granting them extraterritoriality was signed by the Nine Cities, not by the Terran Empire.

'So you revolted, you resident aliens. And we discovered to our dismay that the rebellion was well prepared. Multiple tons of war supplies, multiple thousands of troops, had been smuggled beforehand into wilderness areas . . . from Aruli!'

'That is not true,' the prisoner said. 'Of course our mother world favors our righteous cause, but – '

'But we have census figures, remember. The registered Arulian-descended Freeholders do not add up to anything like the total in your "Sacred Horde." You yourself, my friend, whose ancestors supposedly lived here for generations, cannot speak the language! Oh, I understand Aruli's desire to avoid an open clash with Terra, and Terra's willingness to indulge this desire. But let us not waste our personal time with transparent hypocrisies, you and I.'

The prisoner refused response.

Ridenour sighed. 'Your sacrifices, what victories you have had, everything you have done is for nothing,' he went on. 'Suppose you did succeed. Suppose you actually did win your "independent world in pheromone association with the Holy Ancestral Soil" – do you really think your species would benefit? No, no. The result would mean nothing more than a new weapon for Merseia to use against Terra . . . a rather cheaply acquired one.' His smile was weary. 'We're familiar with the process, we humans. We've employed it against each other often enough in our past.'

'As you like,' the Arulian said. By instinct he was less combative as an individual than a human is, though possibly more so in a collectivity. 'Your opinions make scant difference. The great objective will be achieved before long.'

Ridenour regarded him with pity. 'Have your superiors really kept on telling you that?'

'Surely. What else?'

'Don't you understand the situation? The Empire is putting less effort into the campaign than it might, true. This *is* a distant frontier, however critical. Two hundred light-years make a long way from Terra. But our lack of energy doesn't matter in the long run, except to poor tormented Freehold.

'Because this system has in fact been taken by us. You aren't getting any more supplies from outside. You can't. Small fast courier boats might hope to run our blockade, I suppose, if they aren't too many and accept a high percentage of loss. But nothing except a full-sized task force would break it. Aruli cannot help you further. She hasn't that kind of fleet. Merseia isn't going to. The game isn't worth the candle to her. You are cut off. We'll grind you away to nothing if we must; but we hope you'll see reason, give up and depart.'

'Think. You call it yaro fever, do you not – that disease which afflicts your species but not ours – for which the antibiotic must be grown on Aruli itself where the soil bacteria are right? We capture more and more of you who suffer from yaro. When did you last see a fresh lot of antibiotic?'

The prisoner screamed. He cast his cigar at Ridenour's feet, sprang from his chair and ran to the office door. 'Take me back to the stockade,' he wept.

Ridenour's mouth twisted. Oh, well, he thought, I didn't really hope to learn anything new from any of those pathetic devils.

Besides, the savages are what I'm supposed to investigate. Though I've speculated if perhaps, in the two centuries they lived here, the Arulians had some influence on the outback people. Everybody knows they traded with them to some extent. Did ideas pass, as well as goods?

For certainly the savages have become troublesome.

* * *

47

The next day Ridenour was lucky and got a direct lead. The mayor of Domkirk arrived in Nordyke on official business. And word was that the Domkirk militia had taken prisoners after beating off a raid from the wilderness dwellers. Ridenour waited two days before he got to see the mayor, but that was about par for the course in a project like this, and he found things to do meanwhile.

Rikard Uriason proved to be a short, elegantly clad, fussy man. He was obviously self-conscious about coming from the smallest recognized community on the planet. He mentioned a visit he had once made to Terra and the fact that his daughter was studying on Ansa, twice in the first ten minutes after Ridenour entered his hotel room. He kept trying to talk the Emperor's Anglic and slipping back into Freeholder dialect. He fussed about, falling between the stools of being a gracious host and a man of the universe. Withal, he was competent and well informed where his own job was concerned.

'Yes, sir, we of Domkirk live closer to the outback than anyone else. For various reasons,' he said, after they were finally seated with drinks in their hands. A window stood open to the breeze off Catwick – always slightly alien-scented, a hint of the smell that wet iron has on Terra – and the noise of streets and freight-belts, and the view of waters glittering out to the dunes of Longenhook. 'Our municipality does not yet have the manpower to keep a radius of more than about two hundred kilometers under cultivation. Remember, Terran crops are fragile on this planet. We can mutate and breed selectively as much as we like. The native life forms will nonetheless remain hardier, eh? And, while robotic machines do most of the physical work, the requirement for supervision, decision-making human personnel is inevitably greater than on a more predictable world. This limits our range. Then, too, we are on a coastal plateau. Onyx Heights falls steeply to the ocean, westward to the Windhook, into marsh – unreclaimable – by us at our present stage of development, at any rate.'

Good Lord, Ridenour thought, I have found a man who can out-lecture me. Aloud: 'Are those tidelands inhabited by savages, then?'

'No, sir, I do not believe so. Certainly not in any significant degree. The raiders who plague our borders appear to be centered in the Windhook Range and the Upwoods beyond. That was where the recent trouble occurred, on that particular margin. We have been fortunate in that the war's desolation has passed us by. But we feel, on this very account, our patriotic duty is all the more pressing, to make up the agricultural losses caused elsewhere. Some expansion is possible, now that refugees augment our numbers. We set about clearing land in the foothills. A valley, actually, potentially fertile once the weeds and other native pests have been eradicated. Which, with modern methods, takes only about one year. A Freehold year, I mean, circa about twenty-five per cent longer than a Terran year. Ah . . . where was I? . . . yes. A band of savages attacked our pioneers. They might have succeeded. They did succeed in the past, on certain occasions, as you may know, sir. By surprise, and numbers, and proximity – for their weapons are crude. Necessarily so, iron and similar metals being scarce. But they did manage, for instance, several years ago, to frustrate an attempt on settling on Moon Garnet Lake, in spite of the attempt being supplied by air and backed by militia with reasonably modern small arms. Ahem! This time we were forewarned. We had our guards disguised as workers, their weapons concealed. Not with any idea of entrapment. Please understand that, sir. Our wish is not to lure any heathen to their deaths, only to avoid conflict. But neither had we any wish for them to spy out our capabilities. Accordingly, when a gang attacked, our militiamen did themselves proud, I may say. They inflicted casualties and drove the bulk of the raiders back into the forest. A full twenty-seven prisoners were flitted to detention in our city jail. I expect the savages will think twice before they endeavour to halt progress again.'

Even Uriason must stop for breath sometime. Ridenour took the opportunity to ask, 'What do you plan to do with your prisoners?'

The mayor looked a little embarrassed. 'That is a delicate question, sir. Technically they are criminals – one might say traitors, when Freehold is at war. However, one is almost obliged morally, is one not, to regard them as hostiles protected by the Covenant? They do by now, unfortunately, belong to a foreign culture; and they do not acknowledge our planetary government. Ah . . . in the past, rehabilitation was attempted. But it was rarely successful, short of outright brainscrub, which is not popular on Freehold. The problem is much discussed. Suggestions from Imperial experts will be welcomed, once the war is over and we can devote attention to sociodynamic matters.'

'But isn't this a rather longstanding problem?' Ridenour said.

'Well, yes and no. On the one hand, it is true that for several centuries people have been leaving the cities for the outback. Their reasons varied. Some persons were mere failures; remember, the original colonists held an ideal of individualism and made scant provision for anyone who could not, ah, cut the mustard. Some were fugitive criminals. Some were disgruntled romantics, no doubt. But the process was quite gradual. Most of those who departed did not vanish overnight. They remained in periodic contact. They traded things like gems, furs, or their own itinerant labor for manufactured articles. But their sons and grandsons tended, more and more, to adopt a purely uncivilized way of life, one which denied any need for what the cities offered.'

'Adaptation,' Ridenour nodded. 'It's happened on other planets. On olden Terra, even – like the American frontier.' Seeing that Uriason had never heard of the American frontier, he went on a bit sorrowfully: 'Not a good process, is it? The characteristic human way is to adapt the environment to oneself, not oneself to the environment.'

'I quite agree, sir. But originally, no one was much concerned in the Nine Cities. They had enough else to think about. And, indeed, emigration to the wilderness was a safety valve. Thus, when the anti-Christian upheavals occurred three hundred years ago, many Christians departed. Hence the Mechanists came to power with relatively little bloodshed – including the blood of Hedonists, who also disappeared rather than suffer persecution. Afterward, when the Third Constitution decreed tolerance, the savages were included by implication. If they wished to skulk about in the woods, why not? I suppose we, our immediate ancestors, should have made ethnological studies on them. A thread of contact did exist, a few trading posts and the like. But . . . well, sir, our orientation on Freehold is pragmatic rather than academic. We are a busy folk.'

'Especially nowadays,' Ridenour observed.

'Yes. Very true. I presume you do not speak only of the war. Before it started, we had large plans in train. Our incorporation into His Majesty's domains augured well for the furtherance of civilization on Freehold. We hope that, when the war is over, those plans may be realized. But admittedly the savages are a growing obstacle.'

'I understand they sent embassies telling this and that city not to enlarge its operations further.'

'Yes. Our spokesman pointed out to them that the Third Constitution gave each city the right to exploit its own hinterland as its citizens desired – a right which our Imperial charter has not abrogated. We also pointed out that they, the savages, were fellow citizens by virtue of residence. They need only adopt the customs and habits of civilization – and we stood ready to lend them educational, financial, even psychotherapeutic assistance toward this end. They need only meet the simple, essential requirements for the franchise, and they too could vote on how to best develop the land. Uniformly they refused. They denied the authority of the mayors and laid claim to all unimproved territory.'

Ridenour smiled, but with little mirth. 'Cultures, like individuals, die hard,' he said.

'True,' Uriason nodded. 'We civilized people are not unsympathetic. But after all! The outbacker population, their number, is unknown to us. However, it must be on the same order of magnitude as the cities', if not less. Whereas the potential population of a Freehold properly developed is – well, I leave that to your imagination, sir. Ten billion? Twenty? And not any huddled masses, either. Comfortable, well fed, productive, happy human beings. May a few million ignorant woodsrunners deny that many souls the right to be born?'

51

'None of my business,' Ridenour said. 'My contract just tells me to investigate.'

'I might add,' Uriason said, 'that Terra's rivalry with Merseia bids fair to go on for long generations. A well populated highly industrialized large planet here on the Betelgeusean frontier would be of distinct value to the Empire. To the entire human species, I believe. Do you not agree?'

'Yes, of course,' Ridenour said.

He readily got permission to return with Uriason and study the savage prisoners in depth. The mayor's car flitted back to Domkirk two days later – two of Freeholder's twenty-one hour days. And thus it happened that John Ridenour was on hand when the city was destroyed.

* * *

Karlsarm loped well in among the buildings, with his staff and guards, before combat broke loose. He heard yells, crack of blasters, hiss of slugthrowers, snap of bowstrings, sharp bark of explosives, and grinned. For they came from the right direction, as did the sudden fire-flicker above the roofs. The airport was first struck. Could it be seized in time, no dragons would fly.

Selene light had drenched and drowned pavement luminosity. Now windows were springing to life throughout the town. Karlsarm's group broke into a run. The onduty militiamen, barracked at the airport, were few. Wolf's detachment should be able to handle them in the course of grabbing vehicles and that missile emplacement which Terran engineers had lately installed. But Domkirk was filled with other men, and some of them kept arms at home. Let them boil out and get organized, and the result would be slaughterous. But they couldn't organize without communications, and the electronic center of the municipality was in the new skyscraper.

A door opened, in the flat front of an apartment house. A citizen stood outlined against the lobby behind, pajama-clad, querulous at being roused. 'What the hell d'you think – '

Light spilled across Karlsarm. The Domkirker saw: a man in bast and leather, crossbow in hands, crossbelts sagging with edged weapons; a big muscular body, weatherbeaten counte-

52

nance, an emblem of authority which was not a decent insigne but the skull and skin of a catavray crowning that wild head. '*Savages*!' the Domkirker shrieked. His voice went eunuch high with panic.

Before he had finished the word, the score of invaders were gone from his sight. More and more keening lifted, under a gathering battle racket. It suited Karlsarm. Terrified folk were no danger to him.

When he emerged in the cathedral square, he found that not every mind in town had stampeded.

The church loomed opposite, overtopping the shops which otherwise ringed the plaza. For they were darkened and were, in any event, things that might have been seen anywhere in the Empire. But the bishop's seat was raised two centuries ago, in a style already ancient. It was all colored vitryl, panes that formed one enormous many-faceted jewel, so that by day the interior was nothing except radiances – and even by moonlight, the outside flashed and dim spectra played. Karlsarm had small chance to admire. Flames stabbed and bullets sang. He led a retreat back around the corner of another building.

'Somebody's got together,' Link o' the Cragland muttered superfluously. 'Think we can bypass them?'

Karlsarm squinted. The skyscraper poked above the cathedral, two blocks farther on. But whoever commanded this plaza would soon isolate the entire area, once enough men had rallied to him. 'We'd better clean them out right away,' he decided. 'Quick, intelligencers!'

'Aye.' Noach unslung the box on his shoulder, set it down, talked into its ventholes and opened the lid. Lithe little shapes jumped forth and ran soundlessly off among the shadows. They were soon back. Noach chittered with them and reported: 'Two strong squads, one in the righthand street, one in the left. Doorways, walls, plenty of cover. Radiocoms, I think. The commanders talk at their own wrists, anyhow, and we can't jam short-range transmissions, can we? If we have to handle long-range ones too? Other men keep coming to join them. A team just brought what I suppose must be a tripod blastgun.'

Karlsarm rephrased the information in bird language and sent messengers off, one to a chief of infantry, one to the monitors.

The latter arrived first, as proper tactics dictated. The beasts – half a dozen of them, scaled and scuted crocodilian shapes, each as big as two buffalo – were not proof against Imperial-type guns. Nothing was. And being stupid, they were inflexible; you gave them their orders and hoped you had aimed them right, because that was that. But they were hard to kill ... and terrifying if you had never met them before. The blastgunners unleashed a single ill-directed thunderbolt and fled. About half the group barricaded themselves in a warehouse. The monitors battered down the wall, and the defenders yielded.

Meanwhile the Upwoods infantry dealt with the opposition in the other street. Knifemen could not very well rush riflemen. However, bowmen could pin them down until the monitors got around to them, after which a melee occurred, and everyone fought hand-to-hand anyway. A more elegant solution existed but doctrine stood, to hold secret weapons in reserve. The monitors were expendable, there being no way to evacuate creatures that long and heavy.

Karlsarm himself had already proceeded to capture the sky-scraper and establish headquarters. From the top floor, he had an overview of the entire town. It made him nervous to be enclosed in lifeless plastic, and he had a couple of the big windows knocked out. Grenades were needed to break the vitryl. So his technicians manning the communication panels, a few floors down, must endure being caged.

A messenger blew in from the night and fluted: 'The field of dragons has been taken, likewise a fortress wherein our people were captive – '

Kalrsarm's heart knocked. 'Let Mistress Evagail come to me.'

Waiting, he was greatly busied. Reports, queries, suggestions, crisis; directives, answers, decisions, actions. The streets were a phosphor web, out to the icy moonlands, but most of the buildings hulked lightless again, terror drawn back into itself. Sporadic fire flared, the brief sounds of clash drifted faintly to him. The air grew colder.

When Evagail entered, he needed an instant to disengage his mind and recognize her. They had stripped her. They had stripped off her buckskins and gold furs, swathed the supple height of her in a shapeless prison gown; and a bandage still hid most of the ruddy-coiled hair. But then she laughed at him, eyes and mouth alive with an old joy, and he leaped across a desk to seize her.

'Did they hurt you?' he finally got the courage to ask.

'No, except for this battle wound, and it isn't much,' she said. 'They did threaten us with a . . . what's the thing called? . . . a hypnoprobe, when we wouldn't talk. Just as well you came when you did, loveling.'

His tone shook: 'Better than well. If that horror isn't used exactly right, it cracks apart both reason and soul.'

'You forget I have my Skill,' she said grimly.

He nodded. That was one reason why he had launched his campaign earlier than planned: not only for her sake, but for fear that the Cities would learn what she was. She might not have succeeded in escaping or in forcing her guards to slay her, before the hypnoprobe vibrations took over her brain.

She should never have accompanied that raid on Falconsward Valley. It was nothing but a demonstration, a test . . . militarily speaking. Emotionally, though, it had been a lashing back at an outrage committed upon the land. Evagail had insisted on practicing the combat use of her Skill; but her true reason was that she wanted to avenge the flowers. Karlsarm wielded no authority to stop her. He was a friend, occasionally a lover, some day perhaps to father her children; but was not any woman as free as any man? He was the war chief of Upwoods; but was not any Mistress of a Skill necessarily independent of chiefs?

Though a failure, the attack had not been a fiasco. Going into action for the first time, and meeting a cruel surprise, the outbackers had nonetheless conducted themselves well and retreated in good order. It was sheer evil fortune that Evagail was knocked out by a grazing bullet before she had summoned her powers.

'Well, we got you here in time,' Karlsarm said. 'I'm glad.' Later he would make a ballad about his gladness.

'How stands your enterprise?'

'We grip the place, barring a few holdouts. I don't know if we managed to jam every outgoing message. Mistress Persa's buzzerwave bugs could have missed a transmitter or two. And surely our folk not handling the concenter can't long maintain the pretense of being ordinary, undisturbed Domkirkers. No aircraft have showed thus far. Better not delay any more than we must, though. So we ought to clear out the population – and nobody's stirred from their miserable dens!'

'Um-m, what are you doing to call them forth?'

'An all-phones announcement.'

Evagail laughed anew. 'I can imagine that scene, loveling! A poor, terrified family, whose idea of a wilderness trip is a picnic in Gallows Wood. Suddenly their town is occupied by hairy, skinclad savages – the same terrible people who burned the Moon Garnet camp and bush-whacked three punitive expeditions in succession and don't pay taxes or send their children to school or support the Arulian war or do *anything* civilized – but were supposed to be safe, cozy hundreds of kilometers to the west and never a match for regular troops on open ground – suddenly, here they are! They have taken Domkirk! They whoop and wave their tomahawks in the very streets! What can our families do but hide in their ... apartment, is that the word? ... the apartment, with furniture piled across the door? They can't even phone anywhere, the phone is dead, they can't call for help, can't learn what's become of Uncle Enry. Until the thing chimes. Hope leaps in Father's breast. Surely the Imperials, or the Nordyke militia, or somebody has come to the rescue! With shaking hand, he turns the instruments on. In the screen he sees – who'd you assign? Wolf, I'll wager. He sees a long-haired stone-jawed wild man, who barks in an alien dialect: "Come out of hiding. We mean to demolish your city."'

Evagail clicked her tongue. 'Did you learn nothing about civilization while you were there, Karlsarm?' she finished.

'I was too busy learning something about its machines,' he

56

said. 'I couldn't wait to be done and depart. What would you do here?'

'Let a more soothing image make reassuring noises for a while. Best a woman; may as well be me.' Karlsarm's eyes widened before his head nodded agreement. 'Meanwhile,' Evagail continued, 'you find the mayor. Have him issue the actual order to evacuate.' She looked down at her dress, grimaced, pulled it off and threw it in a corner with a violent motion. 'Can't stand that rag another heartbeat. Synthetic ... dead. Which way is the telephone central?'

Karlsarm told her. Obviously she had already discovered how to use gravshifts and slideways. She departed, striding like a leontine, and he dispatched men on a search for city officialdom.

That didn't take long. Apparently the mayor had been trying to find the enemy leader. Toms led him and another in at the point of a captured blaster. The weapon was held so carelessly that Karlsarm took it and pitched it out the window. But then, Toms was from the Trollspike region – as could be told from his breech-clout and painted skin – and had probably never seen a gun before he enlisted.

Karlsarm dismissed him and stood behind the desk, arms folded, against the dark broken pane, letting the prisoners assess him while he studied them. One looked almost comical, short, pot-bellied, red-faced and pop-eyed, as if the doom of his city were a personal insult. The fellow with him was more interesting, tall, yellow-haired, sharp-featured, neither his hastily donned clothes nor his bearing nor even his looks typical of any place on Freehold that Karlsarm had heard of.

'Who are you?' the little man sputtered. 'What's the meaning of this? Do you realize what you have done?'

'I expect he does,' said his companion dryly. 'Permit introductions. The mayor, Honorable Rikard Uriason: myself, John Ridenour, from Terra.'

An Imperialist! Karlsarm must fight to keep face impassive and muscles relaxed. He tried to match Ridenour's bow. 'Welcome, sirs. May I ask why you, distinguished outworlders, are here?'

'I was in Domkirk to interview, ah, your people,' Ridenour said. 'In the hope of getting an understanding, with the aim of eventual reconciliation. As a house guest of Mayor Uriason, I felt perhaps I could assist him – and you – to make terms.'

'Well, maybe,' Karlsarm didn't bother to sound skeptical. The Empire wasn't going to like what the out-backers intended. He turned to Uriason. 'I need your help quite urgently, Mayor. This city will be destroyed. Please tell everyone to move out immediately.'

Uriason staggered. Ridenour saved him from falling. His cheeks went gray beneath a puce webwork. 'What?' he strangled. 'No. You are insane. Insane, I tell you. You cannot. Impossible.'

'Can and will, Mayor. We hold your arsenal, your missile emplacement – nuclear weapons, which some of us know how to touch off. At most, we have only a few hours till a large force arrives from another town or an Imperial garrison. Maybe less time than that, if word got out. We want to be gone before then; and so must your folk; and so must the city.'

Uriason collapsed in a lounger and gasped for air. Ridenour seemed equally appalled, but controlled it better. 'For your own sakes, don't,' the Terran said in a voice that wavered. 'I know a good bit of human history. I know what sort of revenge is provoked by wanton destruction.'

'Not wanton,' Karlsarm answered. 'I'm quite sorry to lose the cathedral. A work of art. And museums, libraries, laboratories – But we haven't time for selective demolition.' He drove sympathy out of his body and said like one of the machines he hated: 'Nor do we have the foolishness to let this place continue as a base for military operations against us and civilian operations against our land. Whatever happens, it goes up before daybreak. Do you or do you not want the people spared? If you do, get busy and talk to them!'

Evacuation took longer than he had expected. Obedience was swift enough after Uriason's announcement. Citizens moved like cattle, streamed down the streets and out onto the airport expanse, where they milled and muttered, wept and whimpered under the bleak light of waning setting Selene. (With less luminescence to oppose, more stars had appeared, the stars of Empire, but one looked and understood how the gulf gaped between here and them, and shuddered in the pre-dawn wind.) Nevertheless people got in each other's way, didn't grasp the commands of their herders, shuffled, fainted, stalled the procession while they tried to find their kin. Besides, Karlsarm had forgotten there would be a hospital, with some patients who must be carried out and provided for in an outlying latifundium.

But, one by one, the aircraft filled with humans, and ran fifty kilometers upwind, and deposited their cargoes, and returned for more: until at last, when the first eastern paleness began to strengthen, Domkirk stood empty of everything save the wind.

Now the Upwoods army boarded and was flown west. Most of their pilots were city men, knives near to throats. Karlsarm and his few technicians saw the last shuttling vehicle off. It would return for them after they were through. (He was not unaware of the incongruity: skin-clad woodsrunners with dirks at their belts, proposing to sunder the atom!) Meanwhile it held Evagail, Wolf and Noach – his cadre – together with Uriason and Ridenour, who were helping control the crowds.

The mayor seemed to have crumpled after the pressure was off him. 'You can't do this,' he kept mumbling. 'You can't do this.' He was led up the gangway into the belly of the flyer.

Ridenour paused, a shadow in the door, and looked down. Was his glance quizzical? 'I must admit to puzzlement about your method,' he said. 'How will you explode the town without exploding yourselves? I gather your followers have only the sketchiest notion of gadgetry. It isn't simple to jury-rig a timing device.'

'No,' Karlsarm said, 'but it's simple to launch a missile at any angle you choose.' He waved to unseen Evagail. 'We'll join you shortly.'

The bus took off and dwindled among the last stars. Karlsarm directed his crew in making preparations, then returned outside to watch the first part of the spectacle. Beyond the squat turret at his back, the airfield stretched barren gray to the ruined barracks. How hideous were the works of the Machine People!

But when the missiles departed, that was a heart-stopping sight.

They were solid-fuel rockets. There had been no reason to give expensive gravitic jobs to a minor colonial town so far from the battlefront that the Arulians couldn't possibly attack it in force. The weapons lifted out of their three launchers some distance away ... with slow majesty, spouting sun-fire and white clouds, roaring their thundersong that clutched at the throat until Karlsarm gripped his crossbow and glared in defiance of the terror they roused ... faster, though, streaking off at a steep slant, rising and rising until the flames flickered out ... still rising, beyond his eyes, but drawing to a halt, caught now by the upper winds that twisted their noses downward, by the very rotation of the planet that aimed them at the place they should have defended –

And heavenward flew the second trio. And the third. Karlsarm judged he had better get into shelter.

He was at the bottom of the bunker with his men – tons of steel, concrete, force-screen generator shutting away the sky – when the rockets fell; and even so, he felt the room tremble around him.

Afterward, emerging, he saw a kilometers-high tree of dust and vapor. The command aircraft landed, hastily took on his group and fled the radioactivity. From the air he saw no church, no Domkirk, nothing but a wide, black, vitrified crater ringed in with burning fields.

He shook, as the bombproof had shaken, and said to no one and everyone: 'This is what they would do to us!'

* * *

Running from the morning, they returned to a dusk before dawn. The other raiders were already there. This was in the eastern edge of wilderness, where hills lifted sharply toward the Windhook Mountains.

Ridenour walked some distance off. He didn't actually wish to be alone; if anything, he wanted a companion for a shield

60

between him and the knowledge that two hundred light-years reached from here to Lissa and the children, their home and Terra. But he must escape Uriason or commit violence. The man had babbled, gobbled, orated and gibbered through their entire time in the air. You couldn't blame him, maybe, His birthplace as well as his job had gone up in lethal smoke. But Ridenour's job was to gather information; and that big auburn-haired Evagail woman, whom he'd met not unamicably while she was still captive, had appeared willing to talk if she ever got a chance.

No one stopped Ridenour. Where could he flee? He climbed onto a crest and looked around.

The valley floor beneath him held only a few trees and they small, probably the result of a forest fire, though nature — incredibly vigorous when civilization has not sucked her dry — had covered all scars with a thick blanket of silvery-green trilobed 'grass' and sapphire blossoms. No doubt this was why the area had been set for a rendezvous. Aircraft landed easily. Hundreds of assorted tools must have been stacked here before-hand or stolen from the city, for men were attacking the vehicles like ants. Clang, clatter, hails, cheerful oaths profaned the night's death-hush.

Otherwise there was great beauty in the scene. Eastward, the first color stole across a leaf-roof that ran oceanic to the edge of sight, moving and murmuring in the breeze. Westward, the last few stars glistened in a plum-dark sky, above the purity of Windhook's snowpeaks. Everywhere dew sparkled.

Ridenour took out pipe and tobacco and lit up. It made him hiccough a bit, on an empty stomach, but comforted him in his chilled weariness. And in his dismay. He had not imagined the outbackers were such threats. Neither had anyone else, apparently. He recalled remarks made about them in Nordyke and (only yesterday?) Domkirk. 'Impoverished wretches . . . Well, yes, I'm told they eat well with little effort. But otherwise, just think, no fixed abodes, no books, no schools, no connection with the human mainstream, hardly any metal, hardly any energy source other than brute muscle. Wouldn't you call that an impoverished existence? Culturally as well as materially?'

'Surly, treacherous, arrogant. I tell you, I've dealt with them. In trading posts on the wilderness fringe. They do bring in furs, wild fruits, that sort of thing to swap, mostly for steel tools – but only when they feel like taking the trouble, which isn't often, and then they treat you like dirt.'

But a much younger man had had another story. 'Sure, if one of us looks down on the woodsrunners, they'll look down right back at him. But I was interested and acted friendly, and they invited me to overnight in their camp . . . Their songs are plain caterwauling, but I've never seen better dancing, not even on Imperial Ballet Corps tapes, and afterwards, the girls – ! I think I might get me some trade goods and return some day.'

'Swinish. Lazy. Dangerous also, I agree. Look what they've done every time someone tried to start a real outpost of civilization in the mid-wilderness. We'll have to clean them out before we can expand. Once this damned Arulian war is over – No, don't get me wrong, I'm not vindictive. Let's treat them like any other criminal: rehabilitation, re-integration into society. I'll go further; I'll admit this is a case of cultural conflict rather than ordinary lawbreaking. So why not let the irreconcilables live out their lives peacefully on a reservation somewhere? As long as their children get raised civilized –

'If you ask me, I think heredity comes into the picture. It wasn't easy to establish the Cities, maintain and enlarge them, the first few centuries on an isolated, metal-poor world like this. Those who couldn't stand the gaff opted out. Once the disease and nutrition problems were licked, you could certainly live with less work in the forests – if you didn't mind turning into a savage and didn't feel any obligation toward the civilization that had made your survival possible. Later, through our whole history, the same thing continued. The lazy, the criminal, the mutinous, the eccentric, the lecherous, the irresponsible, sneaking off . . . to this very day. No wonder the outbackers haven't accomplished anything. They never will, either. I'm not hopeful about rehabilitating them, myself, not even any of their brats that we institutionalized at birth. Scrub stock!

'Well, yes, I did live with them a while. Ran away when I was sixteen. Mainly, I think now, my reason was – you know, girls –

and that part was fine, if you don't wonder about finding some girl you can respect when you're ready to get married. And I thought it'd be romantic. Primitive hunter, that sort of thing. Oh, they were kind enough. But they set me to learning endless nonsense – stuff too silly and complicated to retain in my head – rituals, superstitions – and they don't really hunt much, they have some funny kind of herding – and no stereo, no cars, no air-conditioning – hiking for days on end, and have you ever been *out* in a Freehold rainstorm? – and homesickness, after a while; they don't talk or behave or think like us. So I came back. And mighty draggle-tailed, I don't mind admitting. No, they didn't forbid me. One man guided me to the nearest cultivated land.

'Definitely an Arulian influence, Professor Ridenour. I've observed the outbackers at trading posts, visited some of their camps, made multisensory tapes. Unscientific, no doubt, I'm strictly an amateur as an ethnologist. But I felt somebody must try. They are more numerous, more complicated, more important than Nine Cities generally realize. Here, I'll play some of my recordings to you. Pay special attention to the music and some of the artwork. Furthermore, what little I could find out about their system of reckoning kinship looks as if it's adopted key Arulian notions. And remember, too, the savages – not only on this continent, but on both others, where they seemed to have developed similarly. Everywhere on Freehold, the savages have grown more and more hostile in these past years. Not to our Arulian enemies, but to us! When the Arulians were marshalling in various wilderness regions, did they have savage help? I find it hard to believe they did not.'

Ridenour drank smoke and shivered.

He grew peripherally aware of an approach and turned. Evagail joined him on panther feet. She hadn't yet bothered to dress, but the wetness and chill didn't seem to inconvenience her. Ridenour scolded himself for being aware of how good she looked. Grow up, he thought; you're a man with a task at hand.

'Figured I'd join you.' Her husky voice used the Upwoods dialect, which was said to be more archaic than that of the

63

Cities. The pronunciation was indeed different, slower and softer. But Ridenour had not observed that vocabulary and grammar had suffered much. Maybe not at all. 'You look lonesome. Hungry, too, I'll bet. She offered him a large gold-colored sphere.

'What's that?' he asked.

'Steak apple, we call it. Grows everywhere this time of year.'

He lay down his pipe and bit. The fruit was delicious, sweet, slightly smoky, but with an underlying taste of solid protein. Ravenous, he bit again. 'Thank you,' he said around a mouth-ful. 'This should be a meal by itself.'

'Well, not quite. It'll do for breakfast, though.'

'I, uh, understand the forests bear ample food the year around.'

'Yes, if you know what to find and how. Was necessary to introduce plants and animals from offworld, mutated forms that could survive on Freehold, before humans could live here without any synthetics. Especially urgent to get organisms that concentrate what iron the soil has, and other essential trace minerals. Several vitamins were required as well.'

Ridenour stopped chewing because his jaw had fallen. Savages weren't supposed to talk like that! Hastily, hoping to keep her in the right mood, he recovered his composure and said: 'I believe the first few generations established such species to make it easier to move into the wilderness and exploit its resources. Why didn't they succeed?'

'Lots of reasons,' Evagail said. 'Including, I think, a pretty deep-rooted fear of ever being alone.' She scowled. Her tone grew harsh. 'But there was a practical reason, too. The new organisms upset the ecology. Had no natural enemies here, you see. They destroyed enormous areas of forests. That's how the desert south of Startop originated, did you know? *Our* first generations had a fiend's time restoring balance and fertility.'

Again Ridenour gaped, not sure he had heard right.

'Of course, the sun helped,' she went on more calmly.

'Beg pardon?'

'The sun.' She pointed east. The early light was now like molten steel, and spears of radiance struck upward. Her hair was made copper, her body bronze. 'F-type star. Actinic and ionizing radiation gets through in quantity, even with this dense an atmosphere. Bio-chemistry is founded on highly energetic compounds. Freehold life is more vigorous than Terran, evolves faster, finds more new ways to be what it wants.' Her voice rang. 'You learn how to become worthy of the forest, or you don't last long.'

Ridenour looked away from her. She aroused too much within him.

The work of demolishing the aircraft went apace, despite the often primitive equipment used. He could understand why their metal was often desired. The outbackers were known to have mines of their own, but few and poor; they employed metal only where it was quite unfeasible to substitute stone, wood, glass, leather, bone, shell, fiber, glue . . . But the vehicles were being stripped with unexpected care. Foremen who obviously knew what they were doing supervised the removal, intact, of articles like transceivers and power cells.

Evagail seemed to follow his thought. 'Oh, yes, we'll use those gadgets while they last,' she said. 'They aren't vital, but they're handy. For certain purposes.'

Ridenour finished his apple, picked up his pipe and rekindled it. She wrinkled her nose. Tobacco was not a vice of the woodsfolk, though they were rumored to have many others, including some that would astonish a jaded Terran. 'I never anticipated that much knowledgeability,' he said. 'Including if I may make bold, your own.'

'We're not all provincials,' she answered, with a quirk of lips. 'Quite a few, like Karlsarm, for instance, have studied offplanet. They'd be chosen, you see, as having the talent for it. Afterwards they'd come back and teach others.'

'But – how –'

She studied him for a moment, with disconcertingly steady hazel eyes, before saying: 'No harm in telling you, I suppose. I believe you're an honest man, John Ridenour – intellectually honest – and we do need some communicators between us and the Empire.

'Our people took passage on Arulian ships. This was before the rebellion, of course. It began generations ago. The humans of the Nine Cities paid no attention. They'd always held rather aloof from the Arulians: partly from snobbishness, I suppose, and partly from lack of imagination. But the Arulians traded directly with us, too. That wasn't any secret. Nor was it a secret that we saw more of them more intimately, learned more from them, than the City men did. It was only that the City men weren't interested in details of that relationship. They didn't ask what their "inferiors" were up to. Why should we or the Arulians volunteer lectures about it?'

'And what were you up to?' Ridenour asked softly.

'Nothing, at first, except that we wanted some of our people to have a look at galactic civilisation – real civilization, not those smug, ingrown Nine – and the Arulians were willing to sell us berths on their regular cargo ships. In the nature of the case, our visits were mainly to planets outside the Empire, which is why Terra never heard what was going on. At last, though, some, like Karlsarm, did make their way to Imperial worlds, looked around, enrolled in schools and universities . . . By that time, however, relations on Freehold were becoming strained. There was no predicting what might happen. We thought it best to provide our students with cover identities. That wasn't hard. No one inquired closely. No one can remember all the folkways of all the colonies. This is such a big galaxy.'

'It is that,' Ridenour whispered. The sun climbed aloft, too brilliant for him to look anywhere near.

'What are you going to do now?' he asked.

'Fade into the woods before enemy flyers track us down. Cache our plunder and start for home.'

'But what about your prisoners? The men who were forced to pilot and – '

'Why, they can stay here. We'll show them what they can eat and where a spring is. And we'll leave plenty of debris. A searcher's bound to spot them before long. Of course, I hope some will join us. We don't have as many men with civilized training as we could use.'

'Join you?' Ridenour choked. 'After what you have done?'

Again she regarded him closely and gravely. 'What did we do that was unforgiveable? Killed some men, yes – but in honest battle, in the course of war. Then we risked everything to spare the lives of everybody else.'

'But what about their livelihoods? Their homes? Their possessions, their – '

'What about ours?' Evagail shrugged. 'Never mind. I suspect we will get three or four recruits. Young men who've felt vaguely restless and unfulfilled. I had hopes about you. But maybe I'd better go talk with someone more promising.'

She turned, not brusquely or hostilely, and rippled back downhill. Ridenour stared after her.

* * *

He stood long alone, thinking, while the sun lifted and the sky filled with birds and the work neared an end below him. It was becoming more and more clear that the outbackers – the Free People, as they seemed to call themselves – were not savages.

Neither Miserable Degraded Savages nor Noble Happy Savages. All their generations, shaped by these boundless shadowy whispering woodlands and by what they learned from beings whose species and mode of life were not human: that alchemy had transmuted them into something so strange that their very compatriots in the Nine Cities had failed to identify it.

But what was it?

Not a civilization, Ridenour felt sure. You could not have a true civilization without ... libraries, scientific and artistic apparatus, tradition-drenched buildings, reliable transportation and communication ... the cumbersome necessary impedimenta of high culture. But you could have a barbarism that was subtle, powerful and deathly dangerous. He hearked back to ages of history, forgotten save by a few scholars. Hyksos in Egypt, Dorians in Achaea, Lombards in Italy, Vikings in England, Crusaders in Syria, Mongols in China, Aztecs in Mexico. Barbarians, to whom the malcontents of civilization often deserted – who gained such skills that incomparably more sophisticated societies fell before them.

Granted, in the long run the barbarian was either absorbed by his conquests or was himself overcome. Toward the end of the pre-space travel era, civilization had been the aggressor, crushing and devouring the last pathetic remnants of barbarism. It was hard to see how Karlsarm's folk could hold out against atomic weapons and earthmoving machinery, let alone prevail over them.

And yet the outbackers had destroyed Domkirk.

And they had no immediate fear of punitive expeditions from Cities or Empire. Why should they? The wilderness was theirs, roadless, townless, mapped only from above and desultorily at that – three-fourths of Freehold's land surface! How could an avenger *find* them?

Well, the entire wilderness could be destroyed. High altitude multimegaton bursts can set a whole continent ablaze. Or, less messily, disease organisms can be synthesized that attack vegetation and soon create a desert.

But no. Such measures would ruin the Nine Cities, too. Though they might be protected from direct effects, the planetary climate would be changed, agriculture become impossible, the economy crumble and the people perforce abandon their world. And the Cities were the sole thing that made Freehold valuable, to Terra or Merseia. They formed a center of population and industry on a disputed frontier. Without them, this was simply one more undeveloped globe: because of its metal poverty, not worth anyone's trouble.

Doubtless Karlsarm and his fellow chiefs understood this. The barbarians could only be obliterated gradually, by the piecemeal conquest, clearing and cultivation of their forests. Doubtless they understood that, too, and were determined to forestall the process. Today there remained just eight Cities, of which two were in the hands of their Arulian friends(?) and two others crippled by the chances of war. Whatever the barbarians planned next, and whether they succeeded or not, they might well bring catastrophe on civilised Freeholder man.

Ridenour's mouth tightened. He started down the hill.

*

Halfway, he met Uriason coming up. He had heard the mayor some distance off, raving over his shoulder while several listening outbackers grinned:

' – treason! I say the three of you are traitors! Oh, yes, you talk about "attempted rapprochment" and "working for a detente". The fact remains you are going over to the monsters who destroyed your own home! And why! Because you aren't fit to be human. Because you would rather loaf in the sun, and play with unwashed sluts, and pretend that a few superstitious ceremonies are "autochthonous" than take the trouble to cope with this universe. It won't last, gentlemen. Believe me, the glamor will soon wear off. You will come skulking back like many other runaways, and expect to be received as indulgently as they were. But I warn you. This is war. You have collaborated with the enemy. If you dare return, I, your mayor, will do my best to see you prosecuted for treason!'

Puffing hard, he stopped Ridenour. 'Ah, sir.' His voice was abruptly low. 'A word, if you please.'

The xenologist suppressed a moan and waited.

Uriason looked back. No one was paying attention. 'I really am indignant,' he said after he had his breath. 'Three of them! Saying they had long found their work dull and felt like trying something new . . . But no matter. My performance was merely in character.'

'What?' Ridenour almost dropped his pipe from his jaws.

'Calm, sir, be calm, I beg you.' The little eyes were turned up, unblinking, and would not release the Terran's. 'I took for granted that you also will accompany the savages from here.'

'Why – why – '

'An excellent opportunity to fulfill your mission, really to learn something about them. Eh?'

'But I hadn't – Well, uh, the idea did cross my mind. But I'm no actor. I'd never convince them I was suddenly converted to their cause. They might believe that of a bored young provincial who isn't very bright to begin with. Even in those cases, I'll bet they'll keep a wary eye out for quite some time. But me, a Terran, a scientist, a middle-aged paterfamilias? The outbackers aren't stupid, Mayor.'

'I know, I know,' Uriason said impatiently. 'Nevertheless, if you offer to go with them — telling them quite frankly that your aim is to collect information — they will take you. I am sure of it. I kept my ears open down yonder, sir, as well as my mouth. The savages are anxious to develop a liaison with the Empire. They will let you return whenever you say. Why should they fear you? By the time you, on foot, reach any of the cities, whatever military intelligence you can offer will be obsolete. *Or so they think.*'

Ridenour gulped. The round red face was no longer comical. It pleaded. After a while, it commanded.

'Listen, Professor,' Uriason said. 'I played the buffoon in order to be discounted and ignored. Your own best role is probably that of the impractical academician. But you may thus gain a chance for an immortal name. If you have the manhood!

'Listen, I say. I listened, to them. And I weighed in my mind what I overheard. The annihilation of Domkirk was part of some larger scheme. It was advanced ahead of schedule in order to rescue those prisoners we held. What comes next, I do not know. I am only certain that the plan is bold, large-scale and diabolical. It seems reasonable, therefore, that forces must be massed somewhere. Does it not? Likewise, it seems reasonable that these murderers will join that force. Does it not? Perhaps I am wrong. If so, you have lost nothing. You can simply continue to be the absent-minded scientist, until you decide to go home. And that will be of service per se. You will bring useful data.

'However, if I am right, you will accompany this gang to some key point. And when you arrive . . . Sir, warcraft of the Imperial Navy are in blockading orbit. When I reach Nordyke, I shall speak to Admiral Cruz. I shall urge that he adopt my plan — the plan that came to me when I saw — here.' Uriason reached under his cloak. Snake swift, he thrust a small object into Ridenour's hand. 'Hide that. If anyone notices and asks you about it, dissemble. Call it a souvenir or something.'

'But . . . but what — ' Like an automaton, Ridenour pocketed the hemicylinder. He felt a pair of super-contacts on either end and a grille on the flat side and assumed that complex micro-circuitry was packed into the plastic case.

'A communication converter. Have you heard of them?'

'I – yes. I've heard.'

'Good. I doubt that any of the savages have, although they are surprisingly well informed in certain respects. The device is not new or secret, but with galactic information flow as inadequate as it is, especially here on what was a sleepy backwater . . . Let me refresh your memory, sir. Substitute this device for the primary modulator in any energy weapon of the third or fourth class. The weapon will thereupon become a maser communicator, projecting the human voice to a considerable distance. I shall ask Admiral Cruz to order at least one of his orbital ships brought low and illuminated for the next several weeks, so that you may have a target to aim at. If you find yourself in an important concentration of the enemy's – where surely stolen energy weapons will be kept – and if you get an opportunity to call down a warcraft . . . Do you follow me?'

'But,' Ridenour stammered. 'But. How?'

'As mayor, I knew that such devices were included in the last consignment of defensive materials that the Navy sent to Domkirk. I knew that one was carried on every military aircraft of ours. And several military aircraft were among those stolen last night. I watched my chance, I made myself ridiculous, and – '

Uriason threw out his chest, thereby also throwing out his belly – 'at the appropriate moment, I palmed this one from beneath the noses of the wrecking crew.'

Ridenour wet his lips. They felt sandpapery. 'I could've guessed that much,' he got out. 'But me – I – how – '

'It would not be in character for me to accompany the savages into their wilderness,' Uriason said.

'They would be entirely too suspicious. Can I, can Freehold, can His Majesty and the entire human species rely upon you, sir?'

The man was short and fat. His words rose like hot-air balloons. Nevertheless, had he dared under possible observation, Ridenour would have bowed most deeply. As matters were, the Terran could just say, 'Yes, Citizen Mayor, I'll try to do my best.'

* * *

These were the stages of their journey:

Karlsarm walked beside Ridenour, amicably answering questions. But wariness crouched behind. He wasn't altogether convinced that this man's reasons for coming along were purely scientific and diplomatic. At least, he'd better not be, yet. Sometimes he thought that humans from the inner Empire were harder to fathom than most nonhumans. Being of the same species, talking much the same language, they ought to react in the same ways as your own people. And they didn't. The very facial expressions, a frown, a smile, were subtly foreign.

Ridenour, for immediate example, was courteous, helpful, even genial: but entirely on the surface. He showed nothing of his real self. No doubt he loved his family and was loyal to his Emperor and enjoyed his work and was interested in many other aspects of reality. He spoke of such things. But the emotions didn't come through. He made no effort to share his feelings, rather he kept them to himself with an ease too great to be conscious.

Karlsarm had encountered the type before, offplanet. He speculated that reserve was more than an aristocrat's idea of good manners; it was a defense. Jammed together with billions of others, wired from before birth into a network of communication, coordination, impersonal omnipotent social machinery, the human being could only protect his individuality by making his inner self a fortress. Here, in the outback of Freehold, you had room; neither people nor organizations pressed close upon you; if anything, you grew eager for intimacy. Karlsarm felt sorry for Terrans. But that did not help him understand or trust them.

'You surprise me pleasantly,' he remarked. 'I didn't expect you'd keep up with us the way you do.'

'Well, I try to stay in condition,' Ridenour said. 'And remember, I'm used to somewhat higher gravity. But to be honest, I expected a far more difficult trip – narrow muddly trails and the like. You have a road here.'

'Hm, I don't think a lot of it. We do better elsewhere. But then, this is a distant marchland for us.'

Both men glanced around. The path crossed a high hillside, smoothly graded and switchbacked, surface planted in a mossy growth so tough and dense that no weeds could force themselves in. (It was a specially bred variety which, among other traits, required traces of manganese salt. Maintenance gangs supplied this from time to time, and thus automatically kept the moss within proper bounds). The path was narrow, over-arched by forest, a sun-speckled cool corridor where birds whistled and a nearby cataract rang. Because of its twistings, few other people were visible, though the party totalled hundreds.

Most of them were on different courses anyhow. Karlsarm had explained that the Free People laid out as many small, interconnected, more or less parallel ways as the traffic in a given area demanded, rather than a single broad highroad. It was easier to do, less damaging to ecology and scenery, more flexible to changing situations. Also, it was generally undetectable from above. He had not seen fit to mention the other mutant plant types, sown throughout this country, whose exudates masked those of human metabolism and thereby protected his men from airborne chemical sniffers. 'I've heard you use beasts of burden in a limited fashion,' Ridenour said.

'Yes, horses and stathas have been naturalized here,' Karlsarm said. 'And actually, in our central regions, we keep many. City folk see just a few, because we don't often bring them to our thinly populated borderlands. No reason for it. You can go about as fast on foot, when you aren't overloaded with gear. But at home you'll see animals, wagons — boats and rafts, for that matter — in respectable totals.'

'Your population must be larger than is guessed, then.'

'I don't know what the current guess is in the Cities. And we don't bother with, uh, a census. But I'd estimate twenty million of us on this continent, and about the same for the others. Been stable for a long time. That's the proper human density. We don't crowd each other or press hard on natural resources. And so we've got abundant free food and stuff. No special effort involved in satisfying the basic needs. At the same time, there

73

are enough of us for specialization, diversity, large-scale projects like road building. And, I might add, gifted people. You know, only about ten per cent of mankind are born to be leaders or creators in any degree. We'd stagnate if we were too few, same as we'd grow cramped and over-regulated if we became too many.'

'How do you maintain a level population? You don't appear to have any strong compulsion mechanism.'

'No, we haven't. Tradition, public opinion, the need to help your neighbor so he'll help you, the fact that out-and-out bastards get into quarrels and eventually get killed – such factors will do, when you have elbow room. The population-control device is simple. It wasn't planned, it evolved, but it works. Territory.'

'Beg pardon?'

'A man claims a certain territory for his own, to support him and his family and retainers. He passes it on to one son. How he chooses the heir is his business. Anybody who kills the owner, or drives him off, takes over that parcel of land.'

Ridenour actually registered a little shock, though he managed a smile. 'Your society is less idyllic than some young City people told me,' he said.

Karlsarm laughed. 'We do all right – most of us. Can any civilization claim more? The landless don't starve, remember. They're taken on as servants, assistants, guards and the like. Or they become itinerant laborers, or entrepreneurs, or something. Let me remind you, we don't practice marriage. Nobody needs to go celibate. It's only that few women care to have children by a landless man.' He paused. 'Territorial battles aren't common any more, either. The landholders have learned how to organize defenses. Besides, a decent man can count on help from his neighbors. So not many vagabonds try to reave an estate. Those that do, and succeed – well, haven't they proven they're especially fit to become fathers?'

The paths ranged above timberline. The land became boulder-strewn, chill and stark. Ridenour exclaimed, 'But this road's been blasted from the cliffside!'

'Why, of course,' said Rowlan. 'You didn't think we'd chip it out by hand, did you?'

'But what do you use for such jobs?'

'Organics. Like nitroglycerine. We compound that – doesn't take much apparatus, you know – and make dynamite from it. Some other explosives, and most fuels, we get from vegetables we've bred.' Rowlan tugged his gray beard and regarded the Terran. 'If you want to make a side trip,' he offered, 'I'll show you a hydroelectric plant. You'll call it ridiculously small, but it beams power to several mills and an instrument factory. We are not ignorant, John Ridenour. We adopt from your civilization what we can use. It simply doesn't happen to be a particularly large amount.'

Even in this comparatively infertile country, food was plentiful. There were no more fruits for the plucking, but roots and berries were almost as easily gotten in the low brush, and animals – albeit of different species from the lowlands – continued to arrive near camp for slaughter. Ridenour asked scholarly little Noach how that was done, he being a beast operator himself. 'Are they domesticated and conditioned?'

'No, I wouldn't call them that, exactly,' Noach replied. 'Not like horses or dogs. We use the proper stimuli on them. Those vary, depending on what you're after and where you are. For instance, in Brenning Dales you can unstopper a bottle of sex attractant, and every gruntleboar within ten kilometers rushes straight toward your bow. Around the Mare we've bred instincts into certain species to come when a sequence of notes is played on a trumpet. If nothing else, you can always stalk for yourself, any place. Hunting isn't difficult when critters are abundant. We don't want to take the time on this journey, though, so Mistress Jenith has been driving those cragbuck with her fire bees.' He shrugged. 'There are plenty of other ways. What you don't seem to realise, as yet, is that we're descended from people who applied scientific method to the problem of living in a wilderness.'

For once, the night was clear above Foulweather Pass. Snow glistened on surrounding peaks, under Selene, until darkness lay drenched with an unreal brilliance. Not many stars shone through. But Karlsarm scowled at one, which was new and moved visibly, widdershins over his head.

'They've put up another satellite.' The words puffed ghost white from his lips; sound was quickly lost, as if it froze and tinkled down onto the hoarfrosted road. 'Or moved a big spaceship into near orbit without camouflage. Why?'

'The war?' Evagail shivered beside him and wrapped her fur cloak tighter about her. (It was not her property. Warm outfits were kept for travelers in a shed at the foot of the pass, to be returned on the other side, with a small rental paid to the servant of the landholder.) 'What's been happening?'

'The news is obscure, what I get of it on that mini-radio we took along,' Karlsarm said. 'A major fight's developing near Sluicegate. Nuclear weapons, the whole filthy works. By Oneness, if this goes on much longer we won't be left with a planet worth inhabiting!'

'Now don't exaggerate.' She touched his hand. 'I grant you, territory's that's fought on, or suffers fallout, is laid waste. But not forever, and it isn't any big percentage of the total.'

'You wouldn't say that if you were the owner. And what about the ecological consequences? The genetic? Let's not get overconfident about these plant and animal species we've modified to serve our needs while growing wild. They're still new and unstable. A spreading mutation could wipe them out. Or we might have to turn farmers to save them!'

'I know. I know. I do want you to see matters in perspective. But agreed, the sooner the war ends, the better.' Evagail turned her gaze from that sinister, crawling spark in the sky. She looked down the slope on which they stood, to the camp. Oilwood fires were strewn along the way, each economically serving a few people. They twinkled like red and orange constellations. A burst of laughter, a drift of song came distantly to her ears.

Karlsarm could practically read her thought. 'Very well, what about Ridenour?' he challenged.

'I can't say. I talk with him, but he's so locked into himself, I get no hint of what his real purpose may be. I could almost wish my Skill were of the love kind.'

'Why yours?' Karlsarm demanded. 'Why don't you simply wish, like me, that we had such a Mistress with us?'

Evagail paused before she chuckled. 'Shall I admit the truth? He attracts me. He's thoroughly a man, in his quiet way; and he's exotic and mysterious to boot. Must you really sic an aphrodite onto him when we reach Moon Garnet?'

'I'll decide that at the time. Meanwhile, you can help me decide and maybe catch forewarning of any plot against us. He can't hide that he's drawn to you. Use the fact.'

'I don't like to. Men and women — of course, I mean women who don't have that special Skill — they should give to each other, not take. I don't even know if I could deceive him.'

'You can try. If he realizes and gets angry, what of it?' Beneath the shadowing carnivore headpiece, Karlsarm's features turned glacier stern. 'You have your duty.'

'Well . . .' Briefly, her voice was forlorn. 'I suppose.' Then the wide smooth shoulders tightened. Moonfrost sparkled on a mane lifted high. 'It could be fun, too, couldn't it?' She turned and walked from him.

Ridenour sat at one campfire, watching a dance. The steps were as intricate as the music that an improvised orchestra made. He seemed not only glad but relieved when Evagail seated herself beside him.

'Hullo,' she greeted. 'Are you enjoying the spectacle?'

'Yes,' he said, 'but largely in my professional capacity. I'm sure it's high art, but the conventions are too alien for me.'

'Isn't your business to unravel alien symbolisms?'

'In part. Trouble is, what you have here is not merely different from anything I've ever seen before. It's extraordinarily subtle — obviously the product of a long and rigorous tradition. I've discovered, for instance, that your musical scale employs smaller intervals than any other human music I know of. Thus you make and use and appreciate distinctions and combinations that I'm not trained to hear.'

'I think you'll find that's typical,' Evagail said. 'We aren't innocent children of nature, we Free People. I suspect we elaborate our lives more, we're fonder of complication, ingenuity, ceremoniousness, than Terra herself.'

'Yes, I've talked to would-be runaways from the Cities.'

She laughed. 'Well, the custom is that we give recruits a tough apprenticeship. If they can't get through that, we don't want them. Probably they wouldn't survive long. Not that life's harder among us than in the Cities. In fact, we have more leisure. But life is altogether different here.'

'I've scarcely begun to grasp how different,' Ridenour said. 'The questions are so many, I don't know where to start.' A dancer leaped, his feather bonnet streaming in Selene light, flame light, and shadow. A flute twittered, a drum thuttered, a harp trilled, a bell rang, chords intertwining like ripple patterns on water. 'What arts do you have besides . . . this?'

'Not architecture, or monumental sculpture, or murals, or multi-sense taping.' Evagail smiled. 'Nothing that requires awkward masses. But we do have schools of – oh, scrimshaw, jewelry, weaving, painting and carvings, that sort of thing – and they are genuine, serious arts. Then drama, literature, cuisine . . . and things you don't have – to call them contemplation, conversation, integration – but those are poor words.'

'What I can't understand is how you can manage without those awkward masses,' Ridenour said. 'For example, everyone seems to be literate. But what's the use? What is there to read?'

'Why, we probably have more books and periodicals than you do. No electronics competing with them. One of the first things our ancestors did, when they started colonizing the outback in earnest, was develop plants with leaves that dry into paper and juice that makes ink. Many landholders keep a little printing press in the same shed as their other heavy equipment. It doesn't need much metal, and wind or water can power it. Don't forget, each area maintains schools. The demand for reading matter is a source of income – yes, we use iron and copper slugs for currency – and the transporters carry mail as well as goods.'

'How about records, though? Libraries? Computers? Information exchange?'

'I've never met anybody who collects books, the way some do

in the Cities. If you want to look at a piece again, copies are cheap.' (Ridenour thought that this ruled out something he had always considered essential to a cultivated man – the ability to browse, re-read on impulse, to be serendipitous among the shelves. However, no doubt these outbackers thought he was uncouth because he didn't know how to dance or to arrange a meteor-watching festival.) 'Messages go speedily enough for our purposes. We don't keep records like you. Our mode of life doesn't require it. Likewise, we have quite a live technology, still developing. Yes, and a pure science. But they concentrate on areas of work that need no elaborate apparatus: the study of animals, for instance, and ways to control them.'

Evagail leaned closer to Ridenour. No one else paid attention; they were watching the performance. 'But do me a favor tonight, will you?' she asked.

'What? Why, certainly.' His gaze drifted across the ruddy lights in her hair, the shadows under her cloak, and hastily away. 'If I can.'

'It's easy.' She laid a hand over his. 'Just for tonight, stop being a research machine. Make small talk. Tell me a joke or two. Sing me a Terran song, when they finish here. Or walk with me to look at the moon. Be human, John Ridenour . . . only a man . . . this little while.'

* * *

West of the pass, the land became a rolling plateau. Again it was forested, but less thickly and with other trees than in the warm eastern valleys. The travelers met folk more often, as population grew denser; and these were apt to be mounted. Karlsarm didn't bother with animals. A human in good condition can log fifty kilometers a day across favorable terrain, without difficulty. Ridenour remarked, highly centralized empires were held together on ancient Terra with communication no faster than this.

Besides, the outbackers possessed them: not merely an occasional aircar for emergency use, but a functioning web. He broke into uncontrollable laughter when Evagail first explained the system to him.

79

'What's so funny?' She cocked her head. Though they were much together, to the exclusion of others, they still lacked mutual predictability. He might now be wearing outbacker garb and be darkened by Freehold's harsh sunlight and have let his beard grow because he found a diamond-edge razor too much trouble. But he remained a stranger.

'I'm sorry. Old saying.' He looked around the glen where they stood. Trees were stately above blossom-starred grasses; leaves murmured in a cool breeze and smelled like spice. He touched a green tendril that curled over one trunk and looped to the next. 'Grapevine telegraph!'

'But . . . well, I don't recognize your phrase, John, but that kind of plant does carry signals. Our ancestors went to a vast amount of work to create the type and sow and train it, over the entire mid-continent. I confess the signals don't go at light speed, only neural speed; and the channel isn't awfully broad – but it suffices for us.'

'How do you, uh, activate it?'

'That requires a Skill. To send something, you'd go to the nearest node and pay the woman who lives there. She'd transmit.'

Ridenour nodded. 'I see. Actually, I've met setups on non-human planets that aren't too different from this.' He hesitated. 'What do you mean by a Skill?'

'A special ability, inborn, cultivated, disciplined. You've watched Skills in action on our route, haven't you?'

'I'm not certain. You see, I'm barely starting to grasp the pattern of your society. Before, everything was a jumble of new impressions. Now I observe meaningful differences between this and that. Take our friend Noach, for one, with his spying quasi-weasels; or Karlsarm and the rest, who use birds for couriers. Do they have Skills?'

'Of course not. I suppose you might say their animals do. That is, the creatures have been bred to semi-intelligence. They have the special abilities and instincts, the *desire*, built into their chromosomes. But as for the men who use them, no, all they have is training in language and handling. Anybody could be taught the same.'

*

Ridenour looked at her, where she stood like a lioness in the filtered green light, stillness and strange odors at her back. 'Only women have Skills, then,' he said finally.

She nodded. 'Yes.'

'Why? Were they bred too?'

'No.' Astonishingly, she colored. 'Whatever we may do with other men, we seldom become pregnant by anyone but a landholder. We want our children to have a claim on him. But somehow, women seem able to do more with hormones and pheromones. A biologist tried to explain why, but I couldn't follow him terribly well. Let's say the female has a more complex biochemistry, more closely involved with her psyche, than a male. Not that any woman can handle any materials. In fact, those who can do something with them are rare. When identified, in girlhood, they're carefully trained to use what substances they can.'

'How?'

'It depends. A course of drugs may change the body secretions . . . delicately; you wouldn't perceive any difference; but some-one like Mistress Jenith will never be stung by her fire bees. Rather, they'll always live near her. And she has ways to control them, make them go where she commands and – No, I don't know how. Each Skill keeps its secrets. But you must know how. Each few parts per million in the air will lure insects for kilometers around, to come and mate. Other insects, social ones, use odor signals to coordinate their communities. Man himself lives more by trace chemicals than he realizes. Think how little of some drugs is needed to change his metabolism, even his personality. Think how some smells recall a past scene to you, so vividly you might be there again. Think how it was proven, long ago, that like, dislike, appetite, fear, anger . . . every emotion . . . are conditioned by just such faint cues. Now imagine what can be done, as between a woman who knows precisely how to use those stimuli – some taken from bottles, some created at will by her own glands – between her and an organism bred to respond.'

'An Arulian concept?'

'Yes, we learned a lot from the Arulians,' Evagail said.

'They call you Mistress. I've heard. What's your Skill?'

She lost gravity. Her grin was impudent. 'You may find out one day. Come, let's rejoin the march.' She took his hand. 'Though we needn't hurry,' she added.

As far as could be ascertained, Freehold had never been glaciated. The average climate was milder than Terra's, which was one reason the outbackers didn't need fixed houses. They moved about within their territories, following the game and the fruits of the earth, content with shelters erected here and there, or with bedrolls. By Ridenour's standards, it was an austere life.

Or it had been. He found his canon gradually changing. The million sights, sounds, smells, less definable sensations of the wilderness, made a city apartment seem dead by contrast, no matter how many electronic entertainers you installed.

(Admittedly, the human kinds of fun were limited. A minstrel, a ball game, a chess game, a local legend, a poety reading, were a little pallid to a man used to living at the heart of Empire. And while the outbackers could apparently do whatever they chose with drugs and hypnotism, so could the Terrans. Lickerish rumor had actually underrated their uninhibited inventiveness in other departments of pleasure. But you had only a finite number of possibilities there too, didn't you? And he wasn't exactly a young man any more, was he? And damn, but he missed Lissa! Also the children, of course, the tobacco he'd exhausted, friends, tall towers, the gentler daylight of Sol and familiar constellations after dark, the sane joys of scholarship and teaching: everything, everything.)

But life could not be strictly nomadic. Some gear was not portable, or needed protection. Thus, in each territory, at least one true house and several outbuildings had been erected, where the people lived from time to time.

Humans needed protection too. Ridenour found that out when he and Evagail were caught in a storm.

She had led him off the line of march to show him such a center. They had been enroute for an hour or two when she began casting uneasy glances at the sky. Clouds rose in the north, unbelievably high thunderheads with lightning in their

82

blue-black depths. A breeze chilled and stiffened; the forest moaned. 'We'd better speed up,' she said at length. 'Rainstorm headed this way.'

'Well?' He no longer minded getting wet.

'I don't mean those showers we've had. I mean the real thing.'

Ridenour gulped and matched her trot. He knew what kind of violence a deep, intensely irradiated atmosphere can breed. Karlsarm's folk must be hard at work, racing to chop branches and make rough roofs and walls for themselves. Two alone couldn't do it in time. They'd normally have sought refuge under a windfall or in a hollow trunk or anything else they found. But a house was obviously preferable.

The wind worsened. Being denser than Terra's, air never got to hurricane velocity; but it thrust remorselessly, a quasi-solid, well-nigh unbreathable mass. Torn-off leaves and boughs started to fly overhead, under a galloping black cloud wrack. Darkness thickened, save when lightning split the sky. Thunder, keenings, breakings and crashings, resounded through Ridenour's skull.

He had believed himself in good shape, but presently he was staggering. Any man must soon be exhausted, pushing himself against that horrible wind. Evagail, though, continued, easy of breath. *How?* he wondered numbly, before he lost all wonder in the cruel combat to keep running.

The first raindrops fell, enormous, driven by the tempest, stinging like gravel when they struck. You could be drowned in a flash flood, if you were not literally flayed by the hail that would soon come. Ridenour reeled toward unconsciousness – no, he was helped, Evagail bore him, he leaned on her and –

And they reached the hilltop homestead.

It consisted of low, massive log-and-stone buildings, whose overgrown sod roofs would hardly be visible from above. Everything stood unlighted, empty. But the door to the main house opened at Evagail's touch; no place in the woodlands had a lock. She dragged Ridenour across the threshold and closed the door again. He lay in gloom and gasped his way back to consciousness. As if across light-years, he heard her say, 'We didn't arrive any too soon, did we?' There followed the canno-nade of the hail.

After a while he was on his feet. She had stimulated the lamps, which were microcultures in glass globes, to their bright phos-phorescence and had started a fire on the hearth. The principal heat source, however, was fuel oil, a system antique but adequate. 'We might as well figure on spending the night,' she said from the kitchen. 'This weather will last for hours, and the roads will be rivers for hours after that. Why don't you find yourself a hot bath and some dry clothes? I'll have dinner ready soon.'

Ridenour swallowed a sense of inadequacy. He wasn't an outbacker and couldn't be expected to cope with their country. How well would they do on Terra? Exploring, he saw the house to be spacious, many-roomed, beautifully paneled, draped and furnished. Evagail's advice was sound. He returned to her as if reborn.

She had prepared an excellent meal out of what was in the larder; including a heady red wine. White tablecloth, crystal goblets, candlelight were almost a renaissance of a Terra which had been more gracious than today's. (Almost. The utensils were horn, the knifeblades obsidian. The paintings on the walls were of a stylized, unearthly school; looking closely, you could identify Arulian influence. No music lilted from a taper; instead came the muffled brawling of the storm. And the woman who sat across from him wore a natural-fiber kilt, a fringed leather bolero, a dagger and tomahawk.)

They talked in animated and friendly wise, though since they belonged to alien cultures they had little more than question-and-answer conversation. The bottle passed freely back and forth. Being tired and having long abstained, Ridenour was quickly affected by the alcohol. When he noticed that, he thought, what the hell, why not? It glowed within him. 'I owe you an apology,' he said. 'I classed your people as barbarians. I see now you have a true civilization.'

'You needed this much time to see that?' she laughed. 'Well, I'll forgive you. The Cities haven't realized it, yet.'

'That's natural. You're altogether strange to them. And,

isolated as they are from the galactic mainstream, they . . . haven't the habit of thinking something different . . . can be equal or superior to what they take for granted is the civilized way.'

'My, that was a sentence! Do you acknowledge, then, we are superior?'

He shook his head with care.

'No. I can't say that. I'm a city boy myself. A lot of what you do shocks me. Your ruthlessness. Your unwillingness to compromise.'

She grew grave. 'The Cities never tried to compromise with us, John. I don't know if they can. Our wise men, those who've studied history, say an industrial society must keep expanding or go under. We've got to stop them before they grow too strong. The war's given us a chance.'

'You can't rebel against the Empire!' he protested.

'Can't we? We're a goodly ways from Terra. And we are rebelling. No one consulted us about incorporation.' Evagail shrugged. 'Not that we care about that in itself. What difference to us who claims the over-lordship of Freehold, if he lets us alone? But the Cities have not let us alone. They cut down our woods, dam our rivers, dig holes in our soil, and get involved in a war that may wreck the whole planet.'

'M-m, you could help end the war if you mobilized against the Arulians.'

'To whose benefit? The Cities'!'

'But when you attack the Cities, aren't you aiding the Arulians?'

'No. Not in the long run. They belong to the Cities also. We don't want to fight them – our relationship with them was mostly pleasant, and they taught us a great deal – but eventually we want them off this world.'

'You can't expect me to agree that's right.'

'Certainly not.' Her tone softened. 'What we want from you is nothing but an honest report to your leaders. You don't know how happy I am that you admit we are civilized. Or post-civilized. At any rate, we aren't degenerate, we are progressing on our own trail. I can hope you'll go between us and the Empire, as a friend of both, and help work out a settlement. If you do that, you'll live in centuries of ballads: the Peacebringer.'

'I'd like that better than anything,' he said gladly.

She raised her brows. 'Anything?'

'Oh, some things equally, no doubt. I am getting homesick.'

'You needn't stay lonely while you're with us,' she murmured.

Somehow, their hands joined across the table. The wine sang in Ridenour's veins. 'I've wondered why you stood apart from me,' she said. 'Surely you could see I want to make love with you.'

'Y-yes.' His heart knocked.

'Why not? You have a . . . a wife, yes. But I can't imagine an Imperial Terran worries about that, two hundred light-years from home. And what harm would be done her?'

'None.'

She laughed anew, rose and circled the table to stand beside him and rumpled his hair. The odor of her was sweet around him. 'All right, then, silly,' she said, 'what have you been waiting for?'

He remembered. She saw his fists clench and stepped back. He looked at the candle flames, not her, and mumbled: 'I'm sorry. It mustn't be.'

'Why not?' The wind raved louder, nearly obliterating her words.

'Let's say I do have idiotic medieval scruples.'

She regarded him for a space. 'Is that the truth?'

'Yes.' But not the whole truth, he thought. I am not an observer, not an emissary, I am he who will call down destruction upon you if I can. The thing in my pocket sunders us, dear. You are my enemy, and I will not betray you with a kiss.

'I'm not offended,' she said at last, slowly. 'Disappointed and puzzled, though.'

'We probably don't understand each other as well as we believed,' he ventured.

'Might be. Well, let's let the dishes wait and turn in, shall we?' Her tone was less cold than wary.

Next day she was polite but aloof, and after they had rejoined the army she conferred long with Karlsarm.

* * *

Moon Garnet Lake was the heart of the Upwoods: more than fifty kilometers across, walled on three sides by forest and on the fourth by soaring snowpeaks. At every season it was charged with life, fish in argent swarms, birds rising by thousands when a bulligator bellowed in a white-plumed stand of cockatoo reed, wildkine everywhere among the trees. At full summer, microphytons multiplied until the waters glowed deep red, and the food chain which they started past belief in size and diversity. As yet, the year was too new for that. Wavelets sparkled clear to the escarpments, where mountaintops floated dim blue against heaven.

'I see why you reacted violently against the attempt to found a town here,' Ridenour said to Karlsarm. They stood on a beach, watching most of the expedition frolic in the lake. Those boisterous shouts and lithe brown bodies did not seem out of place; a cruising flock of fowl overhead was larger and made more clangor. The Terran drew a pure breath. 'And it would have been a pity, esthetically speaking. Who owns this region?'

'None,' Karlsarm answered. 'It's too basic to the whole country. Anyone may use it. The numbers that do aren't great enough to strain the resources, similar things being available all over. So it's a natural site for our periodic head-of-household gatherings.' He glanced sideways at the other man and added: 'Or for an army to rendezvous.'

'You are not disbanding, then?'

'Certainly not. Domkirk was a commencement. We don't intend to stop till we control the planet.'

'But you're daydreaming! No other City's as vulnerably located as Domkirk was. Some are on other continents – '

'Where Free People also live. We're in touch.'

'What do you plan?'

Karlsarm chuckled. 'Do you really expect me to tell you?'

Ridenour made a rueful grin, but his eyes were troubled. 'I

don't ask for military secrets. In general terms, however, what do you foresee?'

'A war of attrition,' Karlsarm said. 'We don't like that prospect either. It'll taste especially sour to use biologicals against their damned agriculture. But if we must, we must. We have more land, more resources of the kind that count, more determination. And they can't get at us. We'll outgrind them.'

'Are you quite sure? Suppose you provoke them – or the Imperial Navy – into making a real effort. Imagine, say, one atomic bomb dropped into this lake.'

Anger laid tight bands around Karlsarm's throat and chest, but he managed to answer levelly: 'We have defenses. And means of retaliation. This *is* a keystone area for us. We won't lose it without exacting a price – which I think they'll find too heavy. Tell them that when you go home!'

'I shall. I don't know if I'll be believed. You appear to have no concept of the power that a single, minor-class spaceship can bring to bear. I beg you to make terms before it's too late.'

'Do you aim to convince a thousand leaders like me and the entire society that elected us? I wish you luck, John Ridenour.' Karlsarm turned from the pleading gaze. 'I'd better get busy. We're still several kilometers short of our campsite.'

His brusqueness was caused mainly by doubt of his ability to dissemble much longer. What he, with some experience of Imperialists, sensed in this one's manner, lent strong support to the intuitive suspicions that Evagail had voiced. Ridenour had more on his mind than the Terran admitted.

It was unwise to try getting the truth out of him with drugs. He might be immunized or counter-conditioned. Or his secret might turn out to be something harmless. In either case, a potentially valuable spokesman would have been antagonized for nothing.

An aphrodite? She'd boil the ice water in his veins, for certain! And, while possessors of that Skill were rare, several were standing by at present in case they should be needed on some intelligence mission.

It might not work, either. But the odds were high that it

would. Damned few men cared for anything but the girl – the woman – the hag – whatever her age, whatever her looks – once she had turned her pheromones loose on him. She could ask what she would as the price of her company. But Ridenour might belong to that small percentage who, otherwise normal, were so intensely inner-directed that it didn't matter how far in love they fell; they'd stick by their duty. Should this prove the case he could not be allowed to leave and reveal the existence of that powerful a weapon. He must be killed, which was repugnant, or detained, which was a nuisance.

Karlsarm's brain labored on, while he issued his orders and led the final march. Ridenour probably did not suspect that he was suspected. He likeliest interpreted Evagail's avoidance of him as due to pique, despite what she had claimed. (And in some degree it no doubt is, Karlsarm snickered to himself.) Chances were he attributed the chief's recent gruffness to preoccupation. He had circulated freely among the other men and women of the force; but not having been told to doubt his good faith, they did not and he must realise it.

Hard to imagine what he might do. He surely did not plan on access to an aircar or a long-range radio transmitter! Doubtless he'd report anything he had seen or heard that might have military significance. But he wouldn't be reporting anything that made any difference. Well before he was conducted to the agrolands, the army would have left Moon Garnet again; and it would not return, because the lake was too precious to use for a permanent base. And all this had been made explicit to Ridenour at the outset.

Well, then, why not give him free rein and see what he did? Karlsarm weighed risks and gains for some time before he nodded to himself.

The encampment was large. A mere fraction of the Upwoods men had gone to Domkirk. Thousands stayed behind, training. They greeted their comrades with envious hilarity. Fires burned high that night, song and dance and clinking goblets alarmed the forest.

At sunset, Karlsarm and Evagail stood atop a rocky bluff,

overlooking water and trees and a northward rise to the camp. Behind them was a cave, from which projected an Arulian howitzer. Several other heavy-duty weapons were placed about the area, and a rickety old war boat patrolled overhead. Here and there, a man flitted into view, bow or blade on shoulder, and vanished again into the brake. Voices could be heard, muted by leaves, and smoke drifted upward. But the signs of man were few, virtually lost in that enormous landscape. With the enemy hundreds of kilometers off, guns as well as picket-posts were untended; trees divided the little groups of men from each other and hid them from shore or sky; the evening was mostly remote bird cries and long golden light.

'I wonder what our Terran thinks of this,' Karlsarm said. 'We must look pretty sloppy to him.'

'He's no fool. He doesn't underrate us much. Maybe not at all.' Evagail shivered, though the air was yet warm. Her hand crept into his, her voice grew thin. 'Could he be right? Could we really be foredoomed?'

'I don't know,' Karlsarm said.

She started. The hazel eyes widened. 'Loveling! You are always – '

'I can be honest with you,' he said. 'Ridenour accused me today of not understanding what power the Imperialists command in a single combat unit. He was wrong. I've seen them and I do understand. We can't force terms on them. If they decide the Cities must prevail, well, we'll give them a hard guerrilla war, but we'll be hunted down in the end. Our aim has to be to convince them it isn't worthwhile – that, at the least, their cheapest course of action is to arrange and enforce a status quo settlement between us and the Cities.' He laughed. 'Whether or not they'll agree remains to be seen. But we've got to try, don't we?'

'Do we?'

'Either that or stop being the Free People.'

She leaned her head on his shoulder. 'Let's not spend the night in this hole,' she begged. 'Not with that big ugly gun looming over us. Let's take our bedrolls into the forest.'

'I'm sorry. I must stay here.'

'Why?'

'So Noach can find me . . . if his animals report anything.'

* * *

Karlsarm woke before the fingers had closed on his arm to shake him. He sat up. The cave was a murk, relieved by a faint sheen off the howitzer; but the entrance cut a blue-black starry circle in it. Noach crouched silhouetted. 'He lay awake the whole night,' the handler breathed. 'Now he's sneaked off to one of the blaster cannon. He's fooling around with it.'

Karlsarm heard Evagail gasp at his side. He slipped weapon belts and quiver strap over the clothes he had slept in, took his crossbow and glided forth. 'We'll see about that,' he said. Anger stood bleak within him. 'Lead on.' Silent though they were, slipping from shadow, he became aware of the woman at his back.

Selene was down, sunrise not far off, but the world still lay nighted, sky powdered with stars and lake gleaming like a mirror. An uhu wailed, off in the bulk of the forest. The air was cold. Kalrsarm glanced aloft. Among the constellations crept that spark which had often haunted his thoughts. The orbit he estimated from angular speed was considerable. Therefore the thing was big. And if the Imperialists had erected some kind of space station, the grapevine would have brought news from the Free People's spies inside the Cities; therefore the thing was a spaceship – huge. Probably the light cruiser *Isis*: largest man-of-war the Terrans admitted keeping in this system. (Quite enough for their purposes. A heavier craft couldn't land if needed. This one could handle any probable combination of lesser vessels. If Aruli sent something more formidable, the far-flung scoutboats would detect that in time to arrange reinforcements from a Navy base before the enemy arrived. Which was ample reason to expect that Aruli would not 'intervene in a civil conflict, though denouncing this injustice visited upon righteously struggling kinfolk.')

Was it coincidence that she took her new station soon after Ridenour joined the raiders? Tonight we find out, Karlsarm vowed.

*

The blaster cannon stood on a bare ridge, barrel etched gaunt across the Milky Way. His group crouched under the last tree and peered. One of Noach's beasts could go unobserved among the scattered bushes, but not a man. And the beasts weren't able to describe what went on at the controls of a machine.

'Could he – '

Karlsarm chopped off Evagail's whisper with a hiss. The gun was in action. He saw the thing move through a slow arc and heard the purr of its motor. It was tracking. But what was it locked onto? And why had no energy bolt stabbed forth?

'He's not fixing to shoot up the camp,' Karlsarm muttered. 'That'd be ridiculous. He couldn't get off more than two shots before he was dead. But what else?'

'Should I rush?' Evagail asked.

'I think you'd better,' Karlsarm said, 'and let's hope the damage hasn't already been done.'

He must endure the agony of a minute or two while she gathered the resources of her Skill – not partially, as she often did in everyday life, but totally. He heard a measured intake of breath, sensed rhythmic muscular contractions, smelled sharp adrenalin. Then she exploded.

She was across the open ground in a blur. Ridenour could not react before she was upon him. He cried out and ran. She overhauled him in two giantess bounds. Her hands closed. He struggled, and he was not a weak man. But she picked him up by the wrists and ankles and carried him like a rag doll. Her face was a white mask in the starlight. 'Lie still,' she said in a voice not her own, 'or I will break you.'

'Don't. Evagail, please.' Noach dared stroke an ironhard arm. 'Do be careful,' he said to Ridenour's aghast upside-down stare. 'She's dangerous in this condition. It's akin to hysterical rage, you know – mobilization of the body's ultimate resources, which are quite astounding – but under conscious control. Nevertheless, the personality is affected. Think of her as an angry catavray.'

'Amok,' rattled in Ridenour's throat. 'Berserk.' He shivered.

'I don't recognize those words,' Noach said, 'but I repeat, her Skill consists in voluntary hysteria. At the moment, she could crush your skull between her hands. She might do it, too, if you provoke her.'

They reached the gun. Evagail cast the Terran to earth, bone-rattlingly hard, and yanked him back on his feet by finger and thumb around his nape. He was taller than she, but she appeared to tower over him, over all three men. Starlight crackled in her coiled hair. Her eyes were bright and blind.

Noach leaned close to Ridenour, read the terror upon him, and said mildly, 'Please tell us what you were doing.'

In some incredible fashion, Ridenour got the nerve to yell, 'Nothing! I couldn't sleep, I c-came here to pass the time – '

Karlsarm turned from his examination of the blaster. 'You've got this thing tracking that ship in orbit,' he said.

'Yes. I – foolish of me – I apologize – only for fun – '

'You had the trigger locked,' Karlsarm said. 'Energy was pouring out of the muzzle. But no flash, no light, no ozone smell.' He gestured. 'I turned it off. I also notice you've opened the chamber and replaced the primary modulator with this little gadget. Did you hear him talk, Evagail, before you charged?'

Her strange flat tone said: ' " – entire strength of the outbacker army on this continent is concentrated here and plans to remain for several days at least. I don't suggest a multi-megatonner. It'd annihilate them, all right, but they *are* subjects of His Majesty and potentially more valuable than most. It'd also do great ecological damage – to Imperial territory – and City hinterlands would get fallout. Not to mention the effect on your humble servant, me. But a ship could land without danger. I suggest the *Isis* herself, loaded with marines, aircraft and auxiliary gear. If the descent is sudden, the guerrillas won't be able to flee far. Using defoliators, sonics, gas, stun-beam sweeps and the rest, you should be able to capture most of them inside a week or two. Repeat, capture, not kill, wherever possible. I'll explain after you land. Right now I don't know how long I've got till I'm interrupted, so I'd better describe terrain. We're on the northeast verge of Moon Garnet Lake – " At that point,' Evagail concluded, 'I interrupted him.' The most chilling thing was that she saw no humor.

93

'Her Skill heightens perceptions and data storage too,' Noach said in a shocked, mechanical fashion.

'Well,' Karlsarm sighed, 'no real need to interrogate Ridenour, is there? He converted this gun into some kind of maser and called down the enemy on our heads.'

'They may not respond, if they heard him cut off the way he was,' Noach said with little hope.

'Wasn't much noise,' Karlsarm answered. 'They probably figure he did see somebody coming and had to stop in a hurry. If anything, they'll arrive as fast as may be, before we can disperse the stockpiles that'll give a scent to their metal detectors.'

'We'd better start running,' Noach said. Above the bristly beard, his nutcracker face had turned cold.

'Maybe not.' Excitement rose in Karlsarm.

'I need at least an hour or two to think – and, yes, talk with you, Ridenour.'

The Terran straightened. His tone rang. 'I didn't betray you, really,' he said. 'I stayed loyal to my Emperor.'

'You'll tell us a few things, though,' Karlsarm said. 'Like what procedure you expect a landing party to follow. No secrets to that, are there? Just tell us about newscasts you've seen, books you've read, inferences you've made.'

'No!'

Roused by the noise, other men were drifting up the hill, lean leather-clad shapes with weapons to hand. But Karlsarm ignored them. 'Evagail,' he said.

Her cold, cold fingers closed on Ridenour. He shrieked. 'Slack off,' Karlsarm ordered. 'Now – *slack off, woman*! – have you changed your mind? Or does she unscrew your ears, one by one, and other parts? I don't want you hurt, but my whole civilization's at stake, and I haven't much time.'

Ridenour broke. Karlsarm did not despise him for that. Few men indeed could have defied Evagail in her present mood, and they would have had to be used to the Mistresses of War.

In fact, Karlsarm needed a lot of courage himself, later on, when he laid arms around her and mouth at her cheek and crooned, 'Come back to us, loveling.' How slowly softness, warmth and – in a chill dawn-light – color reentered her skin: until at last she sank down before him and wept.

He raised her and led her to their cave.

* * *

At first the ship was a gleam, drowned in sun-glare. Then she was a cloud no bigger than a man's hand. But swiftly and swiftly did she grow. Within minutes, her shadow darkened the land. Men saw her from below as a tower that descended upon them, hundreds of meters in height, flanks reflecting with a metallic brilliance that blinded. Through light filters might be seen the boat housings, gun turrets and missile tubes that bristled from her. She was not heavily armored, save at a few key points, for she dealt in nuclear energies and nothing could withstand a direct hit. But the perceptors and effectors of her fire-control system could intercept virtually anything that a lesser mechanism might throw. And the full power of her own magazines, vomited forth at once, would have incinerated a continent.

The engines driving that enormous mass were deathly quiet. But where their countergravity fields touched the planet, trees snapped to kindling and the lake roiled white. Her advent was dancer graceful. But it went so fast that cloven air roared behind, one continuous thunderclap between stratosphere and surface. Echoes crashed from mountain to mountain; avalanches broke loose on the heights, throwing ice plumes into the sky; the risen winds smelled scorched.

Emblazoned upon her stood *HMS Isis* and the sunburst of chastising Empire.

Already she had discharged her auxiliaries, aircraft that buzzed across the lakeland in bright quick swarms, probing with instruments, firing random lightning bolts, shouting through amplifiers that turned human voices into an elemental force: 'Surrender, surrender!'

At the nexus of the cruiser's multiple complexity, Captain Chang sat in his chair of command. The screens before him flickered with views, data, reports. A score of specialist officers held to their posts behind him. Their work – speech, tap on signal buttons, clickdown of switches – made a muted buzz. From time to time, something was passed up to Chang himself. He listened, decided and returned to studying the screens. Neither his inflection nor his expression varied. Lieutenant-Commander Hunyadi, his executive officer, punched an appropriate control on the communications board in front of him and relayed the order to the right place. The bridge might have been an engineering center on Terra, save for the uniforms and the straining concentration.

Until Chang scowled. 'What's that, Citizen Hunyadi?' He pointed to a screen in which the water surface gleamed, amidst green woods and darkling cliffs. The view was dissolving.

'Fog rising, sir, I think,' Hunyadi had already tapped out a query to the meteorological officer in his distant sanctum.

'No doubt, Citizen Hunyadi,' Chang said. 'I do not believe it was predicted. Nor do I believe it is precedented – such rapid condensation – even on this freak planet.'

The M.O.'s voice came on. Yes, the entire target area was fogging at an unheard-of rate. No, it had not been forecast and, frankly, it was not understood. Possibly, at this altitude, given this pressure gradient, high insolation acted synergistically with the colloidogenic effect of countergravity beams on liquid. Should the question be addressed to a computer?

'No, don't tie facilities up on academic problem,' Chang said. 'Will the stuff be troublesome?'

'Not very, sir. In fact, aircraft reports indicate it's forming a layer at about five hundred meters. An overcast, should be reasonably clear at ground level. Besides, we have instruments that can see through fog.'

'I am aware of that latter fact, Citizen Nazarevsky. What concerns me is that an overcast will hide us from visual observation at satellite distance. You will recall that picket ships are supposed to keep an eye on us.' Chang drummed fingers on the arm of his chair for a second before he said: 'No matter. We will still have full communication, I trust. And it's necessary to exploit surprise, before the bandits have scattered over half this countryside. Carry on, gentlemen.'

'Aye, aye, sir.' Hunyadi returned to the subtle, engrossing ballet that was command operations.

After a while, Chang stirred himself and asked, 'Has any evidence been reported of enemy willingness to surrender?'

'No, sir,' the exec replied. 'But they don't appear to be marshalling for resistance, either. I don't mean just that they haven't shot at us. The stockpiles of metallic stuff that we're zeroing in on haven't been moved. Terrain looks deserted. Every topographical and soni-probe indication is that it's normal, safe, not booby-trapped.'

'I wish Ridenour had been able to transmit more,' Chang complained. 'Well, no doubt the bandits are simply running in panic. I wonder if they stopped to cut his throat.'

Hunyadi understood that no answer was desired from him.

The ship passed through the new-born clouds. Uncompensated viewports showed thick, swirling gray formlessness. Infrared, ultraviolet and microwave scopes projected a peaceful scene beneath. It was true that an unholy number of tiny flying objects were registered in the area. Insects, no doubt, probably disturbed by the ship. Time was short in which to think about them, before *Isis* broke through. Ground was now immediately below: that slope on the forest edge, overlooking the lake and near the enemy weapon depots, which Chang had selected. It would have been a lovely sight, had the sky not been so low and gloomy, the tendrils and banks of fog drifting so many and stealthy among trees. But everyone on *Isis* was too busy to admire, from the master in his chair of command to the marines ranked before the sally locks.

Aircraft that had landed for final checks of the site flew away like autumn leaves. The cruiser hung until they were gone, extending her landing jacks, which were massive as cathedral buttresses. Then slowly she sank down upon them. For moments the engines loudened, ringing through her metal corridors. Words flew, quiet and tense: ' – stability achieved . . . air cover complete . . . weapons crew standing by . . . detectors report negative . . . standing by . . . standing by . . . standing by . . .'

97

'Proceed with Phase Two,' Chang ordered.

'*Now hear this*,' Hunyadi chanted to the all-points intercom. The engines growled into silence. The air locks opened. Inhuman in helmets, body armor, flying harness, the weapons they clutched, the marine squadrons rushed forth. First they would seize the guerrilla arsenals, and next cast about for human spoor.

The bridge had not really fallen still. Data continued to flow in, commands to flow out; but by comparison, sound was now a mutter, eerie as the bodies of fog that moved out of undertree shadows and across the bouldery hillside. Hunyadi looked into the screens and grimaced. 'Sir,' he said uneasily, 'if the enemy's as skilled in moving about through the woods as I've heard, someone could come near enough to fire a small nuclear missile at us.'

'Have no worries on that score, Citizen Huyadi,' Chang said. 'Nothing material, launched from a projector that one or two men might carry, could reach us before it was detected and intercepted. A blaster beam might scorch a hull plate or two. But upper and lower gun turrets would instantly triangulate on the source.' His tone was indulgent: like most Navy men serving on capital ships, Hunyadi was quite new to ground operations. 'Frankly, I could hope for a show of resistance. The alternative is a long, tedious airborne bushbeating.'

Hunyadi winced. 'Hunting men like animals. I don't like it.'

'Nor I,' Chang admitted. The iron came back into him. 'But we have our orders.'

'Yes, sir.'

'Read your history, Citizen Huyadi. Read your history. No empire which tolerated rebellion ever endured long thereafter. And we are the wall between humanity and Merseian – '

A scream broke through.

And suddenly war was no problem in logistics, search patterns, or games theory. It entered the ship with pain in one hand and blood on the other; and its footfalls thundered.

'*Bees, millions of things like bees, out of the woods – oh, God, coming inboard, the boys're doubled over, one sting hurts enough to knock you crazy – Yaaahhhh!*'

'Close all locks! Seal all compartments! All hands in spacesuits!'

'*Marine Colonel Deschamps to Prime Command. Detachments report small groups of women, unarmed, as they land. Women appear anxious to surrender. Request orders.*'

'Take them prisoners, of course. Stand around them. You may not be attacked then. But if a unit notes a dense insect swarm, the men are to seal their armor and discharge lethal gas at once.'

'*Lock Watch Four to bridge! We can't shut the lock here! Some enormous animal – like a, a nightmare crocodile – burst in from the woods – blocking the valves with its body –* '

'Energy weapons, sweep the surrounding forest. All aircraft, return to bomb and strafe this same area.'

Atomic warheads and poisons could not be used, when the ship would be caught in their blast or the gases pour in through three airlocks jammed open by slain monsters. But some gunners had buttoned up their turrets in advance of the bees. Their cannon hurled bolt after bolt, trees exploded and burned and fell, rocks fused . . . and fog poured in like an ocean. Simultaneously, the instrumentation and optical aids that should have pierced it failed. The crews must fire at random into horrible wet smoke, knowing they could not cover the whole ground about them.

'*Radio dead. Radar dead. Electromagnetic 'scopes dead. Blanketed by interference. Appears to emanate from . . . from everywhere . . . different insects, clouds of them! What scanning stuff we've got that still works, sonics, that kind of thing, gives insufficient definition. We're deaf, dumb, and blind!*'

Aircraft began to crash. Their instruments were likewise gone; and they were not meant to collide with entire flocks of birds.

'*Marine Colonel Deschamps – reporting – reports received – catastrophe. I don't know what, except . . . those women . . . they turned on our men and –* '

Troopers who escaped flew wildly through fog. Birds found them and betrayed them to snipers in treetops. They landed, seeking cover. Arrows whistled from brush, or hellhounds fell upon them.

'Stand by to raise ship.'

'*Lock Watch Four reporting – they've got in through the fog, under our fire – swarming in, wild men and animals – good-by, Maria, good-by, universe –'*

Most aircraft pilots managed to break free. They got above the clouds and ran from that lake. But they were not equipped to evade ground fire of energy weapons with which there was no electronic interference such as continued to plague them. It had been assumed that the marines would take those emplacements. The marines were now dead, or disabled, or fleeing, or captured. The women called their men back to the guns. Stars blossomed and fell through the daylight sky.

'This is Wolf, commanding the Free People group assigned to HMS Isis. A prisoner tells me this thing communicates with the bridge. Better give up, Captain. We're inside. We hold the engine room. We can take your whole ship at our leisure – or plant a nuclear bomb. Your auxiliary forces are rapidly being destroyed. I hope you'll see reason and give up. We don't want to harm you. It's no discredit to you, sir, this defeat. Your intelligence service let you down. You met weapons you didn't know about, uniquely suited to very special circumstances. Tell your men to lay down their arms. We'll lift the interference blanket if you agree – not skyward, but on ground level, anyhow, so you can call them. Let's stop spilling lives and begin talking terms.'

Chang felt he had no choice.

Soon afterward, he and his principal officers stood outside. The men who guarded them were clad and equipped like savages; but they spoke with courtesy. 'I would like you gentlemen to meet some friends,' said the one named Karlsarm. From the forest, toward the captured flying tower, walked a number of women. They were more beautiful than could be imagined.

* * *

Ridenour was among the last to go aboard. Not that there were many – a skeleton staff of chosen Imperialist officers, for the aphrodites could not make captives of more in the short time available, those women themselves, whoever of the army possessed abilities even slightly useful in space warships. But perhaps the measure of Karlsarm's audacity was his drafting of a known spy.

Whose loyalties had not been altered.

Standing in cold, blowing fogbanks. Ridenour shuddered. The cruiser was dim to his eyes, her upper sections lost. Water soaked the earth and dripped from a thousand unseen trees; the insects that made this weather flitted ceaselessly between lake and air, in such myriads that their wingbeats raised an underlying sussuration; a wild beast bellowed, a wild bird shrilled — tones of the wilderness. But the outback reaches were not untamed nature. Like some great animal, they had been harnessed for man, and in turn, something of theirs had entered the human heart.

A Terran went up a gangway, into the ship. His uniform was still neat blue, emblemmed with insignia and sunburst. He still walked with precision. But his eyes scarcely left the weather-beaten, leather-kilted woman at his side, though she must be twenty years his senior.

'There but for the grace of God,' Ridenour whispered.

Evagail, who had appeared mutely a few minutes ago, gave him a serious look. 'Is their treatment so dreadful?' she asked.

'What about their people at home? Their home itself? Their own shame and self-hate for weakness – ' Ridenour broke off.

'They'll be released ... against their wills, I'm sure; they'll plead to stay with us. You can make it part of your job to see that their superiors understand they couldn't help themselves. Afterward, you have reconditioning techniques, don't you? Though I expect most cases will recover naturally. They'll have had just a short exposure.'

'And the, the women?'

'Why, what of them? They don't want to be saddled with a bunch of citymen. This is their wartime duty. Otherwise they have their private affairs.'

'Their Skills,' Ridenour edged away from her.

Her smile was curiously timid. 'John,' she said, 'we're not monsters. We're only the Free People. An aphrodite doesn't use her Skill for unfair gain. It has therapeutic applications. Or I – I don't like raising my strength against fellow humans. I want to use it for their good again.'

He fumbled out the tobacco he had begged from a Terran and began to stuff his pipe. It would give some consolation.

Her shoulders slumped. 'Well,' she said in a tired voice, 'I think we'd better go aboard now.'

'You're coming too?' he said. 'What for? To guard me?'

'No. Perhaps we'll need my reaction speed. Though Karlsarm did hope I'd persuade you — Come along, please.'

She led him to the bridge. Terran officers were already posted among the gleaming machines, the glittering dials. Hunyadi sat in the chair of command. But Karlsarm stood beside him, the catavray head gaping across his brow; and other men of the forest darkened that scene.

'Stand by for liftoff.' Hunyadi must recite the orders himself. 'Close airlocks. All detector stations report.'

Evagail padded over to Karlsarm. Ridenour could not help thinking that her ruddy hair, deep curves, bare bronze, were yet more an invasion of this metal-and-plastic cosmos than the men were. A faint odor of woman lingered behind her on the sterile air.

'What's our situation with the enemy?' she asked.

'Fair, as near as we can learn,' Karlsarm said. 'You haven't followed events since the last fight?'

'No. I was too busy making arrangements for prisoners. Like medical care for the injured, shelter for everyone. They were too wretched, out in this mist.'

'Can't say I've enjoyed it either. I'll be glad when we can let it up . . . Well. We didn't try an aphrodite on old Chang. Instead, we had him call the Terran chief, Admiral Cruz, and report the capture of his ship. Naturally, having no idea we'd be able to raise her, he didn't give that fact away. Supposedly we'll hold vessel and personnel for bargaining counters. The stratosphere's full of aircraft above us, but they won't do anything as long as they think we're sitting with our hostages. Only one spaceship has moved to anything like immediate striking range of us.'

'Are you certain?'

'About as certain as you can be in war, whatever that means. We gave the chief communications officer to an aphrodite, of course. He listened in and decoded orders for the main fleet to stand out to space. That was a logical command for Cruz to issue, once the evacuation notice went out.'

'Evacuation – ?'

'Loveling, you didn't think I'd vaporize the Cities *and* their people, did you? The instant I foresaw a chance to grab this boat, I got in touch with the Grand Council – by radio, for the other continents, because time was short, so short that it didn't matter the Terrans would hear. They're good codebreakers, but I think the languages we used must've puzzled them!' Karlsarm grinned. 'As soon as we'd made this haul, orders went out to our agents in every City, whether Terran- or Arulian-occupied. They were to serve notice that in one rotation period, the Cities would be erased. But they were to imply the job will be done from space.'

Fright touched Evagail. 'The people did evacuate, didn't they?' she breathed.

'Yes. We've monitored communications. The threat's convincing, when there's been so much fear of intervention from Aruli or from Merseia herself. An invading fleet can't get past the blockade. But a certain percentage of fast little courier boats can. Likewise a flight of robot craft with nuclear weapons aboard: which wouldn't be guaranteed to distinguish between friendly and unfriendly target areas.'

'But has no one thought that we, in this ship, might – '

'I trust not, or we're dead,' Karlsarm stated. 'Our timing was phased with care. The fog, and interference, and our ground fire, kept the Terrans from finding out what had happened to their cruiser. We informed them immediately that she was disabled, and they doubtless supposed it was logical. How could anyone take an undamaged Imperial warcraft, without equipment they know we don't have? In fact, they probably took for granted we'd had outside technical assistance in rigging a trap. Remember, the City warning was already preoccupying their thoughts. Chang's call was a precaution against their growing frantic and bombing us in the hope of getting our supposed Merseian or Arulian allies. He made it a few hours ago; and I made certain that he didn't say the ship was captured *intact*.'

'They'll know better now,' Hunyadi said. His face was white, his voice tormented.

'Correct. Lift as soon as you're able,' Karlsarm said. 'If we're hit, your woman will die too.'

The executive officer jerked his head. 'I know! Bridge to all stations. Lift at full power. Be prepared for attack.'

Engines growled. The deck quivered with their force. *Isis* climbed, and the sun blazed about her.

'Communications to bridge,' said the intercom. 'Calls picked up from Imperialists.'

'I expected that,' Karlsarm said dryly. 'Broadcast a warning. We don't want to hurt them, but if they bother us, we'll swat.'

Sickly, Ridenour saw the planet recede beneath him.

Flame blossomed a long way off. 'Missile barrage from one air squadron stopped,' said the intercom. 'Shall fire be returned?'

'No,' Karlsarm said. 'Not unless we absolutely must.'

'Thank you, sir! Those are . . . my people yonder.' After a moment. 'They were my people.'

'They will be again,' Evagail murmured to Ridenour. 'If you help.'

'What can I do?' he choked.

She touched him. He winced aside. 'You can speak for us,' she said. 'You're respected. Your loyalty is not in doubt. You proved it afresh, that night when – We don't belong to your civilization. We don't understand how it thinks, what it will compromise on and what it will die for, the nuances, the symbols, the meanings it finds in the universe. And it doesn't understand us. I think you know us a little, though, John. Enough to see that we're no menace.'

'Except to the Cities,' he said. 'And now the Empire.'

'No, they threatened us. They wouldn't leave our forests alone. As for the Empire, can't it contain one more way of living? Won't mankind be the richer for that?'

They looked at each other, and a thrumming aloneness enclosed them. A screen showed space and stars on the rim of the world.

'I suppose,' he said finally, 'no man can compromise on the basics of his culture. They're the larger part of his identity. To give them up is a kind of death. Many people would rather die in the body. You won't stop fighting until you're utterly crushed.'

'And must that be?' Her speech fell gently on his ears. 'Don't you Terrans want an end of war?'

An earthquake rumble went through the ship. Reports and orders seethed on the bridge. She was in long-range combat with a destroyer.

Undermanned, *Isis* could not stand off Cruz's whole fleet. But those units were scattered, would not reach Freehold for hours. Meanwhile, a solitary Imperial craft went against her with forlorn gallantry. Her fire-control men wept as they lashed back. But they must, to save the women who held them.

'What can I do?' Ridenour said.

'We'll call as soon as we're finished, and ask for a parley,' Evagail told him. 'We want you to urge that the Terrans agree. Afterward we want you to – no, not help plead our cause. Help explain it.'

'Opposition attack parried,' said a speaker. 'Limited return broadside as per orders appears to have inflicted some damage. Opposition sheering off. Shall she be annihilated?'

'No, let her go,' Karlsarm said.

Ridenour nodded at Evagail. 'I'll do what I can,' he said.

She took his hands, gladness bursting through her own tears, and this time he did not pull away.

Isis swung back into atmosphere. Her turrets flew loose. A doomed, empty City went skyward in flame.

* * *

Admiral Fernando Cruz Manqual stood high in the councils of this Imperial frontier, but he was a Terran merely by citizenship and remote ancestry. Military men have gone forth from Nuevo Mexico since that stark planet first was colonized. His manner toward Ridenour was at once curt and courteous.

'And so, Professor, you recommend that we accept their terms?' He puffed hard on a crooked black cigar. 'I am afraid that that is quite impossible.'

Ridenour made a production of starting his pipe. He needed time to find words. Awareness pressed in on him of his surroundings.

The negotiating commissions (to use a Terran phrase, the Free People called them mind-wrestlers) had met on neutral ground, an island in the Lawrencian Ocean. Though uninhabited thus far, it was beautiful with its full feathery trees, blossoming vines, deep cane-brakes, wide white beaches where surf played and roared. But there was little chance to enjoy what the place offered. Perhaps later, if talks were promising and tension relaxed, a young Terran spaceman might encounter a lightfoot outbacker girl in some glen.

But discussion had not yet even begun. It might well never begin. The two camps were armed, separated by three kilometers of forest and, on the Terran side, a wall of guns. Ridenour was the first who crossed from one to another.

Cruz's reception had been so cold that the xenologist half expected arrest. However, the admiral appeared to comprehend why he was there and invited him into his dome for private, unofficial conversation.

The dome was open to a mild, sea-scented breeze, but also to the view of other domes, vehicles, marines on sentry-go, aircraft at hover. Wine stood on the table between the two men, but except for a formal initial toast it had not been poured. Ridenour had stated the facts, and his words had struck unresponding silence.

Now:

'I think it's best sir,' Ridenour ventured. 'They can be conquered, if the Empire makes the effort. But that war would be long, costly, tying up forces we need elsewhere, devastating the planet, maybe making it unfit for human habitation; they'll retaliate with some pretty horrible biological capabilities. The prisoners they hold will not be returned. Likewise the *Isis*. You'll be compelled to order her knocked out, an operation that won't come cheap.'

He looked straight into the hard, mustached face. 'And for what? They're quite willing to remain Terran subjects.'

'They rebelled,' Cruz bit off; 'they collaborated with an enemy; they resisted commands given in His Majesty's name; they occasioned loss to His Majesty's Navy; they destroyed nine Imperial communities; thereby they wrecked the economy of an entire Imperial world. If this sort of behavior is let go unpunished, how long before the whole Empire breaks apart? And they aren't satisfied with asking for amnesty. No, they demand the globe be turned over to them!'

He shook his head. 'I do not question your honesty, Professor – someone had to be messenger boy, I suppose – but if you believe an official in my position can possibly give a minute's consideration to those wood-runners' fantasy, I must question your judgment.'

'They are not savages, sir,' Ridenour said. 'I've tried to explain to you something of their level of culture. My eventual written report should convince everyone.'

'That is beside the point.' His faded, open-throated undress uniform made Cruz look more terrible than any amount of braid and medals. The blaster at his hip had seen much use in its day.

'Not precisely, sir.' Ridenour shifted in his chair. Sweat prickled his skin. 'I've had a chance to think a lot about these issues, and a death-strong motivation for doing so and a career that's trained me to think in impersonal, long-range terms. What's the real good of the Empire? Isn't it the solidarity of many civilized planets? Isn't it, also the stimulus of diversity between those planets? Suppose we did crush the Free – the outbackers. How could the Cities be rebuilt, except at enormous cost? They needed centuries to reach their modern level unaided, on this isolated, metal-impoverished world. If we poured in treasure, we could recreate them, more or less, in a few years. But what then would we have? Nine feeble mediocrities, just productive enough to require guarding, because Merseia considers them a potential threat on her Arulian flank. Whereas if we let the *real* Freeholders, the ones who've adapted until they can

107

properly use this environment, if we let them flourish . . . we'll get, at no cost, a strong, self-supporting, self-defending outpost of Empire.'

That may not be strictly true, he thought. The outbackers don't mind acknowledging Terran suzerainty, if they can have a charter that lets them run their planet the way they want. They're too sensible to revive the nationalistic fallacy. They'll pay a bit of tribute, conduct a bit of trade. On the whole, however, we will be irrelevant to them.

They may not always be so to us, of course. We may learn much from them. If we ever fall, they'll carry on something of what was ours. But I'd better not emphasize this.

'Even if I wanted to accommodate them,' Cruz said, 'I have no power. My authority is broad, yes. And I can go well beyond its formal limits, in that a central government with thousands of other worries will accept any reasonable recommendation I make. But do not exaggerate my latitude, I beg you. If I suggested that the City people, loyal subjects of His Majesty, be moved off the world of their ancestors, and that rebels, no matter how cultivated, be rewarded with its sole possession . . . why, I should be recalled for psychiatric examination, no?'

He sounds regretful, leaped within Ridenour. He doesn't want a butcher's campaign. If I can convince him there is a reasonable and honorable way out – The xenologist smiled carefully around his pipestem. 'True, Admiral,' he said. 'If the matter were put in those words. But need they be? I'm no lawyer. Still, I know a little about the subject, enough that I can sketch out an acceptable formula.'

Cruz raised one eyebrow and puffed harder on his cigar.

'The point is,' Ridenour said, 'that juridicially we have not been at war. Everybody knows Aruli sent arms and troops to aid the original revolt, no doubt at Merseian instigation. But to avoid a direct collision with Aruli and so possibly with Merseia, we haven't taken official cognizance of this. We were content to choke off further influx and reduce the enemy piecemeal. In short, Admiral, your task here has been to quell an internal, civil disturbance.'

'Hm.'

'The outbackers did not collaborate with an external enemy, because legally there was none.'

Cruz flushed. 'Treason smells no sweeter by any other name.'

'It wasn't treason, sir,' Ridenour argued. The outbackers were not trying to undermine the Empire. They certainly had no wish to become Arulian or Merseian vassals!

'Put it this way: Freehold contained three fractions, the human City dwellers, the Arulian City dwellers, and the out-backers. The charter of Imperial incorporation was negotiated by the first of these parties exclusively. Thus it was unfair to the other two. When amendment was refused, social difficulties resulted. The outbackers had some cooperation with the Arul-ians, as a matter of expediency. But it was sporadic and never affected their own simple wish for justice. Furthermore, and more important, it was not cooperation with outsiders, but rather with some other Imperial subjects.

'Actually,' he added, 'when one stops to think about it, the Nine Cities have not at all been innocent martyrs. Their discrimination against the Arulians, their territorial aggressions against the outbackers, were what really brought on the trouble. Merseia then exploited the opportunity – but didn't create it in the first place.

'Why then should the heedlessness of the Cities, that proved so costly to the Empire, not be penalized?'

Cruz looked disappointed. 'I suppose the Policy Board could adopt some such formula,' he said. 'But only if it wanted to. And it won't want to. Because what formula can disguise the fact of major physical harm inflicted in sheer contumacy?'

'The formula of over-zealousness to serve His Majesty's interests,' Ridenour cast back. He lifted one palm. 'Wait! Please! I don't ask you, sir, to propose an official falsehood. The zeal was not greatly misguided. And it did serve Terra's best interest.'

'What? How?'

'Don't you see?' Tensely, Ridenour leaned across the table. Here we go, he thought, either we fly or we crash in the fire. 'The outbackers ended the war for us.'

Cruz fell altogether quiet.

'Between you and me alone, I won't insult your intelligence by claiming this outcome was planned in detail,' Ridenour hurried on. 'But that is the effect. It was Nine Cities, their manufacturing and outworld commerce, their growth potential, that attracted the original Arulian settlers, and that lately made Freehold such a bait. With the Cities gone, what's left to fight about? The enemy has no more bases. I'm sure he'll accept repatriation to Aruli, including those of him who were born here. The alternative is to be milled to atoms between you and the outbackers.

'In return for this service, this removal of a bleeding wound on the Empire, a wound which might have turned into a cancer – surely the outbackers deserve the modest reward they ask. Amnesty for whatever errors they made, in seizing a chance that would never come again; a charter giving them the right to occupy and develop Freehold as they wish, though always as loyal subjects of His Majesty.'

Cruz was unmoving for a long time. When he spoke, he was hard to hear under the military noise outside. 'What of the City humans?'

'They can be compensated for their losses and resettled elsewhere,' Ridenour said. 'The cost will be less than for one year of continued war, I imagine; and you might well have gotten more than that. Many will complain, no doubt. But the interest of the Empire demands it. Quite apart from the problems in having two irreconcilable cultures on one planet, there's the wish to keep any frontier peaceful. The outbackers are unprofitably tough to invade; I rather believe their next generation will furnish some of our hardiest marine volunteers; but at the same time, they don't support the kind of industrial concentration – spaceships, nuclear devices – that makes our opposition worried or greedy.'

'Hm.' Cruz streamed smoke from his lips. His eyes half closed. 'Hm. This would imply that my command, for one, can be shifted to a region where we might lean more usefully on Merseia . . . yes-s-s.'

Ridenour thought in a moment that was desolate: Is that why I'm so anxious to save these people? Because I hope one day

110

they'll find a way out of the blind alley that is power politics? . . .

Cruz slammed a fist on the table. The bottle jumped. 'By the Crown, Professor, you might have something here!' he exclaimed. 'Let me pour. Let us drink together.'

Nothing would happen overnight, of course. Cruz must ponder, and consult, and feel out the other side's representatives. Both groups must haggle, stall, quibble, orate, grow calculatedly angry, grow honestly weary. And from those weeks of monkey chatter would emerge nothing more than a 'protocol.' This must pass up through a dozen layers of bureaucrats and politicians, each of whom must assert his own immortal importance by some altogether needless and exasperating change. Finally, on Terra, the experts would confer; the computers spin out reels of results that nobody quite understood or very much heeded; the members of the Policy Board and the different interests that had put them there use this issue as one more area in which to jockey for a bit more power; the news media make inane inflammatory statements (but not many – Freehold was remote – the latest orgy given by some nobleman's latest mistress was more interesting) . . . and a document would arrive here, and maybe it would be signed but maybe it would be returned for 'further study as recommended . . .'

I won't be leaving soon, Ridenour thought. They'll need me for months. Final agreement may not be ratified for a year or worse.

Some hours passed before he left the Terran camp and walked toward the other. He'd doubtless best stay with the outbackers for a while. Evagail had been waiting for him. She ran down the path. 'How did it go?'

'Very well, I'd say,' he said.

She cast herself into his arms, laughing and weeping. He soothed her, affectionately but just a little impatiently. His prime desire at the moment was to find a place by himself, that he might write a letter home.

Concealed and ignored at the time, the Freeholders' rebellion was a signal that the Empire's long afternoon was drawing to a close. However, other vigorous folk, both human and non-human, had learned the same lessons from history and were individually preparing to survive their effete overlords. In the meantime, Terra's reign had generations yet to run, thanks in no little measure to the cunning and valor of men like Dominic Flandry, the naval intelligence officer turned Imperial advisor.

Yet sunset could not be postponed forever. Terra and Merseia wore each other into oblivion. Their exhausted dominions were devastated by rebellions from within and attacks from without. By the middle of the fourth millennium, the fearful Long Night fell.

A TRAGEDY OF ERRORS

Once in ancient days, the then King of England told Sir Christopher Wren, whose name is yet remembered, that the new Cathedral of St Paul which he had designed was 'awful, pompous and artificial.' Kings have seldom been noted for perspicacity.

Later ages wove a myth about Roan Tom. He became their archetype of those star rovers who fared forth while the Long Night prevailed. As such, he was made to fit the preconceptions and prejudices of whoever happened to mention him. To many scholars, he was a monster, a murderer and thief, bandit and vandal, skulking like some carrion animal through the ruins of the Terran Empire. Others called him a hero, a gallant and romantic leader of fresh young peoples destined to sweep out of time the remnants of a failed civilization and build something better.

He would have been equally surprised, and amused, by either legend.

'Look,' one can imagine his ghost drawling, 'we had to eat. For which purpose, it's sort o' helpful to keep your throat uncut, no? That was a spiny-tail period. Society'd fallen. And havin' so far to fall, it hit bottom almighty hard. The ee-economic basis for things like buildin' spaceships wasn't there any more. That meant little trade between planets. Which meant trouble on most of 'em. You let such go on for a century or two, snowballin', and what've you got? A kettle o' short-lived dwarf nations, that's what – one-planet, one-continent, one-island nations; all of 'em one-lung for sure – where they haven't collapsed even further. No more information-collatin' services, so nobody can keep track o' what's happenin' amongst those millions o'suns. What few spaceships are left in workin' order

113

are naturally the most valuable objects in sight. So they naturally get acquired by the toughest men around who, bein' what they are, are apt to use the ships for conquerin' or plunderin' . . . and complicate matters still worse.

'Well,' and he pauses to stuff a pipe with Earthgrown tobacco, which is available in this particular Valhalla, 'like everybody else, I just made the best o' things as I found 'em. Fought? Sure. Grew up fightin'. I was born on a spaceship. My dad was from Lochlann, but outlawed after a family feud went sour. He hadn't much choice but to turn pirate. One day I was in a landin' party which got bushwhacked. Next I heard, I'd been sold into slavery. Had to take it from there. Got some lucky breaks after a while and worked 'em hard. Didn't do too badly, by and large.

'Mind you, though, I never belonged to one o' those freaky cultures that'd taken to glorifyin' combat for its own sake. In fact, once I'd gotten some power on Kraken, I was a lot more int'rested in startin' trade again than in anything else. But neither did I mind the idea o' fightin', if we stood to gain by it, nor o' collectin' any loose piece o' property that wasn't too well defended. Also, willy-nilly, we were bound to get into brawls with other factions. Usually those happened a long ways from home. I saw to that. Better there than where I lived, no?

'We didn't always win, either. Sometimes we took a clobberin'. Like finally, what I'd reckon as about the worst time I found myself skyhootin' away from Sassania, in a damaged ship, alone except for a couple o' wives. I shook pursuit in the Nebula. But when we came out on the other side, we were in a part o' space that wasn't known to us. Old Imperial territory still, o' course, but that could mean anything. And we needed repairs. Once my ship'd been self-fixin', as well as self-crewin', self-pilotin', self-navigatin', aye-ya, even self-aware. But that computer was long gone, together with a lot of other gear. We had to find us a place with a smidgin of industrial capacity, or we were done for.'

*

The image in the viewscreens flickered so badly that Tom donned armor and went out for a direct look at the system he had entered.

He liked being free in space anyway. He had more esthetic sense than he publicly admitted. The men of Kraken were quick to praise the beauty of a weapon or a woman, but would have considered it strange to spill time admiring a view rather than examining the scene for pitfalls and possibilities. In the hush and dreamlike liberty of weightlessness, Tom found an inner peace; and from this he turned outward, becoming one with the grandeur around him.

After he had flitted a kilometer from it, *Firedrake's* lean hull did not cut off much vista. But reflections, where energy beams had scored through black camouflage coating to the steel beneath, hurt his eye ... He looked away from ship and sun alike. It was a bright sun, intrinsic luminosity of two Sols, though the color was ruddy, like a gold and copper alloy. At a distance of one and a half astronomical units, it showed a disc thirty-four minutes wide; and no magnification, only a darkened faceplate, was necessary to see the flares that jetted from it. Corona and zodiacal light made a bronze cloud. That was not a typical main sequence star, Tom thought, though nothing in his background had equipped him to identify what the strangeness consisted of.

Elsewhere glittered the remoter stars, multitudinous and many-colored in their high night. Tom's gaze circled among them. Yes, yonder was Capella. Old Earth lay on the far side, a couple of hundred light-years from here. But he wanted home, to Kraken: much less of a trip, ten parsecs or so. He could have picked out its sun with the naked eye, as a minor member of that jewel-swarm, had the Nebula not stood between. The thunder-cloud mass reared gloomy and awesome athwart a quarter of heaven. And it might as well be a solid wall, if his vessel didn't get fixed.

That brought Tom's attention back to the planet he was orbiting. It seemed enormous at this close remove, a thick crescent growing as the ship swung dayward, as if it were toppling upon him. The tints were green, blue, brown, but with an underlying red in the land areas that wasn't entirely due to the sunlight color. Clouds banded the brightness of many seas; there was no true ocean. The southern polar cap was extensive. Yet it couldn't be very deep, because its northern counterpart had almost disappeared with summer, albeit the axial tilt was a mere ten degrees. Atmosphere rimmed the horizon with purple. A tiny disc was heaving into sight, the farther of the two small moons.

Impressive, yes. Habitable, probably according to the spectroscope, certainly according to the radio emissions on which he had homed. (They'd broken off several light-years away, but by then no doubt remained that this system was their origin, and this was the only possible world within the system.) Nonetheless – puzzling. In a way, daunting.

The planet was actually a midget. Its equatorial diameter was 6810 kilometers, its mass 0.15 Terra. Nothing that size ought to have air and water enough for men.

But there were men there. Or had been. Feeble and distorted though the broadcasts became, away off in space, Tom had caught Anglic words spoken with human mouths.

He shrugged. One way to find out. Activating his impellers, he flitted back. His boots struck hull and clung. He free-walked to the forward manlock and so inboard.

The interior gee-field was operational. Weight thrust his armor down onto his neck and shoulders. Yasmin heard him clatter and came to help him unsuit. He waved her back. 'Don't you see the frost on me? I been in planet shadow. Your finger'd stick to the metal, kid.' Not wearing radio earplugs, she didn't hear him, but she got the idea and stood aside. Gauntleted, he stripped down to coverall and mukluks and lockered the space equipment. At the same time, he admired her.

She was slight and dark, but prettier than he had realized at first. That was an effect of personality, reasserting itself after what happened in Anushirvan. The city had been not only the most beautiful and civilized, but the gayest on all Sassania; and her father was Nadjaf Kuli, the deputy governor. Now he was dead and his palace sacked, and she had fled for her life with one of her Shah's defeated barbarian allies. Yet she was getting back the ability to laugh. Good stock, Tom thought; she'd bear him good sons.

'Did you see trace of humans?' she asked. He had believed her Anglic bore a charming accent – it was not native to her – until he discovered that she had been taught the classical language. Her gazelle eyes flickered from the telescope he carried in one fist on to his battered and weatherbeaten face.

'Trace, yes,' he answered bluntly. 'Stumps of a few towns. They'd been hit with nukes.'

'Oh-h-h . . .'

'Ease off, youngster.' He rumpled the flowing hair. 'I couldn't make out much, with nothin' better'n these lenses. We'd already agreed the planet was likely raided, that time the broadcasts quit. Don't mean they haven't rebuilt a fair amount. I'd guess they have. The level o', shall I say in two words, radio activity –' Tom paused. 'You were supposed to smile at that,' he said in a wounded tone.

'Well, may I smile at the second joke, instead?' she retorted impishly. They both chuckled. Her back grew straighter, in the drab one-piece garment that was all he had been able to give her, and somehow the strength of the curving nose dominated the tenderness of her mouth. 'Please go on, my lord.'

'Uh, you shouldn't call me that. They're free women on Kraken.'

'So we were on Sassania. In fact, plural marriage –'

'I know, I know. Let's get on with business.' Tom started down the corridor. Yasmin accompanied him, less gracefully than she had moved at home. The field was set for Kraken weight, which was 1.25 standard. But she'd develop the muscles for it before long.

* * *

He had gone through a wedding ceremony with her, once they were in space, at Dagny's insistence. 'Who else will the poor child have for a protector but you, the rest of her life? Surely you won't turn her loose on any random planet. At the same time, she *is* aristocratic born. It'd humiliate her to become a plain concubine.'

117

'M-m-m . . . but the heirship problem – '

'I like her myself, what little I've seen of her; and the Kuli barons always had an honorable name. I don't think she'll raise boys who'll try to steal house rule from my sons.'

As usual, Dagny was no doubt right.

Anxious to swap findings with her, Tom hurried. The passage reached empty and echoing; air from the ventilators blew loud and chilled him; the stylized murals of gods and sea beasts had changed from bold to pathetic – now that only three people crewed this ship. But they were lucky to be alive – would not have been so, save for the primitive loyalty of his personal guardsmen, who died in their tracks while he ran through the burning city in search of Dagny – when the Pretender's non-human mercenaries broke down the last defenses. He found his chief wife standing by the ship with a Mark IV thunderbolter, awaiting his return. She would not have left without him. Yasmin huddled at her feet. They managed to loose a few missiles as they lifted. But otherwise there was nothing to do but hope to fight another day. The damage that *Firedrake* sustained in running the enemy space fleet had made escape touch and go. The resulting absence of exterior force-fields and much interior homeostasis made the damage worse as they traveled. Either they found the wherewithal for repair here, or they stayed here.

Tom said to Yasmin while he strode: 'We couldn't've picked up their radio so far out's we did, less'n they'd had quite a lot, both talk and radar. That means they had a pretty broad industrial base. You don't destroy that by scrubbin' cities. Too many crossroads machine shops and so forth; too much skill spread through the population. I'd be surprised if this planet's not on the way back up.'

'But why haven't they rebuilt any cities?'

'Maybe they haven't gotten that far yet. Been less'n ten years, you know. Or, 'course they might've got knocked clear down to savagery. I've seen places where it happened. We'll find out.'

Walking beside the girl, Roan Tom did not look especially note-worthy, certainly not like the rover and trader chieftain

118

whose name was already in the ballads of a dozen planets. He was of medium height, though so broad in shoulders and chest as to look stocky. From his father, he had the long head, wide face, high cheekbones, snub nose and beardlessness of the Lochlanna. But his mother, a freedwoman said to be of Hermetian stock, had given him dark-red hair, which was now thinning, and star-blue eyes. Only the right of those remained; a patch covered where the left had been. (Some day, somewhere, he'd find someone with the knowledge and facilities to grow him a new one!) He walked with the rolling gait of a Krakener, whose planet is mostly ocean, and bore the intertwining tattoos of his adopted people on most of his hide. A blaster and knife hung at his waist.

Dagny was in the detector shack. Viewscreens might be malfunctioning, along with a lot else, but such instruments as the radionic, spectroscopic, magnetic and sonic were not integrated with ship circuitry. They had kept their accuracy, and she was expert – not educated, but rule-of-thumb expert – in their use.

'Well, there,' she said, looking around the console at which she sat. 'What'd you see?'

Tom repeated in more detail what he had told Yasmin. Since Dagny spoke no Pelevah and only a little pidgin Anglic, while Yasmin had no Eylan, these two of his wives communicated with difficulty. Maybe that was why they got along so well. 'And how 'bout you?' he finished.

'I caught a flash of radiocast. Seemed like two stations communicating from either end of a continental-size area.'

'Still, somebody is able to chat a bit,' Tom said. 'Hopeful.' He lounged against the doorframe. 'Anyone spot us, d' you think?'

Dagny grinned. 'What do you think?'

His lips responded. A positive answer would have had them in action at once, he to the bridge, she to the main fire control turret. They couldn't be sure they had not been noticed – by optical system, quickly brushing radar or maser, gadget responsive to the neutrino emission of their proton converter, several other possible ways – but it was unlikely.

'Any further indications?' Tom asked. 'Atomic powerplants?'

'I don't know.'

'How come?'

'I don't know what the readings mean that I get, particle flux, magnetic variations and the rest. This is such a confoundedly queer sun and planet. I've never seen anything like them. Have you?'

'No.'

They regarded each other for a moment that grew very quiet. Dagny, Od's-daughter in the House of Brenning, was a big woman, a few years his senior. Her shoulder-length yellow mane was fading a bit, and her hazel eyes were burdened with those contact lenses that were the best help anyone on Kraken knew how to give. But her frame was still strong and erect, her hands still clever and murderously quick. It had been natural for an impoverished noble family to make alliance with an energetic young immigrant who had a goodly following and a spaceship. But in time, voyages together, childbirths and child-rearings, the marriage of convenience had become one of affection.

'Well . . . s'pose we better go on down,' Tom said. 'Sooner we get patched, sooner we can start back. And we'd better not be gone from home too long.'

Dagny nodded. Yasmin saw the grimness that touched them and said, 'What is wrong, my . . . my husband?'

Tom hadn't the heart to explain how turbulent matters were on Kraken also. She'd learn that soon enough, if they lived. He said merely, 'There's some kind o' civilization goin' yet around here. But it may exist only as traces o' veneer. The signs are hard to figure. This is a rogue planet, you see.'

'Rogue?' Yasmin was bemused. 'But that is a loose planet – sunless – isn't it?'

'You mean a bandit planet. A rogue's one that don't fit in with its usual type, got a screwball orbit or composition or whatever. Like this'n.'

'Oh. Yes, I know.'

'What?' He caught her shoulder, not noticing how she winced at so hard a grip. 'You've heard o' this system before?'

'No . . . please . . . no, my people never came to this side of the Nebula either, with what few ships we had. But I studied some astro-physics and planetography at Anushirvan University.'

'Huh?' He let her go and gaped. 'Science? Real, Imperial-era science, not engineerin' tricks?' She nodded breathlessly. 'But I thought – you said – you'd studied classics.'

'Is not scientific knowledge one of the classic arts? We had a very complete collection of tapes in the Royal Library.' Forlornness came upon her. 'Gone, now, into smoke.'

'Never mind. Can you explain how come this globe is as it is?'

'Well, I . . . well, no. I don't believe I could. I would need more information. Mass, and chemical data, and – And even then, I would probably not be able. I am not one of the ancient experts.'

'Hardly anybody is,' Tom sighed. 'All right. Let's get us a snack, and then to our stations for planetfall.'

* * *

Descent was tricky. Sensor-computer-autopilot linkups could no longer be trusted. Tom had to bring *Firedrake* in on manual controls. His few instruments were of limited use, when he couldn't get precise data by which to recalibrate them for local conditions. With no viewscreens working properly, he had no magnification, infra-red and ultra-violet presentations, any of the conventional aids. He depended on an emergency periscope, on Dagny's radar readings called via intercom and on the trained reflexes of a lifetime.

Yasmin sat beside him. There was nothing she could do elsewhere, and he wanted to be able to assist her in her inexperience if they must bail out. The spacesuit and gravity impellers surrounded her with an awkward bulk that made the visage in the helmet look like a child's. Neither one of them had closed a faceplate. Her voice came small through the gathering throb of power: 'Is it so difficult to land? I mean, I used to watch ships do it, and even if we are partly crippled – we could travel between the stars. What can an aircar do that we can't?'

'Hyperdrive's not the same thing as kinetic velocity, and most particular not the same as aerodynamic speed,' Tom grunted. 'To start with, I know the theory o' sublight physics.'

'You do?' She was frankly astounded.

121

'Enough of it, anyhow. I can read and write, too.' His hands played over the board. Vibration grew in the deck, the bulkheads, his bones. A thin shrilling was heard, the first cloven atmosphere. 'A spaceship's a sort o' big and clumsy object, once out o' her native habitat,' he said absently. 'Got quite a moment of inertia, f'r instance. Means a sudden, hard wind can turn her over tip and she don't right easy. When you got a lot o' sensitive machinery to do the work, that's no problem. But we don't.' He buried his face in the periscope hood. Cloudiness swirled beneath. 'Also,' he said, 'we got no screens and nobody at the guns. So we'd better be choosy about where we can sit down. And . . . we don't have any way to scan an area in detail. Now do be quiet and let me steer.'

Already in the upper air, he encountered severe turbulence. That was unexpected, on a planet which received less than 0.9 Terran . . . insolation, with a lower proportion of UV to boot. It wasn't that the atmosphere was peculiar. The spectroscope readout had said the mixture was ordinary oxy-nitro-CO_2, on the thin and dry side – sea-level pressure around 600 mm. – but quite breathable. Nor was the phenomenon due to excessive rotation; the period was twenty-five and a half hours. Of course, the inner moon, while small, was close in and must have considerable tidal effect – Hoy!

The outercom buzzed. Someone was calling. 'Take that, Yasmin,' Tom snapped. The ship wallowed. He felt it even through the cushioning internal gee-field, and the altitude meters were wavering crazily. Wind screamed louder. The clouds roiled near, coppery-headed blue-shadowed billows on the starboard horizon, deep purple below him. He had hoped that night and overcast would veil his arrival, but evidently a radar had fingered him. Or – 'The knob marked A, you idiot! Turn it widdershins. I can't let go now!'

Yasmin caught her lower lip between her teeth and obeyed. The screen flickered to life. 'Up the volume,' Tom commanded. 'Maybe Dagny can't watch, but she'd better hear. You on, Dagny?'

'Aye.' Her tone was crisp from the intercom speaker. 'I doubt if I'll understand many words, though. Hadn't you better start aloft and I leave the radar and take over fire control?'

'No, stand where you are. See what you can detect. We're not after a tussle, are we?' Tom glanced at the screen for the instant he dared. It was sidewise to him, putting him outside the pickup arc, but he could get a profile of the three-dimensional image.

The man who gazed out was so young that his beard was brownish fuzz. Braids hung from beneath a goggled fiber crash helmet. But his features were hard; his background appeared to be an aircraft cockpit; and his green tunic had the look of a uniform.

'Who are you?' he challenged. Seeing himself confronted by a girl, he let his jaw drop. 'Who *are* you?'

'Might ask the same o' you,' Tom answered for her. 'We're from offplanet.'

'Why did you not declare yourselves?' The Anglic was thickly accented but comprehensible, roughened with tension.

'We didn't know anybody was near. I reckon you had to try several bands before hittin' the one we were tuned to. Isn't a standard signal frequency any more.' Tom spoke with careful casualness, while the ship bucked and groaned around him and lightning zigzagged in the clouds he approached. 'Don't worry about us. We mean no harm.'

'You trespass in the sky of Karol Weyer.'

'Son, we never heard o' him. We don't even know what you call this planet.'

The pilot gulped. 'N-Nike,' he said automatically. 'The planet Nike. Karol Weyer is our Engineer, here in Hanno. Who are you?'

Dagny's voice said in Eylan. 'I've spotted him on the scope, Tom. Coming in fast at eleven o'clock low.'

'Let me see your face,' the pilot demanded harshly. 'Hide not by this woman.'

'Can't stop to be polite,' Tom said. 'S'pose you let us land, and we'll talk to your Engineer. Or shall we take our business elsewhere?'

Yasmin's gauntlet closed convulsively on Tom's sleeve. 'The look on him grows terrible,' she whispered.

'Gods damn,' Tom said, 'we're friends!'

'What?' the pilot shouted.

'Friends, I tell you! We need help. Maybe you – '

'The screen went blank,' Yasmin cried.

Tom risked yawing *Firedrake* till he could see in the direction Dagny had bespoken. The craft was in view. It was a one- or two-man job, a delta wing whose contrail betrayed the energy source as chemical rather than atomic or electric. However, instruments reported it as applying that power to a gravity drive. At this distance he couldn't make out if the boat had guns, but hardly doubted that. For a moment it glinted silvery against the darkling clouds, banked and vanished.

'Prob'ly hollerin' for orders,' Tom said. 'And maybe reinforcements. Chil'ren, I think we'd better hustle back spaceward and try our luck in some place more sociable than Hanno.'

'Is there any?' Dagny wondered.

'Remains to be seen. Let's hope it's not our remains that'll be seen.' Tom concentrated on the controls. Lame and weakened, the ship could not simply reverse. She had too much downward momentum and was too deep in Nike's gravity well. He must shift vectors slowly and nurse her up again.

After minutes, Dagny called through the racket and shudderings: 'Several of them – at least five – climbing faster than us, from all sides.'

'I was afraid o' that,' Tom said. 'Yasmin, see if you can eavesdrop on the chit-chat between 'em.'

'Should we not stay tuned for their call?' the Sassanian asked timidly.

'I doubt they aim to call. If ever anybody acted so scared and angry as to be past reckon – No, hold 'er.'

The screen had suddenly reawakened. This time the man who stared forth was middle-aged, leonine, bearded to the waist. His coat was trimmed with fur and, beneath the storm in his voice, pride rang. 'I am the Engineer,' he said. 'You will land and be slaves.'

'Huh?' Tom said. 'Look, we was goin' away – '

'You declared yourselves friends!'

'Yes. We'd like to do business with you. But – '

'Land at once. Slave yourselves to me. Or my craft open fire. They have tommics.'

'Nukes, you mean?' Tom growled. Yasmin stifled a shriek. Karol Weyer observed and looked grimly pleased. Tom cursed without words.

The Nikean shook his head. Tom got a glimpse of that, and wasn't sure whether the gesture meant yes, no or maybe in this land. But the answer was plain: 'Weapons that unleash the might which lurks in matter.'

And our force-screen generator is on sick leave, Tom thought. *He may be lyin'. But I doubt it, because they do still use gravs here. We can't outrun a rocket, let alone an energy beam. Nor could Dagny, by herself, shoot down the lot in time to forestall 'em.*

'You win,' he said. 'Here we come.'

'Leave your transceiver on,' Weyer instructed. 'When you are below the clouds, the fish will tell you where to go.'

'Fish?' Tom choked. But the screen had emptied, save for the crackling and formlessness of static.

'D-d-dialect?' Yasmin suggested.

'Uh, yeh. Must mean somethin' like squadron leader. Good girl.' Tom spared her a grin. The tears were starting forth.

'Slaves?' she wailed. 'Oh, no, no.'

'Course not, if I can help it,' he said, *sotto voce* lest the hostiles be listening. 'Rather die.'

He did not speak exact truth. Having been a slave once, he didn't prefer death – assuming his owner was not unreasonable, and that some hope existed of getting his freedom back. But becoming property was apt to be worse for a woman than a man: much worse, when she was a daughter of Sassania's barons or Kraken's sea kings. As their husband, he was honor bound to save them if he could.

'We'll make a break,' he said. 'Lot o' wild country underneath. One reason I picked this area. But first we have to get down.'

'What's gone by me?' Dagny called.

Tom explained in Eylan while he fought the ship. 'But that doesn't make sense!' she said. 'When they know nothing about us –'

'Well, they took a bad clobberin', ten years back. Can't expect 'em to act terribly sensible about strangers. And s'posin' this is a misunderstandin' ... we have to stay alive while we straighten it out. Stand by for a rough jaunt.'

* * *

The aircraft snarled into sight, but warily, keeping their distance in swoops and circles that drew fantastic trails of exhaust. For a moment Tom wondered if that didn't prove the locals were familiar with space-war techniques. Those buzzeroos seemed careful to stay beyond reach of a tractor or pressor beam, that could have seized them ... But no. They were exposed to his guns and missiles, which had far greater range, and didn't know that these were unmanned.

Nevertheless, they were at least shrewd on this planet. From what Tom had let slip, and the battered condition of the vessel, Weyer had clearly guessed that the newcomers were weak. They could doubtless wipe out one or two aircraft before being hit, but could they handle half a dozen? That Weyer had taken the risk and scrambled this much of what must be a very small air fleet suggested implacable enmity. (Why? He couldn't be so stupid as to assume that everyone from offplanet was a foe. Could he?) What was worse, his assessment of the military situation was quite correct. In her present state, *Firedrake* could not take on so many opponents and survive.

She entered the clouds.

For a while Tom was blind. Thunder and darkness encompassed him. Metal toned. The instrument dials glowed like goblin eyes. Their needles spun; the ship lurched; Tom stabbed and pulled and twisted controls, sweat drenched his coverall and reeked in his nostrils.

Then he was through, into windy but uncluttered air. Fifteen kilometers beneath him lay that part of the north temperate zone he had so unfortunately chosen. The view was of a valley, cut into a checkerboard pattern that suggested large agricultural estates. A river wound through, shining silver in what first dawn-light reddened the eastern horizon. A few villages clustered along it, and traffic moved, barge trains and water-

126

ships. A swampy delta spread at the eastern end of a great bay.

That bay was as yet in the hour before sunrise, but glimmered with reflections. It had a narrow mouth, opening on a sea to the west. Lights twinkled on either side of the gate, and clustered quite thickly on the southern bayshore. Tom's glance went to the north. There he saw little trace of habitation. Instead, hills humped steeply toward a mountain which smoked. Forests covered them, but radar showed how rugged they were.

The outercom flashed with the image of the pilot who had first hailed him. Now that conditions were easier, Tom could have swiveled it around himself to let the scanner cover his own features. Yasmin could have done so for him at any time. But he refrained. Anonymity wasn't an ace in the hole – at most, a deuce or a trey – but he needed every card he had.

'You will bear east-northeast,' the 'fish' instructed. 'About a hundred kilos upriver lies a cave. Descend there.'

'Kilos?' Tom stalled. He had no intention of leaving the refuges below him for the open flatlands.

'Distances. Thousand-meters.'

'But a cave? I mean, look, I want to be a good fellow and so forth, but how'm I goin' to spot a cave from the air?'

'Spot?' It was the Nikean's turn to be puzzled. However, he was no fool. 'Oh, so, you mean espy. A cave is a stronghouse. You will know it by turrets, projectors, setdown fields.'

'Your Engineer's castle?'

'Think you we're so whetless, we'd let you near the Great Cave? You might have a tommic boom aboard. No. Karol Weyer dwells by the bay gate. You go to the stronghouse guarding the Nereid River valley. Now change course, I said, or we fire.'

Tom had used the talk-time to shed a good bit of altitude. 'We can't,' he said. 'Not that fast. Have to get low first, before we dare shift.'

'You go no lower, friend! Those are our folk down there.'

'Be reasonable,' Tom said. 'A spaceship's worth your havin', I'm sure, even a damaged one like ours. Why blang us for somethin' we can't help?'

'Um-m-m . . . hold where you are.'

'I can't. This is not like an aircraft. I've got to either rise or sink. Ask your bosses.'

The pilot's face disappeared. 'But – ' Yasmin began.

'Shhh!' Tom winked his good eye at her.

He was gambling that they hadn't had spacecraft on Nike for a long time. Otherwise they wouldn't have taken such a licking a decade ago; and they'd have sent a ship after him, rather than those few miserable, probably handmade gravplanes. So if they didn't have anyone around who was qualified in the practical problems of handling that kind of vessel –

Not but what *Firedrake* wasn't giving him practical problems of his own. Wind boomed and shoved.

The pilot returned. 'Go lower if you must,' he said. 'But follow my word, go above the northshore hills.'

'Surely.' *Right what I was hopin' for*! Tom switched to Eylan. 'Dagny, get to the forward manlock.'

'What do you say?' rapped the pilot.

'I'm issuin' orders to my crew,' Tom said. 'They don't speak Anglic.'

'No! You'll not triple-talk me!'

Tom let out a sigh that was a production. 'Unless they know what to do, we'll crash. Do you want live slaves and a whole spaceship, or no? Make up your mind, son.'

'Um-m . . . well. At first ill-doing, we shoot.'

Tom ignored him. 'Listen, Dagny. You're not needed here any more. I can land on my altimeter and stuff. But I've got to set us down easy, and not get us hit by some overheated gunner. They must have what we need to make our repairs, but not to build a whole new ship, even s'posin' we knew how. So we can't risk defendin' ourselves, leastwise till we get away from the ship.'

'She will be theirs,' Dagney said, troubled. 'And we will be hunted. Shouldn't we surrender peacefully and bargain with them?'

'What bargainin' power has a slave got? Whereas free, if nothin' else, I bet we're the only two on Nike that can run a spacecraft. Besides, we don't know what these fellows are like.

128

They could be mighty cruel. No, you go stand by that manlock along with Yasmin. The minute we touch dirt, you two get out – fast and far.'

'But Tom, you'll be on the bridge. What about you?'

'Somebody's got to make that landin'. I dunno how they'll react. But you girls won't have much time to escape yourselves. I'll come after you. If I haven't joined you soon, figure I won't, and do whatever comes natural. And look after Yasmin, huh?'

Silence dwelt for a moment amidst every inanimate noise. Until: 'I understand Tom, if we don't see each other again, it was good with you.' Dagny uttered a shaken laugh. 'Tell her to kiss you for both of us.'

'Aye-ya.' He couldn't, of course, with that suspicious countenance glowering out of the screen. But in what little Pelevah he had, he gave Yasmin her orders. She didn't protest, too stunned by events to grasp the implications.

Down and down. The tilted wilderness swooped at him.

'The steerin's quit on me!' Tom yelled in Anglic. 'Yasmin, go fantangle the dreelsprail! Hurry! She flung off her safety webbing and left the bridge, as fast as possible in her clumsy armor. 'I've got to make an emergency landin',' Tom said to the Nikean officer.

Probably that caused them to hold their fire as he had hoped. He didn't know, nor wonder. He was too busy. The sonoprobe said firm solid below. The altimeter said a hundred meters, fifty, twenty-five, ten – Leaves surged around. Boughs and boles splintered. The farther trees closed in like a cage. Impact shook, drummed, went to silence. Tom cut the engines and gee-field. Native gravity, one-half standard, hit him with giddiness. He unharnessed himself. The deck was canted. He slipped, skidded, got up and pounded down the companionway.

* * *

The manlock valves opened at Dagny's control while *Firedrake* was still moving. The drop in air pressure hurt her eardrums. She glimpsed foliage against a sky red with dawn, gray with scattering stormclouds. The earthquake landing cast her to hands and knees. She rose, leaning against a bulkhead. Yasmin stumbled into sight. The faceplate stood open before the terrified young visage. 'Chaos! Dog that thing!' Dagny cried. 'We'll be at top speed.' She was not understood. She grabbed the girl and snapped the plate shut herself. 'You . . . know . . . fly?' she asked in her fragment of Anglic.

'Yes. I think so.' Yasmin wet her lips. Her radio voice was unsteady in the other's earplugs. 'I mean . . . Lord Tom explained how.'

'No practice, though?' Dagny muttered in Eylan. 'You're about to get some.' In Anglic: 'Follow I.'

She leaned out of the lock. High overhead she descried the gleam of a wheeling delta wing. The forest roared with wind. A little clearing surrounded the ship where trees had been flattened. Beyond the shadowy tangle of their trunks and limbs, their neighbors made a wall of night.

'Go!' Dagny touched her impeller stud and launched herself. She soared up. Flight was tricky in these gusts. Curving about, she saw Yasmin's suit helplessly cartwheel. She returned, caught the Sassanian girl, laid one arm around her waist and used the other to operate her drive units for her in the style of an instructor. They moved off, slowly and awkwardly.

A scream split the air. Dagny glanced as far behind as she could. Two of the aircraft were stooping . . . One took a hoverstance above *Firedrake*, the other came after her and Yasmin. She saw the muzzle of an energy gun and slammed the two impeller sets into full forward speed. Alone, she might have dived under the trees. But Yasmin hadn't the skill, and two couldn't slip through those dense branches side by side. Tom had told her to look after Yasmin, and Dagny was his sworn woman.

She tried to summon before her the children they had had together, tall sons and daughters, the baby grandchildren, and Skerrygarth, their home that was the dowry she had brought him, towers steadfast above a surf that played white among the reefs –

Explosion smashed at her. Had she been looking directly aft, she would have been dazzled into momentary blindness. As it was, the spots before her eyes and the tolling in her ears lasted for minutes. A wave of heat pushed through her armor.

She yelled, clung somehow to Yasmin, and kept the two of

them going. Fury spoke again and again. It dwindled with distance as they fled.

Finally it was gone. By that time the women had covered some twenty kilometers, more or less eastward. The sea-level horizon of Nike was only about six kilometers off; and this was not flat country. They were well into morning light and far beyond view of the spaceship. Dagny thought she could yet identify an aircraft or two, but maybe those sparks were something else.

Beneath her continued hills and ravines, thickly wooded, and rushing streams. The volcano bulked in the north; smoke plumed from a frost-rimmed crater. Southward the land rolled down to the quicksilver sheet of the bay. Its shore was marshy – an effect of the very considerable tides that the nearer moon raised – but a village of neat wooden houses stood there on piles. Sailboats that doubtless belonged to fishermen were putting out. They must exist in such numbers because of a power shortage rather than extreme backwardness; for Dagny saw a good-sized motorship as well, crossing the bay from the gate to the lower, more populous south side. Its hull was of planks and its wake suggested the engine was minimal. At the same time, its lines and the nearly smokeless stack indicated competent design.

Here the wind had gentled and the clouds were dissipating fast. (Odd to have such small cells of weather, she thought in a detached logical part of herself. Another indication of an atmosphere disturbed by violent solar conditions?) They shone ruddy-tinted in a deep purple vault of sky. The sun stood bright orange above mists that lay on the Nereid River delta.

'Down we go, lass,' Dagny said, 'before we're noticed.'

'What happened? Lord Tom, where is he?'

The sob scratched at Dagny's nerves. She snapped, biting back tears: 'Use your brain, you little beast, if it's anything except blubber! He went first to the main fire-control turret. When he saw us attacked, he cut loose with the ship's weapons. I don't see how he could have gotten all those bastards, though. If they didn't missile him, they've anyhow bottled him up. On *our* account!'

She realized she'd spoken entirely in Eylan. Suppressing a growl, she took over the controls of both suits. With no need for haste, she could ease them past the branches that tried to catch them, down to the forest floor.

'Now,' she said in Anglic. 'Out.' Yasmin gaped. Dagny set the example by starting to remove her own armor.

'Wh-why?'

'Find us. In . . . in . . . in-stru-ments. Smell metal, no? Could be. Not take chance. We got – got to –' Dagny's vocabulary failed her. She had wanted to explain that if they stayed with the suits, they ran the risk of detection from afar. And even if the Nikeans didn't have that much technology left, whatever speed and protection the equipment lent wasn't worth its conspicuousness.

She was almost grateful for every difficulty. It kept her mind – somewhat – off the overwhelming fact that Tom, her Roan Tom, was gone.

Or maybe not. Just maybe not. He might be a prisoner, and she might in time contrive to bargain for his release. No, she would not remember what she had seen done to prisoners, here and there in her wanderings, by vengeful captors!

Were that the case, though . . . Her hand went first to the blaster at one coveralled hip, next to the broad-bladed knife; and there it lingered. If she devoted the rest of her days to the project, and if the gods were kind, she might eventually get his murderers into her clutch.

Yasmin shed the last armor. She hugged herself and shivered in a chill breeze. 'But we haven't any radios except in our helmets,' she said. 'How can he contact us?'

Dagny framed a reply: 'If he'd been able to follow us, he'd already be here, or at least have called. I left my squealer circuit on, for him to track us by. That was safe; its frequency varies continuously, according to synchronized governors in both our suits. But he hasn't arrived, and we daren't stay near this much metal and resonant electronic stuff.' Somehow, by words and gestures, she conveyed the gist. Meanwhile she filled their pockets with rations and medications, arranged the weapons beneath their garments, checked footgear. Last she hid the armor under leaf mould and canebrake, and took precise note of landmarks.

Yasmin's head drooped until the snarled dark locks covered her face. 'I am so tired,' she whispered.

Think I'm not? My lips are numb with it. 'Go!' Dagny snapped:

She had to show the city-bred girl how to conceal their trail through the woods.

After a couple of hours, unhounded, the air warming and brightening around them, both felt a little better. It was up-and-down walking, but without much underbrush to combat, for the ground was densely carpeted with a soft mossy growth. Here and there stood clumps of fronded gymnosperm plants. This native vegetation was presumably chlorophyl-bearing, though its greenness was pale and had a curious bluish overcast. Otherwise the country had been taken over by the more efficient, highly developed species that man commonly brought with him. Oaks cast sun-speckled shadows; birches danced and glistened; primroses bloomed in meadows, where grass had overwhelmed a pseudo-moss that apparently had a competitive advantage only in shade. A sweet summery smell was about, and Yasmin spoke of her homeland. Even Dagny, bred in salt winds and unrestful watery leagues, felt a stirring of ancient instinct.

She was used to denser atmosphere. Sounds – sough in leaves, whistle of birds, rilling of brooks they crossed, thud of her own feet – came as if muffled to her ears; and on a steep upgrade, her heart was apt to flutter. But oxygen shortage was more or less compensated for by a marvelous, almost floating low-gravity lightness.

A good many animals were to be seen. Again, terrestroid forms had crowded out most of the primitive native species. With a whole ecology open to them, they were now in the process of explosive evolution. A few big insect-like flyers, an occasional awkward amphibian, gave glimpses of the original biosphere. But thrushes, bulbuls, long-winged hawks rode the wind. Closer down swarmed butterflies and bees. A wild boar, tusked and rangy, caused Dagny to draw her blaster; but he went by, having perhaps learned to fear man. Splendid was the more distant sight of mustangs, carabao, an entire herd of antlered six-legged tanithars.

A measure of peace came upon Dagny, until at last she could say, 'All right, we stop, eat, rest.'

They sat under a broad-spreading hilltop cedar, that hid them from above while openness, halfway down the heights to the forest, afforded ample ground vision. They had made for the bay and were thus at a lower altitude. The waters sheened to south, ridges and mountains stood sharply outlined to north. In this clear air, the blueness of their distance was too slight to hide the basic ocherous tint of rocks and soil.

Dagny broke out a packet of dehydrate. She hesitated for a moment before adding water to the tray from a canteen she had filled en route. Yasmin, slumped exhausted against the tree trunk, asked, 'What is the matter?' And, her eyes and mind wandering a little, she tried to smile. 'See, yonder, apples. They are green but they can be dessert.'

'No,' Dagny said.

'What? Why not?'

'Heavy metal.' Dagny scowled. How to explain? 'Young planet. Dense. Lots heavy metal. Not good.'

'Young? But – '

'Look around you,' Dagny wanted to say. 'That sun, putting out radiation like an early Type F – in amount – but the color and spectral distribution are late G or early K. I've never seen anything like it. The way it flares, I don't believe it's quite stabilized at its proper position on the main sequence yet. Because of anomalous chemical composition, I suppose. You get that with very young suns, my dear. They've condensed out of an interstellar medium made rich in metals by the thermonuclear furnaces of earlier star generations. Or so I've been told.

'I know for fact that planets with super-abundant heavy elements can be lethal to men. So much . . . oh, arsenic, selenium, radioactives. Slow poison in some areas, fast and horrible deaths in others. This water, that fruit, may have stuff to kill us.'

But she lacked words or inclination. She said, 'Iron. Makes red in rocks. No? Lots iron. Could be lots bad metal. Young planet. Lots air, no?'

She had, in truth, never heard of a dwarf world like this, getting such an amount of sunlight, that had hung onto a proper atmosphere. Evidently, she thought, there had not been time for the gas to leak into space. The primitive life forms were another proof of a low age.

Beyond this, she didn't reason. She did not have the knowledge on which to base logic, nor did she have the scientific way of thinking. What little cosmology and cosmogony she had learned, for instance, was in the form of vague, probably distorted tradition – latter-day myth. And she was intelligent enough to recognize this.

Once, she imagined, any Imperial space officer had been educated in the details of astrophysics and planetology. And he would have seen, or read about, a far greater variety of suns than today's petty travels encompassed. So he would have known immediately what sort of system this was; or, if not, he would have known how to find out.

But that was centuries ago. The information might not actually be lost. It might even be moldering in the damp, uncatalogued library of her own Skerrygarth. Surely parts of it were taught in the universities of more civilized planets, though as a set of theoretical ideas, to be learned by rote without any need for genuine comprehension.

Practical spacefarers, like her and Tom, didn't learn it. They didn't get the chance. A rudiment of knowledge was handed down to them, largely by word of mouth, the minimum they needed for survival.

And speaking of survival –

She reached her decision. 'Eat,' she said. 'Drink.' She took the first sample. The water had a woodsy taste, nothing unfamiliar.

After all, humans did flourish here. Perhaps they were adapted to metal-rich soil. But the adaptation could scarcely be enormous. Had that been the case, terrestroid species would not be so abundant and dominant, after a mere thousand years or whatever on this planet.

Thus Nike was biochemically safe – at least, in this general region – at least, for a reasonable time. Perhaps, if outworlders stayed as long as one or two decades, they might suffer from cumulative poisoning. But she needn't worry that far ahead, when a hunt was on immediately and when Tom –

Grimly, she fueled her body. Afterward she stood watch while Yasmin caught a nap. What she thought about was her own affair.

When the Sassanian awoke, they held a lengthy conference. The order Dagny had to issue was not complicated:

'We're in enemy territory. But I don't believe it covers the whole planet, or even the whole area between this sea and the next one east. "The Engineer of Hanno" is a typical feudal title. I've not heard before that "engineer" changed meaning to the equivalent of "duke" or "king", but it's easy to see how that could've happened, and I've met odder cases of wordshift. Well, our darling Engineer made it plain he regarded us as either the worst menace or the juiciest prey that'd come by in years. Maybe both. So he'd naturally call his full air power, or most of it, against us. Which amounted to half a dozen little craft, with gravmotors so weak they need wings! And look at those sailboats, and the absence of real cities, and the fact there's scarcely any radio in use . . . yes, they've fallen far on Nike. I'm sure that raid from space was only the latest blow. They must have a small half-educated class left, and some technicians of a sort; but the bulk of the people must've been poor and ignorant for many generations.

'And divided. I swear they must be divided. I've seen so many societies like this, I can practically identify them by smell. A crazy-quilt pattern of feudalisms and sovereignties, any higher authority a ghost. If as rich a planet as this one potentially is were united, it'd have made a far greater recovery by now, after the space attack, than it has done. Or it would have beaten the raiders off at least.

'So, if we have enemies here in Hanno, we probably have

automatic friends somewhere else. And not dreadfully far away. At any rate, we're not likely to be pursued beyond the nearest border, nor extradited back here. In fact, the Engineer's rivals are apt to be quite alarmed when they learn he's clapped hands on a real space warship. They're apt to join forces to get it away from him. Which'll make you and me, my dear, much-sought-after advisors. We may or may not be able to get Tom back unhurt. I vow the gods a hundred Blue Giant seabeasts if we do! But we'll be free, even powerful.

'Or so I hope. We've nothing to go on but hope. And courage and wits and endurance. Have you those, Yasmin? Your life was too easy until now. But he asked me to care for you.

'You'll have to help. Our first and foremost job is to get out of Hanno. And I don't speak their damned language for diddly squat. You'll talk for both of us. Can you? We'll plan a story. Then, if and when you see there must be a false note in it, you'll have to cover – at once – with no ideas from me. Can you do that, Yasmin? You must!'

   – But conference was perforce by single words, signs, sketches in the red dirt. It went slowly. And it was repeated, over and over, in every possible way, to make certain they understood each other.

In the end, however, Yasmin nodded. 'Yes,' she said, 'I will try, as God gives me strength . . . and as you do.' The voice was almost inaudible, and the eyes she turned on the bigger, older woman were dark with awe.

* * *

In midafternoon they reached a farm. Its irregular fields were enclosed by forest, through which a cart track ran to join a dirt road that, in turn, twisted over several kilometers until it entered the fisher village.

Dagny spent minutes peering from a thicket. Beside her, Yasmin tried to guess what evaluations the Krakener was making. *I should begin to learn these ways of staying alive,* the Sassanian thought. *More is involved than my own welfare. I don't want to remain a burden on my companions, an actual danger to them.*

137

And to think, not one year ago I took for granted the star rovers were ignorant, dirty, cruel, quarrelsome barbarians!

Yasmin had been taught about philosophic objectivity, but she was too young to practice it consistently. Her universe having been wrecked, herself cast adrift, she naturally seized upon the first thing that felt like a solid rock and began to make it her emotional foundation. And that thing happened to be Roan Tom and Dagny Od's-daughter.

Not that she had intellectual illusions. She knew very well that the Krakeners had come to help the Shah of Sassania because the Pretender was allied with enemies of theirs. And she knew that, if successful, they would exact good pay. She had heard her father grumble about it.

Nevertheless, the facts were: First, compatriots of hers, supposedly civilized, supposedly above the greed and short-sightedness that elsewhere had destroyed civilization . . . had proven themselves every bit as animalistic. Second, the star-rover garrison in Anushirvan turned out to be jolly, well-scrubbed, fairly well-behaved. Indeed, they were rather glamorous to a girl who had never been past her planet's moon. Third, they had stood by their oaths, died in their ships and at their guns, for her alien people. Fourth, two of them had saved her life, and offered her the best and most honorable way they could think of to last out her days. Fifth (or foremost?), Tom was now her husband.

She was not exactly infatuated with him. A middle-aged, battle-beaten, one-eyed buccaneer had never entered her adolescent dreams. But he was kind in his fashion, and a skillful lover, and . . . and perhaps she did care for him in a way beyond friendship . . . if he was alive — oh, let him be alive!

In any event, here was Dagny. She certainly felt grief like a sword in her. But she hid it, planned, guided, guarded. She had stood in the light of a hundred different suns, had warred, wandered, been wife and mother and living sidearm. She knew everything worth knowing (what did ancient texts count for?) except one language. And she was so brave that she trusted her life to what ability an awkward weakling of a refugee might possess.

Please don't let me fail her.

Thus Yasmin looked forth too and tried to make inferences from what she saw.

The house and outbuildings were frame, not large, well-built but well-weathered. Therefore they must have stood here for a good length of time. Therefore Imperial construction methods – alloy, prestressed concrete, synthetics, energy webs – had long been out of general use in these parts, probably everywhere on Nike. That primitiveness was emphasized by the agromech system. A couple of horses drew a haycutter. It also was wooden; even the revolving blades were simply edged with metal. From its creaking and bouncing, the machine had neither wheel bearings nor springs. A man drove it. Two half-grown boys, belike his sons, walked after. They used wooden-tined rakes to order the windrows. The people, like the animals, were of long slim deep-chested build, brown-haired and fair-complexioned. Their garments were coarsely woven smock and trousers.

No weapons showed, which suggested that the bay region was free of bandits, and vendettas. Nevertheless Dagny did not approach. Instead, she led a cautious way back into the woods and thence toward the house, so that the building screened off view of the hayfield.

The Krakener woman scowled. 'Why?' she muttered.

'Why what . . . my lady?'

'Why make – ' Dagny's hands imitated whirling blades. 'Here. Planet . . . canted? . . . little. No cold?'

'Oh. Do you mean, why do they bother making hay? Well, there must be times when their livestock can't pasture.'

Dagny understood. Her nod was brusque. 'Why that?'

'Um-m-m . . . oh, dear, let me think. Lord Tom explained to me what he – what you two had learned about this planet. Yes. Not much axial tilt. I suppose not an unusually eccentric orbit. So the seasons oughtn't to be very marked. And we are in a rather low latitude anyway, on a seacoast at that. It should never get too cold for grass. Too dry? No, this *is* midsummer time. And, well, they'd hardly export hay to other areas, would they?'

Dagny shrugged.

It is such a strange world, Yasmin thought. *All wrong. Too dense. That is, if it had a great many heavy metals, humans would never have settled here permanently. So what makes it dense should be a core of iron, nickel and things, squeezed into compact quantum states. The kind that terrestroid planets normally have. Yes, and the formation of a true core causes tectonic processes, vulcanism, the outguessing of a primitive atmosphere and water. Later we get chemical evolution, life, photosynthesis, free oxygen –*

But Nike is too small for that! It's Mars type. We have a Mars type planet in our own system – oh, lost and loved star that shines upon Sassania – *and it's got a bare wisp of unbreathable air. Professor Nasruddin explained to us. If a world is small, it has weak gravity. So the differential migration of elements down toward the center, that builds a distinct core, is too slow. So few gas molecules get unlocked from mineral combination by heat . . . Nike isn't possible!*

(How suddenly, shockingly real came back to her the lecture hall, and the droning voice, young heads bent above notebooks, sunlight that streamed in through arched windows, and the buzz of bees, odor of roses, a glimpse of students strolling across a greensward that stretched between beautiful buildings.)

Dagny's fingers clamped about Yasmin's arm. 'Heed! Fool!'

Yasmin started from her reverie. They were almost at the house. 'Heavens, I'm sorry.'

'Talk well.' Dagny's voice was bleak with doubt of her.

Yasmin swallowed and stepped forth into the yard. She felt dizzy. The knocking of her heart came remote as death. Penned cows, pigs, fowl were like things in a dream. There was something infinitely horrible about the windmill that groaned behind the barn.

Neither shot nor shout met her. The door opened a crack, and the woman who peered out did so fearfully.

Why, she's nervous of us!

Relief passed through Yasmin in a wave of darkness. But an odd, alert calm followed. She perceived with utter clarity. Her

140

thoughts went in three or four directions at once, all coherent. One chain directed her to smile, extend unclenched hands, and say: 'Greeting to you, good lady.' Another observed that the boards of the house were not nailed but pegged together. A third paid special heed to the windmill. It too was almost entirely of wood, with fabric sails. She saw that it pumped water into an elevated cistern, whence wooden pipes ran to the house and a couple of sheds. Attachments outside one of the latter indicated that there the water, when turned on, drove various machines, like the stone quern she could see.

No atomic or electric energy, then. Nor even solar or combustion power. And yet the knowledge of these things existed: if not complete, then sufficient to make aircraft possible, radio, occasional motorships, doubtless some groundcars. Why was it no longer applied by the common people? The appearance of this farm and of the fisher village as seen from a distance suggested moderate prosperity. The Engineer's rule could not be unduly harsh.

Well, the answer must be, Nike's economy had collapsed so far that hardly anyone could afford real power equipment.

But why not? Sunlight, wood, probably coal and petroleum were abundant. A simple generator, some batteries . . . Such things took metal. A broken-down society might not have the resources to extract much . . . Nonsense! Elements like iron, copper, lead, and uranium were surely simple to obtain, even after a thousand years of industrialization. Hadn't Dagny, who knew, said this was a young planet? Weren't young planets metal-rich?

Meanwhile the woman mumbled, 'Day. You're from out-country?'

'Yes,' Yasmin said. No use trying to conceal that. Quite apart from accent and garments (the Hannoan woman wore a broad-sleeved embroidered blouse and a skirt halfway to her ankles), they were not of the local racial type. But it was presumably not uniform over the whole planet. One could play on a peasantry's likely ignorance of anything beyond its own neighborhood.

141

'I am from Kraken,' Yasmin said. 'My friend is from Sassania.' If no one on those comparatively cosmopolitan planets had heard of Nike, vice versa was certain. 'We were flying on a mission when our aircraft crashed in the hills.'

'That ... was the flare ... noises ... this early-day?' the woman asked. Yasmin confirmed it. The woman drew breath and made a shaky sign in the air. 'High 'Uns I thank! We feared, we, 'twas *them* come back.'

Obvious who 'they' were, and therefore impossible to inquire about them. A little hysterical with relief, the wife flung wide her door. 'Enter you! Enter you! I call the men.'

'No need, we thank you,' Yasmin said quickly. The fewer who saw them and got a chance later to wonder and talk about them, the better. 'Not time. We must hurry. Do you know of our countries?'

'Well, er, far off.' The woman was embarrassed. Yasmin noted that the room behind her was neat, had a look of primitive well-being – but how primitive! Two younger children stared half frightened from an inner doorway. 'Yes, far, and I, poor farm-wife, well, hasn't so much as been to the Silva border – '

'That's the next country?' Yasmin pounced.

'Why ... next cavedom, yes, 'tother side of the High Sawtooths east'ard ... Well, we're both under the Empr'ror, but they do say as the Prester of Silva's not happy with our good Engineer ... You! A-travel like men!'

'They have different customs in our part of the world,' Yasmin said. 'More like the Empire. Not your Empire. The real one, the Terran Empire, when women could do whatever a man might.' That was a safe claim. Throughout its remnants, no one questioned anything wonderful asserted about the lost Imperium – except, perhaps, a few unpleasant scholars, who asked why it had fallen if it had been so great. 'Yes, we're from far parts. My friend speaks little Anglic. They don't, in her country.' That was why Dagny, clever Dagny, had said they should switch national origins. Krakener place names sounded more Anglic than Sassanian ones did, and Yasmin had a ready-made supply.

142

'We have to get on with our mission as fast as possible,' she said. 'But we know nothing about these lands.'

'Storm blow you off track?' the woman queried. As she relaxed, she became more intelligent. 'Bad storm-time coming, we think. Lots rain already. Hope the hay's not ruined before it dries.'

'Yes, that's what happened.' *Thank you, madam for inventing my explanation.* Yasmin could not resist probing further the riddle of Nike. 'Do you really expect many storms?'

* * *

One child hustled after his father while they went in and took leather-covered chairs. The woman made a large to-do about coffee and cakes. Her name was Elanor, she said, and her husband was Petar Landa, a freeholder. One must not think them backwoods people. They were just a few hours from the town of Sea Gate, which lay nigh the Great Cave itself and was visited by ships from this entire coast. Yes, the Landa family went there often; they hadn't missed a Founders' Festival in ten years, except for the year after the friends came, when there had been none –

'You only needed a year to recover from something like that?' Yasmin exclaimed.

Dagny showed alarm, laying a hand on the Sassanian's and squeezing hard. Elanor Landa was surprised. 'Well, Sea Gate wasn't hit. Not that important. Nearest place was . . . I forgot, all the old big cities went, they say, bombed after being looted, but seems to me I heard Terrania was nearest to Hanno. Far off, though, and no man I know was ever there, because 'twas under the Mayor of Bollen and he wasn't any camarado to us western cavedoms, they say – '

Yasmin saw her mistake. Unthinkingly, she had taken 'year' to mean a standard Terran year. It came the more natural to her because Sassania's wasn't very different. *Well,* thought the clarified brain within her, *we came here to get information that might help us escape. And surely, if we're to pretend to be Nikeans, we must know how the planet revolves.*

'I've forgotten,' she said. 'Exactly when was the attack?'

Elanor was not startled. Such imprecision was common in a largely illiterate people. Indeed, it was somewhat astonishing that she should say, 'A little over five years back. Five and a quarter, abs'lut, come Petar's father's birthday. I remember, for we planned a feast, and then we heard the news. We had radio news then. Everyone was so scared. Later I saw one black ship roar over us, and waited for my death, but it just went on.'

'I think we must use a different calendar from you in Kraken,' Yasmin said. 'And – being wealthier, you understand – not that Hanno *isn't* – but we did suffer worse. We lost records and – Well, let's see if Kraken and Sassania were attacked on the same day you heard about it. That was . . . let me think . . . dear me, now, how many days in a year?'

'What? Why, why, five hundred and ninety-one.'

Yasmin allayed Elanor's surprise by laughing. 'Of course. I was simply trying to recollect if an intercalary date came during the period since.'

'A what?'

'You know. The year isn't an exact number of days long. So they have to put in an extra day or month or something, every once in a while.' That was a reasonable bet.

It paid off, too. Elanor spoke of an extra day every eleventh Nikean year. Yasmin related how in Kraken they added a month – 'What do you call the moons hereabouts? . . . I mean by a month, the time it takes for them both to get back to the same place in the sky . . . We add an extra one every twentieth year.' Her arithmetic was undoubtedly wrong, but who was going to check? The important point was that Nike circled its sun in 591 days of 25.5 hours each, as near as made no difference.

And hadn't much in the way of seasons, but did suffer from irregular, scarcely predictable episodes when the sun grew noticeably hotter or cooler.

And was poor in heavy metals. Given all the prior evidence, what Yasmin wormed from the chattersome Elanor was conclusive. Quite likely iron oxides accounted for the basic color. But they were too diffuse to be workable. Metals had never been

144

mined on this globe; they were obtained electrochemically from the sea and from clays. (Aluminum, beryllium, magnesium and the like; possibly a bit of heavy elements too, but only a bit. For the most part, iron, copper, silver, uranium, etc., had been imported from outsystem, in exchange for old-fashioned Terrestrial agroproducts that must have commanded good prices on less favored worlds. This would explain why, to the very present, Nike had such a pastoral character).

The Empire fell. The starships came less and less often. Demoralization ruined the colonies in their turn; planets broke up politically; in the aftermath, most industry was destroyed, and the social resources were no longer there to build it afresh. Today, on Nike, heavy metals were gotten entirely through reclaiming scrap. Consequently they were too expensive for anything but military and the most vital civilian uses. Even the lighter elements came dear; some extractor plants remained, but not enough.

Elanor did not relate this directly. But she didn't need to. Trying to impress her distinguished guests, she made a parade of setting an aluminum coffeepot on the ceramic stove and mentioning the cost. (A foreigner could plausibly ask what that amounted to in real wages. It was considerable.) And, yes, Petar's grandmother had had a lot of ironware in her kitchen. When he inherited, Petar was offered enormous sums for his share. But he had it made into cutting-edge implements. He cared less about money than about good tools, Petar did. Also for his wife. See, ladies, see right here, I use a real steel knife.

'Gold,' Dagny said, low and harsh in Yasmin's ear. 'Animals, buy, ride.'

The younger girl jerked to alertness. Tired, half lulled by Elanor's millwheel voice, she had drifted off into contemplation. Dagny said this was a young world. Nevertheless it was metal-poor. The paradox had an answer. This system could have formed in the galactic halo, where stars were few and the interstellar dust and gas were thin, little enriched. Yes, that must be the case. It had drifted into this spiral arm . . . But wouldn't it, then, have an abnormal proper motion? Tom hadn't mentioned observing any such thing. Nor had he said there was anything peculiar about Nike's own orbit. Yet he had remarked on less striking facts . . .

'Tell! Buy!'

Yasmin nodded frantically. 'I understand. I understand.' They carried a number of Sassanian gold coins. In an age when interstellar currency and credit had vanished, the metal had resumed its ancient economic function. The value varied from place to place, but was never low, and should be fabulous on Nike.

'Good lady,' Yasmin said, 'we are grateful for your kindness. But we have imposed too much. We should not take any of your men away from the hayfields when storms may be coming. If you will spare us two horses, we can make our own way to Vala and thence, of course, to your Engineer.'

Like fun we will! We'll turn east. Maybe we'll ride horseback, maybe we'll take passage on a river boat – whatever looks safest – but we're bound for his enemy, the Prester of Silva!

'We'll pay for them,' Yasmin said. 'Our overlords provided us well with money. See.' She extended a coin. 'Will this buy two horses and their gear?'

Elanor gasped. She made a sign again, sat down and fanned herself. Her youngest child sensed his mother's agitation and whimpered.

'Is that gold?' she breathed. 'Wait. Till Petar comes. He comes soon. We ask him.'

That was logical. But suppose the man got suspicious.

Yasmin glanced back at Dagny. The Krakener made an imperceptible gesture. Beneath their coveralls were holstered energy weapons.

No! We can't slaughter a whole, helpless family!
I hope we won't need to.
I won't! Not for anything!

* * *

Tom reached the fire-control turret as two aircraft peeled off their squadron and dove.

The skyview was full of departing stormclouds, tinged bloody with dawn. Against them, his space-armored women looked tiny. Not so their hunters. Those devilfish shapes swelled at an appalling speed. Tom threw himself into a manual-operation seat and punched for Number Two blastcannon. A cross-hair screen lit for him with what that elevated weapon 'saw'. He twisted verniers. The auxiliary motors whirred. The vision spun giddily. There ... the couple was separating ... one to keep guard on him, its mate in a swoop after Dagny and Yasmin. Tom got the latter centered and pressed the discharge button.

The screen stepped down the searing brightness of the energy bolt. Through the open manlock crashed the thunderclap that followed. The Hannoan craft exploded into red-hot shards that rained down upon the trees.

'Gotcha!' Tom exulted. He fired two or three more times, raking toward the other boat where it hung on its negafield some fifty meters aloft. His hope was to scare it off and bluff its mates into holding their bombs – or whatever they had to drop on him. He didn't want to kill again. The first shot had looked necessary if the girls were to live. But why add to the grudge against him?

Not that he expected to last another five minutes.

No! Wait! Tom swiveled around to another set of controls. Why hadn't he thought of this at once?

The nearby pilot had needed a couple of seconds to recover from the shock of what happened to his companion. Now he was bound hastily back upward. He was too late. Tom focused a tractor beam on him. Its generator hummed with power. Ozone stung the nostrils; rewiring job needed, a distant aspect of Tom took note. Most of him was being a fisherman. He'd gotten his prey, and on a heavy line – the force locked onto the airboat was meant to grab kilotons moving at cosmic velocities – but his catch was a man-eater. And he wanted to land it just so.

The vessel battled futilely to escape. Tom pushed it down near *Firedrake's* hull, into the jumble of broken trees and canebrake that his own landing had made. Their branches probably damaged wings and fuselage, but their leaves, closing in above, hid any details of what was going on from the pilots overhead.

Having jammed his capture against a fence of logs and brush, he held it there with a beam sufficiently narrow that the cockpit canopy wouldn't be pulled shut. Quickly, with a second tractor-pressor projection, he rearranged the tangle in the clearing, shifting trunks, snapping limbs and tossing them about, until he had a fairly good view through a narrow slot that wouldn't benefit observers in heaven. He trusted they were too poorly instrumented – or too agitated, or both – to see how useful the arrangement was for him, and would take the brief stirring they noticed as a natural result of a crash, heaped wood collapsing into a new configuration.

Thereafter he left the turret and made his way to the forward manlock. It was rather high off the ground; the access ladder had automatically extruded, plunging down into the foliage that fluttered shadowy around the base of the hull. Tom placed himself in the chamber, invisible from the sky, hardly noticeable from beneath, and studied his fish more closely.

Fish: yes, indeed. In two senses.

The pilot was that youthful squadron leader with whom he had spoken before. Tom tuned his helmet radio in on the frantic talk that went between the downed man, his companions and Karol Weyer in Sea Gate. He gathered they had no prehensile force-beams on Nike, and only vaguely inferred the existence of such things from their experience with 'friends.'

Friends? The raiders from space? Tom scowled.

But he couldn't stop to think beyond this moment. His notion had been to take a man and an aircraft – the latter probably the more highly valued – as hostages. They'd not nuke him now. But as for what followed, he must play his cards as he drew them. At worst, he'd gotten the girls free. Perhaps he could strike some kind of bargain, though it was hard to tell why any Nikean should feel bound to keep a promise made to an outworlder. At best . . .

Hoy!

The canopy slid back. Tom got a look at the plane's interior.

There was room for two in the cockpit, if one scrooched and aft of the seat was a rack of – something or other, he couldn't see what, but it didn't seem welded in place. His pulse leaped.

The pilot emerged, in a dive flattening himself at once behind a fallen tree. Weyer had said after several fruitless attempts to get a reply from Tom: 'You in the ship! You killed one of ours. Another, and your whole ship goes. Do you seize me?' (That must mean 'understand.') Next, to the flyboy: 'Fish Aran, use own discretion.'

So the young man, deciding he couldn't sit where he was forever, was trying to reach the woods. That took nerve. Tom laid his telescope to his good eye – his face plate was open – and searched out details. Fiber helmet, as already noted; green tunic with cloth insignia, no metal; green trousers tucked into leather boots; a side-arm, but no indication of a portable communicator or, for that matter, a watch. Tom made sure his transmitter was off, trod a little further out in the lock chamber, and bawled from lungs that had often shouted against a gale at sea:

'Halt where you are! Or I'll chop the legs from under you!'

The pilot had been about to scuttle from his place. He froze. Slowly, he raised his gaze. Tom's armored shape was apparent to him, standing in the open lock, but not discernible by his mates. Likewise the blaster Tom aimed. The pilot's hand hovered at the butt of his own weapon.

'Slack off, son,' the captain advised. 'You wouldn't come near me with that pipgun – I said "pip," not even "pop" – before I sizzled you. And I don't want to. C'mon and let's talk. That's right; on your feet; stroll over here and use this nice ladder.'

The pilot obeyed, though his scramble across the log jam was hardly a stroll. As he started up, Tom said: 'They'll see in a minute what you're doin', I s'pose, when you come above the foliage . . . Belay, there, *I* can see you quite well already . . . I want you to draw your gun, as if you'd decided to come aboard and reconnoiter 'stead o' headin' for the nearest beer hall. Better not try shootin' at me, though. My friends'd cut you down.'

The Hannoan paused a moment, rigid with outrage, before he yielded. His face, approaching, showed pale and wet in the first

149

light. He swung himself into the lock chamber. For an instant, he and Tom stood with guns almost in each other's bellies. The spaceman's gauntleted left hand struck like a viper, edge on, and the Nikean weapon clattered to the deck.

'You – you broke my wrist!' The pilot lurched back, clutching his arm and wheezing.

'I think not. I gauge these things pretty good if I do say so myself. And I do. March on ahead o' me, please.' Tom conducted his prisoner into the passageway, gathering the fallen pistol en route. It was a slug-thrower, ingeniously constructed with a minimum of steel. Tom found the magazine release and pressed it one-handed. The clip held ten high-caliber bullets. But what the hoo-hah! The cartridge cases were wood, the slugs appeared to be some heavy ceramic, with a mere skirt of soft metal for the rifling in the barrel to get a grip on!

'No wonder you came along meek-like,' Tom said. 'You never could've dented me.'

The prisoner looked behind him. Footfalls echoed emptily around his words. 'I think you are alone,' he said.

'Aye-ya. I told you my chums *could* wiff you . . . if they were present. In here.' Tom indicated the fire control turret. 'Sit yourself. Now, I'm goin' t'other side o' this room and shuck my armor, which is too hot and heavy for informal wear. Don't get ideas about plungin' across the deck at me. I can snatch my blaster and take aim quicker'n that.'

The young man crouched in a chair and shuddered. His eyes moved like a trapped animal's, around and around the crowding machines. 'What do you mean to do?' he rattled. 'You can't get free. You're alone. Soon the Engineer's soldiers come, with 'tillery, and ring you.'

'I know. We should be gone by then, however. Look here, uh, what's your name?'

An aristocrat's pride firmed the voice. 'Yanos Aran, third son of Rober Aran, who's chief computerman to Engineer Weyer's self. I am a fish in the air force of Hanno – and you are a dirty friend!'

'Maybe so. Maybe not.' Tom stripped fast, letting the pieces

150

lie where they fell. He hated to abandon his suit, but it was too bulky and perhaps too detectable for his latest scheme.

'Why not? Didn't you business Evin Sato?'

'You mean that plane I gunned?'

'Yes. Evin Sato was my camarado.'

'Well, I'm sorry about that, but wasn't he fixin' to shoot two o' my people? We came down frien' – intendin' no harm, and you set on us like hungry eels. I don't want to hurt you, Yanos, lad. In fact, I hope betwixt us we can maybe settle this whole affair. But –' Tom's features assumed their grimmest look which had terrified stronger men than Aran – 'you try any fumblydiddles and you'll find out things about friendship that your mother never told you.'

The boy seemed to crumple. 'I . . . yes, I slave me to you,' he whispered.

He wouldn't stay crumpled long, Tom knew. He must be the scion of a typical knightly class. Let him recover from the dismay of the past half hour and the unbalancing effect of being surrounded by unknown power and he'd prove a dangerous pet. It was necessary to use him while he remained useable.

Wherefore Tom, having peeled down to coveralls, gave him his orders in a few words. A slight demurral fetched a brutal cuff on the cheek. 'And if I shoot you with this blaster, short range low intensity,' Tom added, 'you won't have a neat hole drilled through your heart. You'll be cooked alive, medium rare, so you'll be some days about dying. Seize me?'

He didn't know if he'd really carry out his threat, come worst to worst. Probably not.

Having switched off the tractor beam, he brought Aran far down into the ship, to an emergency lock near the base. It was well hidden by leaves. The vague dawn-light aided concealment. They crept forth, and thence to the captured aircraft.

It had taken a beating, Tom saw. The wingtips were crumpled, the fuselage punctured. (The covering was mostly some fluoro-synthetic. What a metal shortage they must have here!) But it ought to fly anyhow, after a fashion. Given a gravity drive, however weak, airfoils were mainly for auxiliary lift and control.

'In we go,' Tom said. He squeezed his bulky form behind

Aran's seat so that it concealed him. The blaster remained in his fist, ready to fire through the back.

But there was no trouble. Aran followed instructions. He called his squadron: ' – Yes, you're right, I did 'cide I'd try looking at the ship. And no one! None aboard. 'Least, none I saw. Maybe robos fought us, or maybe the rest of the crew got away on foot, not seen. I found a switch, looked like a main powerline breaker, and opened it. Maybe now I can rise.'

And he started the engine. The airboat climbed, wobbling on its damaged surfaces. A cheer sounded from the receiver. Tom wished he could see the faces in the screen, but he dared not risk being scanned himself.

'You land, if Engineer Weyer approves,' Aran directed. 'Go aboard. Be careful. Me, best I take my craft back to base immediately.

Tom had figured that would be a natural move for a pilot on Nike, even a squadron leader. A plane was obviously precious. It couldn't get to the repair shop too fast.

He must now hope that Aran's expression and tone didn't give him away. The 'fish' was no actor. But everyone was strung wire-taut. Nobody noticed how much more perturbed this fellow was. After a few further words had passed, Aran signed off and started west.

'Keep low,' Tom said. 'Like you can't get much altitude. Soon's you're out o' their sight here, swing north. Find us a good secret place to land. I think we got a bucketful to say to each other, no?'

One craft was bound eagerly down. The rest stayed at hover. They'd soon learn that the spaceship was, indeed, deserted. Hence they wouldn't suspect what had happened to Aran until he failed to report. However, that wasn't a long time. He, Roan Tom, had better get into a bolt-hole quick!

* * *

The volcano's northern side was altogether wild. On the lower flanks, erosion had created a rich lava soil and vegetation was dense. For some reason it was principally native Nikean, dominated by primitive but tree-sized 'ferns'. An antigrav flyer could push its way under their soft branches and come to rest beneath the overhang of a cliff, camouflaged against aerial search.

Tom climbed out of the cockpit and stretched to uncramp himself. The *abri* was rough stone at his back, the forest brooded shadowy before him. Flecks of copper sunlight on bluish-green fronds and the integuments of bumbling giant pseudo-insects made the scene look as if cast in metal. But water rilled nearby, and the smells of damp growth were organic enough.

'C'mon, son. Relax with me.' Tom invited. 'I won't eat you. 'Specially not if you've packed along a few sandwiches.'

'Food? No.' Yanos Aran spoke as stiffly as he moved.

'Well, then we'll have to make do with what iron rations I got in my pockets.' Tom sighed. He flopped down on a chair-sized boulder, took out pipe and tobacco pouch, and consoled himself with smoke.

He needed consolation. He was a fugitive on an unknown planet. His ship had been taken, his wives were out of touch; an attempt to raise Dagny on the plane's transmitter, using a Krakener military band, had brought silence. She must already have discarded her telespace armor.

'And all 'count of a stupid lingo mistake!' he groaned.

Aran sat down on another rock and regarded him with eyes in which alertness was replacing fear. 'You say you are not truly our friend?'

'Not in your sense. Look, where I come from, the Aran word "friend" means ... well, fellow you like, and who likes you. When I told your Engineer we were friends, I wanted him to understand we didn't aim him any harm, in fact we could do good business with him.'

'Business!' Aran exploded.

'Whoops-la. Sorry. Said the wrong thing again, didn't I?'

'I think,' Aran replied slowly, 'what you have in mind is what we would call "change". You wanted to "change goods and services with our people. And to you, a "friend" is what we call a "camarado."'

'Reckon so. What're your definitions?'

'A friend is a space raider such as did business with our planet some five years agone. They destroyed the last great cities we had left from the Terran Empire days, and none knows how many million Nikeans they killed.'

'Ah, now we're gettin' somewhere. Let's straighten out for me what did happen.'

Aran's hostility had not departed, but it had diminished. He was intelligent and willing to cooperate within the limits of loyalty to his own folk. Information rushed out of him.

Nike did not appear to be unique, except in its planetology. Tom asked about that. Aran was surprised. Was his world so unusual per se?

He knew only vague traditions and a few fragmentary written accounts of other planetary systems. Nike was discovered and colonized five hundred-odd years ago – about a thousand standard years. It was always a backwater. Fundamentally agricultural because of its shortage of heavy metals, it had no dense population, no major libraries or schools. Thus, when the Empire fell apart, knowledge vanished more quickly and thoroughly here than most places. Nikean society disintegrated; what had been an Imperial sub-province became hundreds of evanescent kingdoms, fiefs and tribes.

The people were on their way back, Aran added defiantly. Order and a measure of prosperity had been restored in the advanced countries. As yet, they paid mere lip service to an 'Emperor', but the concept of global government did now exist. Technology was improving. Ancient apparatus was being repaired and put back into service, or being reproduced on the basis of what diagrams and manuals could be found. Schemes had been broached for making interplanetary ships. Some dreamers had hoped that in time the Nikeans might end their centuries-long isolation themselves, by re-inventing the lost theory and practice of hyperdrive.

For that, of course, as for much else, the tinkering of technicians was insufficient. Basic scientific research must be done. But this was also slowly being started. Had not Aran remarked that his father was head computerman in the Engineer's court?

He used a highly sophisticated machine which had survived to the present day and which two generations of modern workers had finally learned how to operate.

Its work at present was mainly in astronomy. While some elementary nucleonics had been preserved through the dark ages – being essential to the maintenance of what few atomic power plants remained – practically all information about the stars had vanished. Today's astronomers had learned that their sun (as distinguished from their planet) was not typical of its neighborhood. It was unpredictably variable, and not even its ground state could be fitted onto the main sequence diagram. No one had yet developed a satisfactory theory as to what made this sun abnormal, but the consensus was that it must be quite a young star.

One geologist had proposed checking this idea by establishing the age of the planet. Radioactive minerals should provide a clock. The attempt had failed, partly because of the near-nonexistence of isotopes with suitable half-lives and partly, Tom suspected, because of lousy laboratory technique. But passing references in old books did seem to confirm the idea held by latterday theorists, that stars and planets condensed out of interstellar gas and dust. If so, Nike's sun could be very new, as cosmic time went, and not yet fully stabilized.

'Aye, I'd guess that myself,' Tom nodded.

'Good! Important to be sure. You seize, can we make a mathematical model of our sun, then we can predict its variations. Right? And we will never predict our weather until then. Unforeseen storms are our greatest natural woe. Hanno's self, a southerly land, can get killing frosts any season.'

'Well, don't take my authority, son, I'm no scientist. The Imperialists must've known for sure what kind o'star they had here. And a scholar of astronomy, from a planet where they still keep universities and such, could tell you. But not me.' Tom struck new fire to his pipe. 'Uh, we'd better stay with less fun topics. Like those "friends."'

Aran's enthusiasm gave way to starkness. He could relate little. The raiders had not come in any large fleet, a dozen ships at most. But there was no effective opposition to them. They smashed defenses from space, landed, plundered, raped, tortured, burned, during a nightmare of weeks. After sacking a major city, they missiled it. They were human, their language another dialect of Anglic. Whether in sarcasm or hypocrisy or because of linguistic change, they described themselves to the Nikeans as 'your friends, come to do business with you.' Since 'friend' and 'business' had long dropped out of local speech, Tom saw the origin of their present meaning here.

'Do you know who they might have been?' Aran asked. His tone was thick with unshed tears.

'No. Not sure. Space's full o' their kind.' Tom refrained from adding that he too wasn't above a bit of piracy on occasion. After all, he observed certain humane rules with respect to those whom he relieved of their portable goods. The really bestial types made his flesh crawl, and he'd exterminated several gangs of them with pleasure.

'Will they return, think you?'

'Well . . . prob'ly not. I'd reckon they destroyed your big population centers to make sure no one else'd be tempted to come here and start a base that might be used against 'em. They bein' too few to conquer a whole world, you see. 'Course, I wouldn't go startin' major industries and such again without husky space defenses.'

'No chance. We hide instead,' Aran said bitterly. 'Most leaders dare allow naught that might draw other friends. Radio a bare minimum; no rebuilding of cities; yes, we crawl back to our dark age and cower.'

'I take it you don't pers'nally agree with that policy.'

Aran shrugged. 'What matter my thoughts? I am but a third son. The chiefs of the planet had 'cided. They fought a war or two, forcing the rest to go with them in this. I myself bombed soldiers of Silva, when its Prester was made stop building a big atomic power plant. Our neighbor cavedom! And we had to fight them, not the friends!'

Tom wasn't shocked. He'd seen human politics get more

hashed than that. What pricked his ears up was the information that, right across the border, lived a baron who couldn't feel overly kindly toward Engineer Weyer.

'You can seize, now, why we feared you,' Aran said.

'Aye-ya. A sad misunderstandin'. If you hadn't been so bloody impulsive, though – if you'd been willin' to talk – we'd've quick seen what the lingo problem was.'

'No! You were the ones who refused talk. When the Engineer called on you to be slaves – '

'What the muck did he expect us to do after that?' Tom rumbled. 'Wear his chains?'

'Chains? Why . . . wait – oh, oh!'

'Oh-oh, for sure,' Tom said. 'Another little shift o' meanin', huh? All right, what does "slave" signify to you?'

It turned out that, on Nike, to be 'enslaved' was nothing more than to be taken into custody: perhaps as a prisoner, perhaps merely for interrogation or protection. In Hanno, as in every advanced Nikean realm, slavery in Tom's sense of the word had been abolished a lifetime ago.

The two men stared at each other. 'Events got away from both sides,' Tom said. 'After what'd happened when last spacemen came, you were too spooked to give us a chance. You reckoned you had to get us under guard right away. And we reacted to that. We've seen a lot o' cruelty and treachery. We couldn't trust ourselves to complete strangers, 'specially when they acted hostile. So . . . neither side gave the other time to think out the busi – the matter o' word shift. If there'd been a few minutes' pause in the action, I think I, at least, would've guessed the truth. I've seen lots o' similar cases. But I never had any such pause, till now.'

He grinned and extended a broad hard hand. 'All's well that ends well, I'm told,' he said. 'Let's be camarados.'

Aran ignored the gesture. The face he turned to the out-worlder was only physically youthful. 'We cannot,' he said. 'You wrecked a plane and stole another. Worse, you killed a man of ours.'

'But – well, self-defense!'

*

157

'I might pardon you,' Aran said. 'I do not think the Engineer would or could. It is more than the damage you worked. More than the anger of the powerful Sato family, who like it not if a son of theirs dies unavenged because of a comic mix in s'mantics. It is the policy that he, Weyer's self, strove to bring.'

'You mean . . . nothin' good can come from outer space . . . wall Nike off . . . treat anyone that comes as hostile . . . right?' Tom rubbed his chin and scowled sullenly.

Weyer was probably not too dogmatic, nor too tightly bound by the isolationist treaty, to change his mind in time. But Tom had scant time to spare. Every hour that passed, he and his womenfolk risked getting shot down by some hysteric. Also, a bunch of untrained Nikeans, pawing over his spaceship, could damage her beyond the capacity of this planet's industry to repair.

Also, he was needed back on Kraken *soon*, or his power there would crumble. And that would be a mortally dangerous situation for his other wives, children, grandchildren, old and good comrades . . .

In short, there was scant value in coming to terms with Weyer eventually. He needed to reach agreement fast. And, after what had happened this day, he didn't see how he could.

Well, the first thing he must do was reunite his party. Together, they might accomplish something. If nothing else, they could seek refuge in the adjacent country, Silva. Though that was doubtless no very secure place for them, particularly if Weyer threatened another war.

'You should slave yourself,' Aran urged. 'Afterward you can talk.'

'As a prisoner – a slave – I'd have precious little bargainin' leverage,' Tom said. 'Considerin' what that last batch o' spacers did, I can well imagine me bein' tortured till I cough up for free everything I've got to tell. S'posin' Weyer himself didn't want to treat me so inhospitable, he could break down anyhow under pressure from his court or his fellow bosses.'

'It may be,' Aran conceded, reluctantly, but too idealistic at his age to violate the code of his class and lie.

'Whereas if I can stay loose, I can try a little pressure o' my own. I can maybe find somethin' to offer that's worth makin' a deal with me. That'd even appease the Sato clan, hm?' Tom fumed on his pipe. 'I've got to contact my women. Right away. Can't risk their fallin' into Weyer's hands. If they do, he's got me! Know any way to raise a couple o' girls who don't have a radio and 're doin' their level best to disappear?'

* * *

Sunset rays turned the hilltop fiery. Farther down, the land was already blue with a dusk through which river, bay, and distant sea glimmered argent. Cloud banks towered in the east, blood-colored, dwarfing the Sawtooth Mountains that marked Hanno's frontier.

At the lowest altitude when this was visible – the highest to which a damaged, overloaded flyer could limp – the air was savagely cold. It wasn't too thin for breathing; the atmosphere's density gradient is less for small than for large planets. But it swept through the cracked canopy to sear Tom's nostrils and numb his fingers on the board. Above the drone of the combustion powerplant, he heard Yano Aran's teeth clatter. Stuffed behind the pilot chair, the boy might have tried to mug his captor. But he wasn't dressed for this temperature and was chilled half insensible. Tom's clothes were somewhat warmer. Besides, he felt he could take on any two Nikeans hand-to-hand.

The controls of the plane were simple to a man who'd used as wide a variety of machines as he. Trickiness came from the broken and twisted airfoil surfaces. And, of course, he must keep a watch for Weyer's boys. He didn't think they'd be aloft, nor that they would scramble and get here in the few minutes he needed. But you never knew. If one did show up maybe Tom could pot him with a lucky blast from the guns.

He swung through another carousel curve. That should be that. Now to skate away. He throttled the engine back. The megafield dropped correspondingly, and he went into a glide. But he was no longer emitting enough exhaust for a visible trail.

The tracks he had left were scribbled over half the sky. The sun painted them gold-orange against that deepening purple.

159

Abruptly, turbulence across the buckled delta wing gained mastery. The glide became a tailspin. Aran yelled.

'Hang on,' Tom said. 'I can ride 'er.'

Crazily whirling, the dark land rushed at him. He stopped Aran's attempt to grab the stick with a karate chop and concentrated on his altimeter. At the last possible moment, allowing for the fact that he must coddle this wreck lest he tear her apart altogether, he pulled out of his tumble. A prop, jet or rocket would never had made it, but you could do special things with gravs if you had the knack in your fingers. Or whatever part of the anatomy it was.

Finally the plane whispered a few meters above the bay. Its riding lights were doused, and the air here was too warm for engine vapor to condense. Tom believed his passage had a fair chance of going unnoticed.

Hills shouldered black around the water. Here and there among them twinkled house lamps. One cluster bespoke a village on the shore. Tom's convoluted contrail was breaking up, but slowly. It glowed huge and mysterious, doubtless frightening peasants and worrying the military.

Aran stared at it likewise, as panic and misery left him. 'I thought you wrote a message to your camarados,' he said. 'That's no writing.'

'Couldn't use your alphabet, son, seein' I had to give 'em directions to a place with a local name. Could I, now? Even Karken's letters look much like yours. But those're Momotaroan phonograms. Dagny can read 'em. I hope none o' Weyer's folk'll even guess it is a note. Maybe they'll think I went out o' control tryin' to escape and, after staggerin' around a while, crashed . . . Now, which way is this rendezvous?'

'Rendez – oh. The togethering I advised. Follow the north shore eastward a few more kilos. At the end of a headland stands Orgino's Cave.'

'You absolutely sure nobody'll be there?'

'As sure as may be; and you have me for hostage. Orgino was a war chief of three hundred years agone. They said he was so wicked he must be in pact with the Wanderer, and to this day the commons think he walks the ruins of his cave. But it's a landmark. Let your camarados ask shrewdly, and they can find how to get there with none suspecting that for their wish.'

The plane sneaked onward. Twilight was short in this thin air. Stars twinkled splendidly forth, around the coalsack of the Nebula. The outer moon rose, gradually from the eastern cloudbanks, almost full but its disk tiny and corroded-bronze dark. An auroral glow flickered. This far south? Well, Nike had a fairly strong magnetic field – which, with the mean density, showed that it possessed the ferrous core it wasn't supposed to – but not so much that charged solar particles couldn't strike along its sharp curvature clear to the equator.

If they were highly energetic particles, anyhow. And they must be. Tom had identified enormous spots as well as flares on that ruddy sun disk. Which oughtn't to be there! Not even when output was rising. A young star, its outer layers cool and reddish because they were still contracting shouldn't have such intensity. Should it?

Regardless, Nike's sun did.

Well, Tom didn't pretend to know every kind of star. His travels had really not been so extensive, covering a single corner of the old Imperium which itself had been insignificant compared to the whole galaxy. And his attention had naturally always been focused on more or less Sol-type stars. He didn't know what a very young or very old or very large or very small sun was like in detail.

Most certainly he didn't know what the effects of abnormal chemical composition might be. And the distribution of elements in this system was unlike that of any other Tom had ever heard about. Conditions on Nike bore out what spectroanalysis had indicated in space: impoverishment with respect to heavy elements. Since it had formed recently, the sun and its planets must therefore have wandered here from some different region. Its velocity didn't suggest that. However, Tom hadn't determined the galactic orbit with any precision. Besides, it might have been radically changed by a close encounter with another orb. Improbable as the deuce, yes, but then the whole crazy situation was very weird.

The headland loomed before him, and battlements against the Milky Way. Tom made a vertical landing in a courtyard. 'All right.' His voice sounded jarringly loud. 'Now we got nothin' much to do but wait.'

'What if they come not?' Aran asked.

'I'll give 'em a day or two,' Tom said. 'After that, we'll see.' He didn't care to dwell on the possibility. His unsentimental soul was rather astonished to discover how big a part of it Dagny had become. And Yasmin was a good kid, he wished her well.

He left the crumbling flagstones for a walk around the walls. Pseudo-moss grew damp and slippery on the parapet. Once mail-clad spearmen had tramped their rounds here, and the same starlight sheened on their helmets as tonight, or as in the still more ancient, vanished glory of the Empire, or the League before it, or – And what of the nights yet to come? Tom shied from the thought and loaded his pipe.

Several hours later, the nearer moon rose from the hidden sea; its apparent path was retrograde and slow. Although at half phase, with an angular diameter of a full degree it bridged the bay with mercury.

Rising at the half – local midnight, more or less – would the girls never show? He ought to get some sleep. His eyelids were sandy. Aran had long since gone to rest in the tumbledown keep. He must be secured, of course, before Tom dozed off . . . *No. I couldn't manage a snooze even if I tried. Where are you, Dagny?*

The cold wind lulled, the cold waves lapped, a winged creature fluttered and whistled. Tom sat down where a portcullis had been and stared into the woods beyond.

There came a noise. And another. Branches rustled. Hoofbeats clopped. Tom drew his blaster and slid into the shadow of a tower. Two riders on horseback emerged from the trees. For a moment they were unrecognizable, unreal. Then the moon's light struck Dagny's tawny mane. Tom shouted.

Dagny snatched her own gun forth. But when she saw who lumbered toward her, it fell into the rime-frosted grass.

* * *

Afterward, in what had been a feasting hall, with a flashlight from the aircraft to pick faces out of night, they conferred. 'No, we had no trouble,' Dagny said. 'The farmers sold us those animals without any fuss.'

'If you gave him a thirty-gram gold piece, on this planet, I reckon so,' Tom said. 'You could prob'ly've gotten his house thrown into the deal. He's bound to gossip about you, though.'

'That can't be helped,' Dagny said. 'Our idea was to keep traveling east and hide in the woods when anyone happened by. But we'd no strong hope, especially with that wide cultivated valley to get across. Tom, dear, when I saw your sky writing, it was the second best moment of my life.'

'What was the first?'

'You were involved there too,' she said. 'Rather often, in fact.'

Yasmin stirred. She sat huddled on the floor, chilled, exhausted, wretched, though nonetheless drawing Aran's appreciative gaze. 'Why do you grin at each other?' she wailed. 'We're hunted!'

'Tell me more,' Tom said.

'What can we *do*?'

'You can shut up, for the gods' sake, and keep out o' my way!' he snapped impatiently. She shrank from him and knuckled her eyes.

'Be gentle,' Dagny said. 'She's only a child.'

'She'll be a dead child if we don't get out o' here,' Tom retorted. 'We got time before dawn to slip across the Silvan border in yon airboat. After that, we'll have to play 'er as she lies. But I been pumpin' my — shall I say, my friend, about politics and geography and such. I think with luck we got a chance o' staying free.'

'What chance of getting our ship back, and repaired?' Dagny asked.

'Well, that don't look so good, but maybe somethin'll come down the slot for us. Meanwhile let's move.'

They went back to the courtyard. The inner moon was so bright that no supplement was needed for the job on hand. This was to unload the extra fuel tanks, which were racked aft of the cockpit. The plane would lose cruising range, would indeed be unable to go past the eastern slope of the Sawtooths. But it would gain room for two passengers.

'You stay behind, natural,' Tom told Aran. 'You been a nice lad, and here's where I prove I never aimed at any hurt for you. Have a horse on me, get a boat from the village to Weyer's place, tell him what happened – and to tell him we want to be his camarados and 'change with him.'

'I can say it.' Aran shifted awkwardly from foot to foot. 'I think no large use comes from my word.'

'The prejudice against spacemen – '

'And the damage you worked. How shall you repay that? Since 'tis been 'cided there's no good in spacefaring, I expect your ship'll be stripped for its metal.'

'Try, though,' Tom urged.

'Should you leave now?' Aran wondered. 'Weather looks twisty.'

'Aye, we'd better. But thanks for frettin' 'bout it.'

A storm, Tom thought, was the least of his problems. True, conditions did look fanged about the mountains. But he could sit down and wait them out, once over the border, which ought to remain in the bare fringes of the tempest. Who ever heard of weather moving very far west, on the western seacoast of a planet with rotation like this? What was urgent was to get beyond Weyer's pursuit.

Yasmin and Dagny fitted themselves into the rear fuselage as best they could, which wasn't very. Tom took the pilot's seat again. He waved good-by to Yanos Aran and gunned the engine. Overburdened as well as battered, the plane lifted sluggishly and made no particular speed. But it flew, and could be out of Hanno before dawn. That sufficed.

Joy at reunion, vigilance against possible enemies, concentration on the difficult task of operating his cranky vessel, drove weariness out of him. He paid scant attention to the beauties of the landscape sliding below, though they were considerable — mist-magical delta, broad sweep of valley, river's sinuous glow, all white under the moons. He must be one with the wind that blew across this sleeping land.

And blew.

Harder.

The plane bucked. The noise around it shrilled more and more clamorous. Though the cloud wall above the mountains must be a hundred kilometers distant, it was suddenly boiling zenithward with unbelievable speed.

It rolled over the peaks and hid them. Its murk swallowed the outer moon and reached tendrils forth for the inner one. Lightning blazed in its caverns. Then the first raindrops were hurled against the plane. Hail followed, and the snarl of a hurricane.

East wind! Couldn't be! Tom had no further chance to think. He was too busy staying alive.

As if across parsecs, he heard Yasmin's scream, Dagny's profane orders that she curb herself. Rain and hail made the cockpit a drum, himself a cockroach trapped between the skins. The wind was the tuba of marching legions. Sheathing ripped loose from wings and tail. Now and then he could see through the night, when lightning burned. The thunder was like bombs, one after the next, a line of them seeking him out. What followed was doomsday blackness.

His instrument panel went dark. His altitude control stick waggled loose in his hand. The airflaps must be gone, the vessel whirled leaf-fashion on the wind. Tom groped until his fingers closed on the grav-drive knobs. By modulating fields and thrust beams, he could keep a measure of command. Just a measure; the powerplant had everything it could do to lift this weight, without guiding it. But let him get sucked down to earth, that was the end!

He must land somehow, and survive the probably hard impact. How?

The river flashed lurid beneath him. He tried to follow its course. Something real, in this raving night — There was no more inner moon, there were no more stars.

*

165

The plane groaned, staggered, and tilted on its side. The starboard wing was torn off. Had the port one gone too, Tom might have operated the fuselage as a kind of gravity sled. But against forces as unbalanced as now fought him, he couldn't last more than a few seconds. Minutes, if he was lucky.

Must be back above the rivermouths, thought the tiny part of him that stood aside and watched the struggle of the rest. *Got to set down easy-like. And find some kind o' shelter. Yasmin wouldn't last out this night in the open.*

Harshly: *Will she last anyway? Is she anything but a dangerous drag on us? I can't abandon her. I swore her an oath, but I almost wish –*

The sky exploded anew with lightnings and showed him a wide vista of channels among forested, swampy islands. Trees tossed and roared in the wind, but the streams were too narrow for great waves to build up and – Hoy!

Suddenly, disastrously smitten, a barge train headed from Sea Gate to the upriver towns had broken apart. In the single blazing moment of vision that he had, Tom saw the tug itself reel toward safety on the northern side of the main channel. Its tow was scattered, some members sinking, some flung around, and one – yes, driven into a tributary creek, woods and waterplants closing behind it, screening it –

Tom made his decision.

He hoped for nothing more than a bellyflop in the drink, a scramble to escape from the plane and a swim to the barge. But lightning flamed again and again, enormous sheets of it that turned every raindrop and hailstone into brass. And once he was down near the surface of that natural canal, a wall of trees on either side, he got some relief. He was actually able to land on deck.

The barge had ended on a sandbar and lay solid and stable. Tom led his women from the plane. He and Dagny found some rope and lashed their remnant of a vehicle into place. The cargo appeared to be casks of petroleum. A hatch led below, to a cabin where a watchman might rest. Tom's flashlight picked out bunk, chair, a stump of candle.

'We're playin' a good hand,' he said.

166

'For how long?' Dagny mumbled.

'Till the weather slacks off.' Tom shrugged. 'What comes after that, I'm too tired to care. I don't s'pose . . . gods, yes!' he whooped. 'Here, on the shelf! A bottle – lemme sniff – aye-ya, booze! Got to be booze!' And he danced upon the deckboards till he cracked his pate on the low overhead.

Yasmin regarded him with a dull kind of wonder. 'What are you so happy about?' she asked in Anglic. When he had explained, she slumped. 'You can laugh . . . at that . . . tonight? Lord Tom, I did not know how alien you are to me.'

Through hours the storm continued.

They sat crowded together, the three of them, in the uneasy candlelight, which threw huge misshapen shadows across the roughness of bulkheads. Rather Dagny sat on the chair, Tom on the foot of the bunk, while Yasmin lay. The wind-noise was muffled down here, but the slap of water on hull came loud. From time to time, thunder cannonaded, or the barge rocked and grated on the sandbar.

Wet, dirty, haggard, the party looked at each other. 'We should try to sleep,' Dagny said.

'Not while I got this bottle,' Tom said. 'You do what you like. Me, though, I think we'd better guzzle while we can. Prob'ly won't be long, you see.'

'Probably not,' Dagny agreed, and took another pull herself.

'What will we do?' Yasmin whispered.

Tom suppressed exasperation – she had done a good job in Petar Landa's house, if nowhere else – and said, 'Come mornin', we head into the swamps. I s'pose Weyer'll send his merry men lookin' for us, and whoever owns this hulk'll search after it, so we can't claim squatter's rights. Maybe we can live off the country, though, and eventually, one way or another, reach the border.'

'Would it not be sanest . . . they do seem to be decent folk . . . should we not surrender to them and hope for mercy?'

'Go ahead if you want,' Tom said. 'You may or may not get the mercy. But you'll for sure have no freedom. I'll stay my own man.'

167

Yasmin tried to meet his hard gaze, and failed. 'What has happened to us?' she pleaded.

He suspected that she meant, 'What has become of the affection between you and me?' No doubt he should comfort her. But he didn't have the strength left to play father image. Trying to distract her a little, he said, with calculated misunderstanding of her question:

'Why, we hit a storm that blew us the exact wrong way. It wasn't s'posed to. But this's such a funny planet. I reckon, given a violent kind o' sun, you can get weather that whoops out o' the east, straight seaward. And, o' course, winds can move almighty fast when the air's thin. Maybe young Aran was tryin' to warn me. He spoke o' twisty weather. Maybe he meant exactly this, and I got fooled once more by his Nikean lingo. Or maybe he just meant what I believed he did, unreliable weather. He told me himself, their meteorology isn't worth sour owl spit, 'count o' they can't predict the solar output. Young star, you know. Have a drink.'

Yasmin shook her head. But abruptly she sat straight. 'Have you something to write with?'

'Huh?' Tom gaped at her.

'I have an idea. It is worthless,' she said humbly, 'but since I cannot sleep, and do not wish to annoy my lord, I would like to pass the time.'

'Oh. Sure.' Tom found a paper and penstyl in a breast pocket of his coverall and gave them to her. She crossed her legs and began writing numbers in a neat foreign-looking script.

'What's going on?' Dagny said in Eylan.

Tom explained. The older woman frowned. 'I don't like this, dear,' she said. 'Yasmin's been breaking down, closer and closer to hysteria, ever since we left those peasants. She's not prepared for a guerrilla existence. She's used up her last resources.'

'You reckon she's quantum-jumpin' already?'

'I don't know. But I do think we should force her to take a drink, to put her to sleep.'

'Hm.' Tom glanced at the dark head, bent over some arithmetical calculations. 'Could be. But no. Let her do what she

168

chooses. She hasn't bubbled her lips yet, has she? And – we are the free people.'

He went on with Dagny in a rather hopeless discussion of possibilities open to them. Once they were interrupted, when Yasmin asked if he had a trigonometric slide rule. No, he didn't. 'I suppose I can approximate the function with a series,' she said, and returned to her labors.

Has she really gone gollywobble? Tom wondered. *Or is she just soothin' herself with a hobby?*

Half an hour later, Yasmin spoke again. 'I have the solution.'

'To what?' Tom asked, a little muzzily after numerous gulps from the bottle. They distilled potent stuff in Hanno. 'Our problem?'

'Oh, no, my lord. I couldn't – I mean, I am nobody. But I did study science, you remember, and . . . and I assumed that if you and Lady Dagny said this was a young system, you must be right, you have traveled so widely. But it isn't.'

'No? What're you aimed at?'

'It doesn't matter, really. I'm being an awful picky little nuisance. But this *can't* be a young system. It has to be old.'

Tom put the bottle down with a thud that overrode the storm-yammer outside. Dagny opened her mouth to ask what was happening. He shushed her. Out of the shadows across his scarred face, the single eye blazed blue. 'Go on,' he said, most quietly.

Yasmin faltered. She hadn't expected any such reaction. But, encouraged by him, she said with a waxing confidence:

'From the known average distance of the sun, and the length of the planet's year, anyone can calculate the sun's mass. It turns out to be almost precisely one Sol. That is, it has the mass of a G_2 star. But it has twice the luminosity, and more than half again the radius, and the reddish color of a late G or early K type. You thought those paradoxes were due to a strange composition. I don't really see how that could be. I mean, any star is something like 98 per cent hydrogen and helium. Variations in other elements can affect its development some, but surely not this much. Well, we know from Nikean biology that this system must be at least a few billion years old. So the star's instability cannot be due to extreme youth. Any solar mass must settle down on the main sequence far quicker than that. Otherwise we would have many, many more variables in the universe than we do.

'And besides, we can explain all the paradoxes so simply if we assume this system is old. Incredibly old, maybe almost as old as the galaxy itself.'

'Belay!' Tom exclaimed, though not loudly. 'How could this planet have this much atmosphere after so long a time? If any? Don't sunlight kick gases into space? And Nike hasn't got the gravity to nail molecules down for good. Half a standard Gee; and the potential is even poorer, the field strength dropping off as fast as it does.'

'But my lord,' Yasmin said, 'an atmosphere comes from within a planet. At least, it does for the smaller planets, that can't keep their original hydrogen like the Jupiter types. On the smaller worlds, gas gets forced out of mineral compounds. Vulcanism and tectonism provide the heat for that, as well as radioactivity. But the major planetological forces originate in the core. And the core originates because the heavier elements, like iron, tend to migrate toward the center. We know Nike has some endowment of those. Perhaps more, even than the average planet of its age.

'Earth-sized planets have strong gravity. The migration is quick. The core forms in their youth. But Mars-sized worlds . . . the process has to be slow, don't you think? So much iron combines first in surface rocks that they are red. Nike shows traces of this still today. The midget planets can't outgas more than a wisp until their old age, when a core finally has taken shape.'

Tom shook his head in a stunned fashion. 'I didn't know. I took for granted – I mean, well, every Mars-type globe I ever saw or heard of had very little air – I reckoned they'd lost most o' their gas long ago.'

'There are no extremely ancient systems in the range that your travels have covered,' Yasmin deduced. 'Perhaps not in the whole Imperial territory. They aren't common in the spiral arms

170

of the galaxy, after all. So people never had much occasion to think about what they must be like.'

'Uh, what you been sayin', this theory . . . you learned it in school?'

'No. I didn't major in astronomy, just took some required basic courses. It simply appeared to me that some such idea is the only way to explain this system we're in.' Yasmin spread her hands. 'Maybe the professors at my university haven't heard of the idea either. The truth must have been known in Imperial times, but it could have been lost since, not having immediate practical value.' Her smile was sad. 'Who cares about pure science any more? What can you buy with it?

'Even the original colonists on Nike – Well, to them the fact must have been interesting, but not terribly important. They knew the planet was so old that it had lately gained an atmosphere and oxygen-liberating life. So old that its sun is on the verge of becoming a red giant. Already the hydrogen is exhausted at the core, the nuclear reactions are moving outward in a shell, the photosphere is expanding and cooling while the total energy output rises. But the sun won't be so huge that Nike is scorched for – oh, several million years. I suppose the colonists appreciated the irony here. But on the human time-scale, what difference did it make? No wonder their descendants have forgotten and think, like you, this has to be a young system.'

Tom caught her hands between his own. 'And . . . that's the reason . . . the real reason the sun's so rambunctious?' he asked hoarsely.

'Why, yes. Red giants are usually variable. This star is in a transition stage, I guess, and hasn't "found" its period yet.' Yasmin's smile turned warm. 'If I have taken your mind off your troubles, I am glad. But why do you care about the aspect of this planet ten megayears from now? I think best I do try to sleep, that I may help you a little tomorrow.'

Tom gulped. 'Kid,' he said, 'you don't know your own strength.'

'What's she been talking about?' Dagny demanded.

171

Tom told her. They spent the rest of the night laying plans.

* * *

Now and then a mid-morning sunbeam struck copper through the fog. But otherwise a wet, dripping, smoking mystery enclosed the barge. Despite its chill, Tom was glad. He didn't care to be interrupted by a strafing attack.

To be sure, the air force might triangulate on the radio emission of his ruined plane and drop a bomb. However –

He sat in the cockpit, looked squarely into the screen, and said, 'This is a parley. Agreed?'

'For the moment.' Karol Weyer gave him a smoldering return stare. 'I talked with Fish Aran.'

'And he made it clear to you, didn't he, about the lingo scramble? How often your Anglic and mine use the same word different? Well, let's not keep on with the farce. If anybody thinks t'other's said somethin' bad, let's call a halt and thresh out what was intended. Aye?'

Weyer tugged his beard. His countenance lost none of its sternness. 'You have yet to prove your good faith,' he said. 'After what harm you worked – '

'I'm ready to make that up to you. To your whole planet.'

Weyer cocked a brow and waited.

'S'pose you give us what we need to fix our ship,' Tom said. 'Some of it might be kind of expensive – copper and silver and such, and handicrafted because you haven't got the dies and jigs – but we can make some gold payment. Then let us go. I, or a trusty captain o' mine, will be back in a few months . . . uh, a few thirty-day periods.'

'With a host of friends to do business?'

'No. With camarados to 'change. Nike lived on trade under the Terran Empire. It can once more.'

'How do I know you speak truth?'

'Well, you'll have to take somethin' on my word. But listen. Kind of a bad storm last night, no? Did a lot o' damage, I'll bet. How much less would've been done if you'd been able to predict it? I can make that possible.' Tom paused before adding cynically, 'You can share the information with all Nike, or keep

172

it your national secret. Could be useful, if you feel like maybe the planet should have a really strong Emperor, name of Weyer, for instance.'

The Engineer leaned forward till his image seemed about to jump from the screen. 'How is this?'

Tom related what Yasmin had told him. 'No wonder your solar meteorologists never get anywhere,' he finished. 'They're usin' exactly the wrong mathematical model.'

Weyer's eyes dwelt long upon Tom. 'Are you giving this information away in hopes of my good will?' he said.

'No. As a free sample, to shake you loose from your notion that every chap who drops in from space is necessarily a hound o' hell. And likewise this. Camarado Weyer, your astronomers'll tell you my wife's idea makes sense. They'll be right glad to hear they've got an old star. But they'll need many years to work out the details by themselves. You know enough science to realise that, I'm sure. Now I can put you in touch with people that *already* know the details — that can come here, study the situation for a few weeks, and predict your weather like dice odds.

'That's my hole card. And you can only benefit by helpin' us leave. Don't think you can catch us and beat what we know out of us. First, we haven't got the information. Second we'll die before we become slaves, in any meanin' o' the word. If it don't look like we can get killed fightin' the men you send to catch us, why, we'll turn on our weapons on ourselves. Then all you've got is a spaceship that to you is nothin' but scrap metal.'

Weyer drew a sharp breath. But he remained cautious. 'This may be,' he said. 'Nonetheless, if I let you go, why should you bring learned people back to me?'

'Because it'll pay. I'm a trader and a warlord. The richer my markets, the stronger my allies, the better off I am.' Tom punched a forefinger at the screen. 'Get rid o' that conditioned reflex o' yours and think a bit instead. You haven't got much left that's worth anybody's lootin'. Why should I bother return-in' for that purpose? But your potential, that's somethin' else entirely. Given as simple a thing as reliable weather forecasts —

you'll save, in a generation, more wealth than the "friends" ever destroyed. And this's only one for instance o' what the outside universe can do for you. Man, you can't afford not to trust me!'

They argued, back and forth, for a long time. Weyer was intrigued but wary. Granted, Yasmin's revelation did provide evidence that Tom's folk were not utter savages like the last visitors from space. But the evidence wasn't conclusive. And even if it was, what guarantee existed that the strangers would bring the promised experts?

The wrangle ended as well as Tom had hoped, in an uneasy compromise. He and his wives would be brought to Sea Gate. They'd keep their sidearms. Though guarded, they were to be treated more or less as guests. Discussions would continue. If Weyer judged, upon better acquaintance, that they were indeed trustworthy, he would arrange for the ship's repair and release.

'But don't be long about makin' up your mind,' Tom warned, 'or it won't do us a lot o' good to come home.'

'Perhaps,' Weyer said, 'you can depart early if you leave a hostage.'

'You'll be all right?' Tom asked for the hundredth time.

'Indeed, my lord,' Yasmin said. She was more cheerful than he, bidding him good-by in the Engineer's castle. 'I'm used to their ways by now, comfortable in this environment – honestly! And you know how much in demand an outworlder is.'

'That could get dull. I won't be back too bloody soon, remember. What'll you do for fun?'

'Oh,' she said demurely. 'I plan to make arrangements with quite a number of men.'

'Stop teasin' me.' He hugged her close. 'I'm goin' to miss you.'

And so Roan Tom and Dagny Od's daughter left Nike.

He fretted somewhat about Yasmin, while *Firedrake* made the long flight back to Kraken, and while he mended his fences there, and while he voyaged back with his scholars and merchants. Had she really been joking, at the very last? She'd for sure gotten almighty friendly with Yanos Aran, and quite a few other young bucks. Tom was not obsessively jealous, but he could not afford to become a laughing stock.

He needn't have worried. When he made his triumphant landing at Sea Gate, he found that Yasmin had been charming, plausible, devious and, in short, had convinced several feudal lords of Nike that it was to their advantage that the rightful Shah be restored to the throne of Sassania. They commanded enough men to do the job. If the Krakeners could furnish weapons, training, and transportation –

Half delighted, half stunned, Tom said, 'So this time we had a lingo scramble without somethin' horrible happenin'? I don't believe it!'

'Happy endings do occur,' she murmured, and came to him. 'As now.'

And everyone was satisfied except, maybe, some few who went to lay a wreath upon a certain grave.

In the case of the King and Sir Christopher, however, a compliment was intended. A later era would have used the words 'awe-inspiring, stately, and ingeniously conceived.'

The histories of Sassania and Nike illustrate how precious knowledge was being lost and reclaimed on a hundred thousand worlds. Sundered by the dark between the stars, Technic civilization's wretched heirs no longer spoke the same language even when they shared a common tongue. Since reopening communications at whatever cost was the first step to lasting recovery, accounts of such problems dominate the annals of the post-Imperial era.

Freebooter that he was, Roan Tom's contributions to the process were haphazard and self-serving, yet his legendary exploits did light the way for more systematic explorers to follow. Natives of his birthworld Lochlann and his adopted homeworld Kraken played crucial roles in rediscovery expeditions during the next four centuries.

Time and again, these contact teams would find that simple ignorance was the least of the barriers to mutual understanding.

THE SHARING OF FLESH

Moru understood about guns. At least the tall strangers had demonstrated to their guides what the things that each of them carried at his hip could do in a flash and a flameburst. But he did not realize that the small objects they often moved about in their hands, while talking in their own language, were audiovisual transmitters. Probably, he thought they were fetishes.

Thus, when he killed Donli Sairn, he did so in full view of Donli's wife.

That was happenstance. Except for prearranged times at morning and evening of the planet's twenty-eight-hour day, the biologist, like his fellows, sent only to his computer. But because they had not been married long and were helplessly happy, Evalyth received his 'casts whenever she could get away from her own duties.

The coincidence that she was tuned in at that one moment was not great. There was little for her to do. As Militech of the expedition – she being from a half barbaric part of Kraken where the sexes had equal opportunities to learn arts of combat suitable to primitive environments – she had overseen the building of a compound; and she kept the routines of guarding it under a close eye. However, the inhabitants of Lokon were as cooperative with the visitors from heaven as mutual mysteriousness allowed. Every instinct and experience assured Evalyth Sairn that their reticence masked nothing except awe, with perhaps a wistful hope of friendship. Captain Jonafer agreed. Her position having thus become rather a sinecure, she was trying to learn enough about Donli's work to be a useful assistant after he returned from the lowlands.

Also, a medical test had lately confirmed that she was pregnant. She wouldn't tell him, she decided, not yet, over all those hundreds of kilometers, but rather when they lay again

177

together. Meanwhile, the knowledge that they had begun a new life made him a lodestar to her.

On the afternoon of his death she entered the biolab whistling. Outside, sunlight struck fierce and brass-colored on dusty ground, on prefab shacks huddled about the boat which had brought everyone and everything down from the orbit where *New Dawn* circled, on the parked flitters and gravsleds that took men around the big island that was the only habitable land on this globe, on the men and the women themselves. Beyond the stockade, plumy treetops, a glimpse of mud-brick buildings, a murmur of voices, and mutter of footfalls, a drift of bitter woodsmoke, showed that a town of several thousand people sprawled between here and Lake Zelo.

The bio-lab occupied more than half the structure where the Sairns lived. Comforts were few, when ships from a handful of cultures struggling back to civilization ranged across the ruins of empire. For Evalyth, though, it sufficed that this was their home. She was used to austerity anyway. One thing that had first attracted her to Donli, meeting him on Kraken, was the cheerfulness with which he, a man from Atheia, which was supposed to have retained or regained almost as many amenities as Old Earth knew in its glory, had accepted life in her gaunt grim country.

The gravity field here was 0.77 standard, less than two-thirds of what she had grown in. Her gait was easy through the clutter of apparatus and specimens. She was a big young woman, good-looking in the body, a shade too strong in the features for most men's taste outside her own folk. She had their blondness and, on legs and forearms their intricate tattoos; the blaster at her waist had come down through many generations. Otherwise she had abandoned Krakener costume for the plain coveralls of the expedition.

How cool and dim the shack was! She sighed with pleasure, sat down, and activated the receiver. As the image formed, three-dimensional in the air, and Donli's voice spoke, her heart sprang a little.

' – appears to be descended from a clover.'

The image was of plants with green trilobate leaves, scattered

178

low among the reddish native pseudo-grasses. It swelled as Donli brought the transmitter near so that the computer might record details for later analysis. Evalyth frowned, trying to recall what . . . Oh, yes. Clover was another of those life forms that man had brought with him from Old Earth, to more planets than anyone now remembered, before the Long Night fell. Often they were virtually unrecognizable; over thousands of years, evolution had fitted them to alien conditions, or mutation and genetic drift had acted on small initial populations in a nearly random fashion. No one on Kraken had known that pines and gulls and rhizobacteria were altered immigrants, until Donli's crew arrived and identified them. Not that he, or anybody from this part of the galaxy, had yet made it back to the mother world. But the Atheian data banks were packed with information, and so was Donli's dear curly head –

And there was his hand, huge in the field of view, gathering specimens. She wanted to kiss it. *Patience, patience* the officer part of her reminded the bride. *We're here to work. We've discovered one more lost colony, the most wretched one so far, sunken back to utter primitivism. Our duty is to advise the Board whether a civilizing mission is worthwhile, or whether the slender resources that the Allied Planets can spare had better be used elsewhere, leaving these people in their misery for another two or three hundred years. To make an honest report, we must study them, their cultures, their world. That's why I'm in the barbarian highlands and he's down in the jungle among out-and-out savages.*

Please finish soon, darling.

She heard Donli speak in the lowland dialect. It was a debased form of Lokonese, which in turn was remotely descended from Anglic. The expedition's linguists had unraveled the language in a few intensive weeks. Then all personnel took a brain-feed in it. Nonetheless, she admired how quickly her man had become fluent in the woods-runners' version, after mere days of conversation with them.

'Are we not coming to the place, Moru? You said the thing was close by our camp.'

'We are nearly arrived, man-from-the-clouds.'

179

A tiny alarm struck within Evalyth. What was going on? Donli hadn't left his companions to strike off alone with a native, had he? Rogar of Lokon had warned them to beware of treachery in those parts. But, to be sure, only yesterday the guides had rescued Haimie Fiell when he tumbled into a swift-running river . . . at some risk to themselves . . .

The view bobbed as the transmitter swung in Donli's grasp. It made Evalyth a bit dizzy. From time to time, she got glimpses of the broader setting. Forest crowded about a game trail, rust-colored leafage, brown trunks and branches, shadows beyond, the occasional harsh call of something unseen. She could practically feel the heat and dank weight of the atmosphere, smell the unpleasant pungencies. This world – which no longer had a name, except World, because the dwellers upon it had forgotten what the stars really were – was ill suited to colonization. The life it had spawned was often poisonous, always nutritionally deficient. With the help of species they had brought along, men survived marginally. The original settlers doubtless meant to improve matters. But then the breakdown came – evidence was that their single town had been missiled out of existence, a majority of the people with it – and resources were lacking to rebuild; the miracle was that anything human remained except bones.

'Now here, man-from-the-clouds.'

The swaying scene grew steady. Silence hummed from jungle to cabin. 'I do not see anything,' Donli said at length.

'Follow me. I show.'

Donli put his transmitter in the fork of a tree. It scanned him and Moru while they moved across a meadow. The guide looked childish beside the space traveler, barely up to his shoulder; an old child, though, near-naked body seamed with scars and lame in the right foot from some injury of the past, face wizened in a great black bush of hair and beard. He who could not hunt but could only fish and trap to support his family, was even more impoverished than his fellows. He must have been happy indeed when the flitter landed near their village and the strangers offered fabulous trade goods for a week or two of being shown around the countryside. Donli had projected the image of Moru's straw hut for Evalyth – the pitiful few possessions, the woman already worn out with toil, the surviving sons who, at ages said to be about seven or eight, which would equal twelve or thirteen standard years, were shriveled gnomes.

Rogar seemed to declare – the Lokonese tongue was by no means perfectly understood yet – that the low-landers would be less poor if they weren't such a vicious lot, tribe forever at war with tribe. *But really*, Evalyth thought, *what possible menace can they be?*

Moru's gear consisted of a loinstrap, a cord around his body for preparing snares, an obsidian knife, and a knapsack so woven and greased that it could hold liquids at need. The other men of his group, being able to pursue game and to win a share of booty by taking part in battles, were noticeably better off. They didn't look much different in person, however. Without room for expansion, the island populace must be highly inbred.

The dwarfish man squatted, parting a shrub with his hands. 'Here,' he grunted, and stood up again.

Evalyth knew well the eagerness that kindled in Donli. Nevertheless he turned around, smiled straight into the transmitter, and said in Atheian: 'Maybe you're watching, dearest. If so, I'd like to share this with you. It may be a bird's nest.'

She remembered vaguely that the existence of birds would be a ecologically significant datum. What mattered was what he had just said to her. 'Oh, yes, oh, yes!' she wanted to cry. But his group had only two receivers with them, and he wasn't carrying either.

She saw him kneel in the long, ill-colored vegetation. She saw him reach with the gentleness she also knew, into the shrub, easing its branches aside.

She saw Moru leap upon his back. The savage wrapped legs about Donli's middle. His left hand seized Donli's hair and pulled the head back. The knife flew back in his right.

Blood spurted from beneath Donli's jaw. He couldn't shout, not with his throat gaping open; he could only bubble and croak while Moru haggled the wound wider. He reached blindly for his gun. Moru dropped the knife and caught his arms; they rolled over in that embrace, Donli threshed and flopped in the spouting of his own blood. Moru hung on. The brush trembled around them and hid them, until Moru rose red and dripping, painted, panting, and Evalyth screamed into the transmitter beside her, into the universe, and she kept on screaming and fought them when they tried to take her away from the scene in the meadow where Moru went about his butcher's work, until something stung her with coolness and she toppled into the bottom of the universe whose stars had all gone out forever.

Haimie Fiell said through white lips: 'No, of course we didn't know till you alerted us. He and that – creature – were several kilometers from our camp. *Why* didn't you let us go after him right away?'

'Because of what we'd seen on the transmission,' Captain Jonafer replied. 'Sairn was irretrievably dead. You could've been ambushed, arrows in the back or something, pushing down those narrow trails. Best stay where you are, guarding each other, till we got a vehicle to you.'

Fiell looked past the big gray-haired man, out the door of the command hut, to the stockade and the unpitying noon sky. 'But what that little monster was doing meanwhile – 'Abruptly he closed his mouth.

With equal haste, Jonafer said: 'The other guides ran away, you have told me, as soon as they sensed you were angry. I've just had a report from Kallaman. His team flitted to the village. It's deserted. The whole tribe's pulled up stakes. Afraid of our revenge, evidently. Though it's no large chore to move, when you can carry your household goods on your back and weave a new house in a day.'

Evalyth leaned forward. 'Stop evading me,' she said. 'What did Moru do with Donli that you might have prevented if you'd arrived in time?'

Fiell continued to look past her. Sweat gleamed in droplets on his forehead. 'Nothing, really,' he mumbled. 'Nothing that mattered . . . once the murder itself had been committed.'

'I meant to ask you what kind of services you want for him, Lieutenant Sairn,' Jonafer said to her. 'Should the ashes be buried here, or scattered in space after we leave, or brought home?'

Evalyth turned her full gaze upon him. 'I never authorized that he be cremated, Captain,' she said slowly.

'No, but – Well, be realistic. You were first under anesthesia, then heavy sedation, while we recovered the body. Time had passed. We've no facilities for, um, cosmetic repair, nor any extra refrigeration space, and in this heat – '

Since she had been let out of sickbay, there had been a kind of numbness in Evalyth. She could not entirely comprehend the fact that Donli was gone. It seemed as if at any instant yonder doorway would fill with him, sunlight across his shoulders, and he would call to her, laughing, and console her for a meaningless nightmare she had had. That was the effect of the psychodrugs, she knew and damned the kindliness of the medic.

She felt almost glad to feel a slow rising anger. It meant the drugs were wearing off. By evening she would be able to weep.

'Captain,' she said. 'I saw him killed. I've seen deaths before, some of them quite messy. We do not mask the truth on Kraken. You've cheated me of my right to lay my man out and close his eyes. You will not cheat me of my right to obtain justice. I demand to know exactly what happened.'

Jonafer's fists knotted on his desktop. 'I can hardly stand to tell you.'

'But you shall, Captain.'

'All right! All right!' Jonafer shouted. The words leaped out like bullets. 'We saw the thing transmitted. He stripped Donli, hung him up by the heels from a tree, bled him into that knapsack. He cut off the genitals and threw them in with the blood. He opened the body and took heart, lungs, liver, kidneys, thyroid, prostate, pancreas, and loaded them up too, and ran off into the woods. Do you wonder why we didn't let you see what was left?'

'The Lokonese warned us against the jungle dwellers,' Fiell said dully. 'We should have listened. But they seemed like pathetic dwarfs. And they did rescue me from the river. When Donli asked about the birds – described them, you know, and asked if anything like that was known – Moru said yes, but they were rare and shy; our gang would scare them off; but if one man would come along with him, he could find a nest and they

183

might see the bird. A house he called it, but Donli thought he meant a nest. Or so he told us. It'd been a talk with Moru when they happened to be a ways offside, in sight but out of earshot. Maybe that should have alerted us, maybe we should have asked the other tribesmen. But we did not see any reason to – I mean, Donli was bigger, stronger, armed with a blaster. What savage would dare attack him? And anyway, they *had* been friendly, downright frolicsome after they got over their initial fear of us, and they'd shown as much eagerness for further contact as anybody here in Lokon has, and – ' His voice trailed off.

'Did he steal tools or weapons?' Evalyth asked.

'No,' Jonafer said. 'I have everything your husband was carrying, ready to give you.'

Fiell said: 'I don't think it was an act of hatred. Moru must have had some superstitious reason.'

Jonafer nodded. 'We can't judge him by our standards.'

'By whose, then?' Evalyth retorted. Supertranquilizer or no, she was surprised at the evenness of her own tone. 'I'm from Kraken, remember. I'll not let Donli's child be born and grow up knowing he was murdered and no one tried to do justice for him.'

'You can't take revenge on an entire tribe,' Jonafer said.

'I don't mean to. But, Captain, the personnel of this expedition are from several different planets, each with its characteristic societies. The articles specifically state that the essential mores of every member shall be respected. I want to be relieved of my regular duties until I have arrested the killer of my husband and done justice upon him.'

Jonafer bent his head. I have to grant that,' he said low.

Evalyth rose. 'Thank you, gentlemen,' she said. 'If you will excuse me, I'll commence my investigation at once.'

– While she was still a machine, before the drugs wore off.

In the drier, cooler uplands, agriculture had remained possible after the colony otherwise lost civilization. Fields and orchards, painstakingly cultivated with neolithic tools, supported a scattering of villages and the capital town Lokon.

Its people bore a family resemblance to the forest dwellers.

184

Few settlers indeed could have survived to become the ancestors of this world's humanity. But the highlanders were better nourished, bigger, straighter. They wore gaily dyed tunics and sandals. The well-to-do added jewelry of gold and silver. Hair was braided, chins kept shaven. Folk walked boldly, without the savages' constant fear of ambush, and talked merrily.

To be sure, this was only strictly true of the free. While *New Dawn's* anthropologists had scarcely begun to unravel the ins and outs of the culture, it had been obvious from the first that Lokon kept a large slave class. Some were sleek household servants. More toiled meek and naked in the fields, the quarries, the mines, under the lash of overseers and the guard of soldiers whose spearheads and swords were of ancient Imperial metal. But none of the space travelers was unduly shocked. They had seen worse elsewhere. Historical data banks described places in olden time called Athens, India, America.

Evalyth strode down twisted, dusty streets, between the gaudily painted walls of cubical, windowless adobe houses. Commoners going about their tasks made respectful salutes. Although no one feared any longer that the strangers meant harm, she did tower above the tallest man, her hair was colored like metal and her eyes like the sky, she bore lightning at her waist and none knew what other godlike powers.

Today soldiers and noblemen also genuflected, while slaves went on their faces. Where she appeared, the chatter and clatter of everyday life vanished; the business of the market plaza halted when she passed the booths; children ceased their games and fled; she moved in silence akin to the silence in her soul. Under the sun and the snowcone of Mount Burus, horror brooded. For by now Lokon knew that a man from the stars had been slain by a lowland brute; and what would come of that?

Word must have gone ahead to Rogar, though, since he awaited her in his house by Lake Zelo next to the Sacred Place. He was not king or council president or high priest, but he was something of all three, and it was he who dealt most with the strangers.

His dwelling was the usual kind, larger than average but dwarfed by the adjacent walls. Those enclosed a huge compound filled with buildings, where none of the outworlders had been admitted. Guards in scarlet robes and grotesquely carved wooden helmets stood always at its gates. Today their number was doubled, and others flanked Rogar's door. The lake shone like polished steel at their backs. The trees along the shore looked equally rigid.

Rogar's major-domo, a fat elderly slave, prostrated himself in the entrance as Evalyth neared. 'If the heaven-borne will deign to follow this unworthy one, *Klev* Rogar is within – ' The guards dipped their spears to her. Their eyes wide and frightened.

Like the other houses, this turned inward. Rogar sat on a dais in a room opening on a courtyard. It seemed doubly cool and dim by contrast with the glare outside. She could scarcely discern the frescos on the walls or the patterns on the carpet; they were crude art anyway. Her attention focused on Rogar. He did not rise, that not being a sign of respect here. Instead, he bowed his grizzled head above folded hands. The major-domo offered her a bench, and Rogar's chief wife set a bombilla of herb tea by her before vanishing.

'Be greeted, *Klev*,' Evalyth said formally.

'Be greeted, heaven-borne.' Alone now, shadowed from the cruel sun, they observed a ritual period of silence.

Then: 'This is terrible what has happened, heaven-borne,' Rogar said. 'Perhaps you do not know that my white robe and bare feet signify mournings as for one of my own blood.'

'That is well done,' Evalyth said. 'We shall remember.'

The man's dignity faltered. 'You understand that none of us had anything to do with the evil, do you not? The savages are our enemies too. They are vermin. Our ancestors caught some and made them slaves, but they are good for nothing else. I warned your friends not to go down among those we have not tamed.'

'Their wish was to do so,' Evalyth replied. 'Now my wish is to get revenge for my man.' She didn't know if this language included a word for justice. No matter. Because of the drugs, which heightened the logical faculties while they muffled the emotions, she was speaking Lokonese quite well enough for her purposes.

'We can get soldiers and help you kill as many as you choose,' Rogar said.

'Not needful. With this weapon at my side I alone can destroy more than your army might. I want your counsel and help in a different matter. How can I find him who slew my man?'

Rogar frowned. 'The savages can vanish into trackless jungles, heaven-borne.'

'Can they vanish from other savages, though?'

'Ah! Shrewdly thought, heaven-borne. Those tribes are endlessly at each other's throats. If we can make contact with one, its hunters will soon learn for you where the killer's people have taken themselves.' His scowl deepened. 'But he must have gone from them, to hide until you have departed our land. A single man might be impossible to find. Lowlanders are good at hiding, of necessity.'

'What do you mean by necessity?'

Rogar showed surprise at her failure to grasp what was obvious to him. 'Why, consider a man out hunting,' he said. 'He cannot go with companions after every kind of game, or the noise and scent would frighten it away. So he is often alone in the jungle. Someone from another tribe may well set upon him. A man stalked and killed is just as useful as one slain in open war.'

'Why this incessant fighting?'

Rogar's look of bafflement grew stronger. 'How else shall they get human flesh?'

'But they do not live on that!'

'No, surely not, except as needed. But that need comes many times as you know. Their wars are their chief way of taking men; booty is good too, but not the main reason to fight. He who slays, owns the corpse, and naturally divides it solely among his close kin. Not everyone is lucky in battle. Therefore these who did not chance to kill in a war may well go hunting on their own, two or three of them together hoping to find a single man from a different tribe. And that is why a lowlander is good at hiding.'

Evalyth did not move or speak. Rogar drew a long breath and continued trying to explain: 'Heaven-borne, when I heard the evil news, I spoke long with men from your company. They told me what they had seen from afar by the wonderful means you command. Thus it is clear to me what happened. This guide — what is his name? Yes, Moru — he is a cripple. He had no hope of killing himself a man except by treachery. When he saw that chance, he took it.'

He ventured a smile. 'That would never happen in the highlands,' he declared. 'We do not fight wars, save when we are attacked, nor do we hunt our fellowmen as if they were animals. Like yours, ours is a civilized race.' His lips drew back from startlingly white teeth. 'But heaven-borne, your man was slain. I propose we take vengeance, not simply on the killer if we catch him, but on his tribe, which we can certainly find as you suggested. That will teach all the savages to beware of their betters. Afterward we can share the flesh, half to your people, half to mine.'

Evalyth could only know an intellectual astonishment. Yet she had the feeling somehow of having walked off a cliff. She stared through the shadows, into the grave old face, and after a long time she heard herself whisper: 'You . . . also . . . here . . . eat men?'

'Slaves,' Rogar said. 'No more than required. One of them will do for four boys.'

Her hand dropped to her gun. Rogar sprung up in alarm. 'Heaven-borne,' he exclaimed. 'I told you we are civilized. Never fear attack from any of us! We – we –'

She rose too, high above him. Did he read judgment in her gaze? Was the terror that snatched him on behalf of his whole people? He cowered from her, sweating and shuddering. 'Heaven-borne, let me show you, let me take you into the Sacred Place, even if you are no initiate . . . for surely you are akin to the gods, surely the gods will not be offended – Come, let me show you how it is, let me prove we have no will and no *need* to be your enemies – '

There was the gate that Rogar opened for her in that massive wall. There were the shocked countenances of the guards and loud promises of many sacrifices to appease the Powers. There was the stone pavement beyond, hot and hollowly resounding underfoot. There were the idols grinning around a central temple. There was the house of the acolytes who did the work and who shrank in fear when they saw their master conduct a foreigner in. There were the slave barracks.

'See, heaven-borne, they are well treated, are they not? We do have to crush their hands and feet when we choose them as children for this service. Think how dangerous it would be otherwise, hundreds of boys and young men in here. But we treat them kindly unless they misbehave. Are they not fat? Their own Holy Food is especially honorable, bodies of men of all degree who have died in their full strength. We teach them that they will live on in those for whom they are slain. Most are content with that, believe me, heaven-borne. Ask them yourself ... though remember, they grow dull-witted, with nothing to do year after year. We slay them quickly, cleanly, at the beginning of each summer – no more than we must for that year's crop of boys entering into manhood, one slave for four boys, no more than that. And it is a most beautiful rite, with days of feasting and merry-making afterward. Do you understand now, heaven-borne? You have nothing to fear from us. We are not savages, warring and raiding and skulking to get our man-flesh. We are civilized – not godlike in your fashion, no, I dare not claim that, do not be angry – but civilized – surely worthy of your friendship, are we not? Are we not, heaven-borne?'

* * *

Chena Darnard, who headed the cultural anthropology team, told her computer to scan its data bank. Like the others, it was a portable, its memory housed in *New Dawn*. At the moment the spaceship was above the opposite hemisphere, and perceptible time passed while beams went back and forth along the strung-out relay units.

Chena leaned back and studied Evalyth across her desk. The Krakener girl sat so quietly. It seemed unnatural, despite the drugs in her bloodstream retaining some power. To be sure, Evalyth was of aristocratic descent in a warlike society. Furthermore, hereditary psychological as well as physiological differences might exist on the different worlds. Not much was known about that, apart from extreme cases like Gwydion – or this planet? Regardless, Chena thought, it would be better if Evalyth gave way to simple shock and grief.

'Are you quite certain of your facts, dear?' the anthropologist asked as gently as possible. 'I mean, while this island alone is habitable, it's large, the topography is rugged, communications are primitive, my group has already identified scores of distinct cultures.'

'I questioned Rogar for more than an hour,' Evalyth replied in the same flat voice, looking out of the same flat eyes as before. 'I know interrogation techniques, and he was badly rattled. He talked.

'The Lokonese themselves are not as backward as their technology. They've lived for centuries with savages threatening their borderlands. It's made them develop a good intelligence network. Rogar described its functioning to me in detail. It can't help but keep them reasonably well informed about everything that goes on. And, while tribal customs do vary tremendously, the cannibalism is universal. That is why none of the Lokonese thought to mention it to us. They took for granted that we had our own ways of providing human meat.'

'People have, m-m-m, latitude in those methods?'

'Oh, yes. Here they breed slaves for the purpose. But most lowlanders have too skimpy an economy for that. Some of them use war and murder. Among others, they settled it within the tribe by annual combats. Or – Who cares? The fact is that, everywhere in this country, in whatever fashion it may be, the boys undergo a puberty rite that involves eating an adult male.'

Chena bit her lip. 'What in the name of chaos might have started it? Computer! Have you scanned?'

'Yes,' said the machine voice out of the case on her desk. 'Data on cannibalism in man are comparatively sparse, because it is a rarity. On all planets hitherto known to us it is banned and has been throughout their history, although it is sometimes considered forgiveable as an emergency measure when no alternative means of preserving life is available. Very limited forms of what might be called ceremonial cannibalism have

190

occurred, as for example the drinking of minute amounts of each other's blood in pledging oath brotherhood among the Falkens of Lochlann – '

'Never mind that,' Chena said. A tautness in her throat thickened her tone. 'Only here, it seems, have they degenerated so far that – Or is it degeneracy? Reversion, perhaps? What about Old Earth?'

'Information is fragmentary. Aside from what was lost during the Long Night, knowledge is under the handicap that the last primitive societies there vanished before interstellar travel begins. But certain data collected by ancient historians and scientists remain.

'Cannibalism was an occasional part of human sacrifice. As a rule, victims were left uneaten. But in a minority of regions, the bodies, or selected portions of them, were consumed, either by a special class, or by the community as a whole. Generally this was regarded as theophagy. Thus, the Aztecs of Mexico offered thousands of individuals annually to their gods. The requirement of doing this forced them to provoke wars and rebellions, which in turn made it easy for the eventual Europeans conqueror to get native allies. The majority of prisoners were simply slaughtered, their hearts given directly to the idols. But in at least one cult the body was divided among the worshippers.

'Cannibalism could be a form of magic, too. By eating a person, one supposedly acquired his virtues. This was the principal motive of the cannibals of Africa and Polynesia. Contemporary observers did report that the meals were relished, but that is easy to understand, especially in protein-poor areas.

'The sole recorded instance of systematic nonceremonial cannibalism was among the Carib Indians of America. They ate man because they preferred man. They were especially fond of babies and used to capture women from the other tribes for breeding stock. Male children of these slaves were generally gelded to make them docile and tender. In large part because of strong aversion to such practices, the Europeans exterminated the Caribs to the last man.'

The report stopped. Chena grimaced. 'I can sympathize with the Europeans,' she said.

Evalyth might once have raised her brows; but her face stayed as wooden as her speech. 'Aren't you supposed to be an objective scientist?'

'Yes. Yes. Still, there is such a thing as value judgment. And they did kill Donli.'

'Not they. One of them. I shall find him.'

'He's nothing but a creature of his culture, dear, sick with his whole race.' Chena drew a breath, struggling for calm. 'Obviously, the sickness has become a behavioral basic,' she said. 'I daresay it originated in Lokon. Cultural radiation is practically always from the more to the less advanced peoples. And on a single island, after centuries, no tribe has escaped the infection. The Lokonese later elaborated and rationalized the practice. The savages left its cruelty naked. But highlander or lowlander, their way of life is founded on that particular human sacrifice.'

'Can they be taught differently?' Evalyth asked without real interest.

'Yes. In time. In theory. But – well, I do know enough about what happened on Old Earth, and elsewhere, when advanced societies undertook to reform primitive ones. The entire structure was destroyed. It had to be.

'Think of the result, if we told these people to desist from their puberty rite. They wouldn't listen. They couldn't. They *must* have grandchildren. They *know* a boy won't become a man unless he has eaten part of a man. We'd have to conquer them, kill most, make sullen prisoners of the rest. And when the next crop of boys did in fact mature, without the magic food . . . what then? Can you imagine the demoralization, the sense of utter inferiority, the loss of that tradition which is the core of every personal identity? It might be kinder to bomb this island sterile.'

Chena shook her head. 'No,' she said harshly, 'the single decent way for us to proceed would be gradually. We could send missionaries. By their precept and example, we could start the natives phasing out their custom after two or three generations . . . And we can't afford such an effort. Not for a long time to come. Not with so many other worlds in the galaxy, so much worthier of what little help we can give. I am going to recommend this planet be left alone.'

192

Evalyth considered her for a moment before asking: 'Isn't that partly because of your own reaction?'

'Yes,' Chena admitted. 'I cannot overcome my disgust. And I, as you pointed out, am supposed to be professionally broadminded. So even if the Board tried to recruit missionaries, I doubt if they'd succeed.' She hesitated. 'You yourself, Evalyth – '

The Krakener rose. 'My emotions don't matter,' she said. 'My duty does. Thank you for your help.' She turned on her heel and went with military strides out of the cabin.

* * *

The chemical barriers were crumbling. Evalyth stood for a moment before the little building that had been hers and Donli's, afraid to enter. The sun was low, so that the compound was filling with shadows. A thing leathery-winged and serpentine cruised silently overhead. From outside the stockade drifted sounds of feet, foreign voices, the whine of a wooden flute. The air was cooling. She shivered. Their home would be too hollow.

Someone approached. She recognized the person glimpse-wise, Alsabeta Mondain from Neuvamerica. Listening to her well-meant foolish condolences would be worse than going inside. Evalyth took the last three steps and slid the door shut behind her.

Donli will not be here again. Eternally.

But the cabin proved not to be empty to him. Rather, it was too full. That chair where he used to sit, reading that worn volume of poetry, which she could not understand and teased him about, that table across which he had toasted her and tossed kisses, that closet where his clothes hung, that scuffed pair of slippers, that bed – it screamed of him. Evalyth went fast into the laboratory section and drew the curtain that separated it from the living quarters. Rings rattled along the rod. The noise was monstrous in twilight.

She closed her eyes and fists and stood breathing hard. *I will not go soft*, she declared. *You always said you loved me for my strength – among numerous other desirable features, you'd add with your slow grin, but I remember that yet – and I don't aim to let slip anything that you loved.*

I've got to get busy, she told Donli's child. *The expedition command is pretty sure to act on Chena's urging and haul mass for home. We've not many days to avenge your father.*

Her eyes snapped open. *What am I doing,* she thought, bewildered, *talking to a dead man and an embryo?*

She turned on the overhead fluoro and went to the computer. It was made no differently from the other portables. Donli had used it. But she could not look away from the unique scratches and bumps on that square case, as she could not escape his microscope, chemanalyzers, chromosome tracer, biological specimens ... She seated herself. A drink would have been very welcome, except that she needed clarity. 'Activate!' she ordered.

The On light glowed yellow. Evalyth tugged her chin, searching for words. 'The objective,' she said at length, 'is to trace a lowlander who has consumed several kilos of flesh and blood from one of this party, and afterward vanished into the jungle. The killing took place about sixty hours ago. How can he be found?'

The least hum answered her. She imagined the links; to the master in the ferry, up past the sky to the nearest orbiting relay unit, to the next, to the next, around the bloated belly of the planet, by ogre sun and inhuman stars, until the pulses reached the mother ship; then down to an unliving brain that routed the question to the appropriate data bank; then to the scanners, whose resonating energies flew from molecule to distorted molecule, identifying more bits of information than it made sense to number, data garnered from hundreds or thousands of entire worlds, data preserved through the wreck of Empire and the dark ages that followed, data going back to an Old Earth that perhaps no longer existed. She shied from the thought and wished herself back on dear stern Kraken. *We will go there,* she promised Donli's child. *You will dwell apart from these too many machines and grow up as the gods meant you should.*

'Query,' said the artificial voice. 'Of what origin was the victim of this assault?'

Evalyth had to wet her lips before she could reply: 'Atheian. He was Donli Sairn, your master.'

'In that event, the possibility of tracking the desired local inhabitant may exist. The odds will now be computed. In the interim, do you wish to know the basis of the possibility?'

'Y-yes.'

'Native Atheian biochemistry developed in a manner quite parallel to Earth's,' said the voice, 'and the early colonists had no difficulty in introducing terrestrial species. Thus they enjoyed a friendly environment, where population soon grew sufficiently large to obviate the danger of racial change through mutation and/or genetic drift. In addition, no selection pressure tended to force change. Hence the modern Atheian human is little different from his ancestors of Earth, on which account his physiology and biochemistry are known in detail.

'This has been essentially the case on most colonized planets for which records are available. Where different breeds of men have arisen, it has generally been because the original settlers were highly selected groups. Randomness, and evolutionary adaptation to new conditions, have seldom produced radical changes in biotype. For example, the robustness of the average Krakener is a response to comparatively high gravity; his size aids him in resisting cold, his fair complexion is helpful beneath a poor sun in ultraviolet. But his ancestors were people who already had the natural endowments for such a world. His deviations from their norm are not extreme. They do not preclude his living on more Earth-like planets or interbreeding with the inhabitants of these.

'Occasionally, however, larger variations have occurred. They appear to be due to a small original population or to unterrestroid conditions or both. The population may have been small because the planet could not support more, or have become small as the result of hostile action when the Empire fell. In the former case, genetic accidents had a chance to be significant; in the latter, radiation produced a high rate of mutant births among survivors. The variations are less apt to be in gross anatomy than in subtle endocrine and enzymatic qualities, which affect the physiology and psychology. Well known cases include the reaction of the Gwydiona to nicotine and certain indoles, and the requirement of the Ifrians for trace amounts of lead. Sometimes the inhabitants of two planets are actually intersterile because of their differences.

'While this world has hitherto received the sketchiest of examinations – ' Evalyth was yanked out of a reverie into which the lecture had led her ' – certain facts are clear. Few terrestrial species have flourished; no doubt others were introduced originally, but died off after the technology to maintain them was lost. Man has thus been forced to depend on autochthonous life for the major part of his food. This life is deficient in various elements of human nutrition. For example, the only Vitamin C appears to be in immigrant plants; Sairn observed that the people consume large amounts of grass and leaves from those species, and that fluoroscopic pictures indicate this practice has measurably modified the digestive tract. No one would supply skin, blood, sputum, or similar samples, not even from corpses.' *Afraid of magic,* Evalyth thought drearily, *yes, they're back to that too.* 'But intensive analysis of the usual meat animals shows these to be under-supplied with three essential amino acids, and human adaptation to this must have involved considerable change on the cellular and sub-cellular levels. The probable type and extent of such change are computable.

'The calculations are now complete.' As the computer resumed, Evalyth gripped the arms of her chair and could not breathe. 'While the answer is subject to fair probability of success. In effect, Atheian flesh is alien here. It can be metabolized, but the body of the local consumer will excrete certain compounds, and these will import a characteristic odor to skin and breath as well as to urine and feces. The chance is good that it will be detectable by neo-Freeholder technique at distances of several kilometers, after sixty or seventy hours. But since the molecules in question are steadily being degraded and dissipated, speed of action is recommended.'

I am going to find Donli's murderer. Darkness roared around Evalyth.

'Shall the organisms be ordered for you and given the appropriate search program?' asked the voice. 'They can be on hand in an estimated three hours.'

'Yes,' she stammered. 'Oh, please – have you any other . . . other . . . advice?'

'The man ought not to be killed out of hand, but brought here for examination, if for no other reason than in order that the scientific ends of the expedition may be served.'

That's a machine talking, Evalyth cried. *It's designed to help research. Nothing more. But it was his.* And its answer was so altogether Donli that she could no longer hold back her tears.

The single big moon rose nearly full, shortly after sundown. It drowned most stars; the jungle beneath was cobbled with silver and dappled with black; the snowcone of Mount Burus floated unreal at the unseen edge of the world. Wind slid around Evalyth where she crouched on her gravsled; it was full of wet acrid odors, and felt cold though it was not, and chuckled at her back. Somewhere something screeched, every few minutes, and something else cawed reply.

She scowled at her position indicators, aglow on the control panel. Curses and chaos, Moru had to be in this area! He could not have escaped from the valley on foot in the time available, and her search pattern had practically covered it. If she ran out of bugs before she found him, must she assume he was dead? They ought to be able to find his body regardless, ought they not? Unless it was buried deep. Here. She brought the sled over to hover, took the next phial off the rack and stood up to open it.

The bugs came out many and tiny, like smoke in the moonlight. Another failure?

No! Wait! Were not those motes dancing back together, into a streak barely visible under the moon, and vanishing downward? Heart thuttering, she turned to the indicator. Its neurodetector antenna was not aimlessly wobbling, but pointed straight west-northwest, declination thirty-two degrees below horizontal. Only a concentration of the bugs could make it behave like that. And only the particular mixture of molecules to which the bugs had been presensitized, in several parts per million or better, would make them converge on the source.

'Ya-a-ah! She couldn't help the one hawk-yell. But thereafter she bit her lips shut – blood trickled unnoticed down her chin – and drove the sled in silence.

197

The distance was a mere few kilometers. She came to a halt above an opening in the forest. Pools of scummy water gleamed in its rank growth. The trees made a solid-seeming wall around. Evalyth clapped her night goggles down off her helmet and over her eyes. A lean-to became visible. It was hastily woven from vines and withes, huddled against a part of the largest trees to let their branches hide it from the sky. The bugs were entering.

Evalyth lowered her sled to a meter off the ground and got to her feet again. A stun pistol slid from its sheath into her right hand. Her left rested on the blaster.

Moru's two sons groped from the shelter. The bugs whirled around them, a mist that blurred their outlines. *Of course*, Evalyth realized, nonetheless shocked into a higher hatred. *I should have known they did the actual devouring.* More than ever did they resemble gnomes – skinny limbs, big heads, the pot bellies of undernourishment. Krakener boys of their age would have twice their bulk and be noticeably on the way to becoming men. These nude bodies belonged to children, except that they had the grotesqueness of eld.

The parents followed them, ignored by the entranced bugs. The mother wailed. Evalyth identified a few words. 'What is the matter, what are those things – oh, help – ' But her gaze was locked upon Moru.

Limping out of the hutch, stooped to clear its entrance, he made her think of some huge beetle crawling from an offal heap. But she would know that bushy head though her brain were coming apart. He carried a stone blade, surely the one that had hacked up Donli. *I will take it away from him, and the hand with it*, Evalyth wept. *I will keep him alive while I dismantle him with these my own hands, and in between times he can watch me flay his repulsive spawn.*

The wife's scream broke through. She had seen the metal thing, and the giant that stood on its platform, with skull and eyes shimmering beneath the moon.

'I have come for you who killed my man,' Evalyth said.

The mother screamed anew and cast herself before the boys. The father tried to run around in front of her, but his lame foot twisted under him, and he fell into a pool. As he struggled out of its muck, Evalyth shot the woman. No sound was heard; she folded and lay moveless. 'Run!' Moru shouted. He tried to charge the sled. Evalyth twisted a control stick. Her vehicle whipped in a circle, heading off the boys. She shot them from above, where Moru couldn't quite reach her.

He knelt beside the nearest, took the body in his arms and looked upward. The moonlight poured relentlessly across him. 'What can you now do to me?' he called.

She stunned him too, landed, got off and quickly hogtied the four of them. Loading them aboard, she found them lighter than she had expected.

Sweat had sprung forth upon her, until her coverall stuck dripping to her skin. She began to shake, as if with fever. Her ears buzzed. 'I would have destroyed you,' she said. Her voice sounded remote and unfamiliar. A still more distant part wondered why she bothered speaking to the unconscious, in her own tongue at that. 'I wish you hadn't acted the way you did. That made me remember what the computer said, about Donli's friends needing you for study.

'You're too good a chance, I suppose. After your doings, we have the right under Allied rules to make prisoners of you, and none of his friends are likely to get maudlin about your feelings.

'Oh, they won't be inhuman. A few cell samples, a lot of tests, anesthesia where necessary, nothing harmful, nothing but a clinical examination as thorough as facilities allow.

'No doubt you'll be better fed than at any time before, and no doubt the medics will find some pathologies they can cure for you. In the end, Moru, they'll release your wife and children.'

She stared into his horrible face.

'I am pleased,' she said, 'that to you, who won't comprehend what is going on, it will be a bad experience. And when they are finished, Moru, I will insist on having you at least, back. They can't deny me that. Why, your tribe itself has, in effect, cast you out. Right? My colleagues won't let me do more than kill you, I'm afraid, but on this I will insist.'

She gunned the engine and started toward Lokon, as fast as

possible, to arrive while she felt able to be satisfied with that much.

* * *

And the days without him and the days without him.

The nights were welcome. If she had not worked herself quite to exhaustion, she could take a pill. He rarely returned in her dreams. But she had to get through each day and would not drown him in drugs.

Luckily, there was a good deal of work involved in preparing to depart, when the expedition was short-handed and on short notice. Gear must be dismantled, packed, ferried to the ship, and stowed. *New Dawn* herself must be readied, numerous systems recommissioned and tested. Her militechnic training qualified Evalyth to double as mechanic, boat jockey, or loading gang boss. In addition, she kept up the routines of defense in the compound.

Captain Jonafer objected mildly to this. 'Why bother, Lieutenant? The locals are scared blue of us. They've heard what you did – and this coming and going through the sky, robots and heavy machinery in action, floodlights after dark – I'm having trouble persuading them not to abandon their town!'

'Let them,' she snapped. 'Who cares?'

'We did not come here to ruin them, Lieutenant.'

'No. In my judgment, though, Captain, they'll be glad to ruin us if we present the least opportunity. Imagine what special virtues *your* body must have.'

Jonafer sighed and gave in. But when she refused to receive Rogar the next time she was planetside, he ordered her to do so and be civil.

The *Klev* entered the biolab section – she would not have him in her living quarters – with a gift held in both hands, a sword of Imperial metal. She shrugged: no doubt a museum would be pleased to get the thing. 'Lay it on the floor,' she told him.

Because she occupied the single chair, he stood. He looked little and old in his robe. 'I came,' he whispered, 'to say how we of Lokon rejoice that the heaven-borne has won her revenge.'

'Is winning it,' she corrected.

200

He could not meet her eyes. She stared moodily at his faded hair. 'Since the heaven-borne could . . . easily . . . find those she wished . . . she knows the truth in the hearts of us of Lokon, that we never intended harm to her folk.'

That didn't seem to call for an answer.

His fingers twisted together. 'Then why do you forsake us?' he went on. 'When first you came, when we had come to know you and you spoke our speech, you said you would stay for many moons, and after you would come others to teach and trade. Our hearts rejoiced. It was not alone the goods you might someday let us buy, nor that your wisemen talked of ways to end hunger, sickness, danger, and sorrow. No, our jubilation and thankfulness were most for the wonders you opened. Suddenly the world was made great, that had been so narrow. And now you are going away. I have asked, when I dared, and those of your men who will speak to me say none will return. How have we offended you, and how may it be made right, heaven-borne?'

'You can stop treating your fellow men like animals,' Evalyth got past her teeth.

'I have gathered . . . somewhat . . . that you from the stars say it is wrong what happens in the Sacred Place. But we only do it once in our lifetimes, heaven-borne, and because we must!'

'You have no need.'

Rogar went on his hands and knees before her. 'Perhaps the heaven-borne are thus,' he pleaded, 'but we are merely men. If our sons do not get the manhood, they will never beget children of their own, and the last of us will die alone in a world of death, with none to crack his skull and let the soul out – ' He dared glance up at her. What he saw made him whimper and crawl backwards into the sun-glare.

Later Chena Darnard sought Evalyth. They had a drink and talked around the subject for a while, until the anthropologist plunged in: 'You were pretty hard on the sachem, weren't you?'

'How'd you – Oh.' The Krakener remembered that the interview had been taped, as was done whenever possible for later study. 'What was I supposed to do, kiss his maneating mouth?'

201

'No.' Chena winced. 'I suppose not.'

'Your signature heads the list, on the official recommendation that we quit this planet.'

'Yes. But – now I don't know. I was repelled. I am. However – I've been observing the medical team working on those prisoners of yours. Have you?'

'No.'

'You should. The way they cringe and shriek and reach to each other when they're strapped down in the lab and cling together afterward in their cell.'

'They aren't suffering any pain or mutilation, are they?'

'Of course not. But can they believe it when their captors say they won't? They can't be tranquilized while under study, you know, if the results are to be valid. Their fear of the absolutely unknown – Well, Evalyth, I had to stop observing. I couldn't take any more.' Chena gave the other a long stare. 'You might, though.'

Evalyth shook her head. 'I don't gloat. I'll shoot the murderer because my family honor demands it. The rest can go free, even the boys. Even in spite of what they ate.' She poured herself a stiff draught and tossed it off in a gulp. The liquor burned on the way down.

'I wish you wouldn't,' Chena said. 'Donli wouldn't have liked it. He had the proverb that he claimed was very ancient – he was from my city, don't forget, and I have known . . . I did know him longer than you, dear. I heard him say, twice or thrice, *Do I not destroy my enemies if I make them my friends?*'

'Think of a venomous insect,' Evalyth replied. 'You don't make friends with it. You put it under your heel.'

'But a man does what he does because of what he is, what his society has made him.' Chena's voice grew urgent; she leaned forward to grip Evalyth's hand, which did not respond. 'What is one man, one lifetime, against all who live around him and all who have gone before? Cannibalism wouldn't be found everywhere over this island, in every one of these otherwise altogether different groupings, if it weren't the most deeply rooted cultural imperative this race has got.'

Evalyth grinned around a rising anger. 'And what kind of race

202

are they to acquire it? And how about according me the privilege of operating on my own cultural imperatives? I'm bound home, to raise Donli's child away from your gutless civilization. He will not grow up disgraced because his mother was too weak to exact justice for his father. Now if you will excuse me, I have to get up early and take another boatload to the ship and get it inboard.'

That task required a while. Evalyth came back toward sunset of the next day. She felt a little more tired than usual, a little more peaceful. The raw edge of what had happened was healing over. The thought crossed her mind, abstract but not shocking, not disloyal: *I'm young. One year another man will come. I won't love you the less, darling.*

Dust scuffed under her boots. The compound was half stripped already, a corresponding number of personnel berthed in the ship. The evening reached quiet beneath a yellowing sky. Only a few of the expedition stirred among the machines and remaining cabins. Lokon lay as hushed as it had lately become. She welcomed the thud of her footfalls on the steps into Jonafer's office.

He sat waiting for her, big and unmoving behind his desk. 'Assignment completed without incident,' she reported.

'Sit down,' he said.

She obeyed. The silence grew. At last he said, out of a still face: 'The clinical team has finished with the prisoners.'

Somehow it was a shock. Evalyth groped for words. 'Isn't that too soon? I mean, well, we don't have a lot of equipment, and just a couple of men who can see the advanced stuff, and then without Donli for an expert on Earth biology – Wouldn't a good study, down to the chromosomal level if not further – something that the physical anthropologists could use – wouldn't it take longer?'

'That's correct,' Jonafer said. 'Nothing of major importance was found. Perhaps something would have been, if Uden's team had any inkling of what to look for. Given that, they could have made hypotheses and tested them in a whole-organism context and come to some understanding of their subjects as functioning beings. You're right, Donli Sairn had the kind of professional

203

intuition that might have guided them. Lacking that, and with no particular clues, and no cooperation from those ignorant, terrified savages, they had to grope and probe almost at random. They did establish a few digestive peculiarities – nothing that couldn't have been predicted on the basis of ambient ecology.'

'Then why have they stopped? We won't be leaving for another week at the earliest.'

'They did so on my orders, after Uden had shown me what was going on and said he'd quit regardless of what I wanted.'

'What – ? Oh.' Scorn lifted Evalyth's head. 'You mean the psychological torture.'

'Yes. I saw that scrawny woman secured to a table. Her head, her body were covered with leads to the meters that clustered around her and clicked and hummed and flickered. She didn't see me; her eyes were blind with fear. I suppose she imagined her soul was being pumped out. Or maybe the process was worse for being something she couldn't put a name to. I saw her kids in a cell, holding hands. Nothing else left for them to hold onto, in their total universe. They're just at puberty; what'll this do to their psychosexual development? I saw their father lying drugged beside them, after he'd tried to batter his way straight through the wall. Uden and his helpers told me how they'd tried to make friends and failed. Because naturally the prisoners know they're in the power of those who hate them with a hate that goes beyond the grave.'

Jonafer paused. 'There are decent limits to everything, Lieutenant,' he ended, 'including science and punishment. Especially when, after all, the chance of discovering anything else is unusual is slight. I ordered the investigation terminated. The boys and their mother will be flown to their home area and released tomorrow.'

'Why not today?' Evalyth asked, foreseeing his reply.

'I hoped,' Jonafer said, 'that you'd agree to let the man go with them.'

'No.'

'In the name of God – '

'Your God.' Evalyth looked away from him. 'I won't enjoy it,

Captain. I'm beginning to wish I didn't have to. But it's not as if Donli's been killed in an honest war or feud – or – he was slaughtered like a pig. That's the evil in cannibalism; it makes a man nothing but another meat animal. I won't bring him back, but I will somehow even things, by making the cannibal nothing but a dangerous animal that needs shooting.'

'I see.' Jonafer too stared long out of the window. In the sunset light his face became a mask of brass. 'Well,' he said finally, coldly, 'under the Charter of the Alliance and the articles of this expedition, you leave me no choice. But we will not have any ghoulish ceremonies, and you will not deputize what you have done. The prisoner will be brought to your place privately after dark. You will dispose of him at once and assist in cremating the remains.'

Evalyth's palms grew wet. *I never killed a helpless man before!*

But he did, it answered. 'Understood, Captain,' she said.

'Very good, Lieutenant. You may go up and join the mess for dinner if you wish. No announcements to anyone. The business will be scheduled for – ' Jonafer glanced at his watch, set to local rotation ' – 2600 hours.'

Evalyth swallowed around a clump of dryness. 'Isn't that rather late?'

'On purpose,' he told her. 'I want the camp asleep.' His glance struck hers. 'And want you to have time to reconsider.'

'No!' She sprang erect and went for the door.

His voice pursued her. 'Donli would have asked you for that.'

* * *

Night came in and filled the room. Evalyth didn't rise to turn on the light. It was as if this chair, which had been Donli's favorite, wouldn't let her go.

Finally she remembered the psychodrugs. She had a few tablets left. One of them would make the execution easy to perform. No doubt Jonafer would direct that Moru be tranquilized – now, at last – before they brought him here. So why should she not give herself calmness?

It wouldn't be right.

205

Why not?

I don't know. I don't understand anything any longer.

Who does? Moru alone. He knows why he murdered and butchered a man who trusted him. Evalyth found herself smiling wearily into the darkness. *He had superstition for his sure guide. He's actually seen his children display the first signs of maturity. That ought to console him a little.*

Odd, that the glandular upheaval of adolescence should have commenced under frightful stress. One would have expected a delay instead. True, the captives had been getting a balanced diet for a change, and medicine had probably eliminated various chronic low-level imfections. Nonetheless the fact was odd. Besides, normal children under normal conditions would not develop the outward signs beyond mistaking in this short a time. Donli would have puzzled over the matter. She could almost see him, frowning, rubbing his forehead, grinning one-sidedly with the pleasure of a problem.

'I'd like to have a go at this myself,' she heard him telling Uden over a beer and a smoke. 'Might turn up an angle.'

'How?' the medic would have replied. 'You're a general biologist. No reflection on you, but detailed human physiology is out of your line.'

'Um-m-m . . . yes and no. My main job is studying species of terrestrial origin and how they've adapted to new planets. By a remarkable coincidence, man is included among them.'

But Donli was gone, and no one else was competent to do his work – to be any part of him, but she fled from that thought and from the thought of what she must presently do. She held her mind tightly to the realization that none of Uden's team had tried to apply Donli's knowledge. As Jonafer remarked, a living Donli might well have suggested an idea, unorthodox and insightful, that would have led to the discovery of whatever was there to be discovered, if anything was. Uden and his assistants were routineers. They hadn't even thought to make Donli's computer ransack its data banks for possibly relevant information. Why should they, when they saw their problem as strictly medical? And, to be sure, they were not cruel. The anguish they were inflicting had made them avoid whatever might lead to ideas demanding further research. Donli would have approached the entire business differently from the outset.

Suddenly the gloom thickened. Evalyth fought for breath. Too hot and silent here; too long a wait; she must do something or her will would desert her and she would be unable to squeeze the trigger.

She stumbled to her feet and into the lab. The fluoro blinded her for a moment when she turned it on. She went to his computer and said: 'Activate!'

Nothing responded but the indicator light. The windows were totally black. Clouds outside shut off moon and stars.

'What – ' The sound was a curious croak. But that brought a releasing gall: *Take hold of yourself, you blubbering idiot, or you're not fit to mother the child you're carrying*. She could then ask her question. 'What explanations in terms of biology can be devised for the behavior of the people on this planet?'

'Matters of that nature are presumably best explained in terms of psychology and cultural anthropology,' said the voice.

'M-m-maybe,' Evalyth said. 'And maybe not.' She marshalled a few thoughts and stood them firm amidst the others roiling in her skull. 'The inhabitants could be degenerate somehow, not really human.' *I want Moru to be.* 'Scan every fact recorded about them, including the detailed clinical observations made on four of them in the past several days. Compare with basic terrestrial data. Give me whatever hypotheses – anything that does not flatly contradict established facts. We've used up the reasonable ideas already.'

The machine hummed. Evalyth closed her eyes and clung to the edge of the desk. *Donli, please help me.*

At the other end of forever, the voice came to her.

'The sole behavioral element which appears to be not easily explicable by postulates concerning environment and accidental historical developments, is the cannibalistic puberty rite. According to the anthropological computer, this might well have originated as a form of human sacrifice. But that computer notes certain illogicalities in the idea, as follows.

'On Old Earth, sacrificial religion was normally associated with agricultural societies, which were more vitally dependent

207

on continued fertility and good weather than hunters. Even for them, the offering of humans proved disadvantageous in the long run, as the Aztec example most clearly demonstrates. Lokon has rationalized the practice to a degree, making it a part of the slavery system and thus minimizing its impact on the generality. But for the lowlanders it is a powerful evil, a source of perpetual danger, a diversion of effort and resources that are badly needed for survival. It is not plausible that the custom, if ever imitated from Lokon, should persist among every one of those tribes. Nevertheless it does. Therefore it must have some value and the problem is to find what.

'The method of obtaining victims varies widely, but the requirement always appears to be the same. According to the Lokonese, one adult male body is necessary and sufficient for the maturation of four boys. The killer of Donli Sairn was unable to carry off the entire corpse. What he did take of it is suggestive.

'Hence a dipteroid phenomenon may have appeared in man on this planet. Such a thing is unknown among higher animals elsewhere, but is conceivable. A modification of the Y chromosome would produce it. The test for that modification, and thus the test of the hypothesis, is easily made.'

The voice stopped. Evalyth heard the blood slugging in her veins. 'What are you talking about?'

'The phenomenon is found among lower animals on several worlds,' the computer told her.

'It is uncommon and so is not widely known. The name derives from the Diptera, a type of dung fly on Old Earth.'

Lightning flickered. 'Dung fly – good, yes!'

The machine went on to explain.

* * *

Jonafer came along with Moru. The savage's hands were tied behind his back, and the spaceman loomed enormous over him. Despite that and the bruises he had inflicted on himself, he hobbled along steadily. The clouds were breaking and the moon shone ice-white. Where Evalyth waited, outside her door, she saw the compound reach bare to the saw-topped stockade and a

208

crane stand above like a gibbet. The air was growing cold – the planet spinning toward an autumn – and a small wind had arisen to whimper behind the dust devils that stirred across the earth. Jonafer's footfalls rang loud.

He noticed her and stopped. Moru did likewise. 'What did they learn?' she asked.

The captain nodded. 'Uden got right to work when you called,' he said. 'The test is more complicated than your computer suggested – but then, it's for Donli's kind of skill, not Uden's. He'd never have thought of it unassisted. Yes, the notion is true.'

'How?'

Moru stood waiting while the language he did not understand went to and fro around him.

'I'm no medic,' Jonafer kept his tone altogether colorless. 'But from what Uden told me, the chromosome defect means that the male gonads here can't mature spontaneously. They need an extra supply of hormones – he mentioned testosterone and androsterone, I forget what else – to start off the series of changes which bring on puberty. Lacking that, you'll get eunuchism. Uden thinks the surviving population was tiny after the colony was bombed out, and so poor that it resorted to cannibalism for bare survival, the first generation or two. Under those circumstances, a mutation that would otherwise have eliminated itself got established and spread to every descendant.'

Evalyth nodded. 'I see.'

'You understand what this means, I suppose,' Jonafer said. 'There'll be no problem to ending the practice. We'll simply tell them we have a new and better Holy Food, and prove it with a few pills. Terrestrial-type meat animals can be reintroduced later and supply what's necessary. In the end, no doubt our geneticists can repair that faulty Y chromosome.'

He could not stay contained any longer. His mouth opened, a gash across his half-seen face, and he rasped: 'I should praise you for saving a whole people. I can't. Get your business over with, will you?'

Evalyth trod forward to stand before Moru. He shivered but met her eyes. Astonished, she said: 'You haven't drugged him.'

'No,' Jonafer said. 'I wouldn't help you.' He spat.

209

'Well, I'm glad.' She addressed Moru in his own language: 'You killed my man. Is it right that I should kill you?'

'It is right,' he answered, almost as levelly as she. 'I thank you that my woman and my sons are to go free.' He was quiet for a second or two. 'I have heard that your folk can preserve food for years without it rotting. I would be glad if you kept my body to give to your sons.'

'Mine will not need it,' Evalyth said. 'Nor will the sons of your sons.'

Anxiety tinged his words: 'Do you know why I slew your man? He was kind to me, and like a god. But I am lame. I saw no other way to get what my sons must have; and they must have it soon, or it would be too late and they could never become men.'

'He taught me,' Evalyth said, 'how much it is to be a man.'

She turned to Jonafer, who stood tense and puzzled. 'I had my revenge,' she said in Donli's tongue.

'What?' His question was a reflexive noise.

'After I learned about the dipteroid phenomenon,' she said. 'All that was necessary was for me to keep silent. Moru, his children, his entire race would go on being prey for centuries, maybe forever. I sat for half an hour, I think, having my revenge.'

'And then?' Jonafer asked.

'I was satisfied and could start thinking about justice,' Evalyth said.

She drew a knife. Moru straightened his back. She stepped behind him and cut his bonds. 'Go home,' she said. 'Remember him.'

Some forms of sharing will remain utterly impossible despite fullness of knowledge, strength of will, or depth of love. Yet whatever disasters befall humankind, heroism has a way of outliving horror.

Consider the colonial planet Vixen. Wrecked by alien invaders in Flandry's time. It not only recovered and survived the Empire's fall, it founded its own highly successful colony, New Vixen. The latter was flourishing in the eighth millennium when the descendants of anti-Imperialist rebels banished by Flandry stumbled upon their distant kindred.

Was any beacon bright enough to guide the exiles home?

STARFOG

'From another universe. Where space is a shining cloud, two hundred light-years across, roiled by the red stars that number in the many thousands, and where the brighter suns are troubled and cast forth great flames. Your spaces are dark and lonely.'

Daven Laure stopped the recording and asked for an official translation. A part of *Jaccavrie's* computer scanned the molecules of a plugged-in memory cylinder, identified the passage, and flashed the Serievan text onto a reader screen. Another part continued the multitudinous tasks of planetary approach. Still other parts waited for the man's bidding, whatever he might want next. A Ranger of the Commonalty traveled in a very special ship.

And even so, every year, a certain number did not come home from their missions.

Laure nodded to himself. Yes, he'd understood the woman's voice correctly. Or, at least, he interpreted her sentences approximately the same way as did the semanticist who had interviewed her and her fellows. And this particular statement was as difficult, as ambiguous as any which they had made. Therefore: (a) Probably the linguistic computer on Serieve had done a good job of unraveling their basic language. (b) It had accurately encoded its findings – vocabulary, grammar, tentative reconstruction of the underlying world-view – in the cylinders which a courier had brought to Sector HQ. (c) The reencoding, into his own neurones, which Laure underwent on his way here, had taken well. He had a working knowledge of the tongue which – among how many others? – was spoken on Kirkasant.

'Wherever that may be,' he muttered.

The ship weighed his words for a nanosecond or two, decided no answer was called for, and made none.

Restless, Laure got to his feet and prowled from the study

cabin, down a corridor to the bridge. It was so called largely by courtesy. *Jaccavrie* navigated, piloted, landed, lifted, maintained, and, if need be, repaired and fought for herself. But the projectors here offered a full outside view. At the moment, the bulkheads seemed cramped and barren. Laure ordered the simulacrum activated.

The bridge vanished from his eyes. Had it not been for the G-field underfoot, he might have imagined himself floating in space. A crystal night enclosed him, unwinking stars scattered like jewels, the frosty glitter of the Milky Way. Large and near, its radiance stopped down to preserve his retinas, burned the yellow sun of Serieve. The planet itself was a growing crescent, blue banded with white, rimmed by a violet sky. A moon stood opposite, worn golden coin.

But Laure's gaze strayed beyond, toward the deeps and then, as if in search of comfort, the other way, toward Old Earth. There was no comfort, though. They still named her Home, but she lay in the spiral arm behind this one, and Laure had never seen her. He had never met anyone who had. None of his ancestors had, for longer than their family chronicles ran. Home was a half-remembered myth; reality was here, these stars on the fringes of this civilization.

Serieve lay near the edge of the known. Kirkasant lay somewhere beyond.

'Surely not outside of spacetime,' Laure said.

'If you've begun thinking aloud, you'd like to discuss it,' *Jaccavrie* said.

He had followed custom in telling the ship to use a female voice and, when practical, idiomatic language. The computer had soon learned precisely what pattern suited him best. That was not identical with what he liked best; such could have got disturbing on a long cruise. He found himself more engaged, inwardly, with the husky contralto that had spoken in strong rhythms out of the recorder than he was with the mezzo-soprano that now reached his ears.

'Well . . . maybe so,' he said. 'But you already know everything in the material we have aboard.'

'You need to set your thoughts in order. You've spent most of our transit time acquiring the language.'

'All right, then, let's run barefoot through the obvious.' Laure paced a turn around the invisible deck. He felt its hardness, he sensed the almost subliminal beat of driving energies, he caught a piny whiff of air as the ventilators shifted to another part of their odor-temperature-ionization cycle; but still the stars blazed about him, and their silence seemed to enter his bones. Abruptly, harshly, he said: 'Turn that show off.'

The ship obeyed. 'Would you like a planetary scene?' she asked. 'You haven't yet looked at those tapes from the elf castles on Jair that you bought – '

'Not now.' Laure flung himself into a chair web and regarded the prosaic metal, instruments, manual over-ride controls that surrounded him. 'This will do.'

'Are you feeling well? Why not go in the diagnoser and let me check you out? We've time before we arrive.'

The tone was anxious. Laure didn't believe that emotion was put on. He refrained from anthropomorphizing his computer, just as he did those nonhuman sophonts he encountered. At the same time, he didn't go along with the school of thought which claimed that human-sensibility terms were absolutely meaningless in such connections. An alien brain, or a cybernetic one like *Jaccavrie's*, could think; it was aware; it had conation. Therefore it had analogies to his.

Quite a few Rangers were eremitic types, sane enough but basically schizoid. That was their way of standing the gaff. It was normal for them to think of their ships as elaborate tools. Daven Laure, who was young and outgoing, naturally thought of him as a friend.

'No, I'm all right,' he said. 'A bit nervous, nothing else. This could turn out to be the biggest thing I . . . you and I have tackled yet. Maybe one of the biggest anyone has, at least on this frontier. I'd've been glad to have an older man or two along.' He shrugged. 'None available. Our service should increase its personnel, even if it means raising dues. We're spread much too thin across – how many stars?'

'The last report in my files estimated ten million planets with a significant number of Commonalty members on them. As for how many more there may be with which these have reasonably regular contact — '

'Oh, for everything's sake, come off it!' Laure actually laughed, and wondered if the ship had planned things that way. But, regardless, he could begin to talk of this as a problem rather than a mystery.

'Let me recapitulate,' he said, 'and you tell me if I'm misinterpreting matters. A ship comes to Serieve, allegedly from far away. It's like nothing anybody has ever seen, unless in historical works. (They haven't got the references on Serieve to check that out, so we're bringing some from HQ.) Hyperdrive, gravity control, electronics, yes, but everything crude, archaic, bare-bones. Fission instead of fusion power, for example . . . and human piloting!

'That is, the crew seem to be human. We have no record of their anthropometric type, but they don't look as odd as people do after several generations on some planets I could name. And the linguistic computer, once they get the idea that it's there to decipher their language and start cooperating with it, says their speech appears to have remote affinities with a few that we know, like ancient Anglic. Preliminary semantic analysis suggests their abstractions and constructs aren't quite like ours, but do fall well inside the human psych range. All in all, then, you'd assume they're explorers from distant parts.'

'Except for the primitive ship,' *Jaccavrie* chimed in. 'One wouldn't expect such technological backwardness in any group which had maintained any contact, however tenuous, with the general mass of the different human civilizations. Nor would such a slow, under-equipped vessel pass through them without stopping, to fetch up in this border region.'

'Right. So . . . if it isn't a fake . . . their gear bears out a part of their story. Kirkasant is an exceedingly old colony . . . yonder.' Laure pointed toward unseen stars. 'Well out in the Dragon's Head sector, where we're barely beginning to explore. Somehow, somebody got that far, and in the earliest days of interstellar travel. They settled down on a planet and lost the trick of making spaceships. Only lately have they regained it.'

215

'And come back, looking for the companionship of their own kind.' Laure had a brief, irrational vision of *Jaccavrie* nodding. Her tone was so thoughtful. She would be a big, calm, dark-haired woman, handsome in middle age though getting somewhat plump ... 'What the crew themselves have said, as communication got established, seems to bear out this idea. Beneath a great many confused mythological motifs, I also get the impression of an epic voyage, by a defeated people who ran as far as they could.'

'But Kirkasant!' Laure protested. 'The whole situation they describe. It's impossible.'

'Might not that Vandange be mistaken? I mean, we know so little. The Kirkasanters keep talking about a weird home environment. Ours appears to have stunned and bewildered them. They simply groped on through space till they happened to find Serieve. Thus might their own theory, that somehow they blundered in from an altogether different continuum, might it not conceivably be right?'

'Hm-m-m. I guess you didn't see Vandange's accompanying letter. No, you haven't, it wouldn't've been plugged into your memory. Anyway, he claims his assistants examined that ship down to the bolt heads. And they found nothing, no mechanism, no peculiarity, whose function and behavior weren't obvious. He really gets indignant. Says the notion of interspace-time transference is mathematically absurd. I don't have quite his faith in mathematics, myself, but I must admit he has one common-sense point. If a ship could somehow flip from one entire cosmos to another ... why, in five thousand years of interstellar travel, haven't we gotten some record of it happening?'

'Perhaps the ships to which it occurs never come back.'

'Perhaps. Or perhaps the whole argument is due to misunderstanding. We don't have any good grasp of the Kirkasanter language. Or maybe it's a hoax. That's Vandange's opinion. He claims there's no such region as they say they come from. Not anywhere. Neither astronomers nor explorers have ever found anything like a ... a space like a shining fog, crowded with stars – '

'But why should these wayfarers tell a falsehood?' *Jaccavrie* sounded honestly puzzled.

'I don't know. Nobody does. That's why the Serievan government decided it'd better ask for a Ranger.'

Laure jumped up and started pacing again. He was a tall young man, with the characteristic beardlessness, fair hair and complexion, slightly slanted blue eyes of the Fireland mountaineers on New Vixen. But since he had trained at Starborough, which is on Aladir not far from Irontower City, he affected a fashionably simple gray tunic and blue hose. The silver comet of his calling blazoned his left breast.

'I don't know,' he repeated. There rose in him a consciousness of that immensity which crouched beyond this hull. 'Maybe they are telling the sober truth. We don't dare not know.'

When a mere few million people have an entire habitable world to themselves, they do not often build high. That comes later, along with formal wilderness preservation, disapproval of fecundity, and inducements to emigrate. Pioneer towns tend to be low and rambling. (Or so it is in that civilization wherein the Commonalty operates. We know that other branches of humanity have their distinctive ways, and hear rumors of yet stranger ones. But so vast is the galaxy – these two or three spiral arms, a part of which our race has to date thinly occupied – so vast, that we cannot even keep track of our own culture, let alone anyone else's.)

Pelogard, however, was founded on an island off the Branzan mainland, above Serieve's arctic circle: which comes down to almost 56°. Furthermore, it was an industrial center. Hence most of its buildings were tall and crowded. Laure, standing by the outer wall of Ozer Vandange's office and looking forth across the little city, asked why this location had been chosen.

'You don't know?' responded the physicist. His inflection was a touch too elaborately incredulous.

'I'm afraid not,' Laure confessed. 'Think how many systems my service has to cover, and how many individual places within each system. If we tried to remember each, we'd never be anywhere but under the neuro-inductors.'

Vandange, seated small and bald and prim behind a large desk, pursed his lips. 'Yes, yes,' he said. 'Nevertheless, I should not think an *experienced* Ranger would dash off to a planet without temporarily mastering a few basic facts about it.'

Laure flushed. An experienced Ranger would have put this conceited old dustbrain in his place. But he himself was too aware of youth and awkwardness. He managed to say quietly, 'Sir, my ship has complete information. She needed only scan it and tell me no precautions were required here. You have a beautiful globe and I can understand why you're proud of it. But please understand that to me it has to be a way station. My job is with those people from Kirkasant, and I'm anxious to meet them.'

'You shall, you shall,' said Vandange, somewhat mollified. 'I merely thought a conference with you would be advisable first. As for your question, we need a city here primarily because updwelling ocean currents make the arctic waters mineral-rich. Extractor plants pay off better than they would farther south.'

Despite himself, Laure was interested. 'You're getting your minerals from the sea already? At so early a stage of settlement?'

'This sun and its planets are poor in heavy metals. Most local systems are. Not surprising. We aren't far, here, from the northern verge of the spiral arm. Beyond is the halo – thin gas, little dust, ancient globular clusters very widely scattered. The interstellar medium from which stars form has not been greatly enriched by earlier generations.'

Laure suppressed his resentment at being lectured like a child. Maybe it was just! Vandange's habit. He cast another glance through the wall. The office was high in one of the buildings. He looked across soaring blocks of metal, concrete, glass, and plastic, interlinked with trafficways and freight cables, down to the waterfront. There bulked the extractor plants, warehouses, and skydocks. Cargo craft moved ponderously in and out. Not many passenger vessels flitted between. Pelogard must be largely automated.

The season stood at late spring. The sun cast brightness across a gray ocean that a wind rumpled. Immense flocks of seabirds dipped and wheeled. Or were they birds? They had wings, anyhow, steely blue against a wan sky. Perhaps they cried or sang, into the wind skirl and wave rush: but Laure couldn't bear it in this enclosed place.

'That's one reason, I can't accept their yarn,' Vandange declared.

'Eh?' Laure came out of his reverie with a start.

Vandange pressed a button to opaque the wall. 'Sit down. Let's get to business.'

Laure eased himself into a lounger opposite the desk. 'Why am I conferring with you?' he counterattacked. 'Whoever was principally working with the Kirkasanters had to be a semanticist. In short, Paeri Ferand. He consulted specialists on your university faculty, in anthropology, history, and so forth. But I should think your own role as a physicist was marginal. Yet you're the one taking up my time. Why?'

'Oh, you can see Ferand and the others as much as you choose,' Vandange said. 'You won't get more from them than repetitions of what the Kirkasanters have already told. How could you? What else have they got to go on? If nothing else, an underpopulated world like ours can't maintain staffs of experts to ferret out the meaning of every datum, every inconsistency, every outright lie. I had hoped, when our government notified your section, headquarters, the Rangers would have sent a real team, instead of – ' He curbed himself. 'Of course, they have many other claims on their attention. They would not see at once how important this is.'

'Well,' Laure said in his annoyance, 'if you're suspicious, if you think the strangers need further investigation, why bother with my office? It's just an overworked little outpost. Send them on to a heart world, like Sarnac, where the facilities and people really can be had.'

'It was urged,' Vandange said. 'I, and a few others who felt as I do, fought the proposal bitterly. In the end, as a compromise, the government decided to dump the whole problem in the lap of the Rangers. Who turn out to be, in effect, you. Now I must persuade you to be properly cautious. Don't you see, if those . . . beings . . . have some hostile intent, the very worst move would

219

be to send them on – let them spy out our civilization – let them, perhaps, commit nuclear sabotage on a vital center, and then vanish back into space.' His voice grew shrill. 'That's why we've kept them here so long, on one excuse after the next, here on our home planet. We feel responsible to the rest of mankind!'

'But what – ' Laure shook his head. He felt a sense of unreality. 'Sir, the League, the troubles, the Empire, its fall, the Long Night . . . every such thing – behind us. In space and time alike. The people of the Commonalty don't get into wars.'

'Are you quite certain?'

'What makes *you* so certain of any menace in – one antiquated ship? Crewed by a score of men and women. Who came here openly and peacefully. Who, by every report, have been struggling to get past the language and culture barriers and communicate with you in detail – what in cosmos' name makes you worry about them?'

'The fact that they are liars.'

Vandange sat awhile, gnawing his thumb, before he opened a box, took out a cigar and puffed it into lighting. He didn't offer Laure one. That might be for fear of poisoning his visitor with whatever local weed he was smoking. Scattered around for many generations on widely differing planets, populations did develop some odd distributions of allergy and immunity. But Laure suspected plain rudeness.

'I thought my letter made it clear,' Vandange said. 'They insist they are from another continuum. One with impossible properties, including visibility from ours. Conveniently on the far side of the Dragon's Head, so that we don't see it here. Oh, yes,' he added quickly, 'I've heard the arguments. That the whole thing is a misunderstanding due to our not having an adequate command of their language. That they're really trying to say they came from – well, the commonest rationalization is a dense star cluster. But it won't work, you know. It won't work at all.'

'Why not?' Laure asked.

'Come, now. Come, now. You must have learned some astronomy as part of your training. You must know that some things simply do not occur in the galaxy.'

'Uh – '

'They showed us what they alleged were lens-and-film photographs taken from, ah, inside their home universe.' Vandage bore down heavily on the sarcasm. 'You saw copies, didn't you? Well, now, where in the real universe do you find that kind of nebulosity – so thick and extensive that a ship can actually lose its bearings, wander around lost, using up its film among other supplies, until it chances to emerge in clear space? For that matter, assuming there were such a region, how could anyone capable of building a hyperdrive be so stupid as to go beyond sight of his beacon stars?'

'Uh . . . I thought of a cluster, heavily hazed, somewhat like the young clusters of the Pleiades type.'

'So did many Serievans,' Vandange snorted. 'Please use your head. Not even Pleiadic clusters contain that much gas and dust. Besides, the verbal description of the Kirkasanters sounds like a globular cluster, insofar as it sounds like anything. But not much. The ancient red suns are there, crowded together, true. But they speak of far too many younger ones.

'And of far too much heavy metal at home. Which their ship demonstrates. Their use of alloying elements like aluminum and beryllium is incredibly parsimonious. On the other hand, electrical conductors are gold and silver, the power plant is shielded not with lead but with inert-coated osmium, and it burns plutonium which the Kirkansanters assert was mined!

'They were astonished that Serieve is such a light-metal planet. Or claimed they were astonished. I don't know about that. I do know that this whole region is dominated by light elements. That its interstellar spaces are relatively free of dust and gas, the Dragon's Head being the only exception and it merely in transit through our skies. That all this is even more true of the globular clusters, which formed in an ultratenuous medium, mostly before the galaxy had condensed to its present shape – which, in fact, practically don't *occur* in the main body of the galaxy, but are off in the surrounding halo!'

Vandange stopped for breath and triumph.

'Well.' Laure shifted uneasily in his seat and wished *Jaccavrie* weren't ten thousand kilometers away at the only spaceport.

'You have a point. There are contradictions, aren't there? I'll bear what you said in mind when I, uh, interview the strangers themselves.'

'And you will, I trust, be wary of them,' Vandange said.

'Oh, yes. Something queer does seem to be going on.'

In outward appearance, the Kirkasanters were not startling. They didn't resemble any of the human breeds that had developed locally, but they varied less from the norm than some. The fifteen men and five women were tall, robust, broad in chest and shoulders, slim in waist. Their skins were dark coppery reddish, their hair blue-black and wavy; males had some beard and mustache which they wore neatly trimmed. Skulls were dolichocephalic, faces disharmonically wide, noses straight and thin, lips full. The total effect was handsome. Their eyes were the most arresting feature, large, long-lashed, luminous in shades of gray, or green, or yellow.

Since they had refused – with an adamant politeness they well knew how to assume – to let cell samples be taken for chromosome analysis, Vandange had muttered to Laure about nonhumans in surgical disguise. But that the Ranger classed as the fantasy of a provincial who'd doubtless never met a live xeno. You couldn't fake so many details, not and keep a viable organism. Unless, to be sure, happenstance had duplicated most of those details for you in the course of evolution . . .

Ridiculous, Laure thought. *Coincidence isn't that energetic.*

He walked from Pelogard with Demring Lodden, captain of the *Makt*, and Demring's daughter, navigator Graydal. The town was soon behind them. They found a trail that wound up into steeply rising hills, among low, gnarly trees which had begun to put forth leaves that were fronded and colored like old silver. The sun was sinking, the air noisy and full of salt odors. Neither Kirkasanter appeared to mind the chill.

'You know your way here well,' Laure said clumsily.

'We should,' Demring answered, 'for we have been held on this sole island, with naught to do but ramble it when the *reyad* takes us.'

'*Reyad*?' Laure asked.

'The need to ... search,' Graydal said. 'To track beasts, or find what is new, or be alone in wild places. Our folk were hunters until not so long ago. We bear their blood.'

Demring wasn't to be diverted from his grudge. 'Why are we thus confined?' he growled. 'Each time we sought an answer, we got an evasion. Fear of disease, need for us to learn what to expect – Ha, by now I'm half minded to draw my gun, force my way to our ship, and depart for aye!'

He was erect, grizzled, deeply graven of countenance and bleak of gaze. Like his men, he wore soft boots, a knee-length gown of some fine-scaled leather, a cowled cloak, a dagger and an energy pistol at his belt. On his forehead sparkled a diamond that betokened authority.

'Well, but, Master,' Graydal said, 'here today we deal with no village witchfinders. Daven Laure is a king's man, with power to act, knowledge and courage to act rightly. Has he not gone off alone with us because you said you felt stifled and spied on in the town? Let us talk as freefolk with him.'

Her smile, her words in the husky voice that Laure remembered from his recordings, were gentle. He felt pretty sure, though, that as much steel underlay her as her father, and possibly whetted sharper. She almost matched his height, her gait was tigerish, she was herself weaponed and diademmed. Unlike Laure's close cut or Demring's short bob, her hair passed through a platinum ring and blew free at full length. Her clothes were little more than footgear, fringed shorts, and thin blouse. However attractive, the sight did not suggest seductive feminity to the Ranger – when he wasn't feeling the cold that struck through his garments. Besides, he had already learned that the sexes were mixed aboard the *Makt* for no other reason than that women were better at certain jobs than men. Every female was accompanied by an older male relative. The Kirkasanters were not an uncheerful folk, on the whole, but some of their ideals looked austere.

Nonetheless, Graydal had lovely strong features, and her eyes, under the level brows, shone amber.

'Maybe the local government was overcautious,' Laure said, 'but don't forget, this is a frontier settlement. Not many light-years hence, in that part of the sky you came from, begins the unknown. It's true the stars are comparatively thin in these parts – average distance between them about four parsecs – but still, their number is too great for us to do more than feel our way slowly forward. Especially when, in the nature of the case, planets like Serieve must devote most of their effort to developing themselves. So, when one is ignorant, one does best to be careful.'

He flattered himself that was a well-composed conciliatory speech. It wasn't as oratorical as one of theirs, but they had lung capacity for a thinner atmosphere than this. He was disappointed when Demring said scornfully, '*Our* ancestors were not so timid.'

'Or else their pursuers were not,' Graydal laughed.

The captain looked offended. Laure hastily asked: 'Have you no knowledge of what happened?'

'No,' said the girl, turned pensive. 'Not in truth. Legends, found in many forms across all Kirkasant, tell of battle, and a shipful of people who fled far until at last they found haven. A few fragmentary records – but those are vague, save the Baorn Codex; and it is little more than a compendium of technical information which the Wisemen of Skribent preserved. Even in that case' – she smiled again – 'the meaning of most passages was generally obscure until after our modern scientists had invented the thing described for themselves.'

'Do you know what records remain in Homeland?' Demring asked hopefully.

Laure sighed and shook his head. 'No. Perhaps none, by now. Doubtless, in time, an expedition will go from us to Earth. But after five thousand trouble-filled years – And your ancestors may not have started from there. They may have belonged to one of the first colonies.'

In a dim way, he could reconstruct the story. There had been a fight. The reasons – personal, familial, national, ideological, economic, whatever they were – had dropped into the bottom of the millennia between then and now. (A commentary on the importance of any such reasons.) But someone had so badly

224

wanted the destruction of someone else that one ship, or one fleet, hounded another almost a quarter way round the galaxy.

Or maybe not, in a literal sense. It would have been hard to do. Crude as they were, those early vessels could have made the trip, if frequent stops were allowed for repair and resupply and refilling of the nuclear converters. But to this day, a craft under hyperdrive could only be detected within approximately a light-year's radius by the instantaneous 'wake' of space-pulses. If she lay doggo for a while, she was usually unfindable in the sheer stupendousness of any somewhat larger volume. That the hunter should never, in the course of many months, either have overhauled his quarry or lost the scent altogether, seemed conceivable but implausible.

Maybe pursuit had not been for the whole distance. Maybe the refugees had indeed escaped after a while, but – in blind panic, or rage against the foe, or desire to practice undisturbed a brand of utopianism, or whatever the motive was – they had continued as far as they possibly could, and hidden themselves as thoroughly as nature allowed.

In any case, they had ended in a strange part of creation: so strange that numerous men on Serieve did not admit it existed. By then, their ship must have been badly in need of a complete overhaul, amounting virtually to a rebuilding. They settled down to construct the necessary industrial base. (Think, for example, how much plant you must have before you make your first transistor.) They did not have the accumulated experience of later generations to prove how impossible this was.

Of course they failed. A few score – a few hundred at absolute maximum, if the ship had been rigged with suspended-animation lockers – could not preserve a full-fledged civilization while coping with a planet for which man was never meant. And they had to content themselves with that planet. Once into the Cloud Universe, even if their vessel could still wheeze along for a while, they were no longer able to move freely about, picking and choosing.

Kirkasant was probably the best of a bad lot. And Laure thought it was rather a miracle that man had survived there. So small a genetic pool, so hostile an environment . . . but the latter

225

might well have saved him from the effects of the former. Natural selection must have been harsh. And, seemingly, the radiation background was high, which led to a corresponding mutation rate. Women bore from puberty to menopause, and buried most of their babies. Men struggled to keep them alive. Often death harvested adults, too, entire families. But those who were fit tended to survive. And the planet did have an unfilled ecological niche: the one reserved for intelligence. Evolution galloped. Population exploded. In one or two millennia, man was at home on Kirkasant. In five, he crowded it and went looking for new planets.

Because culture had never totally died. The first generation might be unable to build machine tools, but could mine and forge metals. The next generation might be too busy to keep public schools, but had enough hard practical respect for learning that it supported a literate class. Succeeding generations, wandering into new lands, founding new nations and societies, might war with each other, but all drew from a common tradition and looked to one goal: reunion with the stars.

Once the scientific method had been created afresh, Laure thought, progress must have been more rapid than on Earth. For the natural philosophers knew certain things were possible, even if they didn't know how, and this was half the battle. They must have got some hints, however oracular, from the remnants of ancient texts. They actually had the corroded hulk of the ancestral ship for their studying. Given this much, it was not too surprising that they leaped in a single lifetime from the first moon rockets to the first hyperdrive craft – and did so on a basis of wildly distorted physical theory, and embarked with such naivete that they couldn't find their way home again!

All very logical. Unheard of, outrageously improbable, but in this big a galaxy the strangest things are bound to happen now and again. The Kirkasanters could be absolutely honest in their story.

If they were.

'Let the past tend the past,' Graydal said impatiently. 'We've tomorrow to hunt in.'

226

'Yes,' Laure said, 'but I do need to know a few things. It's not clear to me how you found us, I mean, you crossed a thousand light-years or more of wilderness. How did you come on a speck like Serieve?'

'We were asked that before,' Demring said, 'but then we could not well explain, few words being held in common. Now you show a good command of the Hobrokan tongue, and for our part, albeit none of these villagers will take the responsibility of putting one of us under your educator machine . . . in talking with technical folk, we've gained various technical words of yours.'

He was silent awhile, collecting phrases. The three people continued up the trail. It was wide enough for them to walk abreast, somewhat muddy with rain and melted snow. The sun was so far down that the woods walled it off; twilight smoked from the ground and from either side, though the sky was still pale. The wind was dying but the chill deepening. Somewhere behind those dun trunks and ashy-metallic leaves, a voice went 'K-kr-r-r-*ruk*!' and, above and ahead, the sound of a river became audible.

Demring said with care: 'See you, when we could not find our way back to Kirkasant's sun, and at last had come out in an altogether different cosmos, we thought our ancestors might have originated there. Certain traditional songs hinted as much, speaking of space as dark for instance; and surely darkness encompassed us now, and immense loneliness between the stars. Well, but in which direction might Homeland lie? Casting about with telescopes, we spied afar a black cloud, and thought, if the ancestors had been in flight from enemies, they might well have gone through such, hoping to break their trail.'

'The Dragon's Head Nebula,' Laure nodded.

Graydal's wide shoulders lifted and fell. 'At least it gave us something to steer by,' she said.

Laure stole a moment's admiration of her profile. 'You had courage,' he said. 'Quite aside from everything else, how did you know this civilisation had not stayed hostile to you?'

'How did we know it ever was in the first place?' she

chuckled. 'Myself, insofar as I believe the myths have any truth, I suspect our ancestors were thieves or bandits, or – '

'Daughter!' Demring hurried on, in a scandalized voice: 'When we had fared thus far, we found the darkness was dust and gas such as pervade the universe at home. There was simply an absence of stars to make them shine. Emerging on the far side, we tuned our neutrino detectors. Our reasoning was that a highly developed civilization would use a great many nuclear power plants. Their neutrino flux should be detectable above the natural noise level – in this comparatively empty cosmos – across several score light-years or better, and we could home on it.'

First they sound like barbarians bards, Laure thought, *and then like radionicians. No wonder a dogmatist like Vandange can't put credence in them.*

Can I?

'We soon began to despair,' Graydal said. 'We were nigh to the limit – '

'No matter,' Demring interrupted.

She looked steadily first at one man, then the other, and said, 'I dare trust Daven Laure.' To the Ranger: 'Belike no secret anyhow, since men on Serieve must have examined our ship with knowledgeable eyes. We were nigh to our limits of travel without refueling and refurbishing. We were about to seek for a planet not too unlike Kirkasant where – But then, as if by Valfar's Wings, came the traces we sought, and we followed them here.

'And here were humans!

'Only of late has our gladness faded as we begin to see how they temporize and keep us half prisoner. Wholly prisoner, maybe, should we try to depart. Why will they not rely on us?'

'I tried to explain that when we talked yesterday,' Laure said, 'Some important men don't see how you could be telling the truth.'

She caught his hand in a brief, impulsive grasp. Her own was warm, slender, and hard. 'But you are different?'

'Yes.' He felt helpless and alone. 'They've, well, they've called for me. Put the entire problem in the hands of my organization.

228

And my fellows have so much else to do that, well, I'm given broad discretion.'

Demring regarded him shrewdly. 'You are a young man,' he said. 'Do not let your powers paralyze you.'

'No. I will do what I can for you. It may be little.'

The trail rounded a thicket and they saw a rustic bridge across the river, which ran seaward in foam and clangor. Halfway over, the party stopped, leaned on the rail and looked down. The water was thickly shadowed between its banks, and the woods were becoming a solid black mass athwart a dusking sky. The air smelled wet.

'You realize,' Laure said, 'it won't be easy to retrace your route. You improvised your navigational coordinates. They can be transformed into ours on this side of the Dragon's Head, I suppose. But once beyond the nebula, I'll be off my own charts, except for what few listed objects are visible from either side. No one from this civilization has been there, you see, what with millions of suns closer to our settlements. And the stars sights you took can't have been too accurate.'

'You are not going to take us to Homeland, then,' Demring said tonelessly.

'Don't you understand? Homeland, Earth, it's so far away that I myself don't know what it's like anymore!'

'But you must have a nearby capital, a more developed world than this. Why do you not guide us thither, that we may talk with folk wiser than these wretched Serievans?'

'Well . . . uh . . . Oh, many reasons. I'll be honest, caution is one of them. Also, the Commonalty does not have anything like a capital, or – But yes, I could guide you to the heart of civilization. Any of numerous civilizations in this galactic arm.' Laure took a breath and slogged on. 'My decision, though, under the circumstances, is that first I'd better see your world Kirkasant. After that . . . well, certainly, if everything is all right, we'll establish regular contacts, and invite your people to visit ours, and – Don't you like the plan? Don't you want to go home?'

'How shall we, ever?' Graydal asked low.

Laure cast her a surprised glance. She stared ahead of her and down, into the river. A fish – some kind of swimming creature – leaped. Its scales caught what light remained in a gleam that was faint but startling against those murky waters. She didn't seem to notice, though she cocked her head instinctively toward the splash that followed.

'Have you not listened?' she said. 'Did you not hear us? How long we searched in the fog, through that forest of suns, until at last we left our whole small bright universe and came into this great one that has so much blackness in it – and thrice we plunged back into our own space, and groped about, and came forth without having found trace of any star, we knew – ' Her voice lifted the least bit. 'We are lost, I tell you, eternally lost. Take us to your home, Daven Laure, that we may try to make ours there.'

He wanted to stroke her hands, which had clenched into fists on the bridge rail. But he made himself say only: 'Our science and resources are more than yours. Maybe we could find a way where you cannot. At any rate, I'm duty bound to learn as much as I can, before I make report and recommendation to my superiors.'

'I do not think you are kind, forcing my crew to return and look again on what has gone from them,' Demring said stiffly. 'But I have scant choice save to agree.' He straightened. 'Come, best we start back toward Pelogard. Night will soon be upon us.'

'Oh, no rush,' Laure said, anxious to change the subject. 'An arctic zone, at this time of year – We'll have no trouble.'

'Maybe you will not,' Graydal said. 'But Kirkasant after sunset is not like here.'

They were on their way down when dusk became night, a light night where only a few stars gleamed and Laure walked easily through a clear gloaming. Graydal and Demring must needs use their energy guns at minimum intensity for flash-casters. And even so, they often stumbled.

Makt was three times the size of *Jaccavrie*, a gleaming torpedo shape whose curve was broken by boat housings and weapon turrets. The Ranger vessel looked like a gig attending her. In actuality, *Jaccavrie* could have outrun, outmaneuvered, or outfought the Kirkasanter with ludicrous ease. Laure didn't emphasize that fact. His charges were touchy enough already. He had suggested hiring a modern carrier for them, and met a glacial negative. This craft was their property and bore the honor of the confederated clans that had built her. She was not to be abandoned.

Modernizing her would have taken more time than increased speed would save. Besides, while Laure was personally convinced of the good intentions of Demring's people, he had no right to present them with up-to-date technology until he had proof they wouldn't misuse it.

One could not accurately say that he resigned himself to accompanying them in his ship at the plodding pace of theirs. The weeks of travel gave him a chance to get acquainted with them and their culture. And that was not only his duty but his pleasure. Especially, he found, when Graydal was involved.

Some time passed before he could invite her to dinner *a deux*. He arranged it with what he felt sure was adroitness. Two persons, undisturbed, talking socially, could exchange information of the subtle kind that didn't come across in committee. Thus he proposed a series of private meetings with the officers of *Makt*. He began with the captain, naturally; but after a while came the navigator's turn.

Jaccavrie phased in with the other vessel, laid alongside and made air-lock connections in a motion too smooth to feel. Graydal came aboard and the ships parted company again. Laure greeted her according to the way of Kirkasant, with a handshake. The clasp lasted a moment. 'Welcome,' he said.

'Peace between us.' Her smile offset her formalism. She was in uniform – another obsolete aspect of her society – but it shimmered gold and molded itself to her.

'Won't you come to the saloon for a drink before we eat?'

'I shouldn't. Not in space.'

'No hazard,' said the computer in an amused tone. 'I operate everything anyway.'

Graydal had tensed and clapped hand to gun at the voice. She had relaxed and tried to laugh. 'I'm sorry. I am not used to . . . you.' She almost bounded on her way down the corridor with Laure. He had set the interior weight at one standard G. The Kirkasanters maintained theirs fourteen percent higher, to match the pull of their home world.

Though she had inspected this ship several times already, Graydal looked wide-eyed around her. The saloon was small but sybaritic. 'You do yourself proud,' she said amidst the draperies, music, perfumes, and animations.

He guided her to a couch. 'You don't sound quite approving,' he said.

'Well – '

'There's no virtue in suffering hardships.'

'But there is in the ability to endure them.' She sat too straight for the form-fitter cells to make her comfortable.

'Think I can't?'

Embarrassed, she turned her gaze from him, toward the viewscreen, on which flowed a color composition. Her lips tightened. 'Why have you turned off the exterior scene.'

'You don't seem to like it, I've noticed.' He sat down beside her. 'What will you have? We're fairly well stocked.'

'Turn it on.'

'What?'

'The outside view.' Her nostrils dilated. 'It shall not best me.'

He spread his hands. The ship saw his rueful gesture and obliged. Space leaped into the screen, star-strewn except where the storm-cloud mass of the dark nebula reared ahead. He heard Graydal suck in a breath and said quickly, 'Uh, since you aren't familiar with our beverages, I suggest daiquiris. They're tart, a little sweet – '

Her nod was jerky. Her eyes seemed locked to the screen. He leaned close, catching the slight warm odor of her, not quite identical with the odor of other women he had known, though the difference was too subtle for him to name. 'Why does that sight bother you?' he asked.

'The strangeness. The aloneness. It is so absolutely alien to home. I feel forsaken and – ' She filled her lungs, forced detachment on herself, and said in an analytical manner:

232

'Possibly we are disturbed by a black sky because we have virtually none of what you call night vision.' A touch of trouble returned. 'What else have we lost?'

'Night vision isn't needed on Kirkasant, you tell me,' Laure consoled her. 'And evolution there worked fast. But you must have gained as well as atrophied. I know you have more physical strength, for instance, than your ancestors could've had.' A tray with two glasses extended from the side. 'Ah, here are the drinks.'

She sniffed at hers. 'It smells pleasant,' she said. 'But are you sure there isn't something I might be allergic to?'

'I doubt that. You didn't react to anything you tried on Serieve, did you?'

'No, except for finding it overly bland.'

'Don't worry,' he grinned. 'Before we left, your father took care to present me with one of your salt-shakers. It'll be on the dinner table.'

Jaccavrie had analyzed the contents. Besides sodium and potassium chloride – noticeably less abundant on Kirkasant than on the average planet, but not scare enough to cause real trouble – the mixture included a number of other salts. The proportion of rare earths and especially arsenic was surprising. An ordinary human who ingested the latter element at that rate would lose quite a few years of life expectancy. Doubtless the first refugee generations had, too, when something else didn't get them first. But by now their descendants were so well adapted that food didn't taste right without a bit of arsenic trioxide.

'We wouldn't have to be cautious – we'd know in advance what you can and cannot take – if you'd permit a chromosome analysis,' Laure hinted. 'The laboratory aboard this ship can do it.'

Her cheeks turned more than ever coppery. She scowled. 'We refused before,' she said.

'May I ask why?'

'It . . . violates integrity. Humans are not to be probed into.'

He had encountered that attitude before, in several guises. To the Kirkasanter – at least, to the Hobrokan clansman; the planet

233

had other cultures – the body was a citadel for the ego, which by right should be inviolable. The feeling, so basic that few were aware of having it, had led to the formation of reserved, often rather cold personalities. It had handicapped if not stopped the progress of medicine. On the plus side, it had made for dignity and self-reliance; and it had caused this civilization to be spared professional gossips, confessional literature, and psychoanalysis.

'I don't agree,' Laure said. 'Nothing more is involved than scientific information. What's personal about a DNA map?'

'Well . . . maybe. I shall think on the matter.' Graydal made an obvious effort to get away from the topic. She sipped her drink, smiled, and said, 'Mn-m-m-, this *is* a noble flavor.'

'Hoped you'd like it. I do. We have a custom in the Commonalty – ' He touched glasses with her.

'Charming. Now we, when good friends are together, drink half what's in our cups and then exchange them.'

'May I?'

She blushed again, but with pleasure. 'Certainly. You honor me.'

'No, the honor is mine.' Laure went on, quite sincere: 'What your people have done is tremendous. What an addition to the race you'll be!'

Her mouth drooped. 'If ever my folk may be found.'

'Surely – '

'Do you think we did not try?' She tossed off another gulp of her cocktail. Evidently it went fast to her unaccustomed head. 'We did not fare forth blindly. Understand that *Makt* is not the first ship to leave Kirkasant's sun. But the prior ones went to nearby stars, stars that can be seen from home. They are many. We had not realized how many more are in the Cloud Universe, hidden from eyes and instruments, a few light-years farther on. We, our ship, we intended to take the next step. Only the next step. Barely beyond that shell of suns we could see from Kirkasant's system. We could find our way home again without trouble. Of course we could! We need but steer by those suns that were already charted on the edge of instrumental perception. Once we were in their neighborhood, our familiar part of space would be visible.'

234

She faced him, gripping his arm painfully hard, speaking in a desperate voice. 'What we had not known, what no one had known, was the imprecision of that charting. The absolute magnitudes, therefore the distances and relative positions of those verge-visible stars . . . had not been determined as well as the astronomers believed. Too much haze, too much shine, too much variability. Do you understand? And so, suddenly, our tables were worthless. We thought we could identify some suns. But we were wrong. Flitting toward them, we must have bypassed the volume of space we sought . . . and gone on and on, more hopelessly lost each day, each endless day –

'What makes you think you can find our home?'

Laure, who had heard the details before, had spent the time admiring her and weighing his reply. He sipped his own drink, letting the sourness glide over his palate and the alcohol slightly, soothingly burn him, before he said: 'I can try. I do have instruments your people have not yet invented. Inertial devices, for example, that work under hyperdrive as well as at true velocity. Don't give up hope.' He paused. 'I grant you, we might fail. Then what will you do?'

The blunt question, which would have driven many women of his world to tears, made her rally. She lifted her head and said – haughtiness rang through the words: 'Why, we will make the best of things, and I do not think we will do badly.'

Well, he thought, *she's descended from nothing but survivor types. Her nature is to face trouble and whip it.*

'I'm sure you will succeed magnificently,' he said. 'You'll need time to grow used to our ways, and you may never feel quite easy in them, but – '

'What are your marriages like?' she asked.

'Uh?' Laure fitted his jaw back into place.

She was not drunk, he decided. A bit of drink, together with these surroundings, the lilting music, odors and pheromones in the air, had simply lowered her inhibitions. The huntress in her was set free, and at once attacked whatever had been most deeply perturbing her. The basic reticence remained. She looked straight at him, but she was fiery-faced, as she said:

'We ought to have had an equal number of men and women along on *Makt*. Had we known what was to happen, we would have done so. But now ten men shall have to find wives among foreigners. Do you think they will have much difficulty?'

'Uh, why no. I shouldn't think they will,' he floundered. 'They're obviously superior types, and then, being exotic – glamorous . . .'

'I speak not of amatory pleasure. But . . . what I overheard on Serieve, a time or two . . . did I miscomprehend? Are there truly women among you who do not bear children?'

'On the older planets, yes, that's not uncommon. Population control – '

'We shall have to stay on Serieve, then, or worlds like it.' She sighed. 'I had hoped we might go to the pivot of your civilization, where your real work is done and our children might become great.'

Laure considered her. After a moment, he understood. Adapting to the uncountably many aliennesses of Kirkasant had been a long and cruel process. No blood line survived which did not do more than make up its own heavy losses. The will to reproduce was a requirement of existence. It, too, became an instinct.

He remembered that, while Kirkasant was not a very fertile planet, and today its population strained its resources, no one had considered reducing the birthrate. When someone on Serieve had asked why, Demring's folk had reacted strongly. The idea struck them as obscene. They didn't care for the notion of genetic modification or exogenetic growth either. And yet they were quite reasonable and noncompulsive about most other aspects of their culture.

Culture, Laure thought. *Yes. That's mutable. But you don't change your instincts; they're built into your chromosomes. Her people must have children.*

'Well,' he said, 'you can find women who want large families on the central planets, too. If anything, they'll be eager to marry your friends. They have a problem finding men who feel as they do, you see.'

Graydal dazzled him with a smile and held out her glass. 'Exchange?' she proposed.

'Hoy, you're way ahead of me.' He evened the liquid levels. 'Now.'

They looked at each other throughout the little ceremony. He nerved himself to ask, 'As for your women, do you necessarily have to marry within your ship?'

'No,' she said. 'It would depend on . . . whether any of your folk . . . might come to care for one of us.'

'That I can guarantee!'

'I would like a man who travels,' she murmured, 'if I and the children could come along.'

'Quite easy to arrange,' Laure said.

She said in haste: 'But we are buying grief, are we not? You told me perhaps you can find our planet for us.'

'Yes. I hope, though, if we succeed, that won't be the last I see of you.'

'Truly it won't.'

They finished their drinks and went to dinner. *Jaccavrie* was also an excellent cook. And the choice of wines was considerable. What was said and laughed at over the table had no relevance to anyone but Laure and Graydal.

Except that, at the end, with immense and tender seriousness, she said: 'If you want a cell sample from me . . . for analysis . . . you may have it.'

He reached across the table and took her hand. 'I wouldn't want you to do anything you might regret later,' he said.

She shook her head. The tawny eyes never left him. Her voice was slow, faintly slurred, but bespoke complete awareness of what she was saying. 'I have come to know you. For you to do this thing will be no violation.'

Laure explained eagerly: 'The process is simple and painless, as far as you're concerned. We can go right down to the lab. The computer operates everything. It'll give you an anesthetic spray and remove a small sample of flesh, so small that tomorrow you won't be sure where the spot was. Of course, the analysis will take a long while. We don't have all possible equipment aboard. And the computer does have to devote most of her – most of its attention to piloting and interior work. But at the end, we'll be able to tell you – '

'Hush.' Her smile was sleepy. 'No matter. If you wish this, that's enough. I ask only one thing.'

'What?'

'Do not let a machine use the knife, or the needle, or whatever it is. I want you to do that yourself.'

'. . . Yes. Yonder is our home sky.' The physicist Hirn Oran's son spoke slow and hushed. Cosmic interference seethed across his radio voice, nigh drowning it in Laure's and Graydal's earplugs.

'No,' the Ranger said. 'Not off there. We're already in it.'

'What?' Silvery against rock, the two space-armored figures turned to stare at him. He could not see their expressions behind the faceplates, but he could imagine how astonishment flickered above awe.

He paused, arranging words in his mind. The star noise in his receivers was like surf and fire. The landscape overwhelmed him.

Here was no simple airless planet. No planet is ever really simple, and this one had a stranger history than most. Eons ago it was apparently a subjovian, with a cloudy hydrohelium and methane atmosphere and an immense shell of ice and frozen gases around the core; for it orbited its sun at a distance of almost a billion and a half kilometers, and though that primary was bright, at this remove it could be little more than a spark.

Until stellar evolution – hastened, Laure believed, by an abnormal infall of cosmic material – took the star off the main sequence. It swelled, surface cooling to red but total output growing so monstrous that the inner planets were consumed. On the farther ones, like this, atmosphere fled into space. Ice melted; the world-ocean boiled; each time the pulsations of the sun reached a maximum, more vapor escaped. Now nothing remained except a ball of metal and rock, hardly larger than a terrestrial-type globe. As the pressure of the top layers were removed, frightful tectonic forces must have been liberated. Mountains – the younger ones with crags like sharp teeth, the older ones worn by meteorite and thermal erosion – rose from a cratered plain of gloomy stone. Currently at a minimum, but nonetheless immense, a full seven degrees across, blue core surrounded and dimmed by the tenuous ruddy atmosphere, the sun smoldered aloft.

Its furnace light was not the sole illumination. Another star was passing sufficiently near at the time that it showed a perceptible disk ... in a stopped-down viewscreen, because no human eye could directly confront that electric cerulean intensity. The outsider was a B_8 newborn out of dust and gas, blazing with an intrinsic radiance of a hundred Sols.

Neither one helped in the shadows cast by the pinnacled upthrust which Laure's party was investigating. Flashcasters were necessary.

But more was to see overhead, astride the dark. Stars in thousands powdered the sky, brilliant with proximity. And they were the mere fringes of the cluster. It was rising as the planet turned, partly backgrounding and partly following the sun. Laure had never met a sight to compare. For the most part, the individuals he could pick out in that enormous spheroidal cloud of light were themselves red: long-lived dwarfs, dying giants like the one that brooded over him. But many glistened exuberant golden, emerald, sapphire. Some could not be older than the blue which wandered past and added its own harsh hue to this land. All those stars were studded through a soft glow that pervaded the entire cluster, a nacreous luminosity into which they faded and vanished, the fog wherein his companions had lost their home but which was a shining beauty to behold.

'You live in a wonder,' Laure said.

Graydal moved toward him. She had had no logical reason to come down out of *Makt's* orbit with him and Hirn. The idea was simply to break out certain large ground-based instruments that *Jaccavrie* carried, for study of their goal before traveling on. Any third party could assist. But she had laid her claim first, and none of her shipmates argued. They knew how often she and Laure were in each other's company.

'Wait until you reach our world,' she said low. 'Space is eldritch and dangerous. But once on Kirkasant – we will watch the sun go down in the Rainbow Desert; suddenly, in that thin air, night has come, our shimmering star-crowded night, and the

239

auroras dance and whisper above the stark hills. We will see great flying flocks rise from dawn mists over the salt marshes, hear their wings thunder and their voices flute. We will stand on the battlements of Ey, under the banners of those very knights who long ago rid the land of the firearms, and watch the folk dance welcome to a new year – '

'If the navigator pleases,' said Hirn, his voice sharpened by an unadmitted dauntedness, 'we will save our dreams for later and attend now to the means of realizing them. At present, we are supposed to choose a good level site for the observing apparatus. But, ah, Ranger Laure, may I ask what you meant by saying we are already back in the Cloud Universe?'

Laure was not as annoyed to have Graydal interrupted as he might normally have been. She'd spoken of Kirkasant so often that he felt he had almost been there himself. Doubtless it had its glories, but by his standards it was a grim, dry, storm-scoured planet where he would not care to stay for long at a time. Of course, to her it was beloved home; and he wouldn't mind making occasional visits if – No, chaos take it, there was work on hand!

Part of his job was to make explanations. He said: 'In your sense of the term, Physicist Hirn, the Cloud Universe does not exist.'

The reply was curt through the static. 'I disputed that point on Serieve already, with Vandange and others. And I resented their implication that we of *Makt* were either liars or incompetent observers.'

'You're neither,' Laure said quickly. 'But communications had a double barrier on Serieve. First, an imperfect command of your language. Only on the way here, spending most of my time in contact with your crew, have I myself begun to feel a real mastery of Hobrokan. The second barrier, though, was in some ways more serious: Vandange's stubborn preconceptions, and your own.'

'I was willing to be convinced.'

'But you never got a convincing argument. Vandange was so dogmatically certain that what you reported having seen was impossible, that he didn't take a serious look at your report to see if it might have an orthodox explanation after all. You naturally got angry at this and cut the discussions off short. For your part, you had what you had always been taught was a perfectly good theory, which your experiences had confirmed. You weren't going to change your whole concept of physics just because the unlovable Ozer Vandange scoffed at it.'

'But we were mistaken,' Graydal said. 'You've intimated as much, Daven, but never made your meaning clear.'

'I wanted to see the actual phenomenon for myself, first,' Laure said. 'We have a proverb – so old that it's reputed to have originated on Earth – "It is a capital mistake to theorize in advance of the data." But I couldn't help speculating and what I see shows my speculations were along the right lines.'

'Well?' Hirn challenged.

'Let's start with looking at the situation from your viewpoint,' Laure suggested. 'Your people spent millennia on Kirkasant. You lost every hint, except a few ambiguous traditions, that things might be different elsewhere. To you, it was natural that the night sky should be like a gently shining mist, and stars should crowd thickly around. When you developed the scientific method again, not many generations back, perforce you studied the universe you knew. Ordinary physics and chemistry, even atomistics and quantum theory, gave you no special problems. But you measured the distances of the visible stars as lightmonths – at most, a few light-years – after which they vanished in the foggy background. You measured the concentration of that fog, that dust and fluorescing gas. And you had no reason to suppose the interstellar medium was not equally dense everywhere. Nor had you any hint of receding galaxies.

'So your version of relativity made space sharply curved by the mass packed together throughout it. The entire universe was two or three hundred light-years across. Stars condensed and evolved – you could witness every stage of that – but in a chaotic fashion, with no particular overall structure. It's a wonder to me that you went on to gravitics and hyperdrive. I wish I were scientist enough to appreciate how different some of the laws and constants must be in your physics. But you did plow ahead. I guess the fact you knew these things were possible was important to your success. Your scientists would keep fudging and finagling, in defiance of theoretical niceties, until they made something work.'

'Um-m-m . . . as a matter of fact, yes,' Hirn said in a slightly abashed tone. Graydal snickered.

'Well, then *Makt* lost her way, and emerged into the outer universe, which was totally strange,' Laure said. 'You had to account somehow for what you saw. Like any scientists, you stayed with accepted ideas as long as feasible – a perfectly correct principle which my people call the razor of Occam. I imagine that the notion of continguous space-times with varying properties looks quite logical if you're used to thinking of a universe with an extremely small radius. You may have been puzzled as to how you managed to get out of one "bubble" and into the next, but I daresay you cobbled together a tentative explanation.'

'I did,' Hirn said. 'If we postulate a multidimensional – '

'Never mind,' Laure said. 'That's no longer needful. We can account for the facts much more simply.'

'How? I have been pondering it. I think I can grasp the idea of a universe billions of light-years across, in which the stars form galaxies. But our home space – '

'Is a dense star cluster. And as such, it has no definite boundaries. That's what I meant by saying we are already in it. In the thin verge, at least.' Laure pointed to the diffuse, jeweled magnificence that was rising higher above these wastes, in the wake of the red and blue suns. 'Yonder's the main body, and Kirkasant is somewhere there. But this system here is associated. I've checked proper motions and I know.'

'I could have accepted some such picture while on Serieve,' Hirn said. 'But Vandange was so insistent that a star cluster like this cannot be.' Laure visualized the sneer behind his faceplate. 'I thought that he, belonging to the master civilization, would know thereof he spoke.'

'He does. He's merely rather unimaginative,' Laure said. 'You see, what we have here is a globular cluster. That's a group made up of stars close together in a roughly spherical volume of space. I'd guess you have a quarter million, packed into a couple of hundred light-years' diameter.

'But globular clusters haven't been known like this one. The ones we do know lie mostly well off the galactic plane. The space within them is much clearer than in the spiral arms, almost a perfect vacuum. The individual members are red. Any normal stars of greater than minimal mass have gone off the main sequence long ago. The survivors are metal-poor. That's another sign of extreme age. Heavy elements are formed in stellar cores, you know, and spewed back into space. So it's the younger suns, coalescing out of the enriched interstellar medium, that contain a lot of metal. All in all, everything points to the globular clusters being relics of an embryo stage in the galaxy's life.

'Yours, however – ! Dust and gas so thick that not even a giant can be seen across many parsecs. Plenty of mainsequence stars, including blues which cannot be more than a few million years old, they burn out so fast. Spectra, not to mention planets your explorers visited, showing atomic abundances far skewed toward the high end of the periodic table. A background radiation too powerful for a man like me to dare take up permanent residence in your country.

'Such a cluster shouldn't be!'

'But it is,' Graydal said.

Laure made bold to squeeze her hand, though little of that could pass through the gauntlets. 'I'm glad,' he answered.

'How do you explain the phenomenon?' Hirn asked.

'Oh, that's obvious . . . now that I've seen the thing and gathered some information on its path,' Laure said. 'An improbable situation, maybe unique, but not impossible. This cluster happens to have an extremely eccentric orbit around the galactic center of mass. Once or twice a gigayear, it passes through the vast thick clouds that surround that region. By gravitation, it sweeps up immense quantities of stuff. Meanwhile, I suppose, perturbation causes some of its senior members to drift off. You might say it's periodically rejuvenated.

'At prsent, it's on its way out again. Hasn't quite left our spiral arm. It passed near the galactic midpoint just a short while back, cosmically speaking; I'd estimate less than fifty million years. The infall is still turbulent, still condensing out into new stars like that blue giant shining on us. Your home sun and its planets must be a product of an earlier sweep. But there've been twenty or thirty such since the galaxy formed, and each one of them was responsible for several generations of giant stars. So Kirkasant has a lot more heavy elements than the normal planet, even though it's not much younger than Earth. Do you follow me?'

'Hm-m-m . . . perhaps. I shall have to think.' Hirn walked off, across the great tilted block on which the party stood, to its edge, where he stopped and looked down into the shadows below. They were deep and knife sharp. The mingled light of red and blue suns, stars, starfog played eerie across the stone land. Laure grew aware of what strangeness and what silence – under the hiss in his ears – pressed in on him.

Graydal must have felt the same, for she edged close until their armors clinked together. He would have liked to see her face. She said: 'Do you truly believe we can enter that realm, and conquer it?'

'I don't know,' he said, slow and blunt. 'The sheer number of stars may beat us.'

'A large enough fleet could search them, one by one.'

'If it could navigate. We have yet to find out whether that's possible.'

'Suppose. Did you guess a quarter million suns in the cluster? Not all are like ours. Not even a majority. On the other coin side, with visibility as low as it is, space must be searched back and forth, light-year by light-year. We of *Makt* could die of eld before a single vessel chanced on Kirkasant.'

'I'm afraid that's true.'

'Yet an adequate number of ships, dividing the task, could find our home in a year or two.'

'That would be unattainably expensive, Graydal.'

He thought he sensed her stiffening. 'I've come on this before,' she said coldly, withdrawing from his touch. 'In your

244

Commonalty they count the cost and the profit first. Honor, adventure, simple charity must run a poor second.'

'Be reasonable,' he said. 'Cost represents labor, skill, and resources. The gigantic fleet that would go looking for Kirkasant must be diverted from other jobs. Other people would suffer need as a result. Some might suffer sharply.'

'Do you mean a civilization as big, as productive as yours could not spare that much effort for a while without risking disaster?'

She's quick on the uptake, Laure thought. *Knowing what machine technology can do on her single impoverished world, she can well guess what it's capable of with millions of planets to draw on. But how can I make her realize that matters aren't that simple?'*

'Please, Graydal,' he said. 'Won't you believe I'm working for you? I've come this far, and I'll go as much farther as need be, if something doesn't kill us.'

He heard her gulp. 'Yes. I offer apology. *You* are different.'

'Not really. I'm a typical Commonalty member. Later, maybe, I can show you how our civilization works, and what an odd problem in political economy we've got if Kirkasant is to be rediscovered. But first we have to establish that locating it is physically possible. We have to make long-term observations from here, and then enter those mists, and – One trouble at a time, I beg you!'

She laughed gently. 'Indeed, my friend. And you will find a way.' The mirth faded. It had never been strong.

'Won't you?' The reflection of clouded stars glistened on her faceplate like tears.

Blindness was not dark. It shone.

Standing on the bridge, amidst the view of space, Laure saw nimbus and thunderheads. They piled in cliffs, they eddied and steamed, their color was a sheen of all colors overlying white – mother-of-pearl – but here and there they darkened with shadows and grottoes; here and there they glowed dull red as they reflected a nearby sun. For the stars were scattered about in their myriads, dominantly ruby and ember, some yellow or

'Oh, yes. But the effects are soon smothered. Too much else is going on. Too many neutrinos from too many different sources, to name one thing. Too many magnetic effects. The stars are so close together, you see; and so many of them are double, triple, quadruple, hence revolving rapidly and twisting the force lines; and irradiation keeps a goodly fraction of the interstellar medium in the plasma state. Thus we get electromagnetic action of every sort; plus sunchroton and betatron radiation, plus nuclear collision, plus – '

'Spare me the complete list,' Laure broke in. 'Just say the noise level is too high for your instruments.'

'And for any instruments that I can extrapolate as buildable,' *Jaccavrie* replied. 'The precision their filters would require seems greater than the laws of atomistics would allow.'

'What about your inertial system? Bollixed up, too?'

'It's beginning to be. That's why I asked you to come take a good look at what's around us and what we're headed into, while you listen to my report.' The robot was not built to know fear, but Laure wondered if she didn't spring back to pedantry as a refuge: 'Inertial navigation would work here at kinetic velocities. But we can't traverse parsecs except by hyperdrive. Inertial and gravitational mass being identical, too rapid a change of gravitational potential will tend to cause uncontrollable precession and nutation. We can compensate for that in normal parts of space. But not here. With so many stars so closely packed, moving among each other on paths too complex for me to calculate, the variation rate is becoming too much.'

'In short,' Laure said slowly, 'if we go deeper into this stuff, we'll be flying blind.'

'Yes. Just as *Makt* did.'

'We can get out into clear space time, can't we? You can follow a more or less straight line till we emerge?'

'True. I don't like hazards. The cosmic ray background is increasing considerably.'

'You have screen fields?'

'But I'm considering the implications. Those particles have to originate somewhere. Magnetic acceleration will only account for a fraction of their intensity. Hence the rate of nova

248

production in this cluster, and of supernovae in the recent past, must be enormous. This in turn indicates vast numbers of lesser bodies – neutron stars, rogue planets, large meteoroids, thick dust banks – things that might be undetectable before we blunder into them.'

Laure smiled at her unseen scanner. 'If anything goes wrong, you'll react fast,' he said. 'You always do.'

'I can't guarantee we won't run into trouble I can't deal with.'

'Can you estimate the odds on that for me?'

Jaccavrie was silent. The air sputtered and sibilated. Laure found his vision drowning in the starfog. He needed a minute to realize he had not been answered. 'Well?' he said.

'The parameters are too uncertain.' Overtones had departed from her voice. 'I can merely say that the probability of disaster is high in comparison to the value for travel through normal regions of the galaxy.'

'Oh, for chaos' sake!' Laure's laugh was uneasy. 'That figure is almost too small to measure. We knew before we entered this nebula that we'd be taking a risk. Now what about coherent radiation from natural sources?'

'My judgment is that the risk is out of proportion to the gain,' *Jaccavrie* said. 'At best, this is a place for scientific study. You've other work to do. Your basic – and dangerous – fantasy is that you can satisfy the emotional cravings of a few semibarbarians.'

Anger sprang up in Laure. He gave it cold shape: 'My order was that you report on coherent radiation.'

Never before had he pulled the rank of his humanness on her.

She said like dead metal: 'I have detected some in the visible and short infrared, where certain types of star excite pseudo-quasar processes in the surrounding gas. It is dissipated as fast as any other light.'

'The radio bands are clear?'

'Yes, of that type of wave, although – '

'Enough. We'll proceed as before, toward the center of the cluster. Cut this view and connect me with *Makt*.'

The hazy suns vanished. Laure was alone in a metal compartment. He took a seat and glowered at the outercom screen before him. What had gotten into *Jaccavrie*, anyway? She'd been making her disapproval of this quest more and more obvious over the last few days. She wanted him to turn around, report to HQ, and leave the Kirkasanters there for whatever they might be able to make of themselves in a lifetime's exile. Well . . . her judgments were always conditioned by the fact that she was a Ranger vessel, built for Ranger work. But couldn't she see that his duty, as well as his desire, was to help Graydal's people?

The screen flickered. The two ships were so differently designed that it was hard for them to stay in phase for any considerable time, and thus hard to receive the modulation imposed on spacepulses. After a while the image steadied to show a face. 'I'll switch you to Captain Demring,' the communications officer said at once. In his folk, such lack of ceremony was as revealing of strain as haggardness and dark-rimmed eyes.

The image wavered again and became the Old Man's. He was in his cabin, which had direct audiovisual connections, and the background struck Laure anew with outlandishness. What history had brought forth the artistic conventions of that bright-colored, angular-figured tapestry? What song was being sung on the player, in what language, and on what scale? What was the symbolism behind the silver mask on the door?

Worn but indomitable, Demring looked forth and said, 'Peace between us. What occasions this call?'

'You should know what I've learned,' Laure said. 'Uh, can we make this a three-way with your navigator?'

'Why?' The question was machine steady.

'Well, that is, her duties – '

'She is to help carry out decisions,' Demring said. 'She does not make them. At maximum, she can offer advice in discussion.' He waited before adding, with a thrust: 'And you have been having a great deal of discussion already with my daughter, Ranger Laure.'

'No . . . I mean, yes, but – ' The younger man rallied. He did have psych training to call upon, although its use had not yet become reflexive in him. 'Captain,' he said. 'Graydal has been helping me understand your ethos. Our two cultures have to see what each other's basics are if they're to cooperate, and that process begins right here, among these ships. Graydal can make things clearer to me, and I believe grasps my intent better, than anyone else of your crew.'

'Why is that?' Demring demanded.

Laure suppressed pique at his arrogance – he was her father – and attempted a smile. 'Well, sir, we've gotten acquainted to a degree, she and I. We can drop formality and just be friends.'

'That is not necessarily desirable,' Demring said.

Laure recollected that, throughout the human species, sexual customs are among the most variable. And the most emotionally charged. He put himself inside Demring's prejudices and said with what he hoped was the right slight note of indignation: 'I assure you nothing improper has occurred.'

'No, no.' The Kirkasanter made a brusque, chopping gesture. 'I trust her. And you, I am sure. Yet I must warn that close ties between members of radically different societies can prove disastrous to everyone involved.'

Laure might have sympathized as he thought, *He's afraid to let down his mask – is that why their art uses the motif so much? – but underneath, he is a father worrying about his little girl.* He felt too harassed. First his computer, now this! He said coolly, 'I don't believe our cultures are that alien. They're both rational-technological, which is a tremendous similarity to begin with. But haven't we got off the subject? I wanted you to hear the findings this ship has made.'

Demring relaxed. The unhuman universe he could cope with. 'Proceed at will, Ranger.'

When he had heard Laure out, though, he scowled, tugged his beard, and said without trying to hide distress: 'Thus we have no chance of finding Kirkasant by ourselves.'

'Evidently not,' Laure said. 'I'd hoped that one of my modern locator systems would work in this cluster. If so, we could have zigzagged rapidly between the stars, mapping them, and had a fair likelihood of finding the group you know within months. But as matters stand, we can't establish an accurate enough grid, and we have nothing to tie any such grid to. Once a given star disappears in the fog, we can't find it again. Not even by straight-line backtracking, because we don't have the navigational feedback to keep on a truly straight line.'

'Lost.' Demring stared down at his hands, clenched on the desk before him. When he looked up again, the bronze face was rigid with pain. 'I was afraid of this,' he said. 'It is why I was reluctant to come back at all. I feared the effect of disappointment on my crew. By now you must know one major respect in which we differ from you. To us, home, kinfolk, ancestral graves are not mere pleasures. They are an important part of our identities. We are prepared to explore and colonize, but not to be totally cut off.' He straightened in his seat and turned the confession into a strategic datum by finishing dry-voiced: 'Therefore, the sooner we leave this degree of familiarity behind us and accept with physical renunciation the truth of what has happened to us – the sooner we get out of this cluster – the better for us.'

'No,' Laure said. 'I've given a lot of thought to your situation. There *are* ways to navigate here.'

Demring did not show surprise. He, too, must have dwelt on contingencies and possibilities. Laure sketched them nevertheless:

'Starting from outside the cluster, we can establish a grid of artificial beacons, I'd guess fifty thousand, in orbit around selected stars, would do. If each has its distinctive identifying signal, a spaceship can locate herself and lay a course. I can imagine several ways to make them. You want them to emit something that isn't swamped by natural noise. Hyperdrive drones, shuttling automatically back and forth, would be detectable in a light-year's radius. Coherent radio broadcasters on the right bands should be detectable at the same distance or better. Since the stars hereabouts are only light-weeks or light-months apart, an electromagnetic network wouldn't take long to complete its linkups. No doubt a real engineer, turned loose on the problem, would find better answers than these.'

'I know,' Demring said. 'We on *Makt* have discussed the matter and reached similar conclusions. The basic obstacle is the work involved, first in producing that number of beacons, then

– more significantly – in planting them. Many man-years, much shipping, must go to that task, if it is to be accomplished in a reasonable time.'

'Yes.'

'I like to think,' said Demring, 'that the clans of Hobrok would not haggle over who was to pay the cost. But I have talked with men on Serieve. I have taken heed of what Graydal does and does not relay of her conversations with you. Yours is a mercantile civilization.'

'Not exactly,' Laure said. 'I've tried to explain –'

'Don't bother. We shall have the rest of our lives to learn about your Commonalty. Shall we turn about, now, and end this expedition?'

Laure winced at the scorn but shook his head. 'No, best we continue. We can make extraordinary findings here. Things that'll attract scientists. And with a lot of ships buzzing around –'

Demring's smile had no humor. 'Spare me, Ranger. There will never be that many scientiests come avisiting. And they will never plant beacons throughout the cluster. Why should they? The chance of one of their vessels stumbling on Kirkasant is negligible. They will be after unusual stars and planets, information on magnetic fields and plasmas and whatever else is readily studied. Not even the anthropologists will have any strong impetus to search out our world. They have many others to work on, equally strange to them, far more accessible.'

'I have my own obligations,' Laure said. 'It was a long trip here. Having made it, I should recoup some of the cost to my organization by gathering as much data as I can before turning home.'

'No matter the cost to my people?' Demring said slowly. 'That they see their own sky around them, but nonetheless are exiles – for weeks longer?'

Laure lost patience. 'Withdraw if you like, Captain,' he snapped. 'I've no authority to stop you. But I'm going on. To the middle of the cluster, in fact.'

Demring retorted in a cold flare: 'Do you hope to find something that will make you personally rich, or only personally famous?' He reined himself in at once. 'This is no place for impulsive acts. Your vessel is undoubtedly superior to mine. I am not certain, either that *Makt's* navigational equipment is equal to finding that advanced base where we must refuel her. If you continue, I am bound in simple prudence to accompany you, unless the risks you take become gross. But I urge that we confer again.'

'Any time, Captain.' Laure cut his circuit.

He sat then, for a while, fuming. The culture barrier couldn't be that high. Could it? Surely the Kirkasanters were neither so stupid nor so perverse as not to see what he was trying to do for them. Or were they? Or was it his fault? He'd concentrated more on learning about them than on teaching them about him. Still, Graydal, at least, should know him by now.

The ship sensed an incoming call and turned Laure's screen back on. And there she was. Gladness lifted in him until he saw her expression.

She said without greeting, winter in the golden gaze: 'We officers have just been given a playback of your conversation with my father. What is your' (outphasing occurred, making the image into turbulence, filling the voice with staticlike ugliness, but he thought he recognized) 'intention?' The screen blanked.

'Maintain contact,' Laure told *Jaccavrie*.

'Not easy in these gravitic fields,' the ship said.

Laure jumped to his feet, cracked fist in palm, and shouted, 'Is everything trying to brew trouble for me? Bring her back or so help me, I'll scrap you!'

He got a picture again, though it was blurred and watery and the voice was streaked with buzzes and whines, as if he called to Graydal across light-years of swallowing starfog. She said – was it a little more kindly? – 'We're puzzled. I was deputed to inquire further, since I am most . . . familiar . . . with you. If our two craft can't find Kirkasant by themselves, why are we going on?'

Laure understood her so well, after the watches when they talked, dined, drank, played music, laughed together, that he saw the misery behind her armor. For her people – for herself –

this journey among mists was crueler than it would have been for him had he originated here. He belonged to a civilization of travelers; to him, no one planet could be the land of lost content. But in them would always stand a certain ridge purple against sunset, march at dawn, ice cloud walking over wind-gnawed desert crags, ancient castle, wingbeat in heaven . . . and always, always, the dear bright nights that no other place in man's universe knew.

They were a warrior folk. They would not settle down to be pitied; they would forge something powerful for themselves in their exile. But he was not helping them forget their uprooted-ness.

Thus he almost gave her his true reason. He halted in time and, instead, explained in more detail what he had told Captain Demring. His ship represented a considerable investment, to be amortized over her service life. Likewise, with his training, did he. The time he had spent coming hither was, therefore, equivalent to a large sum of money. And to date, he had nothing to show for that expense except confirmation of a fairly obvious guess about the nature of Kirkasant's surroundings.

He had broad discretion — while he was in service. But he could be discharged. He would be, if his career, taken as a whole didn't seem to be returning a profit. In this particular case, the profit would consist of detailed information about a unique environment. You could prorate that in such terms as: scientific knowledge, with its potentialities for technological progress; space-faring experience; public relations —

Graydal regarded him in a kind of horror. 'You cannot mean . . . we go on . . . merely to further your private ends,' she whispered. Interference gibed at them both.

'No!' Laure protested. 'Look, only look, I want to help you. But you, too, have to justify yourselves economically. You're the reason I came so far in the first place. If you're to work with the Commonalty, and it's to help you make a fresh start, you have to show that that's worth the Commonalty's while. Here's where we start proving it. By going on. Eventually, by bringing them in a bookful of knowledge they didn't have before.'

Her gaze upon him calmed but remained aloof. 'Do you think that is right?'

'It's the way things are, anyhow,' he said. 'Sometimes I wonder if my attempts to explain my people to you haven't glided right off your brain.'

'You have made it clear that they think of nothing but their own good,' she said thinly.

'If so, I've failed to make anything clear.' Laure slumped in his chair web. Some days hit a man with one club after the next. He forced himself to sit erect again and say:

'We have a different ideal from you. Or no, that's not correct. We have the same set of ideals. The emphases are different. You believe the individual ought to be free and ought to help his fellowmen. We do, too. But you make the service basic, you give it priority. We have the opposite way. You give a man, or a woman, duties to the clan and the country from birth. But you protect his individuality by frowning on slavishness and on anyone who doesn't keep a strictly private side of his life. We give a person freedom, within a loose framework of common-sense prohibitions. And then we protect his social aspect by frowning on greed, selfishness, callousness.'

'I know,' she said. 'You have – '

'But maybe you haven't thought how we *must* do it that way,' he pleaded. 'Civilization's gotten too big out there for anything but freedom to work. The Commonalty isn't a government. How would you govern ten million planets? It's a private, voluntary, mutual-benefit society, open to anyone anywhere who meets the modest standards. It maintains certain services for its members, like my own space rescue work. The services are widespread and efficient enough the local planetary governments also like to hire them. But I don't speak for my civilization. Nobody does. You've made a friend of me. But how do you make friends with ten million times a billion individuals?'

'You've told me before,' she said.

And it didn't register. Not really. Too new an idea for you, I suppose, Laure thought. He ignored her remark and went on:

'In the same way, we can't have a planned interstellar economy. Planning breaks down under the sheer mass of detail when it's attempted for a single continent. History is full of cases. So we rely on the market, which operates as automatically as gravitation. Also as efficiently, as impersonally, and sometimes as ruthlessly – but we didn't make this universe. We only live on it.'

He reached out his hands, as if to touch her through the distance and the distortion. 'Can't you see? I'm not able to help your plight. Nobody is. No individual quadrillionaire, no foundation, no government, no consortium could pay the cost of finding your home for you. It's not a matter of lacking charity. It's a matter of lacking resources for that magnitude of effort. The resources are divided among too many people, each of whom has his own obligations to meet first.

'Certainly, if each would contribute a pittance, you could buy your fleet. But the tax mechanism for collecting that pittance doesn't exist and can't be made to exist. As for free-will donations – how do we get your message across to an entire civilization, that big, that diverse, that busy with its own affairs? – which include cases of need far more urgent than yours.

'Graydal, we're not greedy where I come from. We're helpless.'

She studied him at length. He wondered, but could not see through the ripplings, what emotions passed across her face. Finally she spoke, not altogether ungently, though helmeted again in the reserve of her kindred, and he could not hear anything of it through the buzzings except: '. . . proceed, since we must. For a while, anyhow. Good watch, Ranger.'

The screen blanked. This time he couldn't make the ship repair the connection for him.

At the heart of the great cluster, where the nebula was so thick as to be a nearly featureless glow, pearl-hued and shot with rainbows, the stars were themselves so close that thousands could be seen. The spaceships crept forward like frigates on unknown seas of ancient Earth. For here was more than fog; here were shoals, reefs, and riptides. Energies travailed in the plasma. Drifts of dust, loose planets, burnt-out suns lay in menace behind the denser clouds. Twice *Makt* would have met catastrophe had not *Jaccavrie* sensed the danger with keener instruments and cried a warning to sheer off.

After Demring's subsequent urgings had failed, Graydal came aboard in person to beg Laure that he turn homeward. That she should surrender her pride to such an extent bespoke how worn down she and her folk were. 'What are we gaining worth the risk?' she asked shakenly.

'We're proving that this is a treasure house of absolutely unique phenomena,' he answered. He was also hollowed, partly from the long travel and the now constant tension, partly from the half estrangement between him and her. He tried to put enthusiasm in his voice. 'Once we've reported, expeditions are certain to be organized. I'll bet the foundations of two or three whole new sciences will get laid here.'

'I know. Everything astronomical in abundance, close together and interacting.' Her shoulders drooped. 'But our task isn't research. We can go back now, we could have gone back already, and carried enough details with us. Why do we not?'

'I want to investigate several planets yet, on the ground, in different systems,' he told her. 'Then we'll call a halt.'

'What do they matter to you?'

'Well, local stellar spectra are freakish. I want to know if the element abundances in solid bodies correspond.'

She stared at him. 'I do not understand you,' she said. 'I thought I did, but I was wrong. You have no compassion. You led us, you lured us so far in that we can't escape without your ship for a guide. You don't care how tired and tormented we are. You can't, or won't, understand why we are anxious to live.'

'I am myself,' he tried to grin. 'I enjoy the process.'

The dark head shook. 'I said you won't understand. We do not fear death for ourselves. But most of us have not yet had children. We do fear death for our bloodlines. We *need* to find a home, forgetting Kirkasant, and begin our families. You, though, you keep us on this barren search – why? For your own glory?'

He should have explained then. But the strain and weariness in him snapped: 'You accepted my leadership. That makes me

258

responsible for you, and I can't be responsible if I don't have command. You can endure another couple of weeks. That's all it'll take.'

And she should have answered that she knew his motives were good and wished simply to hear his reasons. But being the descendant of hunters and soldiers, she clicked her heels together and flung back at him: 'Very well, Ranger. I shall convey your words to my captain.'

She left, and did not again board *Jaccavrie*.

Later, after a sleepless 'night' Laure said, 'Put me through to *Makt's* navigator.'

'I wouldn't advise that,' said the woman-like voice of his ship.

'Why not?'

'I presume you want to make amends. Do you know how she – or her father, or her young male shipmates that must be attracted to her – how they will react? They are alien to you, and under intense strain.'

'They're human!'

Engines pulsed. Ventilators whispered. 'Well?' said Laure.

'I'm not designed to compute about emotions, except on an elementary level,' *Jaccavrie* said. 'But please recollect the diversity of mankind. On Reith, for example, ordinary peaceful men can fall into literally murderous rages. It happens so often that violence under those circumstances is not a crime in their law. A Talatto will be patient and cheerful in adversity, up to a certain point: after which he quits striving, contemplates his God, and waits to die. You can think of other cultures. And they are within the ambience of the Commonalty. How foreign might not the Kirkasanters be?'

'Um-m-m'

'I suggest you obtrude your presence on them as little as possible. That makes for the smallest probability of provoking some unforeseeable outburst. Once our task is completed, once we are bound home, the stress will be removed, and you can safely behave toward them as you like.'

'Well ... you may be right.' Laure stared dull-eyed at a bulkhead. 'I don't know. I just don't know.'

Before long, he was too busy to fret much. *Jaccavrie* went at his direction, finding planetary systems that belonged to various stellar types. In each, he landed on an airless body, took analytical readings and mineral samples, and gave the larger worlds a cursory inspection from a distance.

He did not find life. Not anywhere. He had expected that. In fact, he was confirming his whole guess about the inmost part of the cluster.

Here gravitation had concentrated dust and gas till the rate of star production became unbelievable. Each time the cluster passed through the clouds around galactic center and took on a new load of material, there must have been a spate of supernovae, several per century for a million years or more. He could not visualize what fury had raged; he scarcely dared put his estimate in numbers. Probably radiation had sterilized every abode of life for fifty light-years around. (Kirkasant must, therefore, lie farther out – which fitted in with what he had been told, that the interstellar medium was much denser in this core region than in the neighborhood of the vanished world.)

Nuclei had been cooked in stellar interiors, not the two, three, four star-generations which have preceded the majority of the normal galaxy – here, a typical atom might well have gone through a dozen successive supernova explosions. Transformation built on transformation. Hydrogen and helium remained the commonest elements, but only because of overwhelming initial abundance. Otherwise the lighter substances had mostly become rare. Planets were like nothing ever known before. Giant ones did not have thick shells of frozen water, nor did smaller ones have extensive silicate crusts. Carbon, oxygen, nitrogen, sodium, aluminum, calcium were all but lost among ... iron, gold, mercury, tungsten, bismuth, uranium and transuranics – On some little spheres Laure dared not land. They radiated too fiercely. A heavily armored robot might someday set foot on them, but never a living organism.

The crew of *Makt* didn't offer to help him. Irrational in his hurt, he didn't ask them. *Jaccavrie* could carry on any essential communication with their captain and navigator. He toiled until he dropped, woke, fueled his body, and went back to work. Between stars, he made detailed analyses of his samples. That was tricky enough to keep his mind off Graydal. Minerals like these could have formed nowhere but in this witchy realm.

Finally the ships took orbit around a planet that had atmosphere. 'Do you indeed wish to make entry there?' the computer asked. 'I would not recommend it.'

'You never recommend anything I want to do,' Laure grunted. 'I know air adds an extra factor to reckon with. But I want to get some idea of element distribution at the surface of objects like that.' He rubbed bloodshot eyes. 'It'll be the last. Then we go home.'

'As you wish.' Did the artificial voice actually sigh? 'But after this long time in space, you'll have to batten things down for an aerodynamic landing.'

'No, I won't. I'm taking the sled as usual. You'll stay put.'

'You are being reckless. This isn't an airless globe where I can orbit right above the mountaintops and see everything that might happen to you. Why, if I haven't misgauged the ionosphere is so charged that the sled radio can't reach me.'

'Nothing's likely to go wrong,' Laure said. 'But should it, you can't be spared. The Kirkasanters need you to conduct them safely out.'

'I – '

'You heard your orders.' Laure proceeded to discuss certain basic precautions. Not that he felt they were necessary. His objective looked peaceful – dry, sterile, a stone spinning around a star.

Nevertheless, when he departed the main hatch and gunned his gravity sled to kill velocity, the view caught at his breath.

Around him reached the shining fog. Stars and stars were caught in it, illuminating caverns and tendrils, aureoled with many-colored fluorescences. Even as he looked, one such point, steely blue, multiplied its brilliance until the intensity hurt his eyes. Another nova. Every stage of stellar evolution was so

261

richly represented that it was as if time itself had been compressed – cosmos, what an astrophysical laboratory!

(For unmanned instruments, as a general rule. Human flesh couldn't stand many months in a stretch of the cosmic radiation that sleeted through these spaces, the synchroton and betraton and Cerenkov quanta that boiled from particles hurled in the gas across the intertwining magnetism of atoms and suns. Laure kept glancing at the cumulative exposure meter on his left wrist.)

The solar disk was large and lurid orange. Despite thermostating in the sled, Laure felt its heat strike at him through the bubble and his own armor. A stepdown viewer revealed immense prominences licking flame-tongues across the sky, and a heartstoppingly beautiful corona. A Type K shouldn't be that spectacular, but there were no normal stars in sight – not with this element distribution and infall.

Once the planet he was approaching had been farther out. But friction with the nebula, over gigayears, was causing it to spiral inward. Surface temperature wasn't yet excessive, about 50°C., because the atmosphere was thin, mainly noble gases. The entire world hadn't sufficient water to fill a decent lake. It rolled before him as a gloom little relieved by the reddish blots of gigantic dust storms. Refracted light made its air a fiery ring.

His sled struck that atmosphere, and for a while he was busy amidst thunder and shudder, helping the auto-pilot bring the small craft down. In the end, he hovered above a jumbled plain. Mountains bulked bare on the near horizon. The rock was black and brown and darkly gleaming. The sun stood high in a deep purple heaven. He checked with an induction probe, confirmed that the ground was solid – in fact, incredibly hard – and landed.

When he stepped out, weight caught at him. The planet had less diameter than the least of those on which men live, but was so dense that gravity stood at 1.22 standard G. An unexpectedly strong wind shoved at him. Though thin, the air was moving fast. He heard it wail through his helmet. From afar came a rumble, and a quiver entered his boots and bones. Landslide? Earthquake? Unseen volcano? He didn't know what was or was not possible here. Nor, he suspected, did the most expert planetologist. Worlds like this had not hitherto been trodden.

Radiation from the ground was higher than he liked. Better do his job quickly. He lugged forth apparatus. A power drill for samples – he set it up and let it work while he assembled a pyroanalyzer and fed it a rock picked off the chaotic terrain. Crumbled between alloy jaws, flash heated to vapor, the mineral gave up its fundamental composition to the optical and mass spectrographs. Laure studied the printout and nodded in satisfaction. The presence of atmosphere hadn't changed matters. This place was loaded with heavy metals and radioactives. He'd need a picture of molecular and crystalline structures before being certain that they were as easily extractable as he'd found them to be on the other planets; but he had no reason to doubt it.

Well, he thought, aware of hunger and aching feet, *let's relax awhile in the cab, catch a meal and a nap, then go check a few other spots, just to make sure they're equally promising, and then –*

The sky exploded.

He was on his belly, faceplate buried in arms against the flash, before his conscious mind knew what had happened. Rangers learn about nuclear weapons. When, after a minute, no shock wave had hit him, no sound other than a rising wind, he dared sit up and look.

The sky had turned white. The sun was no longer like an orange lantern but molten brass. He couldn't squint anywhere near it. Radiance crowded upon him, heat mounted even as he climbed erect. *Nova,* he thought in his rocking reality, and caught Graydal to him for the moment he was to become a wisp of gas.

But he remained alive, alone, on a plain that now shimmered with light and mirage. The wind screamed louder still. He felt how it pushed him, and how the mass of the planet pulled, and how his mouth was dry and his muscles tautened for a leap. The brilliance pained his eyes, but was not unendurable behind a self-adapting faceplate and did not seem to be growing greater.

263

The infrared brought forth sweat on his skin, but he was not being baked.

Steadiness came. Something almighty strange was happening. It hadn't killed him yet, though. As a check, with no hope of making contact, he tuned his radio. Static brawled in his earplugs.

His heart thudded. He couldn't tell whether he was afraid or exhilarated. He was, after all, quite a young man. But the coolness of his training came upon him. He didn't stop feeling. Wildness churned beneath self-control. But he did methodically begin to collect his equipment, and to reason while he acted.

Not a nova burst. Main sequence stars don't go nova. They don't vary in seconds, either . . . but then, every star around here is abnormal. Perhaps, if I'd checked the spectrum of this one, I'd have seen indications that it was about to move into another phase of a jagged output cycle. Or perhaps I wouldn't have known what the indications meant. Who's studied astrophysics in circumstances like these?

What had occurred might be akin to the Wolf-Rayet phenomenon, he thought. The stars around him did not evolve along ordinary lines. They had strange compositions to start with. And then matter kept falling into them, changing that composition, increasing their masses. That must produce instability. Each spectrum he had taken in his heart of the cluster showed enormous turbulence in the surface layers. So did the spots, flares, prominences, coronas he had seen. Well, the turbulence evidently went deeper than the photospheres. Actual stellar cores and their nuclear furnaces might be affected. Probably every local sun was a violent variable.

Even in the less dense regions, stars must have peculiar careers. The sun of Kirkasant had apparently been stable for five thousand years – or several million, more likely, since the planet had well-developed native life. But who could swear it would stay thus? Destruction! The place had to be found, had to, so that the people could be evacuated if need arose. You can't let little children fry –

Laure checked his radiation meter. The needle climbed ominously fast up the dial. Yonder sun was spitting X rays, in appreciable quantity, and the planet had no ozone layer to block them. He'd be dead if he didn't get to shelter — for choice, his ship and her force-screens — before the ions arrived. Despite its density, the globe had no magnetic field to speak of, either, to ward them off. Probably the core was made of stuff like osmium and uranium. Such a weird blend might well be solid rather than molten. *I don't know about that. I do know I'd better get my tail out of here.*

The wind yelled. It began driving ferrous dust against him, borne from somewhere else. He saw the particles scud in darkling whirls and heard them click on his helmet. Doggedly, he finished loading his gear. When at last he entered the sled cab and shut the air lock, his vehicle was trembling under the blast and the sun was reddened and dimmed by haze.

He started the motor and lifted. No sense in resisting the wind. He was quite happy to be blown toward the night side. Meanwhile he'd gain altitude, then get above the storm, collect orbital velocity and —

He never knew what happened. The sled was supposedly able to ride out more vicious blows than any this world could produce. But who could foretell what this world was capable of? The atmosphere, being thin, developed high velocities. Perhaps the sudden increased irradiation had triggered paroxysm in a cyclone cell. Perhaps the dust, which was conductive, transferred energy into such a vortex at a greater rate than one might believe. Laure wasn't concerned about meteorological theory.

He was concerned with staying alive, when an instant blindness clamped down upon him with a shriek that nigh tore the top off his skull, and he was whirled like a leaf and cast against a mountainside.

The event was too fast for awareness, for anything but reaction. His autopilot and he must somehow have got some control. The crash ruined the sled, ripped open its belly, scattered its cargo, but did not crumple the cab section. Shock harness kept the man from serious injury. He was momentarily unconscious, but came back with no worse than an aching body and blood in his mouth.

Wind hooted. Dust went hissing and scouring. The sun was a dim red disk, though from time to time a beam of pure fire struck through the storm and blazed off metallic cliffsides.

Laure fumbled with his harness and stumbled out. Half seen, the slope on which he stood caught at his feet with cragginess. He had to take cover. The beta particles would arrive at any moment, the protons, within hours, and they bore his death.

He was dismayed to learn the stowed equipment was gone. He dared not search for it. Instead, he made his clumsy way into the murk.

He found no cave – not in this waterless land – but by peering and calculating (odd how calm you can grow when your life depends on your brain) he discovered in what direction his chances were best, and was rewarded. A one-time landslide had piled great slabs of rock on each other. Among them was a passage into which he could crawl.

Then nothing to do but lie in that narrow space and wait.

Light seeped around a bend, with the noise of the storm. He could judge thereby how matters went outside. Periodically he crept to the entrance of his dolmen and monitored the radiation level. Before long it had reached such a count that – space armor, expert therapy, and all – an hour's exposure would kill him.

He must wait.

Jaccavrie knew the approximate area where he intended to set down. She'd come looking as soon as possible. Flitting low, using her detectors, she'd find the wrecked sled. More than that she could not do unaided. But he could emerge and call her. Whether or not they actually saw each other in this mountainscape, he could emit a radio signal for her to home on. She'd hover, snatch him with a forcebeam, and reel him in.

But ... this depended on calm weather. *Jaccavrie* could overmaster any wind. But the dust would blind both her and him. And deafen and mute them; it was conducive, radio could not get through. Laure proved that to his own satisfaction by experimenting with the miniradar built into his armor.

So everything seemed to depend on which came first, the end of the gale or the end of Laure's powerpack. His air renewer drew on it. About thirty hours' worth of charge remained before he choked on his own breath. If only he'd been able to grab a spare accumulator or two, or better still, a hand-cranked recharger! They might have rolled no more than ten meters off. But he had decided not to search the area. And by now, he couldn't go back. Not through the radiation.

He sighed, drank a bit from his water nipple, ate a bit through his chow lock, wished for a glass of beer and a comfortable bed and went to sleep.

When he awoke, the wind had dropped from a full to a half gale; but the dust drift was so heavy as to conceal the glorious starfog night that had fallen. It screened off some of the radiation, too, though not enough to do him any good. He puzzled over why the body of the planet wasn't helping more. Finally he decided that ions, hitting the upper air along the terminator, produced secondaries and cascades which descended everywhere.

The day-side bombardment must really have got fierce!

Twenty hours left. He opened the life-support box he had taken off his shoulder rack, pulled out the sanitary unit, and attached it. Men don't die romantically, like characters on a stage. Their bodies are too stubborn.

So are their minds. He should have been putting his thoughts in order, but he kept being disturbed by recollections of his parents, of Graydal, of a funny little tavern he'd once visited, of a gaucherie he'd rather forget, of some money owing to him, of Graydal – He ate again, and drowsed again, and the wind filled the air outside with dust, and time closed in like a hand.

Ten hours left. No more?

Five. Already?

What a stupid way to end. Fear fluttered at the edge of his perception. He beat it. The wind yammered. How long can a dust storm continue, anyhow? Where'd it come from? Daylight again, outside his refuge, colored like blood and brass. The charged particles and X rays were so thick that some diffused in to him. He shifted cramped muscles, and drank the stench of his unwashed skin, and regretted everything he had wanted and failed to do.

267

A shadow cast on the cornering rock. A rustle and slither conducted to his ears. A form, bulky and awkward as his own, crawling around the tunnel bend. Numb, shattered, he switched on his radio. The air was fairly clear in here and he heard her voice through the static: '. . . you are, you are alive! Oh, Valfar's Wings upbear us, you live!'

He held her while she sobbed, and he wept, too. 'You shouldn't have,' he stammered. 'I never meant for *you* to risk yourself – '

'We dared not wait,' she said when they were calmer. 'We saw, from space, that the storm was enormous. It would go on in this area for days. And we didn't know how long you had to live. We only knew you were in trouble, or you'd have been back with us. We came down. I almost had to fight my father, but I won and came. The hazard wasn't so great for me. Really, no, believe me. She protected me till we found your sled. Then I did have to go out afoot with a metal detector to find you. Because you were obviously sheltered somewhere, and so you could only be detected at closer range than she can come. But the danger wasn't that great, Daven. I can stand much more radiation than you. I'm still well inside my tolerance, won't even need any drugs. Now I'll shoot off this flare, and she'll see, and come so close that we can make a dash – You are all right, aren't you? You swear it?'

'Oh, yes,' he said slowly. 'I'm fine. Better off than ever in my life.' Absurdly, he had to have the answer, however footling all questions were against the fact that she had come after him and was here and they were both alive. 'We? Who's your companion?'

She laughed and clinked her faceplate against his. '*Jaccavrie*, of course. Who else? You didn't think your womenfolk were about to leave you alone, did you?'

The ships began their trek homeward. They moved without haste. Best to be cautious until they had emerged from the nebula, seen where they were, and aimed themselves at the Dragon's Head.

'My people and I are pleased at your safety,' said Demring's image in the outercom screen. He spoke under the obligation to be courteous, and could not refrain from adding: 'We also approve your decision not to investigate that planet further.'

'For the first, thanks,' Laure answered. 'As for the second – ' He shrugged. 'No real need. I was curious about the effects of an atmosphere, but my computer has just run off a probability analysis of the data I already have, which proves that no more are necessary for my purposes.'

'May one inquire what your purposes are?'

'I'd like to discuss that first with your navigator. In private.'

The green gaze studied Laure before Demring said, unsmiling: 'You have the right of command. And by our customs, she having been instrumental in saving your life, a special relationship exists. But again I counsel forethought.'

Laure paid no attention to that last sentence. His pulse was beating too gladly. He switched off as soon as possible and ordered the best dinner his ship could provide.

'Are you certain you want to make your announcement through her?' the voice asked him. 'And to her in this manner?'

'I am. I think I've earned the pleasure. Now I'm off to make myself presentable for the occasion. Carry on.' Laure went whistling down the corridor.

But when Graydal boarded, he took both her hands and they looked long in silence at each other. She had strewn jewels in her tresses, turning them to a starred midnight. Her clothes were civilian, a deep blue that offset her coppery skin, amber eyes, and suppleness. And did he catch the least woodsy fragrance of perfume?

'Welcome,' was all he could say at last.

'I am so happy,' she answered.

They went to the saloon and sat down on the couch together. Daiquiris were ready for them. They touched glasses. 'Good voyage,' he made the old toast, 'and merry landing.'

'For me, yes.' Her smile faded. 'And I hope for the rest. How I hope.'

'Don't you think they can get along in the outside worlds?'

'Yes, undoubtedly.' The incredible lashes fluttered. 'But they will never be as fortunate as . . . as I think I may be.'

'You have good prospects yourself?' The blood roared in his temples.

'I am not quite sure,' she replied shyly.

He had intended to spin out his surprise at length, but suddenly he couldn't let her stay troubled, not to any degree. He cleared his throat and said, 'I have news.'

She tilted her head and waited with that relaxed alertness he liked to see. He wondered how foolish the grin was on his face. Attempting to recover dignity, he embarked on a roundabout introduction.

'You wondered why I insisted on exploring the cluster center, and in such detail. Probably I ought to have explained myself from the beginning. But I was afraid of raising false hopes. I'd no guarantee that things would turn out to be the way I'd guessed. Failure, I thought, would be too horrible for you, if you knew what success would mean. But I was working on your behalf, nothing else.

'You see, because my civilization is founded on individualism, it makes property rights quite basic. In particular, if there aren't any inhabitants or something like that, discoverers can claim ownership within extremely broad limits.

'Well, we . . . you . . . our expedition has met the requirements of discovery as far as those planets are concerned. We've been there, we've proven what they're like, we've located them as well as might be without beacons – '

He saw how she struggled not to be too sanguine. 'That isn't a true location,' she said. 'I can't imagine how we will ever lead anybody back to precisely those stars.'

'Nor can I,' he said. 'And it doesn't matter. Because, well, we took an adequate sample. We can be sure now that practically every star in the cluster heart has planets that are made of heavy elements. So it isn't necessary, for their exploitation, to go to any particular system. In addition, we've learned about hazards and so forth, gotten information that'll be essential to other people. And therefore' – he chuckled – 'I guess we can't file a claim on your entire Cloud Universe. But any court will award you ... us ... a fair share. Not specific planets, since they can't be found right away. Instead, a share of everything. Your crew will draw royalties on the richest mines in the galaxy. On millions of them.'

She responded with thoughtfulness rather than enthusiasm. 'Indeed? We did wonder, on *Makt*, if you might not be hoping to find abundant metals. But we decided that couldn't be. For why would anyone come here for them? Can they not be had more easily, closer to home?'

Slightly dashed, he said, 'No. Especially when most worlds in this frontier are comparatively metal-poor. They do have some veins of ore, yes. And the colonists can extract anything from the oceans, as on Serieve. But there's a natural limit to such a process. In time, carried out on the scale that'd be required when population had grown ... it's be releasing so much heat that planetary temperature would be affected.'

'That sounds farfetched.'

'No. A simple calculation will prove it. According to historical records, Earth herself ran into the problem, and not terribly long after the industrial era began. However, quite aside from remote prospects, people will want to mine these cluster worlds immediately. True, it's a long haul, and operations will have to be totally automated. But the heavy elements that are rare elsewhere are so abundant here as to more than make up for those extra costs.' He smiled. 'I'm afraid you can't escape your fate. You're going to be ... not wealthy. To call you "wealthy" would be like calling a supernova "luminous". You'll command more resources than many whole civilizations have done.'

Her look upon him remained grave. 'You did this for us? You should not have. What use would riches be to us if we lost you?'

He remembered that he couldn't have expected her to carol about this. In her culture, money was not unwelcome, but neither was it an important goal. So what she had just said meant less than if a girl of the Commonalty had spoken. Nevertheless, joy kindled in him. She sensed that, laid her hands across his, and murmured, 'But your thought was noble.'

He couldn't restrain himself any longer. He laughed aloud.

271

'Noble?' he cried. 'I'd call it clever. Fiendishly clever. Don't you see? I've given you Kirkasant back!'

She gasped.

He jumped up and paced exuberant before her. 'You could wait a few years till your cash reserves grow astronomical and buy as big a fleet as you want to search the cluster. But it isn't needful. When word gets out, the miners will come swarming. They'll plant beacons, they'll have to. The grid will be functioning within one year, I'll bet. As soon as you can navigate, identify where you are and where you've been, you can't help finding your home – in weeks!'

She joined him, then, casting herself into his arms, laughing, and weeping. He had known of emotional depth in her, beneath the schooled reserve. But never before now had he found as much warmth as was hers.

Long, long afterward, air locks linked and she bade him good night. 'Until tomorrow,' she said.

'Many tomorrows, I hope.'

'And I hope. I promise.'

He watched the way she had gone until the locks closed again and the ships parted company. A little drunkenly, not with alcohol, he returned to the saloon for a nightcap.

'Turn off that color thing,' he said. 'Give me an outside view.'

The ship obeyed. In the screen appeared stars, and the cloud from which stars were being born. 'Her sky,' Laure said. He flopped on to the couch and admired.

'I might as well start getting used to it,' he said. 'I expect I'll spend a lot of vacation time, at least, on Kirkasant.'

'Daven,' said *Jaccavrie*.

She was not in the habit of addressing him thus, and so gently. He started. 'Yes?'

'I have been – ' Silence hummed for a second. 'I have been wondering how to tell you. Any phrasing, any inflection, could strike you as something I computed to produce an effect. I am only a machine.'

Though unease prickled him, he leaned forward to touch a bulkhead. It trembled a little with her engine energy. 'And I, old girl,' he said. 'Or else you also are an organism. We're both people.'

'T'..ank you,' said the ship, almost too low to be heard.

Laure braced himself. 'What did you have to tell me?'

She forgot about keeping her voice humanized. The words clipped forth: 'I finished the chromosome analysis some time ago. Thereafter I tried to discourage certain tendencies I noticed in you. But now I have no way to avoid giving you the plain truth. They are not human on that planet.'

'What?' he yelled. The glass slipped from his hand and splashed red wine across the deck. 'You're crazy! Records, traditions, artifacts, appearance, behavior – '

The ship's voice came striding across his. 'Yes, they are human descended. But their ancestors had to make an enormous adaptation. The loss of night vision is merely indicative. The fact that they can, for example, ingest heavy metals like arsenic unharmed might be interpreted as simple immunity. But you will recall that they find unarsenated food tasteless. Did that never suggest to you that they have developed a metabolic requirement for the element? And you should have drawn a conclusion from their high tolerance for ionizing radiation. It cannot be due to their having stronger proteins, can it? No, it must be because they have evolved a capacity for extremely rapid and error-free repair of chemical damage from that source. This in turn is another measure of how different their enzyme system is from yours.

'Now the enzymes, of course, are governed by the DNA of the cells, which is the molecule of heredity – '

'Stop,' Laure said. His speech was as flat as hers. 'I see what you're at. You are about to report that your chromosome study proved the matter. My kind of people and hers can't reproduce with each other.'

'Correct,' *Jaccavrie* said.

Laure shook himself, as if he were cold. He continued to look at the glowing fog. 'You can't call them non-human on that account.'

'A question of semantics. Hardly an important one. Except for the fact that Kirkasanters apparently are under an instinctual compulsion to have children.'

273

'I know,' Laure said.

And after a time: 'Good thing, really. They're a high-class breed. We could use a lot of them.'

'Your own genes are above average,' *Jaccavrie* said.

'Maybe. What of it?'

Her voice turned alive again. 'I'd like to have grandchildren,' she said wistfully.

Laure laughed. 'All right,' he said. 'No doubt one day you will.' The laughter was somewhat of a victory.

And now a new cycle turns on Fortune's cosmic wheel. Another brilliant era races to its apogee. What hidden flaws will send the Commonalty spinning downward into darkness like the Empire and the League before it? Let its free and lively people prosper while they may, for as a proverb handed down from Old Earth puts it,

> *Shines the sun ne'er so bright,*
> *In the end must come the night.*

274

A CHRONOLOGY OF
TECHNIC CIVILIZATION

Note: Although Poul Anderson was consulted during the preparation of this chart, he is not responsible for its dating nor in any way specifically committed to it. Stories are listed by their most recently published titles. Rounded dates are quite approximate. Publication dates refer to American editions.

21st C   Century of recovery. 'The Saturn Game,'
                        Analog Science Fiction (cited as ASF),
                        February, 1981.

22nd C   Interstellar exploration the Breakup, formation of the Commonwealth, planting of early colonies including Hermes.

2150   'Wings of Victory' ASF, April, 1972. Ythri discovered. Discovery of Merseia.

23rd C   Establishment of the Polesotechnic League. Colonization of Aeneas and Altai.

24th C   'The Problem of Pain,' *Fantasy and Science Fiction* (cited as F & SF), February, 1973.

2376   Nicholas van Rijn born Colonization of Vixen

2400   Council of Hiawatha Colonization of Dennitza

2406	David Falkayn born
2416	'Margin of Profit', ASF, September, 1956. (van Rijn) 'How to Be Ethnic in One Easy Lesson', in *Future Quest*, ed. Roger Elwood, Avon Books, 1974.
————	'Three-Cornered Wheel,' ASF, October, 1963. (Falkayn)
stories overlap around 2426	'A Sun Invisible,' ASF, April 1966. (Falkayn) *The Man Who Counts*. Ace Books, 1978 as *War of the Wing-Men*. Ace Books, 1958 from 'The Man Who Counts,' ASF, February-April, 1958. (van Rijn)
2427	'Esau,' as 'Birthright,' ASF, February 1970. (van Rijn) 'Hiding Place,' ASF, March 1961. (van Rijn) 'Territory,' ASF, June, 1963. (van Rijn) 'The Trouble Twisters,' as 'Trader Team,' ASF, July-August, 1965. (Falkayn)
2433	'Day of Burning' as 'Supernova,' ASF, January, 1967. (Falkayn) 'The Master Key,' ASF, August, 1971. (van Rijn)
2437	*Satan's World*. Doubleday, 1969 from ASF, May-August, 1968 (van Rijn and Falkayn) 'A Little Knowledge,' ASF, August, 1971. 'The Season of Forgiveness,' *Boy's Life*, December, 1973.

2446	'Lodestar' in *Astounding: The John W. Campbell Memorial Anthology*, ed. Harry Harrison. Random House, 1973. (van Rijn and Falkayn)
2456	*Mirkheim*. Putnam Books, 1977. (van Rijn and Falkayn)
late 25th C	Settlement of Avalon
26th C	'Wingless on Avalon,' *Boy's Life*, July, 1973. 'Rescue on Avalon,' in *Children of Infinity*, ed. Roger Elwood. Franklin Watts, 1973 Colonization of Nyanza Dissolution of the Polesotechnic League
27th C	The Time of Troubles 'The Star Plunderer,' *Planet Stories* (cited as PS), September, 1952
28th C	Foundation of the Terran Empire, Principate phase begins. Colonization of Unan Bator 'Sargasso of Lost Starships,' PS, January, 1952.
29th C	*The People of the Wind*. New American Libary from ASF February-April, 1973.
30th C	The Covenant of Alfzar
3000	Dominic Flandry born
3019	*Ensign Flandry*. Chilton, 1966. Abridged version in *Amazing* (cited as Amz), October, 1966.

3021	*A Circus of Hells*. New American Library, 1970. Incorporates 'The White King's War,' *Galaxy* (cited as *Gal*), October 1969. Flandry is a Lieutenant (j.g.)
3022	Josip succeeds Georgios as Emperor.
3025	*The Rebel Worlds*. New American Library, 1969. Flandry is a Lt. Commander, then promoted to Commander.
3027	'Outpost of Empire,' *Gal*, December, 1967. (non-Flandry)
3028	*The Day of Their Return*. Doubleday, 1973. (non-Flandry)
3032	'Tiger by the Tail,' PS, January, 1951. Flandry is a Captain.
3033	'Honorable Enemies,' *Future Combined with Science Fiction Stories*, May, 1951.
3035	'The Game of Glory,' *Venture*, March, 1958. Flandry has been knighted.
3037	'A Message in Secret,' as *Mayday Orbit*. Ace Books, 1961 from shorter version, 'A Message in Secret,' *Fantastic*, December, 1959.
3038	'A Plague of Masters,' as *Earthman, Go Home*. Ace Books, 1961 from 'A Plague of Masters,' *Fantastic*, December, 1960-January, 1961.

3040	'Hunters of the Sky Cave,' as *We Claim These Stars!* Ace Books, 1959 from abridged version, 'A Handful of Stars,' *Amz*, June, 1959
3041	Interregnum: Josip dies, after three years of civil war. Hans Molitor rules as sole Emperor.
3042	'The Warriors from Nowhere,' as 'The Ambassadors of Flesh,' PS, Summer, 1954.
3047	*A Knight of Ghosts and Shadows.* New American Library, 1975 from *Gal*, September/October–November/December, 1974.
3054	Hans Molitor dies, succeeded by Dietrich, then Gerhart.
3061	*A Stone in Heaven*, Ace Books, 1979. Flandry is a Vice Admiral.
early 4th millennium	Dominate phase Fall of the Terran Empire
mid-4th millennium	The Long Night
3600	'A Tragedy of Errors,' *Gal*, February, 1968
3900	*The Night Face*. Ace Books, 1978 as *Let the Spacemen Beware!* Ace Books, 1963 from shorter version 'A Twelvemonth and a Day,' *Fantastic Universe*, January, 1960.

In a future world of strangers,
the hunter and the hunted are one . . .

ROGER ZELAZNY

Winner of 3 Nebula and 3 Hugo Awards

William Blackhorse Singer, the last Navajo tracker on a future
earth, has stocked the Interstellar Life Institute with its most
exotic creatures. But one of Singer's prizes preys upon his
mind: a metamorph. The one-eyed shapeshifter Cat, whose
home planet has been destroyed. Singer offers Cat freedom to
help him defend Earth against a terrible predator, and Cat
accepts. The price: permission to hunt the hunter. And the
deadly game begins. In a fierce, global hunt, Singer flees his
extra-sentient killer. And suddenly, he is pursuing not life, but
the mysteries of his people, and the blinding vision of his own
primeval spirit . . .

'Zelazny's best book since *Lord of Light*.' *Joe Haldeman.*
'The interweaving of old tales and futuristic adventures is
genuinely moving . . .'
New York Times Book Review.
'The melting together of perceptions of the future and the past
are brilliant, effective and moving.'
Vonda McIntyre.

SCIENCE FICTION   **0 7221 9442 0**   **£1.95**

A selection of bestsellers from SPHERE

FICTION

DEEP SIX	Clive Cussler	£2.25 ☐
MILLENNIUM	John Varley	£1.99 ☐
SMART WOMEN	Judy Blume	£2.25 ☐
INHERITORS OF THE STORM	Victor Sondheim	£2.95 ☐
HEADLINES	Bernard Weinraub	£2.75 ☐

FILM & TV TIE-INS

THE RIVER	Steven Bauer	£1.95 ☐
WATER	Gordon McGill	£1.75 ☐
THE DUNE STORYBOOK	Joan D. Vinge	£2.50 ☐
NO-ONE KNOWS WHERE GOBO GOES	Mark Saltzman	£1.50 ☐
BOOBER FRAGGLE'S CELERY SOUFFLÉ	Louise Gikow	£1.50 ☐

NON-FICTION

PAUL ERDMAN'S MONEY GUIDE	Paul Erdman	£2.95 ☐
THE 1985 FAMILY WELCOME GUIDE	Jill Foster and Malcolm Hamer	£3.95 ☐
THE OXFORD CHILDREN'S DICTIONARY	John Weston and Alan Spooner	£3.25 ☐
THE *WOMAN* BOOK OF LOVE AND SEX	Deidre Sanders	£1.95 ☐
INTO THE REMOTE PLACES	Ian Hibell with Clinton Trowbridge	£2.95 ☐

All Sphere books are available at your local bookshop or newsagent, or can be ordered direct from the publisher. Just tick the titles you want and fill in the form below.

Name_____

Address_____

_____

Write to Sphere Books, Cash Sales Department, P.O. Box 11, Falmouth, Cornwall TR10 9EN

Please enclose cheque or postal order to the value of the cover price plus:

UK: 55p for the first book, 22p for the second book and 14p per copy for each additional book ordered to a maximum charge of £1.75.

OVERSEAS: £1.00 for the first book and 25p per copy for each additional book.

BFPO & EIRE: 55p for the first book, 22p for the second book plus 14p per copy for the next 7 books, thereafter 8p per book.

Sphere Books reserve the right to show new retail prices on covers which may differ from those previously advertised in the text or elsewhere, and to increase postal rates in accordance with the PO.